Praise for
A SUPERIOR DEATH

"Barr writes in a tangled, rich, descriptive language . . . it has an engrossing pull that gives a vivid feel for the terrain and those who have found their niche in this rather forbidding, gloomy, and chilling landscape . . . A wonderfully satisfying read." —*The Washington Post Book World*

"An engrossing story of death and deceit . . . [an] absorbing novel." —*The Dallas Morning News*

"A vivid finish." —*Los Angeles Times*

"Barr crafts a cunning mystery, and, as usual, her writing about the natural landscape and its history is magical." —*The Orlando Sentinel*

"One of the best . . . Barr weaves mystery with social and political themes . . . and consistently entertains." —*U.S. News & World Report*

"Barr is a gifted storyteller with a nice sense of plotting and a near-poet's touch when it comes to describing primitive Superior country, a land of soaring bluffs, coves, deep forests, and beckoning islands." —*The Buffalo News*

"The final revelation of culprit and motive will surprise all but the most alert readers. A crackling good mystery, fleshed out by a detective and a supporting cast far more human than they need to be." —*Kirkus Reviews*

continued . . .

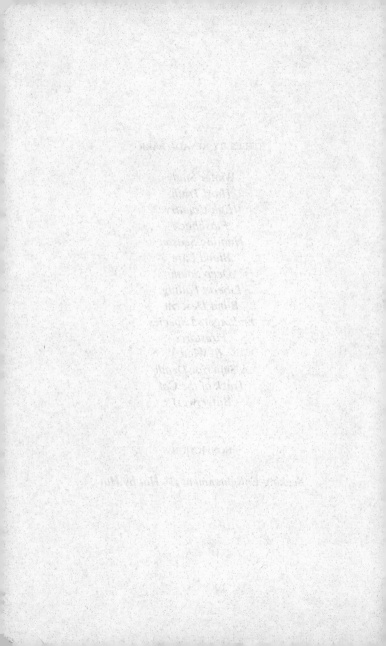

A SUPERIOR DEATH

NEVADA BARR

BERKLEY BOOKS, NEW YORK

A SUPERIOR DEATH

A Berkley Book / published by arrangement with
the author

PRINTING HISTORY
G. P. Putnam's Sons hardcover edition / March 1994
Avon mass-market edition / May 1995
Berkley mass-market edition / September 2003

Copyright © 1994 by Nevada Barr.
Cover design by Wood Ronsaville and Harlin.
Cover illustration by Rob Wood.

ISBN: 978-0-425-19471-3

BERKLEY®
Berkley Books are published by The Berkley Publishing Group,
a division of Penguin Group (USA) Inc.,
375 Hudson Street, New York, New York 10014.
BERKLEY and the "B" design
are trademarks belonging to Penguin Group (USA) Inc.

PRINTED IN THE UNITED STATES OF AMERICA

10 9 8 7 6

For Peter, who always *knows who did it and doesn't think that necessarily makes them bad people*

Special thanks to Daniel Lenihan

CHAPTER 1

These killers of fish, she thought, will do anything.

Through the streaming windscreen Anna could just make out a pale shape bobbing in two-meter waves gray as slate and as unforgiving. An acid-green blip on the radar screen confirmed the boat's unwelcome existence. A quarter of a mile to the northeast a second blip told her of yet another fool out on some fool's errand.

She fiddled irritably with the radar, as if she could clear the lake fog by focusing the screen. Her mind flashed on an old acquaintance, a wide-shouldered fellow named Lou, with whom she had argued the appeal—or lack thereof—of Hemingway. Finally in frustration Lou had delivered the ultimate thrust: "You're a woman. You can't understand Papa Hemingway."

Anna banged open her side window, felt the rain on her cheek, running under the cuff of her jacket sleeve. "We don't understand fishing, either," she shouted into the wind.

The hull of the Bertram slammed down against the back of a retreating swell. For a moment the bow blocked the windscreen, then dropped away; a false horizon falling sickeningly toward an uncertain finish. In a crashing curtain of water, the boat found the lake once more. Anna swore on impact and thought better of further discourse with the elements. The next pounding might slam her teeth closed on her tongue.

Five weeks before, when she'd been first loosed on Superior with her boating license still crisp and new in her wallet, she'd tried to comfort herself with the engineering specs on the Bertram. It was one of the sturdiest twenty-six-foot vessels made. According to its supporters and the substantiating literature, the Bertram could withstand just about anything short of an enemy torpedo.

On a more kindly lake Anna might have found solace in that assessment. On Superior's gun-metal waves, the thought of enemy torpedoes seemed the lesser of assorted evils. Torpedoes were prone to human miscalculation. What man could send, woman could dodge. Lake Superior waited. She had plenty of time and lots of fishes to feed.

The *Belle Isle* plowed through the crest of a three-meter wave and, in the seconds of visibility allowed between the beat of water and wiper blades, Anna saw the running lights of a small vessel ahead and fifty yards to the right.

She braced herself between the dash and the butt-high pilot's bench and picked up the radio mike. "The *Low Dollar,* the *Low Dollar,* this is the *Belle Isle.* Do you read?" Through the garble of static a man's voice replied: "Yeah, yeah. Is that you over there?"

Not for the first time Anna marveled at the number of boaters who survived Superior each summer. There were no piloting requirements. Any man, woman, or child who could get his or her hands on a boat was free to drive it out amid the reefs and shoals, commercial liners and weekend fishing vessels. The Coast Guard's array of warning signs—Diver Down, Shallow Water, Buoy, No Wake— were just so many pretty wayside decorations to half the pilots on the lake. "Go to six-eight." Anna switched her radio from the hailing frequency to the working channel: "Affirmative, it's me over here. I'm going to come alongside on your port side. Repeat: port side. On your left," she threw in for good measure.

"Um . . . ten-four," came the reply.

For the next few minutes Anna put all of her concentration into feeling the boat, the force of the engines, the buck of the wind and the lift of the water. There were people on the island—Holly Bradshaw, who crewed on the dive boat the *3rd Sister,* Chief Ranger Lucas Vega, all of the old-timers from Fisherman's Home and Barnums' Island, who held commercial fishing rights from before Isle Royale had become a national park—who could dock a speedboat to a whirlwind at high tide. Anna was not among this elite.

She missed Gideon, her saddle horse in Texas. Even at his most recalcitrant she could always get him in and out of the paddock without risk of humiliation. The *Belle Isle* took considerably more conning and, she thought grumpily, wasn't nearly as good company.

The *Low Dollar* hove into sight, riding the slick gray back of a wave. Anna reached out of her side window and shoved a fender down to protect the side of the boat. The stern fender was already out. Leaving Amygdaloid Ranger Station, she'd forgotten to pull it in and it had been banging in the water the whole way.

I'll never be an old salt, Anna told herself. Sighing inwardly, she pushed right throttle, eased back on left, and sidled up behind the smaller boat. Together they sank into a trough.

The *Low Dollar* wallowed and heaved like a blowsy old woman trying to climb out of a water bed. Her gunwales lay dangerously close to waterline and Anna could see a bucket, a wooden-backed scrub brush, and an empty Heaven Hill bourbon bottle drowning in their own little sea on the flooded deck.

Two men, haggard with fear and the ice-slap of the wind, slogged through the bilge to grapple at the *Belle Isle* with bare hands and boat hooks. "Stand off, stand off, you turkeys," Anna muttered under her breath. Shouting, even if she could be heard over the wind, would be a waste of time. These men could no more keep their hands off the

Belle Isle than a drowning man could keep his hands off the proverbial straw.

There was a creak of hull against hull as they jerked the boats together, undoing her careful maneuvering.

The man at the bow, wind-whipped in an oversized Kmart slicker, dragged out a yellow nylon cord and began lashing the two boats together as if afraid Anna would abandon them.

She shut down to an idle and climbed up the two steps from the cabin. The fisherman at the *Low Dollar*'s starboard quarter began to tie the sterns together. "Hey! Hey!" Anna shouted. "Don't you tie my boat to that—" "Piece of junk" was the logical end of the sentence, but a fairly recent lecture from Lucas Vega on the importance of positive visitor contact and maintaining a good relationship with the armies of sport fishermen that invaded the island every summer passed through her thoughts.

"Untie that," she shouted against the wind. "Untie it." The man, probably in his mid-forties but looking older in a shapeless sweatshirt and cap with earflaps, turned a blank face toward her. He stopped tying but didn't begin untying. Instead he looked to his buddy, still wrapping loops of line round and round the bow cleats.

"Hal?" he bleated plaintively, wanting corroboration from a proper authority.

Anna waited, her hands on the *Low Dollar*'s gunwale. The old tub had enough buoyancy left that a few more minutes wouldn't make much difference. And, by the sagging flesh of the man's cheeks and his dilated pupils, Anna guessed he was about half shocky with fear and cold.

Hal finished his pile of Boy Scout knots and made his way back the length of the boat. He was younger than the man white-knuckling the stern line, maybe thirty-five. Fear etched hard lines around his eyes and mouth but he looked, if not entirely reasonable, at least able to listen.

"Hi," Anna said calmly. "I'm Anna Pigeon. Hal, I take it?" He nodded dumbly. "Are you the captain of the *Low Dollar*, Hal?" Again the nod. "You've taken on a bit of water, it looks like."

The commonplace words were having their desired effect. The life-and-death look began to fade from his pale blue eyes. He wiped his mouth with his sleeve as if turning on the switch that would allow his lips to function. "Yeah," he managed. "Hit something in Little Todd. Didn't pay much attention. Time we got here we were taking on more'n we could bail. We started radioing then. I think the propeller got dinged and we're taking on water around the shaft."

Normalcy somewhat restored—given the world continued to pitch in a colorless panorama of blustering cloud and billowing wave—Anna spoke again. "Here's what's going to happen, Hal. First put on life jackets. You got any?"

He dragged two disreputable-looking orange vests out from beneath a seat, and the men began buckling them on.

When Hal's hands were free again, Anna said: "You'll need to cut that bow line loose. You . . . ?" She looked at the second man, who was beginning to come to life.

"Kenny. Ken."

"Ken. You untie the stern. Hal, I'm going to hand you my towline. Make it fast to the bow. Then the both of you get aboard my boat. The *Low Dollar*'s riding too low in the water. I'd just as soon nobody was on board. Got all that?"

Kenny started unlooping his line and Hal returned to the bow to tug and jerk at the knots he'd made. The boats climbed a slick cold hill of water, teetered at its summit, then slid down on the other side. Kenny screamed out that his hand was caught between the two hulls, but he was more frightened than hurt.

The yell did a good turn, convincing Hal that slicing through a $1.59 piece of rope might be worth the time saved fumbling with his desperate knots.

In another minute both men were on board the *Belle Isle* and Anna was powering slowly away.

The towline grew taut, was dragged above the churning of the *Belle*'s wake. When the full weight of the sodden *Low Dollar* hit, Anna heard her engines growl over the challenge, then dig deeper into the lake for purchase. The

Bertram might not have the personality of a good horse but it had the power of a sizable herd. Anna was grateful: glad to have a good piece of equipment between her and the bottom of Superior, glad to be leaving the oceanlike expanse for the more protected channels and coves of the north shore.

To the right, amid the waves, she could see the rocky outcrop that was Kamloops Island. Had the water been flatter, or the *Low Dollar* less swamped, she might have towed the damaged vessel north of the little island to Amygdaloid Ranger Station where she had tools. Or even around to Rock Harbor where they had everything including telephones and hot and cold running seaplanes. Today, from the feel of the drag, the crippled boat would be lucky to make landfall.

Hal was stationed on deck watching his boat. Kenny sat on the high bench opposite the pilot's, his fingers clamped around the handholds on the dash. Anna had ordered him inside the cabin where he could warm up. His pallor and the clamminess of his flesh as she'd handed him over the gunwale concerned her. Anna stayed standing, her knees slightly bent, her center of gravity forward over her toes, riding the deck like a surfboard.

The fog was lifting. Several miles of shoreline were coming into hazy focus. The twenty miles of cliffs and coves between Little Todd Harbor and Blake's Point were now as familiar to Anna as the desert trails of the Guadalupe Mountains had been. Hoping to combat fear with knowledge, she'd spent her first two weeks as North Shore Ranger creeping about, chart in one hand, wheel in the other, her head hanging out of the window like a dog's from a pickup truck. She had memorized the shape of every bluff, every bay, the location of every shoal and underwater hazard.

On still, sunny days when the lake was more likely to forgive mistakes, she blanked her windows with old maps and crawled from place to place, eyes glued to the radar screen, ears tuned to the clatter of the depth finder. Like most landlubbers, she was less afraid of shallow waters—

coves full of stones and half-submerged logs—than she was of deep. Though the brutal cold of Superior would drown her a quarter of a mile from shore just as mercilessly as it would ten miles out, Anna seldom came in from open water without a sense of returning to safety. "Safe harbor"—a phrase she'd heard bandied about since childhood—had been given a depth of meaning with Lake Superior's first angry glance.

"You're new," Kenny said as if he echoed her thoughts. "You weren't here last year."

Anna refocused on her passenger. "Displaced desert rat," she replied. "I haven't been warm or dry since I left Texas."

"It's not like it used to be," he went on as if she'd not spoken. "Used to be people on the lake took care of each other. You'd never pass a vessel in distress. Never. We could've sunk out there and nobody'd've so much as thrown us a line. People don't care. All they care about's getting a campsite before the next guy."

"Did somebody pass you?" Anna asked, remembering the other blip on her radar. On such an ugly sea, it struck her as strange, though it was not uncommon. The brotherhood of sport fishermen, if it ever existed, was largely relegated to legend now; another link in the chain memory forged back to the mythical good old days.

"Not passed. A white boat with green—I didn't see the name or I'd report it to the Coast Guard. They were out in the lake near where the *Kamloops* went down, headed east."

"Maybe they didn't see you. The fog's been cat-footing around. Are you sure it wasn't red and white? The *Third Sister* was heading this direction. They're diving the *Emperor* tomorrow."

"Green. And they saw us. They'd've had to. Not a sign. The bastards left us sloshing up to our knees in bilge. They probably heard the rainbow were running in Siskiwit and couldn't wait. When my dad used to bring me out here— oh, twenty years ago at least . . ."

Anna let him ramble, even remembering to grunt or

sigh—listening noises her sister had taught her. "It comforts people," Molly had said. "Besides, it beats me having
to say, 'Anna, are you still there?' into the damn phone
every five minutes."

The noises turned out to be worth a thousand times
what Molly had paid AT&T for the phone time to teach her.
A ranger could get more information from a few well-
placed "oh reallys" and "uh-huhs" than from an hour's by-
the-book interrogation. People wanted to talk. Chewing
over betrayals, disappointments, and unrealized hopes
seemed to do for humans what licking wounds did for animals: a cleansing of poisons, a soothing of hurts.

Anna let Kenny talk, and she made Molly's therapeutic
sounds, but she didn't listen. She had her own wounds to
lick, her own dreams and disappointments. At that moment
she would have given a week's pay for one good hot, dry
day, for the sight of one small fence lizard, the scent of
sage on the wind.

The moment these thoughts blew in, Anna closed her
mind to them. The lake didn't allow for dreamers, not
when the waves were three meters, not when a dilapidated
sea anchor hung off the stern. The desert, with its curtains
of heat and scoured, star-deep skies, was for dreaming.
This land of mist and dark water took all of one's mind up
with the day-to-day chore of staying alive.

In the lee of Kamloops Island the water flattened out re-
assuringly. Even so, the *Low Dollar* was beginning to drag
down the *Belle*'s stern. Anna cut throttle to an idle. All forward motion stopped immediately. She went up onto the
deck where Hal stood staring morosely at the streaming
blue hump that was his boat.

"We aren't going to make the dock at Todd," Anna told
him.

"You can't let her sink," he said pitifully. "She's not
paid for."

For a moment they stood in silence, the deck rocking
gently. There was scarcely any wind, but thin lines of foam
whipping white on the water beyond the *Low Dollar* never
let them forget they were only there on sufferance.

"I can't tow it any further," Anna said. "I've pushed my equipment—and my luck—more than I should have already. Let's pull her up, untie the tow." She pointed to the ragged shoreline where a finger of rock thrust out parallel to Isle Royale, the main island. In the directionless light it was almost indiscernible from the green of the cliffs and the gray of the water. "Behind that's a cove with a sandy bottom. I think I can nudge your boat in there. It'll settle in shallow water and you can salvage her when there's more daylight."

Having unloosed the towline, Anna took the Bertram around behind the *Low Dollar* and, bow to stern, rooted her into the cove like a pig rooting a bucket through the mud. The *Low Dollar* rested on the sand, keeled over on her side. Anna sent Hal wading ashore to tether the boat to a tree so the lake wouldn't work her loose and lure her back to the deep during the night.

Watching him flounder through the frigid waters, Anna was unsympathetic. It was his boat. He could get his own shoes and socks wet. She looked out past Kamloops Island where waves rolled toward Canada, over the waters she had still to traverse before she would be "home."

"I'm not used to so much water all in a row," she said to Kenny, who had finally ventured out on deck.

He looked past her, then returned to the cabin without a word.

Hal scrambled back on board with an armload of canned goods. Their camp gear was all under a foot of water in the hold. "You won't freeze," Anna promised. There were half a dozen spare sleeping bags on the *Belle Isle* and as many army surplus woolen blankets. In hypothermia country it wasn't excessive.

Halfway around the hump of land that separated the cove from Todd Harbor Camp, Kenny came out of his stupor and demanded they return to the *Low Dollar* to retrieve some "personal" things. After medication, food, and shelter had been eliminated, Anna guessed it was booze and, though she could empathize with the need for a good stiff drink, she refused to go back in the rain and growing dusk to fetch it.

Her refusal cost her any goodwill she might have earned for bringing them and their boat in off the lake. By the time they were settled in the shelter at Little Todd Harbor with her assurance that she would return with a Homelite pump in the morning, they'd grown almost surly.

Leaving them to deal with their damaged egos, Anna made her escape. Nine-fifteen P.M.: hers would be a late supper. She'd forgotten she was hungry. So far north, the sun was only just setting. It wouldn't be full dark for another thirty minutes—later, had there been no overcast. In June the days seemed to go on forever.

"Three-zero-two en route to Amygdaloid from Todd Harbor," Anna put in the blind call. The dispatcher in Rock Harbor went off duty at seven, but the call would be taped and, should she go down, at least they'd know where to start diving for the body.

Involuntarily, she shuddered. A body wouldn't be alone down there. There were plenty of ships lying on Superior's bottom. Nearly a dozen provided scuba-diving attractions in the park: the *America, Monarch, Emperor, Algoma, Cox, Congdon, Chisholm, Glenlyon, Cumberland,* the *Kamloops.* Off her port bow a buoy bobbed, marking the deepest of the wrecks: the *Kamloops.* Her stern rested at one hundred and seventy-five feet, her bow at two hundred and sixty. Divers were discouraged: too deep, too cold, too dangerous.

Five sailors still stood guard in the engine room. Anna had seen an underwater photograph of them. Deep, cold, protected from currents, no creatures to eat them, they swam like ghosts in the old ship. For fifty years they'd drifted alone in the dark. Then in 1977 divers found the wreck. Years of submersion had robbed the bodies of most of their corporeal selves and they were translucent as wraiths.

Think of something else, Anna commanded herself. As she entered the familiar channel between Amygdaloid Island and Belle Isle, and saw the ranger station snugged up safe from storms at the foot of the moss-covered cliff, she allowed herself one short dream of cholla cactus and skies without milky veils of moisture, of a sun with fire to it and food hotter even than that.

After the lion incident at Guadalupe Mountains National Park, Anna had felt the need to move on, to start over. At heart, the Park Service was a bureaucracy and, in the wake of the discoveries, there had been much talk and little action. Still, Anna had worn out her welcome in West Texas. The next move, she promised as she eased the Bertram up to the dock, would be back to the Southwest, to the desert. And with a promotion; twenty-two thousand dollars a year was getting harder and harder to live on.

The *3rd Sister*, a handsome forty-foot cabin cruiser with a high-ceilinged pilot's cabin and a flying bridge decked out in red and white pin-striping, was moored across the dock. A hibachi stood unattended on the rough wooden planking of the pier. Anna could smell fish broiling over charcoal.

As she stepped onto the dock, lines in hand, a lithe form bundled in a heavy woolen shirt and a close-fitting fisherman's cap leapt from the deck of the diving boat and took the stern line to make the Bertram fast to the dock.

Anna finished tying the bow, tugging the half-knots snug, then coiling the tail of the line out of tripping distance. "Thanks, Holly," she called down the length of the boat. The wind took her words and flung them out over the channel. Anna was just as glad. As her helper turned, faced the last light from the western sky, she realized it was Holly's brother, Hawk, the third man in the *Sister*'s three-person dive crew.

Many people made the mistake. The twins were so alike they seemed two sides of a coin; male and female brought together just once to share the same species.

At thirty-two, Hawk's sister, Holly, was tall, the cut of her features clean without hardness, her dark hair soft but not fine. Her body was lean and well muscled and her shoulders were broad. Yet only someone crippled with sexual insecurity would have called her mannish.

Hawk was all of this and yet the very essence of masculine. The curve of his shoulders and the blunt efficiency of his wind-chapped hands carried a different message. Where Holly was quick, bright, and strong, he was controlled, thoughtful, exact.

He dropped the line in a perfect coil and came across the planking.

The eyes might take Hawk for Holly, Anna thought, the senses, never. One would have to be as neuter as a snail not to feel the difference.

He stopped beside her, turning to take the sharp edge of the wind onto his own back. "Denny's made too much salad as usual. Plenty of pike," he said, nodding toward the hibachi. "Better join us for supper."

Standing so close, Anna could see the dark stubble on his jaw. A delicate and somehow pleasing scent of Scotch whiskey warmed his breath. She hesitated. Relief at regaining solid ground had released her fatigue.

"No clients today," he added as an incentive. "We dove the *Cox.* Just swam around the bow to get our feet wet. Too rough for tourists. Besides, we needed the dive alone."

"Supper would be good," Anna said. "Bring it inside? I'll light a fire and pour a suitable libation."

Hawk nodded and dropped over the gunwale of the *3rd Sister* as Anna trotted, wind at her back, up the dock and onto the shore of Amygdaloid Island. Home, she thought sourly, but she was glad enough to be there.

The North Shore Ranger Station just missed being utterly charming. Standing foursquare to the dock, the outside was picturesque with a peaked roof and walls of red-brown board and battens. The paint had weathered to almost the same shade as the cliff that backed the building. A central door, flanked by many-paned windows, gave it a look of oldetyme honesty. Two stovepipes, tilted and tin-hatted against the wind, added a sense of roguish eccentricity.

Inside, the age of the building told in many small comfortless ways. It was divided into two large rooms. The front half was the National Park Service office. Under one window was Anna's desk, a marine radio, and a vintage 1919 safe where the revenues from the state of Michigan fishing licenses were kept, as was Anna's .357 service revolver when it was not on board the *Belle*. Across from the desk three Adirondack-style easy chairs nosed up to a cast-iron woodstove. A crib made of lath held firewood and kindling. Maps and charts shared wall space with relics that had accumulated over the years: an oar engraved with the names of two long-dead fishermen who had worked out of the Edison Fishery on the south side of the island, scraps of iron recognizable only to students of lake travel, bits of weathered wood, and three framed, faded photographs.

The first was of the *America*, the pleasure/mail/supply ship that serviced the island in its heyday as a resort community. The second was of the *America*'s bow thrust up through the ice; a pathetic trophy held in the lake's wintery grip long after it had struck a shoal and sunk in the North Gap outside Washington Harbor. The third, a long, glimmering underwater shot, was of the once sleek-sided ship vanishing into the darkness of the lake.

The bow of the *America* was still scarcely a yard beneath the surface, but her stern rested eighty feet down. On a calm day, when the water was clear, it gave Anna vertigo to look down at the old wreck. The last photo captured that dizzy sense of pitching into space.

None of this paraphernalia had been dusted for at least a year and probably longer than that. Rodent droppings, sifting down from the attic over the long winter when Isle Royale was ice-bound and closed to all human occupation, washed the overhead beams with gray. Cobwebs moved faintly in the drafts.

The rear portion of the house was devoted to living quarters. A second woodstove, half the size of the one in the office, was crowded into one corner. Opposite, along the wall beneath a window that faced the cliff, was a crumbling Formica counter with a sink and hand pump. A two-burner gas stove, a gas refrigerator, and an aluminum shower stall lined the short northern wall. A narrow wooden door led out back past the propane tank to the pit toilet.

Anna's bed, dresser, and closet were against the inside wall. Beside the bed, where the cracked blue-and-red-speckled linoleum came to a curling end, was a faded oval rag rug. When Anna's housemate, Christina, had visited from Houghton, she had stood on that rug as a woman might stand on an island in a rising sea of offal and re-marked: "How charming. A Great Room divided into con-versation areas." She'd laughed though, and before she and Alison—her five-year-old daughter—had left, she'd managed to make it a home for Anna.

A patchwork coverlet and handmade pillows brightened the bed. Mexican rugs warmed the walls and kept the drafts out. Alison's contribution—Ally's taste and her mother's money—was a see-through shower curtain be-decked with saxophone-playing alligators in tuxedos.

Christina and her daughter had known Anna less than a year. When she had left Guadalupe, where Chris had been a secretary, they had come with her. Now Anna divided her year between the island in the summer and the park head-quarters in Houghton, Michigan, in the winter, where she shared a house with Chris and Ally. When she'd come out to the island in early May, Anna had been surprised at how much she missed them. She'd always thought of herself as a loner.

Anna lit the oil lamps and laid fires in both stoves, opening dampers and vents to give them a head start. On this drizzly June day the whole place smelled of damp and rat droppings.

Heat and light began to revive her, and overlaid the rickety rooms with a sense of romance. Shelter from the storm, Anna thought as she peeled off the layers of gray and green and pulled on dry fleecy pants and a top with a hood. Given time—and a decent red wine—she believed she might even come to like the place.

The bang of the front door announced the arrival of the *3rd Sister*'s crew, and Anna yelled a superfluous "Come in" as Hawk, Holly, and Denny Castle gusted into the outer office. The wind that carried them smelled of mesquite smoke and whiskey.

Holly was a little drunk—not sloppy drunk, but high. Her eyes burned with alcohol-induced fever and her cheeks were redder than the wind would account for. She carried a bottle of Black & White in her coat pocket, the label showing as if she dared anyone to comment on it. Mist had glued her short dark hair to her forehead in sculpted curls. She looked like a creature of storm and sea, a siren ready to sing some modern-day Ulysses onto the rocks.

Hawk, though he took a glass of Scotch when Holly pressed him, was drinking little. His eyes seldom left his sister's face and he seemed half afraid of the fires that burned so clearly there.

Denny Castle, captain of the *3rd Sister* dive concession, a private venture permitted by the NPS, was older than the Bradshaw twins, close to Anna's age she would have guessed, though he might have been as old as forty-five or as young as thirty-five. Life on the water and under it had weathered his face until it was aged and ageless, like wood that's been worn almost smooth. There was no gray in his hair, but in hair so blond, it would scarcely show as anything more than a subtle fading. He wore it long in the fashion of general Custer. The resemblance to the fabled Indian fighter ended there. No mustache, no beard. Denny Castle's face reflected a deep and abiding care. It was a look that drew women to him like moths to a flame, only to find themselves scorched by his indifference. The care was for the lake; abiding love for Superior in all her moods.

There was a legend that in Superior's storms there sometimes came three waves, each bigger than the last. It was the third that drove ships to their deaths. The waves were called the Three Sisters. It was they, lakers would tell, who had drowned the *Edmund Fitzgerald*. Denny liked to say he had met the third sister and married her. If gossip could be trusted, he had spent more time on board the *3rd*

Sister over the past eleven years than at any woman's breakfast table.

Castle wasn't drinking at all, nor was he talking. As he ran back out into the night to check on dinner, Anna poured herself a glass of Mondavi red and, wondering what the hell was going on, settled close to the stove. The air had an electric feel to it, fueled by alternating currents between the three divers. Anna didn't ask what was up. She had little doubt that some revealing sparks would soon begin to fly.

Within a couple of minutes Denny ducked in out of the drizzle, a plate of blackened fish in his hands. Lamplight caught beads of water on his hair and they flickered orange, a jeweled halo around his face. "Superior," he announced.

"D'Artagnan's last supper. I'll drink to that," Holly said. Despite the liquor, her voice was clear and low, but Denny winced as if she had shrilled at him.

"Forgot the salad—" he said and closed himself again into the night beyond the cabin door.

Hawk leaned down and fed sticks into the woodstove. Anna guessed that whatever gnawed at Holly was eating him. Once more she had the sense that they were two aspects of one person. This night it was the Holly aspect that spoke. Hawk stood back, a reservoir of strength for her to draw on.

"Porthos and Aramis," Anna said aloud. Watching the two faces, so alike, she had put the allusion together. "How long have the three of you been diving together?"

A tear, colored like blood from the fire's light, flashed on Holly's cheek. She swatted it away as if it were a fly. "Always," she said.

"Seven years." Hawk defined "always," but it sounded as if it was always to him as well.

"Since we knew what diving was about. Since the Three Sisters were in pinafores. Since we quit fucking around," Holly said sharply. "Always."

Anna waited, but there was no more. Denny came back with the salad and, seeming to take it for granted that he was to wait on them, cleared Anna's desk and set out plates and flatware. Anna was too tired to help and Hawk and Holly seemed determined to let him serve. When he was finished, he sat down on a stool he'd pulled up. He was the only one at the table, the only one interested, it seemed, in the food.

"This is a celebration," he said, looking not at them but down at his empty plate. "I'm getting married tomorrow."

"To a regular woman?" Anna asked, taken by surprise.

Holly began to laugh.

Hawk turned his face away from Denny, from his sister. There was as much pain in his look as there had been in Holly's laughter.

Anna stood, drained her glass, shook off their misery. She was tired. She was hungry. Maybe they'd been on one too many dives. The deep addled people's brains. She carried her wine bottle to the desk and sat down in the wooden swivel chair. Supper was made and it was free.

"Congratulations, Denny," she said equitably. "Please pass the salad."

CHAPTER 2

Mist lay over Amygdaloid Channel. Humps of pale gray moved lazily over the surface as if ghostly whales swam between air and water. Patches drifted clear and the silver of reflected light glowed till fingers of fog curled back to reclaim the space. To the east, over the green ridges of Belle Isle, the dawn sky was burning into blue, the promise of a beautiful day.

Wrapped against the chill that the forty-eighth parallel would not relinquish even in June, Anna sat on the front steps of the ranger station. Cloaked in a shapeless plaid flannel bathrobe, the tail tucked under her feet to keep them from the dew-bitten planks, she stared through binoculars at the far shore: a thin line of sand and stone, now revealed, now shrouded by the mist. Beside her a mug of coffee curled tiny tendrils of fog into the cold air; a minuscule offering to the gods of the lake.

"Come on," Anna said softly. "Come out. I know you're there. And I know you've got the baby. Show yourselves."

From the silence of the channel a loon called and was answered. The sun pierced the pines on the cliff's top and dyed the mist rose. Open water glittered, bright as new pennies. Again the loon called its haunting liquid warble, this time to be answered by the sound of wings on water.

Now they'll come, Anna thought. "I've seen your tracks," she whispered. "I know you're there."

A shadowy red form darted between her and the dock where gently rocking boats cradled fishermen. She refocused the glasses. The black muzzle of a little fox came into view. Head tilted to one side, pink tongue lolling, she sat less than twenty feet from the station steps ready to beg for her breakfast like a house dog. "Not you, Knucklehead," Anna murmured and again trained the field glasses on the opposite shore.

Somewhere to the north a power boat growled to life and morning's spell was broken. Now they wouldn't come. "Damn." Anna lowered the binoculars. Isle Royale's wolves were the shyest of creatures. Some rangers who'd worked the island for years had never so much as glimpsed them. Scat, tracks, howling, confused reports from hikers startled by foxes—that was all most people ever knew of the wolves in summer.

In winter, when the island's dense foliage dropped its leaves and deep snow made tracking easy, a Winter Study team came to ISRO—Park Service shorthand for Isle Royale—for several weeks and studied the wolf packs. Only two packs remained, twelve wolves in all, with only one new birth in the past year. The wolves were dying and the scientists didn't know why. There was some indication that an outbreak of canine parvovirus, a disease carried by domestic dogs, was a factor in the decline, but inbreeding was the guess most favored at the moment.

The Park Service was doing all it could to preserve the wolves, even to the extremely unpopular extent of denying visitors and staff the privilege of bringing their pets to the island—or even within the park's boundaries four and a half miles out. Still, the wolves did not thrive, did not reproduce.

At least it's not us killing them, not directly, Anna thought, and enjoyed the sense of being one of the good guys, a compatriot instead of a despoiler. It was a proud feeling. And rare as hen's teeth, added her mind's resident cynic.

"Tomorrow," she said to the empty stretch of beach across the channel. "At dawn. Be there or be square. And bring the puppy."

The roar of the motorboat grew louder, wrecking what remained of tranquillity. A glossy wine-colored bow plowed up the mist in the channel. Anna gathered up her cup and crept back inside. It wouldn't do for the public to catch the ranger in her pajamas. Besides, it was her lieu day. If she didn't escape before a tourist happened to her, she'd undoubtedly get roped into some task for which the NPS wouldn't pay overtime.

During the six months the park was staffed, Lucas Vega frowned on rangers leaving the island on their days off. Superior's sudden storms had a habit of turning weekends into paid vacations. Consequently, Anna spent a goodly number of her days off selling fishing licenses, cutting fishhooks out of fingers, and listening to fish stories.

"Attitude, Anna, attitude," she chided herself as she dragged on long underwear and polypropylene trousers, but she had every intention of escaping out the back door unless the approaching vessel could prove problems of a life-and-death nature.

This Tuesday and Wednesday, she'd promised herself a kayak trip, dinner at the lodge, and a phone call to New York. The trip would mix business with pleasure. Anna packed a tent and backcountry gear for several nights out. On the way back, she would spend a couple of days checking the more remote campsites.

The sun was high by the time she shoved off. By Anna's standards it never got warm—not the deep bone-warming temperatures that baked the poisons out down in the Trans-Pecos—but the weather held jewel-bright. A breeze cooled by thirty-nine-degree waters cut across the bow when she nosed her sea kayak into the open water around Blake's Point at the island's northernmost tip, and even through the insulating layers her butt was cold. Hard paddling kept her from feeling the worst of the chill.

Waves, dangerous near the point where shoals broke them, rolled gently half a mile out. Anna kept her bow pointed into the swells and reveled in the sense of being part of the lake instead of a motorized nuisance, a noisy intruder it would shrug from its skin as a horse would twitch free of a fly.

Northeast was Passage Island with its historic lighthouse. To the south, long fingers of land, rock shredded by fifteen centuries of a glacier's feints and retreats, reached into the lake. In the spring sunshine, the peninsulas were clothed in rich greens and the water in the coves was tropical blue. Gold-colored stone, broken into blocks ten and twenty feet on a side, glimmered through the crystal water. Timber, blown over from the mainland or toppled from ISRO's own shores, was scattered like jackstraws on the lake bottom. In places the fissured rock and bleached wood gave the disconcerting illusions of sunken ruins. Castles filled only with fishes, turrets pulled down to make playgrounds for otters.

Anna let the kayak drift down the sheltered channel beside Porter's Island. Shipping her paddles, she ate a lunch of tortillas and beans. Lying back, her legs free of the enclosed bow, she let the sun paint patterns on her eyelids, as the water tapped its music against the sides of the boat.

When she finally paddled into the wake-raddled bustle of Rock Harbor, it was after five o'clock.

Rock Harbor was a nine-mile stretch of water protected from the storms by a chain of islands: Raspberry, Smithwick, Shaw, Tookers, Davidson, Outer Hill, Mott, Caribou. The administrative offices of the National Park Service were clustered on Mott Island, the biggest in the chain. A majority of ISRO's employees were housed there in dormitories or apartments. The island's somewhat gruesome history—it was named for Charlie Mott, who had tried to eat his wife one long and hungry winter—was all but exorcised by the banal necessities of bureaucratic life.

The niche in Rock Harbor that was thought of as the

"real" Rock Harbor was three miles from Mott toward Blake's Point. It was a doubly protected cove shut in an elbow of land. The lodge was there, along with the Visitors' Center, the boat rental concession, and a clapboard windowless hall where National Park Service naturalists like to shut the tourists away from moose and fox and thimbleberry, from rain and wind and mosquitoes and show them slides of Nature.

Gasoline and groceries could be had in Rock, and there was a pumping station for boats. During the height of the summer season the *Voyageur* from Grand Marais, Minnesota, called three times a week, the *Queen* brought passengers from Copper Harbor, Michigan, on Mondays and Fridays, and the *Ranger III* carried fares and supplies from Houghton. The lodge was usually booked weeks ahead and backpackers, disembarking from the ships, often had to hike eight or more miles out before finding a camp for the night.

Bustle and busyness, petty crimes and medical problems had earned the port the nickname of Rock Harlem among park and concessionaire employees. Though Anna enjoyed her occasional forays into this heart of commerce, she always found its urbanity jarring after the isolation of Amygdaloid.

As she dragged her kayak up between the docks that lined the harbor, she saw a blond woman in the khaki and green uniform of the Student Conservation Association. SCAs were volunteers, often college students, who traded their time for the experience and the joy of summering in a park.

Anna knew her slightly from the training provided for all seasonal employees the first week in June. Her name was Tenner, or Tinkle. No, Tinker, Anna remembered. She was married to a man of twenty-four, about ten years younger than she was. It had been the gossip for a day or two. He called himself Damien and leaned toward black capes and cryptic statements.

The woman had a vague and whimsical nature, as if she believed, along with Liza Minnelli, that reality was something she must rise above. At present she was leading a score of tourists around the one-mile paved nature trail.

Anna turned her back on the group and stowed her paddles in the kayak's hull. If it was one of Tinker's first nature walks, Anna didn't want to distract her. Thirty-one years afterward Anna still remembered one devastating moment when she'd looked off stage in the middle of her big moment as Jack Frost to see her grandmother waving from the second row.

On the short walk up from the water, Anna deliberated between a drink and a phone call. The phone call won. ISRO was connected to the mainland by radiophone, and anybody with the right frequency and a passing interest could tune in. But it was the only link with the outside world and Anna was glad to have it.

The booth provided for NPS employees was built of pecky cedar, but after years of use it smelled like a dirty ashtray. Set off in a small clearing in the spruce trees, windows on all four sides, it had the look of the bridge on a tugboat. Several yards away, next to a sixty-watt bulb on a metal post, was a bench for people waiting to use the phone.

Line forms to the right, Anna thought, but she was in luck. There was no one in the booth, and she slipped inside. She shooed a spider off the counter and dragged the phone over. Crackling and whispers grated in the darkness of her inner ear—then finally, faintly, the burr of a phone ringing on the fourteenth floor above Park Avenue and Seventy-sixth Street.

"Park View Clinic," came a toneless voice. But for twelve years of experience, Anna would have waited for the machine's beep.

"Is Dr. Pigeon in?" Anna asked formally. "It's her sister."

"One moment please." Never a spark of recognition, never an "Oh, hello, Anna" in all the years. Hazel—a name Anna found at odds with the cold telephone persona—was the ideal receptionist, Molly said. A woman with an imagination wouldn't have lasted a week in the position.

"Will you hold?" pierced through the static.

"I'll hold." Music, Yo Yo Ma on cello, drifted down the wires through the white noise.

A young man came and sat down on the waiting bench. He had dark thick hair that seemed both wild and well coiffured, the envy of any girl. His eyes were wide-set above chiseled cheekbones. Anna prepared herself to ignore him. Her rare phone calls were too precious to be spoiled by the pressuring eyes of a too-pretty boy. Before she had time to edit him out of her world, he flashed her a smile and she recognized him: Tinker's husband, sans cape.

"Can't talk long. Give me the news."

Molly's voice, sudden and startling, seemed to speak from inside Anna's head. It sounded so faint, so rushed, her isolation felt more complete. A heaviness grew in her chest. She had no news. She was just making contact, drilling a long-distance hole in her loneliness. "You're at the office late," she said.

"My four o'clock had a lot on her mind today. Still afraid her husband will leave her. Been coming to me twice a week for eleven years about it. I must be one hell of a shrink."

"You do her good."

"Maybe. If not for my fees, her husband could've afforded a divorce in 1986. This connection is bloody awful, Anna. Have you found someplace even more godforsaken than West Texas? Tell me you've got flush toilets."

Anna laughed. "Sorry."

"Seven minutes, Anna." There was a short sucking silence; Molly lighting a cigarette.

"Those things'll kill you," Anna said.

"This from a woman who carries a gun," Molly returned.

"Not anymore. It would be more likely to drown you here than save you from the bad guys. I carry it in a briefcase like any self-respecting Manhattan drug dealer."

Molly laughed, almost a cackle. "Six minutes . . . nope. Four."

"Why? What's up?" Anna forced herself to ask, though

suddenly she knew she didn't want to hear of any glittering social event, any cozy gathering.

"Promised to go to a function up in Westchester. A political wine tasting."

"Wine's not your drink."

"Not like it's yours."

Anna ignored that.

"Two reasons: A client of mine is obsessing on it. Can't name names but you'll find his byline in the Girls' Sports section of Sunday's *Times*." Anna laughed—that was how Molly always referred to the Style section. Molly continued: "A rediscovered batch of very pricey long-lost stuff. Supposedly made during Prohibition, the year of the perfect weather in California. When the sun, the grapes, the soil, had reached the mythical moment. Twenty cases were bottled, then mysteriously vanished. Last month a couple of the prodigal bottles returned. My client is most distraught. Swears it's a hoax. As you may have guessed, he wasn't the one to rediscover it.

"Secondly: It's in Westchester County. I haven't been there for a while. I thought I'd stop by Valhalla—" Molly interrupted herself with a snort of laughter. "Valhalla. A good Christian cemetery, no doubt. Look up Zachary. See if the eternal flame still burns or whatever."

"My mother-in-law takes care of that," Anna said.

"Does Edith still think his ashes are under that godawful marble slab? Speaking of mental health," Molly went on without giving Anna time to answer, "do you still have them? Sprinkle them, Anna. Do it. 'Lake Superior, it is said, never gives up her dead.' Do it."

"Don't you have someplace to go?" Anna asked irritably.

"Right. Stay out of Davey Jones's locker."

And the line went dead.

Anna settled the receiver back in the cradle. The heaviness in her chest had grown more oppressive. Maybe she'd been hiding in the wilderness long enough. Maybe it was time to go back to civilization. It would be good to shave her legs, pull on something silk, go to a pretentious party in lipstick and hose.

She looked out the window of the phone box. Damien still inhabited the bench. Not with the air of a man waiting impatiently—or patiently—but of a man with no better place to be. The wide-set eyes were fixed on a pileated woodpecker high in an aspen tree. He watched with the total unaffected concentration of a child.

A red feather floated down through the golden-green leaves and landed a yard or two from his sneakered feet. He picked up the feather and the lovely smile flashed. Not for Anna this time, for the giver of the gift: the woodpecker.

Anna banged open the door of the phone box and the bird flew off in an aerial scramble. "I'm finished," she announced unnecessarily.

"You're Anna Pigeon, aren't you?" Damien's voice was soft and high. Over the phone he would be mistaken for a child. In person, with the clear greenish eyes and styled dark hair, it didn't seem inappropriate.

"You're Damien," Anna replied.

"There's a party tonight in the lodge for Denny Castle of the *Third Sister.* Can you come? Tinker and I must talk to you." He'd dropped his voice to a furtive level and, with a melodramatic flair Anna couldn't help but admire, glanced over his shoulder.

She didn't laugh, but it took some effort. "I'll be there," she replied. "In my official capacity."

If Damien knew she was teasing him, he was not affected by it. "Good," he said, then again, firmly, as if coming to some inner decision: "Good. It is necessary."

As he turned away and walked to the call box, throwing his shoulders as if a cloak swirled down from them, Anna allowed the smile inside to break the neutral set of her mouth.

Officially the party would start at half past eight, when Denny Castle was to bring his new bride into the dining room. Unofficially Anna commenced toasting the happy couple shortly after she got off the phone with her sister. Trying, and fairly successfully, to float the heavy weight off her heart, to water down the loneliness with wine.

Sitting on the lodge's wooden deck, overlooking the harbor, she sipped a mediocre Beaujolais and let the silver of the evening sink into her soul. Sadness didn't seem half bad when there were no human mirrors at hand to reflect it.

"To Piedmont," she said and lifted her glass to the paling sky. The Beaujolais had a lovely color, catching the light without dulling it.

"Piedmont?"

The voice was so calm and well modulated that it made scarcely a ripple in Anna's solitude. "My cat," she said easily and looked up from the deck chair where she sprawled to see who had addressed her.

A small woman—five foot two or so, shorter than Anna—stood a few yards away, her arms crossed against the coming chill. In the pearly evening light her hair shone a pale gold, almost certainly from a bottle, but so artfully done it was hard to tell. She wore it shoulder-length with bangs blunt-cut just above eyebrow level. Her dress, heavy silk from the way it moved in the breeze, was of nearly the same shade, a color close to that of winter sunlight. Her face was heavily lined. Crow's-feet fanned out from the corners of her eyes and partway down her cheeks. There was a pronounced parenthesis around her mouth where the nasolabial folds carved their mark. Faint creases, held at bay by lipstick carefully applied and fixed with powder, cut into her lip-line. But for the wrinkles she showed no age at all. Her body was narrow-hipped, slim as a willow wand, her voice resonant, her gaze direct and challenging.

Anna pegged her as a rich tourist. Maybe a doctor's wife up from the Twin Cities on a tasteful little yacht named the *Kidney Stone* or the *Aqueous Humor.*

The woman smiled, a friendly, pretty smile which gave absolutely nothing away. Anna revised her first impression: maybe the woman was the doctor herself.

"Piedmont's my cat," Anna said, the mutual assessment

over in a heartbeat. "I had to leave him in Houghton with Christina and Ally—my housemates."

"Ah. Yes." The woman spread her skirt around her in a golden circle and sat gracefully on the step. Anna noticed her sandals matched her dress and hair—exactly. They had been dyed the same shade. "We left Pointer in a kennel in Duluth. Carrie writes him once a week. If any dog can learn to read, it'll be Pointer. He's a Lhasa Apso. 'No Domestic Animals on the Island.' As if the comforts here weren't few enough."

An employee. Anna felt she should be able to place the woman, but her brain was in no mood to be racked for once-seen faces, half-heard names. "I know I'm Anna Pigeon, North Shore Ranger, but I don't know who you are. Should I?" The sentence construction was a little tipsy but Anna thought the sentiment sounded reasonable enough.

"At least you know who you are," the woman said and laughed. "That's more than most of the people here know. These Upper Peninsula types aren't given much to introspection. I'm Patience Bittner. I manage the lodge. When I've been guffawed on, jostled, or growled at one too many times, I escape out here to regain my equilibrium."

Anna nodded, took a sip of her drink, turned her mind free again to glide out over the water. She must have made a face, because Patience said: "You're drinking the Beaujolais."

"Yes," Anna said neutrally.

"It's the last of it, I promise. It was ordered without my approval and it seemed a shame to pour it out. It's such an ordeal getting anything good shipped out here back of beyond. I've got quite a decent California red coming in on the *Ranger Three*. Glen Ellen has a nice cabernet sauvignon. Young but nice."

"Nosy without being precocious?" Anna teased, thinking of Molly and her neurotic gourmet.

Patience smiled. "Do I sound pretentious? Habit. I used to manage a winery outside Napa."

"Vodka and beer are the booze ordinaire in this part of the country. Not many people will notice your hard work."

"You will, I expect."

"Only on the first glass," Anna said truthfully, and the woman laughed again, a brittle sound but not unpleasant.

"If I get in anything special, I'll get you in on the first glass." She looked at her watch, a delicate gold band. "Party time. Pleased to meet you, Anna. I hope you'll come by and sit on my deck again sometime soon."

The innkeeper left, trailing a faint scent of perfume. "Privileged," Anna thought, or "Passion." Expensive scents, but neither could compete with the mind-clearing draft that was carried over the water from the ground hemlock and fir on Raspberry Island.

With the fading of the light the guardians of the island began to reclaim her shores. A persistent whining burned in Anna's ear. A stinging itch cut through the thin fabric of her shirt. Again she missed the desert. There, if something bit, one usually died of it. She hated this nickel and diming to death, one bloody sip at a time.

She stood and knocked back the last of her wine. Denny Castle's wedding reception: it would be rude not to make an appearance. And she needed to wheedle an invitation to sleep on someone's floor. Failing that, she'd bed down in the *Lorelei,* the boat belonging to the District Ranger, Ralph Pilcher. More damp sleeping bags and pit toilets.

Inspired—or intimidated—by Patience Bittner's easy elegance, Anna made a stop in the ladies' room. Hair hanging in two gray-streaked braids gave her an aging Rebecca of Sunnybrook Farm look. She wrapped the plaits around her head and secured them in place with pins from her daypack. Too sunburned to wash her face with the harsh industrial soap in the washroom, she limited her toilette to the new coiffure.

The main dining room at the Rock Harbor Lodge made an attempt at being picturesque. The walls were paneled in light-colored wood, the ceiling cross-hatched with redwood beams, and the chandeliers fashioned from brass conning wheels. Other appropriately nautical bits of decor were scattered around, but boxy fifties construction spoiled the overall effect.

Park people were clustered in one corner. Patience floated around like a golden butterfly, refilling glasses. Coffeepot in hand, an awkward-looking girl with dark hair cut in a Prince Valiant shuffled after her from table to table, eyes fixed on the tops of her shoes. Anna wondered if this was the Carrie who wrote letters to Lhasa Apsos. She appeared to be the right age for a daughter of Patience Bittner—twelve or thirteen.

Tinker was there with Damien. They sat near the others but at a table for two. Their hands were clasped together on the white cloth and, instead of the glaring electric table lamps, they shared a candle-lantern which they obviously supplied themselves. Damien tried to catch Anna's eye with a dark and pregnant look, but she pretended not to see him.

Scotty Butkus was sitting at the head of the main table smoking a cigarette, two bottles of Mickey's Big Mouth at his elbow. Scotty, like Anna, was a permanent law enforcement ranger, her counterpart in Rock Harbor. Butkus fancied himself an old cowboy who'd been a ranger when it was still a good job. To hear him talk, he'd helped clean up Dodge City. But he wasn't more than fifty-nine or sixty at most, still a GS-7 making the same salary as Anna.

A few of the younger people thought he was a semiromantic has-been. Anna suspected he was a never-was, drinking and talking to rectify a personal history that was a disappointment. He'd been busted down from somewhere and was starting over: new park, new job, new young wife. The new wife wasn't in evidence.

Next to Butkus was Jim Tattinger, the park's Submerged Cultural Resources Specialist. Anna knew very little about him except that, according to the crew of the *3rd Sister,* he spent all his time playing with computers and never dove any of the wrecks himself. Tattinger looked like a textbook nerd, right down to his skinny neck, thick glasses, and thinning red hair. Anna moved down the table so she wouldn't have to sit opposite him. When he talked or smiled his thin lips stretched too far, turning a moist pink ruffle of nether lip out into the light of day. She didn't want to know him that well.

Between Pizza Dave, the four-hundred-and-fifty-pound maintenance man, and Anna's boss, Ralph Pilcher, the District Ranger for Rock Harbor, she found an empty chair. Lucas Vega wasn't there. One of the perks of being Chief Ranger was being spared some of the employee get-togethers.

Holly and Hawk Bradshaw were conspicuous by their absence.

The pooped-party feel did not surprise Anna. Living in such isolated places, NPS managers felt a responsibility to instill a sense of "family" into their employees and, accordingly, planned endless potlucks, Chrismooses, chocolate pigouts, and receptions. Usually these attempts at building an esprit de corps failed. People came because there was nothing else to do and left as early as good manners—or good politics—allowed.

This get-together had a couple of things going for it. People wanted to see Denny's new wife, and it was held in the lodge within hailing distance of a fully stocked bar.

As Anna wriggled into her chair, Denny Castle and his wife entered the front door, triggering desultory applause. A handful of lodge guests joined in and the sound swelled to a respectable level.

As the popping of hands thinned, and Butkus began another story of how it used to be, Patience took the bride's arm with a natural hostess's charm and walked her and Denny across toward the party.

Denny's wife was five five or six with narrow shoulders and disproportionately wide hips. Lusterless brown hair fell from the center part to below her waist. Her round face was expressionless behind oversized red-framed glasses. As she pulled out the chair next to Ralph, Anna noticed how gnarled and scarred her hands and forearms were. She had seen those blue-black marks before. Looking into the glare of the electric candles, she tried to smooth her mind so the memory would come. After a moment's teasing, it rose to the surface. She'd seen the scars on the arms of a hitchhiker she had given a lift from Santa Barbara to Morro Bay. The man had been an abalone diver. The scars were from where the shells had cut.

"This is the new Mrs. Castle," Patience introduced her. "Jo."

So, the bride, Jo, née God knew what, had opted to be known as Mrs. Denny Castle. Anna thought it an odd choice for a woman with her master's degree in freshwater biology, and the diving scars to prove it. That bit of information Anna had picked up from a Resource Management memorandum. Funded by the park, Jo Castle would spend the summer researching pollution in ISRO's inland waters. Originally she had applied to do her Ph.D. thesis on how much impact sport fishing was having on the island's lake trout population.

That would have been worth knowing, Anna thought. But the NPS wouldn't fund that particular study. Sport fishermen had powerful lobbyists. The fishes did not. So Mrs. Denny Castle would count PCBs and swat mosquitoes in the island's interior for twelve weeks.

A crash and a curse saved Jo from further scrutiny. Scotty had knocked over his beer. Cigarette butts were floating out of the ashtray and down the white tablecloth on a foaming tide. Anna guessed he was drunk. He had the look of a man who's been drunk often enough that he's learned to cover it with a modicum of success. Mopping up the mess with a peach-colored napkin, he was muttering: "Jesus, I'm sorry. I'm not used to eating indoors. No elbowroom. Yes, ma'am"—this to Patience—"I'm sorry as hell. Begging your pardon"—this to Carrie for the rough language. "Let me help you clean up, little lady."

The dialogue was clichéd. Anna lost interest. She cast her eye around for some likely reason to excuse herself from the table.

Damien and Tinker provided it. Damien beckoned with the cock of a wing-shaped eyebrow. Handfast, Tinker's blond hair permed and repermed into a golden frizz, Damien dressed all in black, they looked like the hero and heroine of an *Afterschool Special*.

With a good-bye to Dave, Anna squeaked her chair back, shouldered her daypack, and went over to their table. "Not here," Damien said. Anna waited while, with an odd little ritual that required three taps on the glass and brass of the candle lantern, Tinker blew out the flame and folded the lantern down to stow in a canvas satchel.

They led her out of the restaurant and down to the water. At the end of the first in the row of docks, two-by-twelves, destined to be hauled into the wilderness on the backs of trail crew, were stacked. They settled behind these. Anna squatted down on her heels, balanced easily, and waited. This far out on the water the whine of mosquitoes faded. She took a breath as deep as a sigh. Of necessity the three of them were huddled so close between the lumber and the edge of the pier that her breath moved Tinker's fine hair, silver now in the fluorescent lights over the harbor.

Tinker said: "I know. It's not so much the smoke as the need. It gets hard to breathe."

To her surprise, Anna understood exactly what Tinker was talking about. The air in the lodge felt thick, oppressive with more than just the fumes from Butkus's interminable cigarettes. There was a sense of needs unfulfilled, hopes deferred, a generic discontent.

"People together by necessity, not choice," Anna said. "Makes for strange alliances."

"Yes," Damien said darkly.

Safe in the inky shadow of the lumber, Anna smiled. Had anyone else dragged her out into the damp to play cloak and dagger she would probably have been annoyed. There was something about Tinker and Damien that disarmed her. Though eccentric, even theatrical, they seemed of good heart, as if they did as they did because it was the way in which they could deal with a difficult world. She no more felt they wasted her time than the loons who sang away her mornings.

Gentle people seemed somehow a more natural phenomenon than the greedy bulk of humanity.

"What's the problem?" Anna asked.

"We think Scotty has eaten his wife," Tinker confided.

CHAPTER 3

Anna had recovered her composure. She sat on the floor of Tinker and Damien's room in the old house half a mile from the harbor. Since it had become too run-down for any other use, it had been converted into a dorm for seasonal employees. A dozen or more candles burned, but even this glamorous aura couldn't rid the place of its mildew-and-linoleum seediness. Tinker, her soft hair glittering in the many lights, poured herbal tea into tiny, mismatched Oriental bowls.

"It's made from all natural ingredients," she said as she handed Anna a red lacquered bowl. "Damien and I gathered them here and on Raspberry."

Eye of newt and toe of frog, Anna thought but she took a sip to be polite. The tea tasted of mint and honey with a woody undercurrent reminiscent of the way leaves smell when they're newly fallen. Anna doubted she'd ask for a second cup, but not because the concoction was unpalatable. The strange brew, the black-cloaked boy, the candlelight, put her in mind of other rooms, heavy with incense and dark with Indian-print bedspreads, where the tea and cakes had been laced with more than wild raspberry leaves. She pushed her bowl aside and cleared the cobwebs of the bad old days from her mind.

"So. Scotty's wife—Donna—hasn't been around for a few days?"

"Seven," Damien said, making the number sound like Donna Butkus's death knell. Tinker nodded, her gossamer hair floating in the warm currents from the candles.

"Seven," Anna repeated matter-of-factly.

"We went down to the water on the far side of the dock, down through the tangle of new-growth firs. There's a little cove there where hardly anybody goes. Donna always fed the ducks there mornings," Tinker said.

Anna raised an eyebrow. Feeding wildlife was strictly taboo.

"Yes, it was opportunistic," Tinker agreed. "But sometimes Damien and I would go there later in the day to watch the birds she had attracted." Again Anna was startled at her understanding. Tinker's mind seemed strangely accessible. Either that or Anna was more transparent than she liked to think she was.

"We saw a red-necked grebe, and once a black scooter came to feed." For the first time Damien sounded like a boy. Birds, then, were his passion.

"Last Wednesday, after breakfast, we went birding in the cove. Donna wasn't there. That's when we first suspected she was missing," Damien said.

"Maybe she came earlier, fed them, and had already gone," Anna suggested.

Damien shook his head portentously. "You don't understand. The ducks were *expecting* her." The boy was gone; the wizard was back.

"Did you ask Scotty where she was?"

"He said she'd had the flu and was home watching the soaps and drinking orange juice," Tinker replied, as if that course of events was too farfetched to fool even a child. She folded the tips of long tapered fingers delicately around the lacquered bowl and raised it to her lips, not to drink but to inhale the sweet-smelling steam.

It crossed Anna's mind that perhaps O.J. and *The Young and the Restless* were beyond the pale for Tinker. "Replace the soaps with old Jimmy Stewart movies and that's what I'd do if I had the flu," Anna said. "What's wrong with that?"

"There is no flu going around," Damien declared flatly.

Tinker said: "Donna had promised to cut my hair. In return I was going to teach her how to use some of the herbs here. Just for small things—nothing dangerous," she reassured Anna who, till then, hadn't needed it. "Just hair rinses and facials, decoctions for colds, that sort of thing. Then nothing. Not a word. Not a note. Then we . . ." She looked to her husband for assistance, clearly coming now to what she considered shaky ground.

"We conducted the surveillance warranted by the seriousness of the situation," he said firmly. In his airy voice the statement reminded Anna of the sweet but implacable "Because I said so" that Sister Judette had used to such effect on the class of '69.

"You watched the house," Anna said, careful not to sound judgmental. "And?"

"Nothing," Damien echoed his wife. "Neither days nor nights. We never saw Donna."

A moment's silence was slowly filled with suspense, yet Anna did not doubt their sincerity.

"Then this," Tinker said gravely. She turned to a brick-and-board bookcase filled with field guides to birds, bats, edible plants, herbs, and mammals of Isle Royale, bits of rock, bones, dried plants, and melted candle stubs. From beneath the bookcase she took a small glass container so clean it looked polished. She set it on her palm and offered it up to Anna.

Anna reached for it, then stopped. "May I?" she said, adopting the ceremony that seemed so natural to these two.

"Yes," Damien replied formally. "We would not have come to you had we not found proof Scotty devoured his wife. It is a serious charge."

Anna lifted the jar carefully from Tinker's hand and turned it in the flickering light. It was several inches high, wider at the bottom than the top, and had ridges at the mouth where a screw cap had once fitted. If there had been a label it had been scrubbed off completely.

"A jar," Anna said blankly.

"A pickle relish jar . . ." Damien encouraged her.

Anna began to feel her brain had fogged up somehow. Could there have been something in the tea? Was Tinker a self-styled witch? Damien a warlock hopeful? Or were they merely a couple of eccentrics, the kind-hearted flakes she'd thought them to be? One thing was certain: Anna was not making sense of much of what they were saying. If they did have a puzzle, the pieces they offered didn't seem to fit any picture she could come up with.

"A pickle relish jar," she repeated.

"Heinz," Tinker added.

"That"—Damien pointed to the little bottle as if it were something unclean—"is not an isolated incident. The last food order Scotty Butkus sent to Bob's Foods included an order for an entire case of pickle relish."

ISRO employees ordered their food for a week at a time, sending lists to several markets in Houghton. Every Tuesday the food was shipped back on the *Ranger III*.

"That's a lot of relish," Anna said, wondering what it was she was agreeing with. "I take it you saw his order form?"

"It was in the trash," Tinker explained.

From beyond the screened-in window, Anna could hear muted laughter, the dull-edged variety brought on by vodka. Trail crew must have made a late appearance at the party and were now staggering back to their boats for the short ride home to their bunkhouse on Mott.

Suddenly voices were raised in anger: a brawl, quickly hushed. On Mott they were allowed more freedom; here in the lap of the tourist trade the hard-drinking crew were kept in line.

Another burst of noise, invective. "Rock Harlem" seemed terribly apt at the moment. Anna had a dizzying sense of having been transported to a basement apartment in a bad section of New York City.

"You went through his trash." This time Anna didn't bother to school her voice. Her nerves were becoming frayed. With an effort, she focused on Tinker. She looked hurt. Even her hair seemed to droop. A flower blasted by the cold. Anna felt a stab of remorse. She ignored it.

"We were seeking recyclable materials," Damien said stiffly. "The Butkuses' trash customarily provides seven to ten pounds of recyclable glass and aluminum." He pronounced the word "al-yew-min-ee-um."

"I'll bet," Anna said. Scotty would be a veritable Philemon's pitcher of bottles and cans. Pickle relish wasn't the only thing he ordered by the case. The repetition of thought triggered understanding. "Twenty-seven Bottles of Relish!" Anna exclaimed. It was a short story about a man who had consumed the evidence of his wife's murder, with relish as the condiment.

"That's what we think," Tinker said. She had brightened again, Anna's disapproval a cloud that had passed.

With comprehension, the fog began to lift from Anna's mind and she was mildly ashamed she'd suspected the drugging of her tea. To clear Tinker of an accusation never made, she took a swallow. Cold, it tasted more of earth and root than of mint and honey. She set it aside.

"You've got expectant ducks and an empty pickle jar," Anna summed up the evidence. She knew she sounded abrupt but she was getting tired. Under her collar, her sunburn had begun to chafe and the smoke from the candles was making her eyes water.

"We also have photographs," Damien said. He rose, swirling his calf-length cape alarmingly near the open flames, and took down a tin box from the jumble of bags and boxes that filled the top of the two bunk beds.

Anna's interest pricked up. She eased her back, forcing herself to sit a little straighter.

"We'll need artificial light for this," Damien apologized. Anna was grateful. She could use the nice healthy glare of the overhead electric. Disappointment soon followed: Damien took a flashlight from the upper bunk. Anna allowed herself a small sigh. It was barely even a change in her breathing pattern, but Tinker caught it. She lay one tapered finger on Anna's sleeve as if to lend her patience. Or faith.

Damien sat on the floor again, tailor fashion, the black cape billowing around his knees, then settling like a dark mist. He opened the box with the lid toward Anna so she couldn't see its contents. Some rummaging with the flashlight produced two snapshots. For a long, irritating moment he studied them, then handed the first to Anna.

She took it and the flashlight from his hands. The Polaroid was of Scotty Butkus in his NPS uniform standing on the dock in Houghton. Behind him the hull of the *Ranger III* rose like a blue wall. Suitcases and boxes and canoes littered the pier. Apparently it was loading day; the day most of the staff moved to the island for the season.

"Now look at this one." Damien handed her the second photograph.

Dutifully, Anna trained the flashlight on it: Scotty Butkus leaning against the wall of the Rec Hall on Mott Island. He was wearing Levi's and a white vee-necked undershirt. In his right hand was what was probably a Mickey's Big Mouth. The aspen trees behind him were in full leaf and in the background Anna could just make out Canada dogwood in bloom. The dogwood had only begun to flower in the last week. The picture had been taken recently.

"What am I supposed to be seeing?" she asked.

Tinker, unable to contain herself any longer, leaned over Anna's arm and pointed at Butkus's midsection. "Look how much fatter he is in this picture. He's a blimp. He must've put on fifteen pounds."

Scotty *was* heavier. His belly hung over his belt and his face was puffy. Anna clicked off the flashlight and handed it and the photographs back to Damien. "Given that Scotty, for whatever reason, decided to murder his wife," she began, trying a new tack, "doesn't it seem odd that with access to a boat and hundreds of square miles of deep water, he would choose to dispose of the body by eating it?"

"Not if he was the reincarnation of Charlie Mott,"

Damien said triumphantly. He and Tinker looked at her expectantly, twin Perry Masons having delivered the coup de grâce.

Anna rubbed her face. "Could we have some light in here, please?"

Damien hopped up obediently and switched on the overhead. The room's mystery vanished. For a few moments the three of them blinked at one another like surprised owls.

"I'll look into it," Anna said and dragged herself up on legs numb from sitting so long. "Right now I'm for bed. Thanks for the tea."

"You can stay here," Tinker offered. "Damien and I sleep on the lower bunk."

Damien reached out and took his wife's hand. They shared a smile that made Anna lonely.

"Stay," Damien said. "You can sleep with Oscar if you don't mind cigar smoke. Oscar likes company sometimes."

Anna knew housing for seasonals was tight in the National Park Service but this arrangement shocked even her. The bunks were barely wide enough for one adult. "I'll sleep on the *Lorelei*," she said. "Thanks just the same." She grabbed up her daypack and stepped toward the door.

"Oscar says, 'Anytime,'" Anna followed Tinker's look to the tumbled goods on the top bunk. From within a cave of boxes, they were being watched by two button eyes. The little stuffed bear had a dilapidated red bow tied around his neck and an amiable expression on his face.

"Thanks," Anna said, not knowing whether she addressed Tinker or the bear, and made her escape into the cleansing cold of the night.

Like the southwestern deserts, the northern lake country was a land of extremes. Anna bumbled through the thick dark of the forest like a blinded thing, then, moving onto the open shore between the woods and the dock area, was struck with a light so intense she turned expecting to see a spotlight shining from a fishing vessel. Instead, she saw the moon. It was brighter here than anyplace she'd ever been, fulfilling a long-standing exaggeration: a sharp-eyed person actually could read a newspaper by its light.

The *Lorelei* was moored in the concrete NPS dock, tied at bow and stern. Anna stepped over the gunwale and let herself into the cabin. Pilcher's boat was the twin of the *Belle Isle.* At the forward end of the cabin, between the two high seats and down a step, was a small door. Anna ducked through it into the triangular-shaped space in the bow. Padded benches lined the bulkhead. Beneath them she knew she would find, among the flares, line, and emergency medical supplies, the *Lorelei*'s spare sleeping bags.

She unloosed the bow hatch and propped it open. In a space so familiar, the light of the moon would be adequate. Or would have been had District Ranger Pilcher been more organized. "Pigsty," she grumbled as she cleared a space for herself and unrolled a sleeping bag that smelled of mildew. Everything smelled of damp and was cold to the touch. Fully clothed, she crawled into the bag and thrashed her feet violently to warm it.

As she pulled the stinking cover under her chin, she stared up through the hatch. Seventeen stars pricked the eight-by-sixteen rectangle. They didn't shimmer like desert stars but burned steady and cold: lights for sailors to navigate by. Stars seemed close to the earth in the north woods but not friendly, not the eyes of angels watching over children as they slept.

The Quallofil bag was slowly warming, but it was a moist warmth Anna knew would turn clammy in the coldest part of the night. She would wake shivering with her clothes stuck to her. At least with Oscar she would have been warm.

Her thoughts turned to Tinker and Damien. Tinker was in her thirties—probably not more than five or six years younger than Anna—but she seemed so childlike. She and Damien, with cloaks and candles and bears, playing out some game they might even believe. A game where horror held more of excitement than of nightmares, where danger and adventure were synonymous.

And Scotty Butkus the reincarnation of Charlie Mott;

Anna laughed aloud in the darkness. The story of Charlie and Angelique Mott was a staple on the island. Tales of cold and cannibalism were common in the Northwest. The other end of the island was named for the legendary flesh-eating spirit, the Windigo. Modern thought would have the Windigo a symbol of the cold and the loneliness and the starvation that faced mere humans who dared the northern winters. But some still believed it flew and moaned and consumed the unwary.

Charlie was the personification of the Windigo. The story was true. He and his wife had been left on Mott Island without supplies. As winter wore on, Charlie had begun to look at Angelique with a new hunger, ever sharpening his butcher knife. Finally she had escaped to live in a cave. Charlie had perished, his body kept fresh in the cabin by the awful cold. Angelique survived by snaring rabbits with nooses made from the hair of her head.

Had Scotty that lean and hungry look? Tinker and Damien thought they saw it; saw the result in the fleshy roll around his belly.

In the morning, Anna decided, she would talk with Butkus—nose around—find Donna before Tinker and Damien got themselves crosswise of Scotty. For all his apparent good-old-boy bonhomie, he had a reputation for stabbing people in the back. Anna would not like to see Tinker or Damien hurt.

She thought of them sharing their narrow bunk. They must sleep curled together like kittens. It would be a good night to curl up with someone.

There'd been a man in Texas. Rogelio was a man to curl up with on hot nights. Not a Zachary, not someone to share a life with—or a narrow bunk bed—but a good man. "A warm body," she said to those same stars. "I could do with a couple of those right now."

Maybe Molly was right; maybe it was time to sprinkle Zachary's ashes, give him to the lake. Anna smiled. Zach would be miserable in this wilderness of water and woods. He would have his ashes sprinkled over Manhattan on

New Year's Day. "At least then you'd be on Broadway," Anna said to a memory.

The lake, at least in the harbor, chose to be kind, and rocked Anna gently to sleep before she had time to think too hard.

CHAPTER 4

Anna woke feeling groggy and gummy. The Adminis-tration Building on Mott had an employee shower for the use of guests and backcountry rangers on overnight to the "big city." She paddled her kayak the few miles down-channel and treated herself to a hot shower that wasted enough water to keep her permanently out of the Environ-mentalists' Hall of Fame. It was worth it. The heat steamed away the mildew she felt beginning to grow in her hair and rinsed the sweat, mosquito repellent, and sunblock from her skin.

Dried and refreshed, she cadged a cup of bad coffee from the pot the dispatcher always kept hot, then wandered out to the dock to drink it in with the thin sunshine. The day was fair and promised to be warm—or warm for Isle Royale—somewhere in the sixties. A westerly breeze, smelling of pine and the loamy soil of the boreal forests, trickled in over the island.

Anna leaned back against the warming cement of the quay and closed her eyes.

She was down to the last gulp of coffee, the Cremora

scum clinging to the plastic cup, when Scotty Butkus stomped onto the dock, reminding her of her promise to Tinker and Damien.

As always when in uniform, Scotty looked natty. The creases in his shirt were as sharp as if he ironed them instead of just snatching them out of the dryer before the permapress became permacrunch. His brass badge sparkled and his cowboy boots were polished to a fine gloss.

The boots were an absurdity. There wasn't a horse for hundreds of square miles and anything but soft, white-soled shoes were forbidden on boats—they marked up the decks. But Scotty went booted in the *Cisco,* a nineteen-foot runabout he used for harbor patrol. He'd even worn them in the *Lorelei* the time Anna had ridden with him and the District Ranger to Windigo.

Scotty was also wearing his side arm. Because of the low crime rate and the ever present danger of death by drowning, wearing defensive equipment on ISRO was optional. Butkus was the only ranger who opted to lug the heavy piece around. In concession to water safety he had struck a compromise that was strictly against regulations: he didn't wear the full belt with cuffs and reloaders and holster, but just the pistol in a light-weight breakaway holster on the belt of his trousers.

Cowboy, Anna thought. The gun was just for show.

She'd wondered why Pilcher never called him on his boots, why Lucas Vega hadn't made him adhere to the defensive equipment standards. Then Christina, who worked as a part-time secretary in the main NPS office in Houghton, told her why the brass treated Scotty with kid gloves. When typing the minutes of the last Equal Opportunity meeting, Chris had discovered Scotty was suing ISRO for not giving him Pilcher's position when he'd applied for it. He accused the park of discriminating against him because of his age.

The way he saw it, the fact that he refused to learn the long-range navigation device all the Bertrams were

equipped with, and had let his scuba-diving license lapse
was mere detail.

Anna smiled. She knew altogether too much about
Scotty Butkus. It was handy having someone on the inside.

"Morning, Scotty," she said, shading her eyes to look
up at him.

"Morning. Lieu day?"

She nodded. He looked awful. His face was gray and
puffy and his eyes were bloodshot. The skin on his neck
hung loose. He looked like a man who was drinking heavily, sleeping poorly, and was badly hung over. Anna
doubted he had eaten his wife. In the shape he was in he
probably couldn't keep vanilla yogurt down, much less a
woman.

"Where's Donna?" Anna asked. "I haven't seen her
around this trip. She missed Denny's party."

"God damn him!" Scotty exploded. Anna was so startled by his outburst she twitched the last swallow of coffee
onto her trouser leg. "That son of a bitch ask you to nose
around? Tell him to look after his own goddam wife for a
change."

"No," Anna said calmly. "Denny didn't send me. I was
just making polite conversation. Why? What would Denny
want to know he couldn't ask you himself?"

Scotty chose not to answer for a minute. He jumped
into the *Cisco* with surprising agility. Anna could see she'd
underestimated his physical abilities. He was killing himself with booze and cigarettes but he had kept his strength.
His upper body looked powerful, the arms hard-muscled.

He busied himself checking the fuel levels, the lines,
and a few other things that didn't need checking. Anna
sensed he was itching to gossip, to vent what was evidently
a long-standing gripe. She watched in silence.

"The s.o.b. was pestering Donna. She put a flea in his
ear, by God." He smiled a crooked, inward smile that Anna
could've sworn he'd learned from watching Randolph
Scott movies. "That little gal he married on the rebound is
in for a hell of a life hitched to that bastard."

"Is that why Donna didn't come to the reception?" Anna persisted.

Suddenly Scotty looked wily, his eyes narrowing in an almost cartoon fashion. Suspicious, Anna thought, but it could've just been the hangover biting down. "Donna's gone back to the mainland. Her sister, Roberta, has a ruptured disk. Donna's looking after the kids till she gets on her feet again." He turned the key and the *Cisco* responded with a rattling lawn mower noise. Anna got up and untied his lines for him. "See ya," he said as she dropped them over the side. Without a backward look, he motored out toward the main channel.

Anna picked up her Styrofoam cup. It was time to find out a little more about Donna Butkus. Anna had entered on duty May 3, six days before the early staff had moved to the island. The Butkuses had followed a week or so later. Secreted away on Amygdaloid, she had missed Lucas Vega's getting-to-know-you potluck. Almost everything she knew about her fellow islanders she'd learned second-hand through Christina's letters. As a secretary at the headquarters in Houghton, Chris was in on everything.

Anna carried her cup back to the Administration Building.

The architect hadn't catered to any north woods notion of romantic design. It was purely governmental: a low, boring, wooden building with a concrete walk, a square of exotic grass species mowed short, and a white flagpole flying the Stars and Stripes. Inside, it was made only slightly more interesting by the addition of maps and charts on the walls.

Anna let herself past a counter installed to keep out Unofficial Persons and walked down the linoleum-floored hallway to the third door on the right. The drone of a computer printing out hung in the air like dust and there was the smell of stale coffee. Sandra Fox, ISRO's dispatcher, sat with her back to the door. Sandra was in her mid-fifties with close-cropped red hair and a comfortably rounded body.

"Come for another cup of your fine coffee," Anna said to announce herself.

"Hi, Anna," Sandra said without turning from the keyboard. "Be with you in a sec."

Anna set in the metal folding chair between the wastebasket and the door, watching Sandra's fingers pecking at the keys. Each was pocked with dots. One printer printed the text out in braille, a second in regular print. It was the first machine of its kind Anna had ever seen.

"Can I pet Delphi?" she asked.

"Sure." Sandra went on typing.

The dispatcher's seeing-eye dog, a seven-year-old golden retriever and, as the only dog allowed on the island, a minor celebrity, lay curled neatly under the table that held the printers. Anna crouched and fondled her ears. She cocked one blond eyebrow and looked up with dark liquid eyes. Her tail thumped softly. The warmth of the fur, the nonjudgmental gaze made Anna realize how much a part of her life Piedmont was, how dear and valued a friend.

"There!" Sandra sighed with satisfaction. "So. You finally got those bozos on the *Low Dollar* afloat. Did they limp back to Grand Marais all right?"

"I guess," Anna returned. "Nothing washed up on the north shore." Sandra laughed. Anna wasn't surprised she knew about the foundered vessel. The dispatcher saw nothing but she heard everything; heard and noted every radio transmission on the island. Rumor had it she used her radio to listen in on phone calls when things got slow—her own version of watching the soaps. Since she kept her own counsel nobody ever called her on it.

"Do you know Donna Butkus, Scotty's wife?" Anna asked, staying where she was on the cold linoleum so she could enjoy the company of the dog.

Sandra settled back in her chair, folded her hands over her midriff where it rounded out the green fabric of her uniform trousers.

Settling in for a gossip, Anna thought. Good.

"Oh, yes. Scotty brought her back from his trip home last August. He and his third wife were good friends with her parents." The information was delivered without emotion, but Fox had a lump of tongue in her cheek and the skin around her unseeing eyes crinkled.

"What's she like?" Anna asked. "Tinker and Damien were talking about her last night. She sounds like an interesting person."

"Hard to say what somebody's really like." Sandra warmed to her subject. Between the radio, the phone calls, and the gossip, Anna guessed people were Sandra's hobby. "She's around twenty-nine or thirty, dark hair and eyes. Pretty in an old-fashioned way. 'A darling dumpling of a girl' was how Trixy described her."

Trixy was the seasonal who headed the Interpretive Program. Winters she taught school in Houghton. For the last six summers she'd worked at ISRO. Anna winced at Trixy's choice of "dumpling" to describe the woman Tinker and Damien thought to be both meat and drink to her husband.

Sandra smiled mischievously. "All that, of course, is merely hearsay. I didn't see it with my own eyes. My idea of what Donna's like is less superficial. She's got a real gentle voice, and shaking hands with her is like catching a butterfly—all soft and fluttering you're afraid you'll crush. Very quiet. I think she feels out of place here. Everybody's so rough-and-tumble and always talking shop. She and Trixy got fairly close. Both artsy types. I think she pretty much hero-worshiped Scotty. Then she married him. Oops!" Sandra laughed good-humoredly and Anna laughed with her. "Why are you interested? Lucas got you investigating rangers' wives?"

Anna shook her head. "No. Tinker and Damien hadn't seen her around and were concerned. I asked Scotty about her this morning and he blew up—something about Denny Castle. Piqued my interest. I'm just being nosy."

"Um," Sandra said, the explanation completely satisfactory. "That Denny Castle thing was all the talk this winter. He and Donna spent a lot of time together, I guess. I don't know if there really was ever anything in it, but a man who marries a woman thirty years younger than himself's bound to have a few insecurities. Especially if he's not rich. I guess the romance was mostly on Denny's side. He made kind of a fool of himself. Following her, that kind of thing. Those deep sensitive types get funny yens. Myself, I like bluff hearty types who swat you on the behind."

Anna felt she owed Sandra for the information and paid in kind. She told her the details of the reception. The dispatcher had been on duty that evening. Sandra listened with a concentration that flattered most people, including Anna, into telling her things they'd never really intended to.

"Jo's been around forever," Sandra said when Anna had finished. "Always finding excuses to work with Denny, or at least get to the island. She's been chasing after him since high school. Them what's uncharitable say that's why he took to the water: to get away from her. Then she went to college—double major in freshwater and marine biology. 'Ain't no mountain high enough, ain't no ocean deep enough,' I guess. She's got him now," Sandra concluded philosophically. "More power to her."

"Seven-oh-one, one-two-one," cackled at Sandra's elbow.

"Duty calls," she said to Anna.

"I've got to go too." Anna stayed just long enough to hear what 121—Lucas Vega—was calling about. It didn't concern her, so she gave Delphi a farewell pat and left.

Donna was in Houghton nursing a sister with a ruptured disk.

Case closed.

Despite Tinker and Damien's wishes, ISRO was simply not a hotbed of crime. The only deaths were those of innocent fishes and that was deemed not only legal but admirable. So much so it surprised Anna that it was not written into every ranger's job description that he or she was too ooh and aah over the corpses of what had once been flashing silver jewels enlivening the deep.

To Isle Royale fishermen's credit, Anna forced herself

to admit, they almost always ate what they killed—unlike the trophy hunters in Texas who wanted only heads and racks and skins to display on dusty walls.

Anna waited till the *Ranger III* docked at noon, in the hope there would be a note from Christina. Anna had become friends with Chris and her daughter, Alison, in Texas. The desert had never appealed to Christina and she had missed town living. In the weeks Anna had been out on the island there'd been a note with each *Ranger III* docking. A letter this Wednesday would mean a lot and she waited even at the risk of having to kayak Blake's Point in the dark.

The letter was there. Anna put it away: a treat for later. At the convenience store at Rock she bought half a dozen Snickers bars and two Butterfingers. She didn't bother to track down Tinker and Damien Coggins-Clarke. Next week would be soon enough to tell them of Donna's miraculous recovery from connubial cannibalism. Let them enjoy one more week of the game.

A ll morning clouds had been building in the west. White cumulus laced Greenstone Ridge, peeking up over the wooded slopes of Mount Ojibway. As Anna shoved the kayak out into the calm waters of Rock Harbor, she eyed them with concern. Afternoons were no time to start out onto the lake, but the north end of the island, ripped to a stony fringe by glaciation, provided a lot of sheltered coves and harbors. If she could get around Blake's Point before the water got rough, she could run for the shelter of Duncan or Five Finger Bay.

Anna put her energy into paddling. Between the dock at Rock Harbor and the end of Merrit Lane, she saw nothing of the scenery: she was making time, covering ground. At the tip of Merrit, her little craft held safe between the buffers of Merrit to the southeast and the last of Isle Royale to the northwest, she stopped to rest. Strain burned hot spots into her right elbow and her deltoid muscles where they crossed from arms to back.

Weather moving in from Thunder Bay had reached the island. Out in the lake waves rolled, cresting white with foam. Passage Island, four miles out, had vanished in an encircling arm of fog. Overhead the sun still shone but soon it, too, would be wrapped in cloud.

For long minutes Anna sat in the kayak debating the wisdom of continuing. On the one hand, if she got careless or overtired, she could end up providing a lot of search-and-rescue rangers with a healthy chunk of overtime pay for combing the ragged shores for her body. On the other hand, she could return to Rock and face another grating evening listening to the political maneuvering and gossip inherent in a closed community, and another night mildewing in Pilcher's floating pigsty.

It was not a tough decision. Anna pulled up the water-proof sleeve that fitted into the kayak like a gasket and snugged it around her waist with a drawstring. If she was careful she would probably be safe enough, but there would be no way to stay completely dry.

For another minute she sat in the lane, her paddle across the bow, while she ate a Snickers bar. Never once had she experienced the sugar rush of energy other people swore by as they downed their Cokes and Hersheys before slamming fire line or hiking that last twenty-five-hundred-foot ascent at the end of the day, but it was as good a reason as any to eat chocolate.

Out in open water Anna found the waves were two and three meters high. The sheer immensity of the lake had warped her perspective. The wind turned from fresh to bitter. It snatched up droplets, hard as grains of sand, and rasped them across her face, exacerbating her sunburn and making her eyes tear.

Keeping the nose of the kayak directly into the wind, she dug her way forward. Water carried her up till the kayak balanced high on an uncertain escarpment. Around her were the ephemeral mountain ranges of Lake Superior. As one can from a hilltop, she saw the island spreading away to the south, bibbed now with a collar of white where waves pouring in from Canada broke into foaming lace against the shoals.

The hill of water sank, fell as if to the center of the world. Mountainous slippery-sided waves rose up past the boat, past Anna's head, up till it seemed they must over-balance and crash down on her, driving her meager craft to the bottom with the great metal ships like the *Glenlyon* and the *Cox*, or the *Monarch*, her massive wooden hull broken on the Palisades. But the kayak stayed afloat, climbed hills and slid through valleys with a structural certainty of de-sign that lent her courage. She stroked with clocklike reg-ularity, taking deep, even bites of the lake.

Shoulders ached. Elbows burned. Anna pushed herself harder. There were times that hurting was a part of, times the fatigue and the fear were necessary ingredients: fires to burn away the dead wood, winds to blow away the chaff, closing the gap between body and brain.

That night Anna shared a camp in Lane Cove with half a dozen Boy Scouts from Thief River Falls, Minnesota, who couldn't grasp the concept that it was no longer polit-ically correct to cut boughs for beds and saplings to fash-ion camp tables.

The following night she spent a more pleasant if less productive night on Belle Isle with two retired school-teachers from Duluth who visited the island every summer to watch birds.

The next day Anna kayaked Pickerel Cove and Robin-son Bay. Backcountry patrol—days in the wilderness—those were the assignments Anna lived for, times it made her laugh aloud to think it was being called "work" and she was being paid to do it.

An hour shy of midnight of the third day she finally slid the kayak up onto the shingle at Amygdaloid. The western sky was washed in pale green, enough light to see by. Overhead stars shone, looking premature, as if they'd grown impatient waiting for the sun to set and had crept out early.

It was June 21, Anna realized. The longest day of the year. For a few minutes she sat in the kayak, steadying the little vessel by bracing her paddle against the gravel. Her muscles felt limp and warm. Her butt was numb and her legs were stiff from their long imprisonment. There was a good chance she would fall over when she tried to extricate herself from the boat she had worn like a body stocking for the last eight hours.

"Need some help, eh?"

A squat round-bodied man stood above her on the dock. He had a Canadian look. The closest Anna had come to describing it was "voyageur." Many of the Canadian fishermen who frequented the island had the powerful, compact build of the voyageurs she had seen pictured in woodcuts from the trading days. More telling: he spoke with a distinct Canadian accent.

"Couldn't hurt," Anna replied.

Landing lightly as a cat, he jumped down the four feet from the pier to the shore. Anna untied the drawstring of the waterproof sleeve around her middle. He caught her under the arms, lifted her out of the kayak, and set her up on the dock as easily as she could have lifted the five-year-old Alison.

"Thanks." Rolling over, she pushed herself up on hands and knees, then eased herself to her feet.

"I'm Jon. Are you the ranger here?" the Canadian asked. He had bounced back up onto the dock to stand next to her.

"Just barely." Anna hobbled up the dock like an old woman. "I will be tomorrow."

"Ranger station closed, eh?" Jon followed her off the dock and stood balanced on a rock, his hands in his pockets, watching as she pulled the kayak up onto dry land.

"Yup. Opens at eight tomorrow morning." Anna retrieved her pack and started up the slope toward a bed made with clean flannel sheets.

The Canadian was right on her heels. "Is it too late to get a diving permit? We want to get an early start tomorrow."

Anna gave up. After all, he had plucked her out of her boat and saved her an ignomious end to a glorious paddle. "I'll write you a permit. Give me a minute to unlock and put on some dry clothes."

He trotted happily down the dock to where a well-worn but clean little cabin cruiser nosed gently against her fenders. Her aft deck was piled with scuba gear: tanks and dry suits, flippers, masks, and fins.

"Bobo!" the Canadian called into the cabin window. "She'll do it."

Anna let herself into the ranger station. It was too late to build a fire to drive out the damp. She took half a bottle of Proprietor's Reserve Red out of the refrigerator, poured a glass, and left it on the counter to warm while she changed and wrote the dive permit.

The two men were waiting for her when she re-emerged into the office area. Anna lit a kerosene lamp. The station had Colemans but she didn't plan to spend enough time with the Canadians to make the effort of lighting one worthwhile.

Cold water divers were, of necessity, lovers of equipment. Anna noticed that "Bobo"—the taller of the two but just barely, his round face darkened by a well-trimmed beard—wore a watch that had everything in it but a micro fax machine.

She got the forms from her desk. "Where do you want to dive?"

"The *Emperor*."

Anna started her spiel on danger and difficulty, but the one called Bobo cut her off. "We heard the lecture from the ranger in Windigo. We dove the *Kamloops* today."

The *Kamloops* was the most dangerous dive on the island. At depths from one hundred and seventy-five to two hundred and sixty feet, the wreck was beyond the reach of all but the most experienced divers. Or outlaw divers; people who threw caution—and sometimes their lives—to the wind.

"You've racked up some bottom time," Anna said. "Is this going to give you a long enough surface interval?" The pressures at the depths where the *Kamloops* dwelt were such that oxygen and nitrogen were forced into solution in the human body, dissolved in the blood and fatty liquids much as carbon dioxide is forced under pressure into soda pop. When divers surfaced, returning to the lesser pressure above the water, those gasses re-formed from a liquid to a gaseous state much like the fizz when a soda pop is opened. If divers surfaced slowly, according to established ascent stages, the gasses worked out slowly and were exhaled harmlessly. If not, they formed bubbles in the bloodstream causing symptoms called the bends which were painful and occasionally fatal.

Regardless of the timing of the ascent, there was always a small residue of nitrogen still in the body. Twelve hours was the rule of thumb between dives more than a couple of atmospheres down.

"We know our numbers," Bobo said.

Anna shrugged and wrote "*Emperor*" in the space provided.

"Did you know there were bodies down there?" Jon asked as Anna handed him a copy of the permit. "On the *Kamloops*?" Bobo looked annoyed, as if Jon were telling family secrets.

"Yeah," Anna returned and Bobo looked disappointed. "Part of the crew was trapped on board when she went down."

"They're weird-looking," Jon said. "Like wax."

"The corpses are saponified," Anna told him. "It's called an adipocere formation. It's fairly common with submerged bodies. The soft tissues get converted to a waxy stuff. Don't ask me how. Their still being like that after over sixty years is a little strange, but it's happened before in the Great Lakes."

For divers accustomed to the sometimes centuries-old wooden-hulled vessels in the Caribbean, the preservation of Superior's treasures often surprised them. Geology and geography conspired to entomb the ships in an almost ageless death. In the deep, still, cold, fresh-water canyons beneath the lake's surface no coral could grow, no surf could batter.

"Everything on the ship is like that—in a time warp," Jon went on. "We must've seen a hundred pairs of shoes. They looked like if you dried them out you could wear them home."

"Did you try them on?" Anna asked casually.

Both divers looked offended. "We did not try them on," Bobo said with cold dignity.

"Just asking." Taking artifacts from shipwrecks was a sport—a business for some. Before Isle Royale was made a national park in 1940, it wasn't illegal. By the time most of the wrecks were protected a lot of their scientific and historical value had been destroyed by treasure hunters. As had some of the joy of discovery for the divers who came after the depredations were committed. Vandalism and theft continued to be a problem. The *Kamloops,* so inaccessible, so long lost, was like a time capsule. The Park Service hoped to keep her that way.

"One of the bodies was incredible," Jon said. "He looked like he'd drowned yesterday. Clothes like new, hair—everything was still perfect."

Anna doubted that. The bodies were recognizable as human but in a featureless kind of way. One's head was missing, several had limbs from which the flesh had dissolved away, leaving only stumps of bone protruding. The clothing was preserved but by no stretch of the imagination "like new."

"Mmm," she murmured, willing them to take their permit and go away.

"The other five were a little the worse for wear, eh?" Jon said.

"There's just the five," Anna said. "Total."

"No," Bobo returned, sounding pleased to correct her. "There are six."

"Did you manage to open the stern room?" Anna asked. She couldn't imagine they had. The entrance was blocked with tons of debris. But the NPS Submerged Cultural Resources Unit out of Santa Fe speculated that there could be as many as a dozen more corpses there—men trapped when the ship foundered.

"This was the engine room," Bobo said, his tone daring her to challenge his knowledge of anything underwater.

"Six?" Anna said. "Well, stranger things have happened . . ." She was too tired to stand and argue. Nitrogen narcosis, shadows, imagination—at a hundred and seventy-five feet who knew what they thought they saw? Anna didn't really care.

Her agreeing without believing stung Bobo. "You wait," he commanded and trotted out the door. Jon shrugged his heavy shoulders in a gesture that was so French as to be a parody.

Anna waited, thinking of the wine on the counter, of her flannel sheets. The hands on the desk clock found one another at midnight. Jon hummed a little song to himself and poked through the rack of brochures.

Bobo came back with an underwater videocamera. He pushed the machine at Anna. "Look," he demanded. Anna pressed her eye to the viewfinder. "Body number one," he announced and she saw a pale headless apparition lit by the unforgiving glare of an underwater lamp. Bobo took the camera back and pushed fast forward, his attention fixed on a digital readout window. "Body number two." He thrust the camera into Anna's hands once again. A drift of amorphous remains clad in what looked to be overalls floated on the tape. "Number three," Bobo said after repeating the fast-forwarding process. Another dead Pillsbury doughboy in dark clothes. Anna smiled. The fingers of the left hand had been folded down, all but the middle finger. She'd heard divers sometimes flipped a macabre and ghostly bird to the next guy down. "Four and five," Bobo said, working his video magic again. Two more remnants, faceless, one with no arms. "And six." Bobo handed Anna the camera a final time.

She pressed her eye to the viewfinder until black clouds troubled her vision. Then she set the camera carefully on the desk. "I'm going to need this tape," she said. She reached over the desk and lifted the permit from Jon's fingers. "And I'm going to have to ask that you do not dive the *Emperor* tomorrow morning, that you remain here. I'm sure the Chief Ranger will have some questions to ask you."

Again she lifted the camera and pressed her eye to the viewfinder. Number six was indeed well preserved. Though the clothing was right for a sea captain of the early part of the twentieth century, it looked new. Shadows hid most of the face but the lips and chin were sharply defined and a cloud of light-colored hair floated out from beneath the cap the figure wore.

Number six had not gone down in the storm of 1927.

CHAPTER 5

"Like I said, I couldn't tell who it was—or supposed to be," Anna told Lucas Vega. "Caucasian from the color of the hair. Male attire, if that means anything. It was impossible to tell size from the video. It was just a dark body floating against a darker background. There was nothing close enough—and in focus—to compare it with."

Lucas didn't say anything. He and Anna stood on the deck of the *Lorelei* watching the white vee-shaped wake plowing a furrow in the lake. Diving gear was stacked against the cabin behind them. Pilcher piloted the boat and Jim Tattinger, ISRO's Submerged Cultural Resources Specialist, rode inside as was his custom whenever possible. A light drizzle fell from an iron-gray sky hanging low over the lake. There was no wind and the water was flat and dark.

Anna pulled herself deeper inside her Gore-Tex jacket, keeping her back to the wash of air around the cabin. Vega, bareheaded in the rain, his arms crossed over the green bulk of his life preserver, was lost in thought. Lucas Vega was what Anna considered an Old World ranger. He believed in wilderness, in the Park Service, in the sanctity of the NPS credo: ". . . to conserve the scenery and the natural and historic objects and the wildlife therein and to provide for the enjoyment of the same in such a manner and by such means as will leave them unimpaired for the enjoyment of future generations." A graduate of Stanford with an advanced degree in archaeology, he worked for peanuts. Lucas Vega also believed in noblesse oblige. He could afford to. Lucas was the only son of a woman who owned seventy-five hundred acres of San Diego County, one of the last existing Spanish land grants in southern California.

"I couldn't tell who it was either—or if it was an effigy," Vega said finally. "And I'd hate to guess at this stage of the game. I expect it's a hoax. Martini's Law taking effect. A lot of these guys have a sense of humor that's not of this world. The ecstasy of the deep? Too much weightlessness?"

Anna shrugged. She knew what he meant. Divers, the serious ones with a lot of dives to their credit, had a different way of looking at life. Not as if it were cheap—they strove to stay alive and risked a great deal to keep each other alive—but they seemed to grasp a connectedness that eluded most people, a sense that life and death were two parts of the same whole, like the crests and the valleys of a wave emerging from the same sea.

This realization—if it was a realization—created as many behavior patterns as there were divers; from protective zealots like Denny Castle to hard-living, hard-drinking party divers. The kind who would make a sixty-year-old corpse flip the bird.

The kind who might dress up a mannequin in turn-of-the-century finery and put it in an engine room nearly two hundred feet beneath the water.

"Those Canadians, Jon Diller and Bobo Whatsisname, did they strike you as the type?" Vega's mind seemed to be following in the same channels as Anna's.

She shook her head. Wrestling a mannequin down into the *Kamloops* was dangerous, expensive, and disrespectful—not of human life or human remains but of the lake.

"They seemed fairly legit," Anna said. "And I doubt

they'd have the money for that kind of elaborate joke. Bobo had some expensive equipment, but their boat had that repaired and polished look boats get when love and hard work take the place of money."

"We'll go back through the permits. Yours, ours, and whatever Windigo's got. There can't have been that many divers on that wreck."

The *Kamloops* scared off all but the best or the boldest. She was not a casual dive. "Not that kind of girl," Anna agreed. The corner of the Chief Ranger's mouth twitched in what might have been a smile.

"This isn't my favorite dive," Lucas said. "Too much can go wrong. You get too stupid at six atmospheres. And you're in too much of a hurry to get home."

Every fifty feet down hit the human brain like one dry martini—hence Martini's Law. It had something to do with nitrogen forced into the bloodstream. No one knew exactly how it worked, just as no one knew why laughing gas made people laugh. But two hundred feet down in frigid waters, the lake usually had the last laugh.

"This'll be a bounce dive," Lucas went on. "Ralph and I'll scoot down, look around. Keep our bottom time to the bare minimum. Keep our decompression time on the ascent as short as we safely can. If it turns out I'm risking the lives of two rangers because somebody played a bad joke, we'll find our jokers and slap them with everything the law will allow, including Piracy on the High Seas and Not Working and Playing Well with Others."

Anna smiled. Lucas Vega was just the man who could make the charges stick.

"What's that?" Vega asked suddenly. "There."

Anna looked where he pointed. Softened by veils of mist, the north shore rose up out of the lake. Cliffs, formed when the island's bedrock was fractured and tipped to the southeast, showed dark and forbidding. A litter of boulders chewed the waters at their base.

"Down at waterline, among the rocks," Vega said.

Anna saw what he was looking at then: a boulder, smoother, blacker than the others. As she stared at it she realized it was moving ever so slightly, a barely perceptible bobbing with the breath of the lake.

Anna ducked into the cabin and borrowed Ralph Pilcher's field glasses. Protocol required she hand them to the Chief Ranger, and she did so. He took them without comment, his eyes never leaving the shore.

"It's a vessel all right. A little runabout. Maybe sixteen, eighteen feet long. Black fiberglass hull, red upholstery. I can't see the name, but unless there's another just like it, that's the *Blackduck*." The *Blackduck* was the Resource Management Department's boat. They had lent her to Jo Castle for the duration of her research on the island.

"Tell Ralph to change course." Lucas never altered the tone of his voice, never raised it, but there was that about the man that when he wished to be obeyed instantly, he was. Anna went back into the cabin and pointed the vessel out to the District Ranger. "Shit," he whispered, cut left throttle and pushed full right to turn the *Lorelei* more sharply.

Anna rejoined Lucas on deck. He kept the field glasses, giving a running report as they neared the vessel. "She's not swamped. There's some water on the seats and the dash from this drizzle, but the deck's not awash. There doesn't seem to be any damage to the hull. Maybe some scratches where she's been nudging against the rocks."

The timbre of the inboards changed as Ralph eased the *Lorelei* gingerly into the shallower water along the base of the cliff. Anna and Lucas each took a side of the boat and stared intently down at the unrevealing surface for any tell-tale shadows of submerged snags or boulders.

Ralph cut power completely and the boat drifted slowly forward. "That's it," he shouted. "I'm afraid to take her any further in."

"Close enough," Lucas replied.

A few yards off the *Lorelei*'s bow, moving up and down on the Bertram's fading wake, the *Blackduck* sat in the water. Her outboard motor made a delicate scratching sound as it scraped against a rock.

Feet on the gunwale, Anna eased around the cabin using

the chrome railing on the roof to steady herself. Vega passed her the boat hook and she knelt to fish up the *Blackduck*'s bow line where it trailed down from the cleat. She pulled it dripping from the shallows and Lucas secured it to the *Lorelei*'s stern. As Anna worked her way back aft, the Chief Ranger reeled in their catch.

The *Blackduck* had one full tank of fuel; the other was a quarter full. The engine fired up at a touch of the starter. There was no damage to the hull or the propeller. A complete complement of life jackets was stowed under the pilot's seat. She appeared simply to have been abandoned, left to drift.

They hooked her to the tow line and Pilcher started back out toward the burial place of the *Kamloops*. The light-haired mannequin in the engine room no longer seemed a practical joke.

Pilcher took the *Lorelei* to the long-range navigational, or loran, coordinates where the buoy marking the *Kamloops*' location was secured. Once again Anna and Lucas studied the water.

Pocked by fine rain, the water looked to be made of granite. Anna was glad she was not going down. Technically she was qualified, but she knew there were miles of road between "qualified" and "ready." The scrap of paper with its gold curlicues and typed-in names that certified her as a diver was merely a promissory note. One day, with practice and experience, she might become a diver.

With luck, Anna thought, she'd make it back to a desert park before that fate befell her.

Jim Tattinger dropped a two-hundred-foot line marked off at ten-foot intervals with bright blue bands. When the body swam through cold dark waters and the brain swam through six of Neptune's martinis, getting lost or ascending faster than the prescribed feet per minute were very real dangers. The line helped orientation and timing. On a longer dive it would also hold spare tanks at intervals along the way.

Ralph and Lucas began the cumbersome process of suiting up. Both wore polypropylene long johns and two pairs of heavy socks. Over these they zipped khaki-colored quilted overalls, then added balaclavas. To Anna they resembled nothing so much as Peter Pan's little lost boys. All that was missing were the round ears and fuzzy tails. Next came the thick rubber dry suits with attached booties and rubber hoods, then flippers, weight belts, masks, tanks, gloves. Blue-and-black-bodied, faceless, humped with yellow metal cylinders as they were, all trace of humanity was buried under layers of protective gear.

Anna eyed them askance. She didn't much care to go someplace Mother Nature had gone to such lengths to keep her out of.

Pilcher rolled off the waterline deck at the *Lorelei*'s stern and was swallowed by the liquid granite. Seconds later he surfaced and Anna handed him the underwater light. Vega settled his mask and mouthpiece and followed Pilcher into the lake. When he bobbed back up, Anna gave him the still camera. Tattinger, leaning over the starboard gunwale, deployed the red and white flag that indicated there were divers down. He was remaining on the surface with Anna as a dive tender.

In a pale roiling of bubbles, Pilcher and Vega were gone. There was nothing more to do but wait. Anna went into the cabin where it was dry and, relatively speaking, warm. She settled lengthwise on the bench, her back against the cold plastic of the side window. The divers would be down only ten to twelve minutes. Descending at sixty-five to seventy feet per minute, they'd be at the wreck in about four minutes, then in and out of the engine room and back up. If they stayed down much longer they would have to make prolonged stops on the ascent or they'd risk the bends. The only cure was to go into a hyperbaric chamber and start the long recompression process. The nearest chamber was in Minneapolis, two hours away by low-flying plane.

As the abandoned *Blackduck,* Jo's boat, bobbed gently to the starboard, Jim tried to raise Mrs. Castle on the radio. Sandra Fox answered, reminding him Jo had not yet been issued a handheld Motorola radio.

"Try Scotty," Anna suggested. "He could stop by Davidson and see if she's there." Davidson Island had a lovely rustic cabin the NPS set aside for visiting researchers. Permanent NPS staff had more prosaic quarters with flush toilets and electricity on Mott. Seasonal rangers had lusted after the Davidson house, but it was much too nice for seasonals.

"Scotty's off today," Jim said. His voice was nasal and flat, so much in keeping with his traditional nerd exterior that Anna wondered if all the pencil-neck-geek genes were housed on the same chromosome.

"He got yesterday and today off and he took another day of annual leave so he could go to Houghton and have his ear looked at."

"What's wrong with his ear?" Anna asked because Jim expected her to.

"Scotty's part deaf in his left ear. He wears one of those little bitty hearing aids in it. Did you know that?" Jim asked so sharply Anna wondered if he was telling Scotty's secrets.

"Nope." She'd guessed Scotty was hard of hearing on one side by the way he cocked his head and the number of times he asked people to repeat things, but she'd never given it any thought.

"That damn Denny Castle hit him on his bad ear," Tattinger went on. "Scotty had that little thing in there and it hurt him." Jim sounded angry but had a vocal range that expressed perpetual discontent, and Anna wasn't sure if he had something against Denny or was just making conversation.

"How did Denny happen to hit him?"

"He didn't *happen* to hit him," Jim snapped. Anna didn't take offense. Jim had never learned how to win friends and influence people. "Castle hit him on purpose. After that stupid reception, Castle came over to Mott. I wasn't there, but I guess he was looking for Donna. Scotty wasn't taking any of his crap."

And Scotty was drunk, Anna thought. "A fight?"

"More like a shoving match. Denny Castle doesn't have the gonads to fight."

"Gonads." Not "balls." Anna swallowed a smile. She pictured a little, skinny, red-haired Jimmy Tattinger practicing swearing in the bathroom mirror and never managing to get it quite right.

For a while they sat without talking. Anna got her day-pack and dug out a paperback copy of *Ivanhoe*. It produced a book's inevitable effect. In cats it stimulated the urge to sit on the pages. In humans it stimulated conversation.

"I feel sorry for Jo," Jim said, staring out the window to where the *Blackduck* had nudged up beside the *Lorelei*. "I wouldn't be surprised if this was no accident, if she got upset and came out here and killed herself. It'd be one way of getting away from that damned Denny Castle."

Anna was a little surprised at his vehemence and at his echoing Scotty's words. Why was Tattinger so down on Denny? Jim didn't have any wife to steal. Maybe it was enough that Denny openly expressed the opinion that Tattinger was a lousy diver, an incompetent manager, and showed no concern for the resources he was hired to protect.

She decided to prod a little. "I don't know why anybody would feel sorry for Jo," she said. "There's not many women who'd throw Denny Castle out of bed for eating crackers."

Jim snorted, a sound like old pug dogs make. "Oh, *women* fall for that crap Denny dishes out."

The insult to Denny and all of womankind seemed to be in about equal proportions. Jim exposed a moist ruffled underlip as he smiled at a delicious memory.

A number of retorts came to mind but Anna left them unsaid. She wondered if Jim was trying to needle her into an argument. For a moment she just watched him; the pale restless eyes staring at the gray nothing beyond the windscreen, the bored wanderings of his white-skinned fingers picking at the vinyl seat cover where it was worn through.

No, she decided, he wasn't trying intentionally to provoke her. He was just naturally irritating. At his age—somewhere in the neighborhood of forty—he probably knew he rubbed people the wrong way. Anna suspected he'd never figured out why and somewhere along the line had given up trying and retreated into his computers.

"I used to work on St. John in the Caribbean," he said suddenly. "I didn't mind diving so much there. It's warm."

"Why did you leave the Virgin Islands National Park?" Anna asked. Tattinger was a GS-5 making less than nineteen thousand a year, an entry-level position, so it hadn't been for a promotion.

"The District Ranger was a prick," he said succinctly.

"Ah." He didn't elaborate, and Anna said: "A Submerged Cultural Resource Specialist who doesn't like diving? What happened? Shark bite you?"

"They made me do it in the Navy," he said. "It's a job."

A secure government job with health and retirement benefits. Easy to get for an ex-Navy man with veteran's preference in hiring. Dig a comfortable little air-conditioned niche and wait out the years until retirement while hundreds of overqualified people worked as seasonals, scraping by winters doing odd jobs, because they wanted to save the world—or at least one little corner of it.

It wasn't hard to understand how Denny had come by his contempt for Jim.

Anna picked up *Ivanhoe* again, determined to answer only in grunts until any further attempts at conversation were effectively squashed.

The respite was short-lived. Ralph and Lucas surfaced. She and Jim helped them crawl aboard. For half a minute the divers lay in a puddle on the boat deck like a couple of unpleasant monsters dragged in with the day's catch.

With a popping, sucking noise, Vega pulled off his rubber hood and dropped it on the deck. Anna tossed it against the cabin and knelt to help him with his tanks. Vega's face was almost the same shade of gray as the lake.

"Not a joke?" Anna asked.

Lucas shook his head. "Not a joke. It's Denny, Denny Castle."

Anna rocked back on her heels. She felt as if she'd been punched in the solar plexus. It confused her.

She hadn't known she cared.

CHAPTER 6

J im Tattinger did most of the talking and he was asking questions that neither Ralph nor Lucas wanted to answer: What did Denny look like? Could they tell what killed him? Did they touch him? Were his eyes open? He talked rapidly and his usually pale skin was flushed up to his ears. He babbled like a man trying to cover up a social faux pas.

As a reaction to the death of a colleague, guilty embarrassment seemed singularly inappropriate. Anna wondered if Tattinger was ashamed of having spoken ill of the dead when the dead floated thirty fathoms beneath his feet.

She and Jim had talked of Castle as if he were alive. In their minds—at least in Anna's—he had still lived. It was as if no one could die until she had been informed. In a way that was true. Even now, years after Zachary had been killed, Anna would sometimes forget he was dead. She'd think of a joke she wanted to tell him, a place she wanted to show him, and for that moment he would be alive again, utterly alive. So much so that the next moment, when she remembered, was always a fresh grief, though now blessedly short-lived.

Anna made a mental note to tell Jo Castle that things did get better eventually. She did not expect Jo would believe her.

Lucas Vega thought of Denny's wife at that same moment. He and Ralph were back in dry clothes sitting on the engine box drinking hot coffee from a thermos while Anna and Jim stowed gear and reeled in line. "Anna," Vega said, "I'd like you to come with me to Davidson and give the news to Jo. I'd like a female officer to be present."

Anna nodded. She never felt particularly comfortable when called on to be a female officer. Some arcane, instinctual talents were expected and she'd never figured out exactly what they were. "What then?" she asked.

Lucas wiped a fine-boned brown hand over his face, dragging down the flesh of his cheeks. "I'll call the Feds. This clearly is no accident. The man didn't bump his head diving off the high board and drown. He's a couple of hundred feet down floating around in a Halloween costume.

"Then I guess we go get him. It's a hell of a crime scene to investigate. The standard techniques aren't going to help much. I doubt there's an FBI man in a thousand miles who could even get to the scene, much less function after he did. We're stuck with this one. At least for a while."

Anna wondered if Lucas expected her to make the dive for the body recovery. A dormant claustrophobia began to awaken within her, a cold hard spot just under her breastbone. It was the park's policy that a ranger was never to tackle a task she or he felt unsafe performing for any reason. She would not be forced to go.

"Do you feel you're ready for a dive that technical?" Lucas asked.

"Sure."

He clapped her on the shoulder and went into the cabin.

Ralph Pilcher, still seated on the engine box, drank his coffee as the Bertram powered up. Anna felt him watching her. She coiled the last of the line and stowed it in its niche in the hull by his knees. Ralph had a crooked smile—

rather, his smile was straight but a twice broken nose un-balanced his face till it seemed crooked. His hair, wild from the rubber hood, stood out from his head in a brown tangle. "The lake scare you?" he asked.

"Yup."

"Good. It should. It's one scary place."

Anna stopped what she was doing to look at him. Fit, compact, in his early thirties, he didn't look afraid of any-thing. Except perhaps, if the gossip had any truth to it, being tied down to his new baby and his pretty new wife. "Does the lake scare you?" she returned.

"No. But then it didn't scare Denny either." He threw the last of his coffee over the side of the boat. "Why didn't you tell Lucas you were scared to dive? He'd never razz you about it. He'd give you something else to do, some-thing you're comfortable with."

"The devil you know is better than the devil you don't," Anna replied. "Time I made his acquaintance."

Pilcher nodded. "We'll give you all the help you need. Don't get pigheaded." He stood up, his feet firm and easy on the moving deck. "And stay a little scared. You'll live longer."

The District Ranger went inside. Anna didn't want to think anymore of the dive. I'll jump off that bridge when I come to it, she told herself. She lashed the tanks down so they wouldn't roll, then settled her shoulders against the cabin where she was out of the wind.

The drizzle had stopped and the sun was piercing through a rent in the clouds above the island, pouring gold down onto the treetops until they glowed a rich green against their shadowed fellows. Sparks of sunshine reached the water. Where they touched, the lake turned emerald and azure. Light, life, color: Anna breathed deeply and knew the breath for a miracle, a celebration, an act of devotion.

Sandra Fox's comfortable voice came into her mind, telling her again of a high school girl's relentless love of a boy. How it molded her career, shaped her life even into her early thirties. A week and a half ago Jo had married her high school boy. Now that boy was dead.

At the moment, in Jo's mind, Denny still lived.

The instant Anna's husband died, each minute that he had lived became a memory. The good were golden, the bad like an acid that burned in the mind. She hoped Jo's thoughts these last precious minutes were not the kind that would haunt her for the rest of her life.

By the time they reached Davidson Island the sky was clear and the sun shone down as if it always had. Pilcher and Tattinger had been left at Mott. Anna piloted the *Lorelei* up to the small wooden dock. A gray jay scolded from the branches of an aspen tree and a mallard swam in and out of the pilings with her downy brood scuttling along in her wake. Anna sidled up to the pier as gently as she could so she wouldn't overset the ducklings.

Lucas made the lines fast to the dock cleats and stood in the sun waiting. Both he and Anna did each small unimportant task with a time-consuming precision designed to postpone the inevitable.

As they walked up the wooded path toward the cabin, three bunnies, new-made and too young to be afraid, hopped out of their way. White baneberry blossoms leaned close and the woods were carpeted ankle-deep in bluebeard lilies. A world where rain fell: the abundance of life stunned Anna. This afternoon there was something both reassuring and mocking in such wealth.

The door of the cabin was open. From within came the sound of a woman's tuneless humming. Across the honey-colored wooden floors, Anna could see Jo Castle bent over the counter labeling corked test tubes and storing them upright in a wooden rack. The long hair curved out around the oversized, glasses frames, then fell till it was forced out again by her wide hips.

Jo saw them before they had a chance to knock. And she knew there was bad news before they had a chance to speak.

"What?" she demanded, looking from one to the other. Then more sharply: "What?"

Lucas took an audible breath. In the short eternity while he was collecting his thoughts, forming his sentences, Anna could see the strain rip through the muscles of Jo Castle's face, turning each to stone as it passed.

"It's god-awful, Jo," Anna said. "Denny's been killed." And Anna started to cry. Jo Castle left the test tube she'd been labeling on the counter, its contents slowly seeping out, and walked straight into Anna's arms as if she had always found solace there.

Sandra Fox and Trixy came over at ten-thirty after Trixy's evening program. Sandra had a casserole that smelled enticingly of onion and garlic and cheese. Women could sit with grief, hold its hands, watch it pour from the eyes of friends and children, lie down beside it and help it to rest. Their delicate strength would weave a net strong as spun steel, keep the widow Castle from hitting bottom.

Anna slipped out the kitchen door. She would stay the night in Rock Harbor and check on Jo in the morning before she bummed a ride back to Amygdaloid. For a time Jo would need her. Not because she was a friend, but because Anna, too, had lost her husband. Sandra had only lost her eyes, Trixy her parents. In the arrogance of grief, Jo would not believe that they could understand.

Evidently Lucas had radioed for a lift back to Mott. He had left the *Lorelei* so Anna could get back to Rock, and she blessed him for being a true gentleman.

"Tell me a story," Anna said into the mouthpiece. "I've had a real bad day."

"What kind of a story?" Molly asked. "One where all the bad guys die?"

"One where nobody dies and the girl gets Robert Redford."

"Is this a New York story, or do they live happily ever after?"

Anna laughed. "Does anybody?"

"If they do they never pay me a hundred and fifty bucks an hour to hear about it. What's wrong, Anna?"

"Zach's still dead."

"Zach and Franco."

"Better make it a story with no plot and great costumes," Anna said. "Tell me about your Westchester wine soiree."

"That turned out to be a hoot. At eight hundred and twenty bucks a pop, I wasn't allowed to sip the elixir of the gods, of course. Us peons had to settle for some French stuff. But the Palates sipped and swirled and sniffed. Three of them said it was the True Vintage—not unlike, I gathered from their tone, a splinter from the True Cross—and the other two swore it was a hoax. My client was in the hoax contingent, as you might imagine. Nothing makes a bona fide Seeker more neurotic than having one of his fellows stumble across the holy grail before he does.

"How's that for a story: mystery, romance, tuxedos. And Zach's still dead. What's up, Anna?"

"A diver who worked here was killed on one of the wrecks. I just got done telling his wife."

There was sympathetic silence from New York. In the background Anna could hear police sirens.

"You know the saddest part?" Anna said. "She hasn't got a sister to tell her stories."

After she got off the phone with Molly, Anna sat awhile in the dark. Some enterprising person had disabled the light beside the waiting bench, so the mosquitoes at least had to find their suppers the old-fashioned way.

Nights in the desert had never seemed dark to Anna. Here, under the canopy of trees, the darkness was absolute. At first she had hated it. Over the weeks she had come to know it, to hear its many soft voices. This night it soothed her. It was a night one could immerse oneself in: still seeing, still hearing, still a part of, but unseen. Wrapped in summer darkness, Anna felt safe and alone but not lonely. Shut away from the sometimes forbidding beauty of the heavens, the scent of pine and loam and budding leaves all around her, she felt firmly a part of the earth, and it was a comfort.

Footsteps, muted voices intruded and she stood up, melted into the trees off the path. Two people, walking without a light, came up the trail from the marina. They sat on the bench Anna had vacated. She could hear the whisper of fabric sweeping over the wooden seat. "You go first."

Anna recognized Damien's voice. The whisper was probably his cape. A light flickered as the door to the telephone booth was opened, and for a second Tinker was lit like an actor on a stage. Then all was dark again.

Anna slipped quietly away. She didn't want to talk with Tinker and Damien tonight. This was not their kind of death. This one had a corpse and a widow.

Patience Bittner found Anna on the deck halfway down her third burgundy. The night sky was pricked full of light, but the velvet darkness on the island remained inviolate. Muffled in a dark sweater and black beret, Anna was part of a living shadow beneath the thimbleberry bushes that overhung the deck.

Patience swept out through the double doors like a woman pursued. At the railing she stopped, her hands resting on the wood, her head drooping forward. Anna could see the movement of the pale shining hair. Patience wore white trousers and a light-colored shirt of shimmery material. Not a good outfit for hiding, Anna thought, and decided she had better make her presence known before the woman stumbled across her and scared herself to death.

"Don't be afraid," Anna whispered.

Patience screamed. A short stab of sound.

"Sorry," Anna apologized. "I guess coming out of the dark those are three pretty terrifying words. It's me, Anna Pigeon."

"Oh Lord . . ."

Anna could hear Patience taking deep breaths, lowering her pulse rate.

"Do you always creep about like that?" the woman demanded.

Anna took umbrage. She'd felt it was good of her to have given up a moment of her privacy to save Patience a coronary. The alcohol had made her quite benevolent. "I'm not creeping. I'm sitting and drinking. Not at all the same thing. Creeping suggests the active. I am the personification of the passive. Letting the night soak in."

Patience had recovered herself; her irritation at being startled had passed. Using her hands like a woman still night-blind, she shuffled over from the railing and sat down on the deck near Anna. "You work on the other side of the island, don't you?"

"Amygdaloid."

"Not your days off. I remember."

"No," Anna said. "I was with the group that found Denny. I came back with Lucas to break the news to Jo."

"Found? My God. Tell me!" Anna felt strong fingers grabbing at her, strong arms shaking her. Patience's panic was thick in the air between them and all at once Anna was unpleasantly sober. She caught Patience's hands and held them with difficulty. It had not occurred to her that Patience would not have heard. The news would have shot through the park community within half an hour of Jim and Ralph's setting foot on Mott. But Patience was a concessionaire, the lodge manager. She was not on the grapevine. At least not the evening edition.

"Shh. Shh. It's okay. You're okay," Anna said, wondering what Denny had been to Patience. "Denny's had an accident. We found his body today. I'm sorry. I thought you knew."

"My God," Patience said again and she moaned, a ghostly creaking in the night. "Where was he?"

"Inside the *Kamloops*."

Patience twitched. Anna felt it like an electric shock running through her arms and hands. Patience took a breath, a shushing sound. Anna wished she could see her face but the darkness in the shadow of the thimbleberry was absolute. Patience's hands stopped quivering. She returned Anna's hold with a firm pressure, then tried to withdraw. There was a sense of gathering, of control; a powerful woman remembering who she was.

"Denny was very kind to Carrie—and me—when we first got here. We were such city slickers. Afraid of wolves and the Windigo; hadn't sense enough to come in out of the rain. Denny took us under his wing. That's not going to be forgotten."

Eulogy was the first step toward recovery. Patience Bittner would be all right. Anna loosed her hands.

"Do you have a place to sleep?" Patience asked.

"I'll sleep on the *Lorelei*."

"Ralph's a sweetheart, but his housekeeping leaves something to be desired. Stay with Carrie and me." Anna hesitated. "Please," Patience urged. "I'd like to have someone to talk to."

Patience put the lodge to bed at midnight and Anna followed her home. In the last of the four lodge buildings sprinkled along the western shore of Rock Harbor, she shared an apartment with her daughter. There was nothing rustic or romantic about the decor—the furnishings looked to have been borrowed from a doctor's waiting room—but the sliding glass doors opening out of the living room looked across the harbor to the lush shores of Raspberry Island.

Carrie Bittner wasn't home, a fact that irritated her mother. Patience put her domestic disappointments aside, however, and turned on her hostess's charm. Though it was transparent, it was effective. Patience knew how to put people at their ease, and Anna was glad to have been rescued from a mildewed bed aboard Pilcher's boat. The hot shower, the strains of Rampal on the compact disc player, and the loan of one of Patience's flannel gowns were welcome luxuries at the end of a trying day.

As Anna curled up on the sofa, Patience uncorked a bottle of Pinot Noir. Words of protest were in Anna's mouth but Patience forestalled them.

"This is an excellent wine," she said. "It warms without intoxicating. I promise. Tonight we both need it. Wine is important."

"You've said that before."

Patience smiled without embarrassment. "I suppose I have. I'll probably say it again. Wine is history, comfort and strength, food and drink, art and commerce. You can't say that about much else." She handed Anna a small glass of dark purple liquid. She raised hers to the light, met Anna's eye, and said: "Over the lips and through the gums, look out stomach, here it comes."

Anna enjoyed both the wine and the company. She told Patience all she dared of Denny's whereabouts. The exact details, the 1900s captain's uniform, the lack of any scuba gear, the precise location, Anna kept to herself. She knew that whoever handled the case would want as much information as possible to be known only to themselves and the killer.

It was close to one o'clock in the morning when Carrie Bittner came home. She had the flushed, excited look that can only be explained by young love or other covert night actions. As Patience scolded her off to her room, Anna wondered which of the busboys dared to court the boss's daughter.

Patience apologized unnecessarily and followed her daughter to bed. Though soothed by wine and warmth, Anna still was not sleepy. For the third time that day she dug in her daypack for *Ivanhoe*. So much had transpired since last she'd turned its pages, it seemed that Rebecca must surely have perished from old age by now.

Anna couldn't concentrate. Putting the book away, she came across Christina's letter, brought on the *Ranger III,* unopened, forgotten amid the Sturm and Drang of the past thirty-six hours. She tucked her blankets around her on the sofa and opened the letter. Alison had drawn her a picture of Piedmont. He looked like a yellow and red armadillo but there was an authentic paw print to prove otherwise.

Anna smiled at the struggle that must have ensued before Piedmont had let one of his perfect golden paws be pressed into an ink pad, and laughed aloud when she read Christina's account of trying to scrub vermilion cat tracks off the kitchen counter. Alison was to play Uncle Sam in the Fourth of July pageant, the lilacs were in full bloom, Anna's order for Justin boots had finally been forwarded from Texas, Christina was going bike riding with Bertie on Sunday, the plumber said the outside faucets needed frost-proof somethings. Anna couldn't make out Chris's scrawl.

She put away the letter, looked again at Piedmont-as-armadillo. Christina, as always, had a talent for reaffirming life. She got to the crux of it: Sunday school and plumbers and "What's for dinner?" Everything else was mere affectation.

Anna turned off the light. Life would go on. A five-year-old girl was playing Uncle Sam. Universal peace couldn't be far away.

CHAPTER 7

Lucas had wanted a good long surface interval and he got it. The wheels of justice were grinding slow. Not because they ground exceeding fine, Anna thought, but because they were mired down in red tape.

As Lucas gave Anna a ride back to the north shore he told her of his call to the Federal Bureau of Investigation.

Assured that the corpse would keep as well at the bottom of the lake as it would in the refrigerator at the morgue, the FBI wanted a man on site when the body was brought up. That man was Frederick Stanton out of Detroit. Frederick (known to his intimates, the FBI secretary told Lucas, as "Frederick"; "Fred" or "Freddy" could undermine any potential for an amicable working relationship) specialized in narcotics violations occurring on the American-Canadian border in the midwest region. Officer Stanton had to give a deposition in New Jersey on Wednesday. Thursday he would fly to Houghton, and Friday take the seaplane to Rock. Only after he arrived could the body be recovered.

The Chief Ranger speculated that the FBI smelled big-

time crime. The Feds couldn't conceive of any bizarre
form of death that wasn't either mob- or drug-connected,
and since everyone knew Italians didn't dive, that left
Denny Castle on the drug connections list.

Frederick Stanton's specialty.

Despite the reports of arrogance, Anna developed a bit
of a soft spot for Frederick the Fed: His delays would postpone the dreaded *Kamloops* dive for five days.

As the *Lorelei* motored down Amygdaloid Channel, she
saw the *3rd Sister* moored at the dock in front of the ranger
station. She wondered if anyone had called Hawk and
Holly to tell them of Denny's death. Anna didn't even
know where they lived.

Isle Royale was like a place out of time, out of the ordinary run of lives. No one but the wild creatures really
lived there. The human population appeared for six months
out of each year, a full-blown society with cops and rob-
bers, houses and boats, shovels and Hershey bars, pumping gas and drinking vodka, making love and money.
Then, October 19, humanity closed up shop and left the island to heal itself under the winter snows.

A government-issued Brigadoon. And what is known of
the people of Brigadoon? The ninety-nine years that they
are hidden in the mists, what do they do to pass the time?
Somehow Anna couldn't picture the Bradshaws puttering
around the house, watching television, going to a bed that
didn't rock and bob with the moods of the lake.

"Who told the Bradshaws about Denny?" Anna asked
the Chief Ranger.

"Nobody. Couldn't raise the *Third Sister* by radio. And
we didn't have any luck by phone. The only number we
have for the Bradshaws is the number at the Voyageur Marina in Grand Portage. I left a message with the old guy
that runs the place but they never called me. They don't
know Denny's dead—shouldn't know, anyway."

Anna understood the implication. Denny Castle's body
was found in a place only a handful of people had the
courage or the skill to go. The Bradshaws would top the
list of murder suspects.

"I hear Holly was pretty upset about Denny's marriage to Jo." Lucas began the fishing. "Hell hath no fury? Her and Denny?"

"Holly was unhappy but she wasn't spitting tacks," Anna said carefully. "I'd think if her lover was marrying another woman there'd've been more china through the plate glass, if you know what I mean. Maybe it was just that Jo would break up the Three Musketeers. The Bradshaws have been diving with Denny a long time. I got the feeling they'd be pretty lost without him. Maybe even out of business. Who owns the *Third Sister*?"

"I always assumed it belonged to Denny but I never asked," Lucas replied. "I'll ask."

Including gear, the dive boat would be worth a couple hundred thousand dollars. Anna picked up Lucas's field glasses from the instrument panel and looked at the docked vessel now less than a quarter of a mile away.

"They've got Denny's gear aboard," she said. Castle was what some of the lake divers referred to as a clotheshorse. He had a lot of fancy equipment. Anna recognized his distinctive orange dry suit.

"We knew it wasn't on Denny."

"How in the hell did he get down there?" Anna wondered aloud.

"Either he put himself there, or somebody else did. Maybe the autopsy will tell us something. If there are tire tracks on his chest or a piece of hot dog lodged in his throat, we can figure somebody else did."

"In an antique sailor suit," Anna added.

"In an antique sailor suit. Maybe he borrowed gear, put the costume on, dived, dumped his tanks. Suicide."

"On his honeymoon?"

Lucas said nothing, and Anna was reminded that the Castles' marriage had not been made in heaven but forged from equal parts determination and rebound. Even this "honeymoon" was a working vacation. The *3rd Sister* had clients arriving on the next *Ranger III*.

"In thirty-four-degree water he'd have been dead of hypothermia before he reached the engine room," Anna said.

"Possibly. Maybe he had the costume under the dry suit. No. . . . Nix that theory. Ralph and I didn't see any suit or tanks, and he couldn't have swum far without them. He must have been killed above the water, then the corpse was hidden there."

"In the hope it would get lost in the crowd?" Anna asked dubiously.

"No good either," Lucas contradicted himself. "I don't think the 'hide in plain sight' axiom works with such a celebrated collection of bodies as inhabit the *Kamloops*."

"He could have been put there just for that; to be seen. A warning of some kind," Anna suggested. "Like drug dealers who break legs, or a mob execution."

"Could be. That would make the Feds doubly happy: a drug-connected mob killing."

Anna laughed. Even given the circumstances, it felt good. Especially given the circumstances.

"Do you know Tinker and Damien Coggins-Clarke?" Lucas asked abruptly. "They're SCAs at Rock. Flaky. Naturalists."

"I know them," Anna said. She didn't know whether to bring up Charlie-Mott-cum-reincarnation-and-cannibalism or not, so she waited.

For a moment Lucas didn't go on. He looked as if he struggled with a statement as absurd as the one resting under Anna's tongue. Then he chuckled to himself and shook his head. "I was down at the marina fueling the boat when they heard of Denny's death. They were trying to catch that herring gull—the one that's got a fishhook stuck in its beak—so they could get the hook out before the bird starves. Jim came in on the *Loon,* saw a couple of fresh ears, and started babbling out the story—Tattinger, by the way, spilled the beans about the location of the body. Anyway, Tinker looked at Damien and said: 'The *Kamloops*. Yes. Denny would want to look after his friends.'" The recitation finished, Lucas looked uncomfortable with the telling. He fiddled with the throttles, cutting back to a speed that wouldn't wake the boats moored at the dock.

Anna speculated that he'd taken comfort in Tinker's

offbeat theory and was too much of a man to be easy with that.

"It's as good an explanation as any we've come up with," she said. "It certainly fits with the personality involved better. I can't see Denny Castle dealing with drugs or mobsters, but it's not hard to imagine him standing guard for all eternity over the submerged treasures of Lake Superior."

Lucas snorted genteelly. Though he'd brought the subject up, this line of conversation was to be at an end. Anna fell silent, and Vega turned his attention to docking the *Lorelei.*

Bow and stern lines in hand, Anna jumped ashore and tied off while Vega shut down the engines. Through the cabin window she saw him take off the green NPS baseball cap and put on the flat-brimmed straw hat used on official occasions.

Lucas stepped onto the dock, smoothing his coarse black hair where the hat ruffled it. "Stay close," he said. Obediently, Anna followed him down the dock and stood by as he knocked on the cabin of the *3rd Sister.*

The windows were open but all the curtains were drawn, and when there was no answer, Anna wondered if Hawk and Holly had gone ashore for some reason. Lucas knocked again.

Scarcely louder than the squeaking of the boats as they rubbed their fenders between dock and hull, mutterings leaked through the cabin windows. Hawk and Holly were conferring in whispers.

Anna reminded herself that under scrutiny all human foibles appeared to be suspicious behaviors. She exchanged a look with Lucas and he knocked a third time.

The cabin door opened. Hawk, tousled and blinking, looked up at them.

"Sleeping?" Lucas asked politely.

"No." Hawk looked over his shoulder into the cabin's interior. "No, we were just . . . ." The words trailed off as if he couldn't concentrate long enough to finish the sentence.

"Sorry. Come aboard if you want. We can put on coffee or something, I guess."

Anna had seldom heard a less gracious invitation, but it seemed borne more of embarrassment than malice.

"Holly, we got company," Hawk said and they heard a muted scramble from within as he vanished inside. Lucas followed.

"The quarters are cramped. You stay on deck." The Chief Ranger—half in, half out of the cabin—fixed Anna with a stare to be sure she understood what he wanted.

She did. He closed the door behind him. Through the window Anna heard him saying: "I'm afraid I've got some bad news. Denny's been killed." Only silence answered him. Neither Hawk nor Holly asked how or when, neither cried out.

Anna was glad to be on deck. Other people's angst sawed at the nerves like a dry wind.

Remembering Lucas's pointed stare, she stopped eavesdropping and began searching the deck, not looking for anything, just looking at what was there and what was not.

Gear was piled in every available place. Besides two bottle caps, a bit of braided black nylon cord, one broken thong sandal, and the usual boat supplies, there was full diving paraphernalia for three people and a portable air compressor—the gasoline-driven kind that was the bane of lovers of quietude—for recharging spent tanks. As a rule divers recharged their tanks immediately after use. Six one-hundred-cubic-foot scuba tanks were piled in a pyramid between the box covering the engine and the hull. An oversized single with a Y valve that Anna recognized as Denny's had rolled to one side.

She glanced at the pressure gauges. All the one hundreds were fully charged. The single was only half full. There could be a dozen good reasons the single had not been topped off. Hawk or Holly might have used it on a dive earlier that day. Most ISRO dives didn't require double hundreds. The regulator might have been damaged. They could have run out of fuel for the compressor, or just gotten lazy.

But to a suspicious mind it could suggest that when the Bradshaws had filled the tanks the previous day, they had known Denny would not be needing his.

Lucas's interview with the twins was neither reassuring nor conclusive: The Bradshaws, he said, reacted as if dead inside. Maybe shock, maybe forewarning—Vega was a ranger, not a shrink.

CHAPTER 8

"Dead bodies seem to follow you around, Anna. Are you sure you never auditioned for *Night of the Living Dead* when you lived in New York?"

"I saw it," Alison stuck in. Ally was sitting in Anna's canvas canoe chair between her mother, who occasionally dipped a paddle off the bow, and Anna, who worked all of the mobile magic from the stern. "There were all these dead people with white faces and black lips who walked like this."

"Don't stand up!" Anna and Christina said in unison.

"Like this." Alison demonstrated from her seat, swinging her arms like a chair-bound Frankenstein's monster. "They were supposed to be scary but they were just stupid. It was in black and white," she said as if that explained everything.

"*Night of the Living Dead* scared the pants off me," Anna said. "For weeks afterward all my roommates had to do was walk stiff-legged—"

"Don't stand up!" the two women repeated as Ally squirmed.

"—and I'd turn totally paranoid," Anna finished.

"What's paranoid?" Ally asked.

"Being scared of things that aren't really going to hurt you," her mother replied. "Pair-ah-noyd. P-a-r . . ."

When Tuesday's *Ranger III* had docked, Chris and Ally had been on it. "We needed to be at One with Nature," Chris had said but she'd come because Anna's letters had sounded lonely. Christina hated nature unless it could be pruned into an attractive foundation planting.

Anna smiled. If one couldn't go home, the next best thing was having home come to the wilderness. Christina Walters, with her soft white hands, deplorable J-stroke, and antipathy toward pit toilets, carried homeyness with her the way lilacs carried perfume. Anna knew one day she would lose her housemates to a sweetheart. Christina would not be single long.

"I wish I were gay," she said over Alison's head. Literally over the little girl's head, not figuratively. At five Ally was more sophisticated than Anna had been at thirty.

"Would you marry Ally and me?" Christina asked.

"In a second."

"No good." Christina laughed, caught a crab with her paddle, and splashed her daughter and Anna. "I only go for women with more impressive b-o-s-o-m-s."

"Et tu, Brute," Anna grumbled, and: "You do not."

"You haven't met Bertie."

The bicycling friend: Anna might lose them sooner than she had thought. It would be hard not to meet Chris's date at the door, cross-examine her about her intentions and if she could support Chris and Ally in the manner they had grown accustomed to. Anna smiled wryly. They all three lived on NPS wages. Any greasy-spoon waitress could answer the last question with a resounding "Yes!"

"Don't worry, Aunt Anna," Ally was saying. "If Momma and I get married again you can come live with us. If you bring Piedmont," she added as a condition.

"We'll adopt you," Chris said.

"Paddle," Anna returned. "You guys weigh a ton."

"An-oh-wreck-see-ah," Christina said. "No one in the

Walters family will ever be skinny. It indicates a stinginess of the spirit. We only accept your meagerness because it comes from being a rotten cook, not a bad person."

Anna paddled. She had that rare sense of knowing, at the moment it was happening, that she was happy, that life was okay. She stopped talking to better enjoy it. Ally and Christina's chatter pattered over her like warm rain.

"How much farther?" Ally asked after a few minutes.

"When do you bring it up?" Christina said at almost the same instant. "It" meant Denny Castle's body. Chris knew Denny. She'd met him once in Houghton and again when she'd visited Anna on the island in late May. But Christina chose not to personify death, not to call it by name. Euphemisms—"passed away," "no longer with us"—came naturally to her.

Once Anna had thought it an affectation. In the year she had known Chris it had persisted to such an extent that she now classified it as, if not a religious taboo, at least a superstition. Molly might well have termed it a neurotic denial of human mortality—but that's what Molly was paid for. And though Anna believed everything her sister told her on principle, she tended to look askance at the labeling of the less socially ratified personality traits as "illness" and the therapists, quite profitably, as the "cure."

"Three quarters of a mile and Friday," she answered cheerfully. Even dark thoughts and tedious practicalities took on a different air when shared.

"Do you have to dive so deep?" Christina asked.

"Yup."

"Are you scared?"

"Yup."

"Are you par-ah-noyd?" Ally asked.

"Yup."

"Do you want to talk about it?" Chris asked.

"Nope."

"Nope," Ally echoed, popping the *p* so it sounded like a cork coming out of a bottle.

•   •   •

The weather held all day. The water stayed smooth and flat. Inland it would be humid, buggy, but on the water it was cool. The shoreline in McCargo Cove was just warm enough for a little cautious sunbathing. Christina worked on matching her old tan with her new bathing suit and getting through *Ryan's Daughter* because Bertie had recommended it. Anna skipped stones, tracked foxes in the sand, and annoyed caddis fly larvae with Ally.

Midafternoon they launched the canoe and paddled back up the long narrow cove. Sailboats moved slowly in McCargo's protected waters, their sails as colorful and delicate-seeming as butterfly wings. Three miles long and no more than an eighth of a mile wide, McCargo was a favorite anchorage.

Anna planned an early picnic supper at the Birch campsite. Birch was a pretty little island set at the mouth of Brady Cove, a lagoonlike pocket of water off McCargo. From Birch they could watch the boat traffic and, if they got lucky, Anna could show Chris and Ally a moose. Brady Cove, behind the island, was barely six feet deep and moose often came there to browse. Several boaters had reported seeing a cow with twin calves in the past week.

A more prosaic reason was because fires were allowed on Birch. Open fires had been banned at most of Isle Royale's camps. The areas got so much use, sites had been stripped bare by campers looking for firewood. In places branches and bark had been torn from trees as high as a man could reach. In a year or two fires would probably be banned park-wide. At present Birch was still legal, and Anna wanted a fire for Ally. Marshmallows, the smell of smoke, gathering twigs, being warned half a dozen times a minute by Mom—the core camping experience.

A thin line of smoke drifting out over the water announced that Birch was occupied. Anna couldn't hide her disappointment. Hot dogs fried over the roaring invisible flame of her Peak 1 would be a poor substitute.

"We'll eat down by the water," Chris said. "That way we can see better. Besides, it's always less buggy on the shore out of the trees." She knew Anna and Alison had their hearts set on building a campfire. She was trying to make them feel better. They didn't.

Alison sulked while Anna dragged the canoe up on shore and unloaded it. Anna tried to keep up her end of the day but she felt a childish resentment that her plans had been disrupted. "I'm the ranger," she said peevishly.

"That and a dollar won't even get you a cup of coffee here," Chris returned. She excused herself to find the "ladies' room" and left Anna and Ally sitting with their legs dangling over the edge of the dock, both steadfastly refusing to play the Pollyanna Glad Game.

Anna had just about mustered up the energy to start behaving like an adult, when Christina returned.

"Anybody want to come eat supper by my fire?" she invited.

Anna's first uncharitable thought was that the fire had been left unattended and she cursed herself for leaving her citation book back on Amygdaloid.

"Two very nice people said we could share."

Anna's anger dissolved. Sharing: the obvious solution and one that never would have occurred to her in a thousand years. Following Chris and Alison, she carried the picnic cooler up the trail. The sun was shining again; the clouds she and Ally had been fomenting cleared in an instant. The air smelled of pine and wild lily of the valley, marsh marigolds put their golden heads together along the boardwalk over the swampy areas. Goldthread nodded wisely in the woods.

"It's like Disneyland," Ally reported, running ahead.

Alison had never been to Disneyland, but Anna knew exactly what she meant. In June, Isle Royale was very like the artist's conceptions of the forest where Bambi and Snow White spent the bulk of their days. Now and then mosquitoes whined menacingly from the shadows, but their bloodthirsty hum only served to add the spice of reality.

Lugging the cooler, Anna came last into the clearing. From a low branch of a spruce tree two beady black eyes met hers. Oscar the bear was on watch, protecting Birch Island camp. Ally stood on a stump, a black cloak held vampirelike across the lower half of her face. Their hosts were Tinker and Damien.

"How did you guys get here?" Anna asked in surprise. "There's no boat."

"Pizza Dave brought us over in the *Loon* and dropped us off," Tinker told her. "He was on his way to Thunder Bay on a pizza run."

Taking an NPS boat forty miles across open water to get pizza: it was a firing offense. Anna liked Dave. She hoped she wouldn't be the one to catch him. "I see Oscar's on duty," she said.

"He's promised not to offer Ally cigars," Tinker assured her. Anna eyed the woman narrowly but couldn't tell if she was joking or not.

Before the first marshmallow had melted off the stick and fallen into the ashes, Anna was glad the Fates had seen fit to put them in the way of the Coggins-Clarkes. Ally was completely taken with Damien. For at least a week Christina would be haunted by "Damien said . . ." and "Damien thinks . . ."

Tinker showed Anna a dead bat she'd found. Anna had heard the faint whistling of bats' wings as they cut through the air over the dock at night, but she'd never seen more of them than shadows fleeting over the water. Even Christina was drawn in by Tinker's knowledge and enthusiasm.

Tinker handled the little animal as if it still lived. Anna thought the creature would get a respectful interment for its unwitting service—probably with an appropriate ritual and a tiny headstone—but after Tinker had studied it she left it high in the crotch of a tree for the scavengers.

For some reason—maybe the eccentric clothes or the childlike love of ritual magic—Anna consistently underestimated the Coggins-Clarkes. There was nothing wrong with their minds.

"That reminds me," Anna said, speaking to her own thoughts. "Did anyone ever tell you what happened to Donna Butkus?"

"No," Damien replied and the inflection implied that no

one needed to. He and Ally shared a bench at the picnic table. They'd shoved aside all the condiments, and played some gambling game involving pebbles and elbows of dried macaroni. Oscar looked on.

"The Windigo," Damien intoned.

Mentally, Anna rolled her eyes.

"What's a Windigo?" Ally demanded.

"Shall I tell you a story?" Damien asked the child.

"A scary one," Ally insisted.

"I'll tell the scariest kind of all—the true kind," he promised.

"I don't know . . ." Christina began.

"Please," Ally begged.

Damien waited. Chris sighed. "The Windigo," Damien began. With proper flourishes and a creditable French accent, he told Algernon Blackwood's classic tale of the Windigo, the cannibal spirit who stalked the north woods snatching up unwary travelers and flying them through the air at such incredible speeds their feet were burned away to stumps and their cries echoed through the clear cold skies.

"That was a long time ago," Damien finished. "Things have changed. There are no more voyageurs, hardly any Indians. But the Windigo is still here, still all around us. Anywhere men hunger for what they cannot have, anywhere they will devour others to get their bellies filled with pride or money or land or power, that's where the Windigo waits."

Chris applauded. Tinker beamed: she'd heard the story before. Damien told it at evening programs. Ally was transfixed.

Alison's eyes were a little too round for Anna's comfort. It wasn't a story for a five-year-old. "Does anybody want to know what really happened to Donna Butkus or not?" she asked testily.

"What happened, Damien?" Ally asked to hear him talk. The name Donna Butkus would mean nothing to her.

"She was eaten by her husband, Scotty," Damien explained. "With pickle relish."

Ally squealed with delight. "Was Scotty a Windigo?"

"Yes."

Christina said: "Oh, for heaven's sake!"

Tinker crumbled chocolate into a split banana.

Oscar was unmoved.

"I did talk with Scotty," Anna pushed on doggedly, "the morning after the reception for Denny. Donna's sister, Roberta, ruptured a disk. Scotty told me Donna went to Houghton to give her a hand."

"Scotty *said*." Damien pursed his lips. Obviously that carried no weight with him. "And the case of relish?"

"Didn't ask," Anna admitted.

"Ah."

"Roberta Ingles?" Christina sounded mildly alarmed.

"I don't know her last name," Anna replied. "Donna goes by Butkus. God knows why. But Scotty said 'her sister, Roberta.'"

"When did this happen—the disk?" The concern was still on Christina's face.

"Why?" Anna asked. It all seemed rather far from Chris for her to take such a personal interest.

"Because I went bicycling with Bertie Sunday. She was fine then."

"Bertie is Roberta, Donna's sister?"

"Yes. She told me to say hi if I saw Donna."

"Oh Jesus," Anna breathed. "And Scotty's left the island."

"What is it, Anna?" Chris touched her arm.

"Denny and Donna. Donna disappears. Scotty lies. Castle dies. Scotty leaves the island. Maybe the Houghton police had better start looking for a second body."

"They won't find it," Damien said and he tapped the Durkee relish jar significantly.

"And Scotty never left the island," Tinker added.

"Did you . . ." Anna hesitated to use words like "spy" or "snoop." "Follow up on Donna's disappearance?"

"Some. Scotty's been kind of short with us ever since he ate Donna."

"Sort of spiritual indigestion?" Anna offered. Everyone, including Ally, gave her stern matronly looks. "Sorry. Go on."

"He'd been kind of nasty to Damien a time or two. But when we heard he'd gone to Houghton for a few days, we thought it would be safe to go through his garbage for recyclables."

"You know it's illegal?" Anna asked.

"It's a greater crime to let resources and energy go to waste," Damien said earnestly and Anna caught another glimpse of the boyish intensity usually hidden behind his cloak of mystery.

"Okay. So you went through his trash and . . ."

"For recyclables," Christina reiterated.

"For recyclables. And . . ."

"We found a flier that had come in on Saturday's *Ranger Three*—we know because everybody got one that day. There was a TV dinner, the kind that come with their own plastic plate and you throw the whole thing out. The leftovers were still fresh. Three Jack Daniel's bottles and a couple of six-packs of Mickey's Big Mouths. Dave picks up the garbage on Wednesdays and Saturdays. If Scotty'd gone to Houghton Thursday morning like he said he was going to, his trash would've been empty."

If it was supposed to be empty, Anna wondered, why search for recyclables? But she didn't say anything. "Any relish bottles?" she couldn't resist asking.

"Aunt Anna, she'd already been eaten up!" said Ally with exasperation.

"Right. Did you see Scotty?" Anna asked seriously. "Hear anything?"

Tinker and Damien shook their heads.

"He could be hurt or sick. He's prime heart attack material," Anna said. "I'll radio in as soon as we get back to Amygdaloid and get someone over there to check on him."

"We never thought . . ." Tinker began and she looked so stricken Anna was afraid she would cry or faint. "I should have thought. I haven't changed a bit. What if he's lying there hurt or dead and I didn't even think to look?" Tinker's voice had risen to a wail.

Anna sat rooted to the bench. Christina, making crooning sounds, put an arm around Tinker. Damien just hung his head, helpless with misery.

"It wouldn't be that big a loss," Anna said in an attempt to soothe Tinker. Christina silenced her with a look.

In a few minutes Tinker had recovered herself, but the picnic was over.

As soon as they'd landed at Amygdaloid, Anna radioed two-oh-two, Scotty Butkus's call number. On the second hail, Scotty answered and Anna canceled her plans to radio Pilcher requesting Butkus's quarters be checked. "Just making a radio check, Scotty," Anna said. "I've been having some static here."

"Loud and clear on this end," he assured her.

Anna signed off wondering what Tinker and Damien were up to.

Christina and Ally spent the night at Amygdaloid Ranger Station. Chris took the bed. Anna and Alison camped out on the floor. "Because we're tough," Ally explained. The next morning Anna took them back to Rock Harbor so they could catch the *Ranger III*. It was a six-hour boat trip to Houghton. Anna did not underestimate what it had cost Chris to make the visit. She'd spent twelve hours cooped up on a boat with a five-year-old child. All the coloring books in the state of Michigan couldn't have made it smooth sailing.

Anna remained on dock waving till the *Ranger III* cleared the harbor. Christina had insisted on it on her first visit. "It's the closest a government secretary may ever come to leaving for Europe aboard the *Queen Elizabeth*," she'd said. Anna had made a point of doing it ever since.

Finding Scotty wasn't difficult. He liked to be on hand when the *Ranger III* or the *Queen* set sail. When Anna saw

him he was across the harbor indulging in his favorite pas-
time on duty: swapping fish stories for fishing stories.

For a long time, she sat aboard the *Belle Isle* trying not
to look like a cheap detective on a stakeout. She wasn't
watching Scotty, but trying to think of a way to get answers to her questions without appearing to interrogate a
fellow officer. Till she had more conservative proof than
Tinker and Damien's testimony, she would not go to Ralph
or Lucas.

When inspiration did not come, she decided to play it
by ear. As she walked down the pier to where Scotty stood,
one booted foot on someone's gunwale, talking to a red-
faced man in an orange tractor cap, she could hear the
tones that usually heralded tall tales. "I kid you not, that
son of a bitch was at least . . ."

"Hey ya, Scotty," she said and sauntered up beside the
two men. The fisherman took the interruption as an opportunity to escape, made a quick excuse, and trotted away.
"How was Houghton?"

Scotty looked a little shamefaced. "To tell you the truth,
I never made it," he said with a dry chuckle. He laughed
through tight lips. He always laughed like that, as if at an
off-color joke he'd tell if it weren't for the presence of a
lady.

Anna treated him to the friendly silent stare she had
been taught in law enforcement school. Eyes wide, brows
slightly elevated, she was ready to hang on his every word.
She half expected him to stare right back if for no other
reason than to let her know she couldn't get away with
pulling that trick on him.

"I was a little under the weather. Holed up a few days,"
he told her.

"Flu?" Anna asked solicitously.

"One hell of a bug. I was flat on my back."

Anna thought of the three Jack Daniel's bottles and the
beer. "My mom always said there's nothing for the flu but
to drink plenty of liquids," she said.

That scared up Scotty's Wile E. Coyote look, half embarrassed, half proud. Anna wondered what it meant, but

he was done volunteering information. "I'm trying to track down Donna," she said suddenly. "She's not with her sister. Do you know where I can get in touch with her?"

"I'm getting tired of this," Scotty snapped. "Those little shits better not fuck with me."

"Pardon?"

"You heard me. Tell them to stay the hell away from me and Donna."

"What little shits?"

"Look, you can pull that innocent act all you want but it's not going to work on me. I've been in this business one hell of a lot longer than you have. I can smell a rat a mile away and that little poof and his wife stink to high heaven. They got a hair up their ass about Donna. I can't prove it, but I'll bet dollars to doughnuts they've been through my garbage, peeking in my windows. If I catch them at it, I'll wring their necks for them. They're not harmless little woo-woos. I've seen that Tinker before. I don't remember where, but she wasn't calling herself Tinker then. Satanism—devil worship—is my guess. They had Donna putting together all kinds of muck from leaves and moss. I was about half scared they'd poison her. That's one of the reasons I sent her to stay with her sister."

Anna waited but the outburst was at an end. "Donna's not at her sister's," she reminded him.

"You got something to say to Donna, you say it to me," he growled. When Anna said nothing, he stomped off down the dock. A couple of tourists watched with delight: better than an evening program on wildflowers any day. Anna smiled crookedly and followed Scotty off the quay.

She had a few calls to make. Checking the egress from Isle Royale wasn't difficult. The *Voyageur, Queen, Ranger III,* and the seaplane from Houghton were the only ways out of Rock Harbor.

Donna Butkus hadn't booked passage on any of them.

Anna wished she'd asked Scotty about the case of pickle relish.

CHAPTER 9

Anna had done her duty: She had reported Donna's absence to the District Ranger. Her report had omitted Tinker and Damien's cannibalism-and-reincarnation theory. Pilcher had been given the bare bones: Donna had not been seen on the island for nearly two weeks; Scotty had lied about where she was; there was no record of her leaving ISRO by commercial carrier.

Ralph Pilcher seemed singularly unmoved by the information. His mind was occupied with the imminent arrival of Frederick the Fed on the next morning's seaplane, plans for recovering Denny's body, and investigating a submerged crime scene.

The body recovery and investigation created an interesting problem. It all had to be done in twenty-five minutes of bottom time. More than that and the ascent time began to creep upwards of an hour and a half to decompress. Even in a dry suit, a diver was faced with hypothermia if exposed too long in frigid waters.

Ralph pointed out that Donna had not officially been reported as missing by any of her friends or her family, and he hinted that Tinker and Damien were not among the most highly reliable of sources. After the Castle corpse was recovered and the investigation firmly in the hands of the FBI, he promised, he would nose around, talk with Scotty and Trixy. Trixy was Donna's best friend on the island.

Anna had to satisfy herself with that. It wasn't hard. She didn't enjoy conversations with Scotty. Whether it was knee-jerk hatred of someone twenty years younger, female, and in competition with him for the next pay raise, or whether she just had an irritating quayside manner, she wasn't sure, but every time she tried to talk with him, she set him off.

Pilcher, with his man's man charm and roguish reputation, would probably fare better.

As Anna fired up the *Belle Isle* and headed up Rock Harbor from Mott, she speculated as to whether or not Scotty possessed the courage or the control it would take to murder a wife and her lover.

Scotty and Denny *mano a mano*?

It seemed out of character. Scotty had a vindictive streak but it was usually expressed in unsigned letters and backbiting phone calls just before positions were filled or promotions handed out.

But Scotty drank, and alcohol changes character. Had there been a drunken fight, as Jim had said? Not impossible. There was no denying Butkus had retained his upper-body strength. It was evidenced in the line of muscle under his lightweight summer uniform shirts.

If Scotty had killed Denny, why put the body on the *Kamloops*? Why the sailor suit? That was a touch of macabre whimsy more in keeping with the Coggins-Clarkes' mysticism than Butkus's good-old-boy approach to life. Unless the sailor suit had special meaning for Scotty—or Donna. Perhaps Scotty wanted her to know her lover was found in the costume on the *Kamloops*. Some sort of personal revenge. What sort of meaning? A lover's in-joke? Even for Denny Castle, an engine room nearly two hundred feet below the surface of Lake Superior was an unlikely trysting place. And if Tinker and Damien were right, Donna had vanished before Castle was killed. That would destroy any theory that Denny's bizarre entombment was meant as a message to, or vengeance upon, Donna.

Anna wondered if Scotty could even make a dive as demanding as the *Kamloops*. Physical problems were not the only reason he'd not kept his diving certification. In a rare moment of indiscretion, Lucas Vega had told Anna that Butkus had lost his nerve. From the mix of bravado about the good old days and contempt for the new that Scotty evinced whenever the talk turned to deep diving, Anna suspected Lucas was right.

"Did Denny kill Donna because she rejected him, and then Scotty kill Denny to avenge her?" Anna asked aloud as she used to ask her horse, Gideon, in Texas. The *Belle Isle* didn't have skin to twitch or ears to rotate to signify interest, but hummed on with mechanical indifference.

Speculation was giving Anna a headache. Briefly, she considered reviewing the facts, but they were few in number and absurd in nature. All that was known for certain was that Denny Castle, dressed in an antique captain's uniform, was floating in the engine room of a long-dead ship with sixty-four-year-old ghosts for company. And that Scotty Butkus had ordered a case of Heinz sweet pickle relish.

Denny and Donna's affair, Scotty and Denny's fistfight, even Donna's disappearance, were all just hearsay. Donna could have gotten a ride to the mainland on a private vessel. Denny could have given her a lift himself on the *3rd Sister*.

Davidson Island swam up on Anna's right. Impulsively, she turned from the channel and piloted up to the dock. The *Blackduck* was moored there as well as a sixteen-foot skiff used by Maintenance. Anna tied the *Belle Isle* in behind the skiff and walked up the wooded path toward the cabin Jo had shared with her husband for so short a time.

The door stood open, the screen closed to keep out the blackflies that had come into bloom with the spiky pink fireweed in late June. A luna moth, nearly big enough to

transport Dr. Dolittle to the moon, clung to the wire above
the door handle. Not wanting to disturb it by knocking,
Anna cupped her hands around her eyes and peered into
the gloom.

"Anybody home?"

"Just us chickens," came the reply. Anna's eyes ad-
justed and she saw who had spoken. Sandra Fox, wearing
yellow Bermuda shorts and a Hawaiian print shirt, sat at
the wooden table in Jo's kitchen. Salt and pepper and nap-
kins mixed in with samples of pond slime were shoved to
one side. A leather-bound portfolio lay open over most of
the table. Delphi was circled neatly between the table legs.
"Pizza Dave brought us. He's doing water quality today."
Sandra explained her and the dog's presence.

Anna let herself in. The sink was piled high with dirty
dishes. Half-consumed edibles littered the countertop. A
bee buzzed around a Pepsi can. A torn pizza box was open
on the stove. Three slices, curling up at the edges, lay beside a bowl of soggy corn flakes garnished with the lid of
a petri dish. Heartbreak was not a good homemaker.

"Glad you're here," Sandra said. She sniffed the air and
smiled. "The place could use a little swamping out."

"Looks like home to me," Anna returned. She sat in the
chair next to Sandra. "Where's Jo?"

"Upstairs getting her other picture albums. I guess
there's quite a few."

For the first time Anna looked at the book on the table.
It was an old-fashioned scrapbook. Affixed to the thick
black paper with ornate corner holders, the color snapshots
looked anachronistic. None of the people were familiar at
first. Then the clothes and the hairstyles peeled away the
years and Anna recognized Denny in bell-bottoms and a
beard. Jo had changed very little. The seventies had seen
the same long straight hair and owl-like glasses. In fifteen
years it seemed all Jo had done was exchange her army
surplus jacket for a polypropylene Patagonia.

"We've been looking at photo albums all afternoon,"
Sandra said. "I don't know whether your life flashes before

your eyes the moment before you die, but I'm here to tell you it flashes before everybody else's the moment after."

"Must be kind of weird," Anna said. For a blind woman to sit looking at pictures was the unspoken half of the thought. Unvoiced though it was, Sandra heard it.

"Not really. I'd like to see David, and Joseph Muench's stuff. I'd give my left tit to see Ansel Adams photographs of Yosemite. But album snapshots are for talking over, not looking at." Sandra poked a well-manicured index finger randomly at the open book. " 'There I am with Aunt Gertie in front of the old Packard. That was my first grown-up dress. Mom had to stuff tissue in my bra so the darts wouldn't fold over. My first high heels. Look how my ankles buckle.' "

Anna laughed. "You've made your point. How's Jo doing?"

"Hard to say. She doesn't cry. At least not in front of me. She's not crying over the pictures. She's proving something to herself. That Denny really loved her, is my guess. All that history's got to prove something, right?"

"Something besides persistence?"

"Once they're dead, they can never make it up to you."

"And you can never make it up to them," Anna said. "There's nothing left but to rewrite history."

Maybe next weekend, when the *Kamloops* dive was behind her, she would take Zach's ashes out and sprinkle them in the crystal waters of Five Finger Bay. Molly would be relieved. Christina would cry. What would she do? Anna asked herself. The gesture was purely symbolic. Seven years of memories couldn't be thrown overboard so easily.

"Got them." The voice came at the same instant as Jo's footstep on the stair. Unconsciously Anna and Sandra composed their features into sympathetic lines. "Oh. Hi, Anna. I was just showing Sandra some old pictures of Denny and me." She set two more albums on a coffee table under the picture window. Outside, a snowshoe hare nibbled at the grass beneath the picnic table. A whiskey jack eating crumbs hopped down the bench just over its neatly folded ears. Grief's half-finished sandwiches were a boon to somebody, Anna thought.

Jo closed the album on the table as carefully as if it were one of Shakespeare's original folios and replaced it with another. This one was more what Anna expected to house a young girl's memories: avocado-green padded leatherette with orange flower decals pasted haphazardly over it.

Jo stood between Sandra and Anna and opened the book. She pointed a finger marred with a broken and blackened nail at the first snap. "That's me when I was twenty-four. Isn't that sundress a stitch? That's the sorority house I lived in in Santa Barbara behind me. We never did fix that broken step."

Sandra wasn't missing an image.

Anna and Sandra did all that was required of them, which wasn't much. They nodded and asked meaningless questions, helping Jo to talk herself out. In the days since her husband's death, Jo had lost four or five pounds and hadn't washed her hair. The skin beneath her eyes was puffed and old-looking. Anna touched the gray that ran in zigzag lines through her own braided hair. Death aged people. If they were lucky it left in its wake some grain of wisdom. Usually it left only a sore place, like a weak muscle, a part of the psyche that would buckle first under pressure.

"Here's another one of Denny," Jo was saying. Her voice was hard, as if she kept it that way, knowing his name must be said. "We were going to a dance or something. He had this Viking thing. You know, when they died they were put on their ship and the ship was put out to sea and sunk. Only not quite Viking. He wanted to be put aboard a Spanish galleon or an old Civil War gunboat, all decked out, then sunk where there'd once been a reef. He had this mental picture of the fish coming to live on the wreck with him." She stopped short as if she'd realized the direction her words were going.

Anna snapped out of the trance she'd dropped into. She looked at the photograph that had stimulated the remarks. A young Denny Castle, maybe thirty-one or -two, sporting a handlebar mustache, stood beneath an oak tree in front of a stone building. He was wearing a turn-of-the-century ship captain's uniform. Anna schooled her voice. The information about how the body was dressed had not yet been released. She, Ralph, Lucas, and Tattinger knew. And whoever had put Denny in the engine room. "May I?" She peeled back the clear plastic that held the pictures on the page, lifted the snapshot out, and held it up to the light. The cap, the jacket with black braid at the cuffs, the eight brass buttons, were the same as she remembered them from Jon and Bobo's videotape.

"That's a wonderful costume," she said.

"It's not a costume," Jo told her, retrieving the picture from profaning hands as soon as was polite. "It's authentic. It belonged to Denny's great-uncle. He sailed the Great Lakes in the twenties."

"Did he go down on one of the ships?" Sandra asked.

"No. He lives in Florida. He owns a chain of laundromats there, I think. Or did."

"This picture was taken a while back," Anna said.

"In 1981."

"Did Denny keep the uniform?"

"He must've. Why?" Jo and Sandra were looking at Anna suspiciously, as if they thought she would offer to buy the dead man's clothes for a costume party before the corpse was decently in the ground.

Anna ignored Jo's question. "Do you know where it is?"

"Probably at Mother Gilma's," Jo replied coldly. "He left a lot of things in his mom's attic." As she replaced the picture in the album, the sleeve of her blouse fell away from her arm and Anna saw again the blue-green scars she'd associated with abalone diving on the west coast. Did Jo dive? The man she loved was making a fool of himself over another man's wife. It was the best reason Anna could think of for feeding one's husband to the fishes.

The pathology of humanity, coupled with the smell of decaying food in the kitchen, suddenly threatened to overwhelm. Muttering half-listened-to excuses, Anna stood and let herself out through the screen. The luna moth was still there. The hare and the jay were gone. She trotted to the dock and loosed the *Belle Isle* from the cleats.

Ralph Pilcher could teach her by example. In less than twenty-four hours she would be donning cold water gear with its claustrophobic layers, diving the deepest she had ever gone. Divers—the ones who lived to be old divers—prepared for a dive mentally as well as physically. A mind cluttered with what-ifs and other people's heartaches couldn't tend to the business of survival.

CHAPTER 10

Amygdaloid dock looked like suburbia on a Saturday afternoon. The pier was lined on both sides by boats and one was tethered crosswise at the end. Half a dozen hibachis smoked on the rough planking. Clothes and towels hung from rigging. Beer-bellied men sat in webbed lawn chairs. Two teenage boys played a delicate game of Frisbee over the heads of an unimpressed audience. A little girl tossed bits of hot dog bun to Knucklehead, the camp fox.

Anna counted three minor violations before she'd cut power. Two she would attend to. The black and tan cigarette boat moored in her slot was ousted. The little girl would be educated. The Frisbee players would go unpunished. Park policy insisted Frisbee was an inappropriate activity in the wilderness. Anna knew it for a quick way to Zen and chose to let people worship in their own way.

A couple of fishermen from Two Harbors jumped up from their lawn chairs to tether the *Belle*'s lines to the dock. They were good boaters, the kind the Park Service could count on to bail out their less qualified brethren. Anna was always glad to see them in ISRO's waters.

The *3rd Sister* was moored near the end of the dock, her deck piled with diving gear. Hawk sat on the bow staring into the water. Anna hoped he wasn't seeing too much trash on the channel floor. It had been six weeks since she and Ralph dove around the major docking points, trying to clean up new garbage while leaving undisturbed the garbage old enough to have been transmuted by the passing of years into Important Historical Artifacts. In its four-thousand-year human history, ISRO had been farmed and mined and fished, hunted and burned and logged. The areas where refuse was traditionally tossed could be archaeological treasure troves.

Holly, her dark hair curling close around her face, was bent over a grill all but hidden by inch-thick steaks. Three men, all of an age and dressed alike enough to have come off the same page in an Eddie Bauer catalog, drank Leinenkugels and got in her way.

Despite Denny's death, Holly and Hawk had gone ahead with the trip. Anna doubted it was callousness. Diving would be their way of bidding him goodbye. And they probably needed the money. Summer concessionaires—the smaller individual businesspeople not backed by the big money of the corporations allowed to run concessions in parks, National Parks Concessionaires Incorporated, or T.W. Services—often held on by their fiscal fingertips from one season to the next.

Anna wandered up the dock answering questions, admiring dead fish, and—one of a ranger's most difficult jobs—declining free beers.

"How's it going, Hawk?" she asked when she reached the *3rd Sister*. His eyes left the water briefly, flicked over her face, and returned to whatever had held them before. "Okay," Anna said. "I can live with that." She stood for a moment watching the northern sun play at Midas, turning water and air to burnished gold.

Holly turned the last of the steaks and looked up. "Hawk's being a jerk," she said with a touch of genuine malice Anna had never heard before when she spoke of her brother. Hawk shot his sister a black look. Seeing the Bradshaws at odds was like watching two of the faces of Eve snarl at each other.

At a loss for words, Anna polished the toe of her un-polishable deck shoe against the back of her calf and said nothing. "Don't sulk," Holly ordered her tartly. "It'll only encourage him. Want a steak? Sorry. I forgot you are a veg-etable-arian. Want a carrot stick?"

"No, thanks," Anna declined. "I'm just passing through." She smiled at the young men. They seemed sub-dued for three Type T personalities out on an expensive ad-venture, and she wondered how long Hawk and Holly had been generating foul weather.

She left them under their dark cloud and walked back into the sunlit picnic that had spread its blanket over the re-mainder of the dock. She spent a few minutes sitting on the edge of the pier talking with the child who'd been feeding the fox, explaining that Knucklehead had kits hidden in the woods and she needed to teach them to hunt. If they learned only to beg for hot dog buns, come winter, when the bun market crashed, the kits would starve.

It was only a half-truth, but Anna hoped it would suf-fice. The facts were a little less copacetic with the balance of nature. If the fox became a pest, begging close enough to present the slightest danger of tourists being bitten, of even suffering too many foxy thefts, eventually Lucas Vega would have her killed. Anna told that bedtime story to grown-up perpetrators. Little girls got the whitewashed version. She wanted them all to grow up to be rangers.

"Keeping the faith?" It was Hawk. He watched the girl meandering back toward her home barbecue. "She's prob-ably going for a fresh supply of hot dog buns."

"Probably."

"You're patient," Hawk said.

"On the second offense I shoot them."

Hawk was supposed to laugh but he didn't. "Sorry I was a jerk. Since Denny died there's been a lot of that going around."

"I know what you mean." Anna was thinking of Scotty's alcohol-ravaged face, Jo's eyes swollen with tears shed and unshed, of herself poking at everybody's boils trying to prod them into telling her something that would make sense out of the chaos in the *Kamloops'* engine room.

"Can I buy you a beer?" Hawk asked.

"Let me slip into something less governmental and you're on."

"Meet you at the ranger station," Hawk said. Finally he smiled.

Midas's touch turned both the smile and the man to gold. Anna felt a dangerous melting as she watched him walking back toward his boat. Bulk was of no use to divers. Their bodies were lean and wiry, the proportions natural, the endurance of the career divers just short of supernatural. For a dizzy moment, Anna contemplated the ramifications of that endurance.

"Stop it, you horrid old woman!" she whispered to herself and hurried up to the station feeling neither horrid nor old. She felt better than she had in days, since Chris and Ally had brought their homely comfort into her wilderness. Enjoying being pleasantly foolish, she combed her hair out. Crimped from being confined so long in braids, it fell in waves down around her shoulders. It went against the heat of her mood to put on a lot of clothes, but she'd not yet steeled her thin Texas blood to the northern summer. She pulled on Levi's and a sweatshirt.

Hawk was sitting on the steps when Anna came out. The long brown necks of four Leinenkugel bottles poked up from a paper sack between his knees. The gloom that had hung about him as he'd hunkered on the *3rd Sister's* bow had gathered round again. Anna could see it pushing down the back of his neck, bowing his shoulders. She gathered the copper mass of hair away from her face and stuffed it down the neck of her sweatshirt.

"So, what's up?" she asked as she sat beside him. "You look like a man with the bends."

"Do I?" He opened a bottle of beer and handed it to her but forgot to open one for himself. Anna took a drink. She loved the beers of the Upper Midwest. The Germans had truly mastered the brewer's art.

Hawk stared down the slope toward the water where it shimmered yellow and blue, the sun still clearing the trees though it was after seven. It crossed Anna's mind that he had come not so much to be with her but because on her front steps he would not be with Holly and yet not be alone.

Content to drink his beer and fill the emptiness next to him, she shifted mental gears from romance to contemplation of nature. Humans were herd animals, like the moose. Sometimes even the most independent needed to clump up, hip and shoulder touching, protecting their soft flanks from the wolves.

"Ever seen a wolf here?" Anna asked.

"No. Diving's a noisy business. On shore we're either jamming jugs or hosting a party."

Anna nodded. The sound of the air compressor filling scuba tanks or the chatter of humans would keep the wolves deep in the woods.

"You bringing Denny up tomorrow?" Hawk asked, his eyes still on the glittering channel.

"Yeah. Around noon is my guess. There's an FBI guy flying in from Houghton to be on the scene."

"A diver?"

"No."

Hawk shrugged slightly and Frederick Stanton was dismissed as having no real relevance. "I wish you'd leave him there," Hawk said suddenly. "Jo'll bury him on land. Plant him down in the dirt like a turnip with a slab of marble at his head to hold him there. That's not for Denny. His body pumped full of chemicals to keep it from rotting, a Sunday-go-to-meetin' suit moldering down around his bones. On the *Kamloops* he'd float forever, flipping divers the bird and guarding the lake. Leave him."

"Can't," Anna said. "It's against the law. It's even illegal to scatter the ashes of a cremated corpse in a national park."

"Even if they had a Golden Eagle Pass?" Hawk said,

but he didn't smile and bitterness took the humor out of his words.

Anna didn't reply. She finished her beer and he opened another for her without asking. She took it. "I saw a picture of Denny over at Jo's today. He was wearing an early-twentieth-century ship captain's uniform," Anna said, watching Hawk's face. His expression never changed, only hardened slightly. But their bodies touched from shoulder to hip and Anna felt a current run through him that he could not hide. "Did you ever see that picture?"

"Yeah. Well, no. I think I remember the uniform. Denny might've worn it once or twice." Hawk's voice was heavy with indifference and his eyes focused keenly on nothing. He was not a good liar. Anna liked him for that. She doubted she would like the reason he had to lie.

"What happens to the *Third Sister* now?" she asked. "Does it go to Jo?"

"She's been wanting to get her hands on it, turn it into a research vessel. A floating freshwater lab," Hawk said with disgust. Anna imagined he viewed the *3rd-Sister*-as-lab much as Jacques Cousteau might view a desk job. "She might've eventually weaseled it—and Denny—out of the diving business, but Denny left the boat to Holly and me. It's in his will. He told us so, anyway."

Denny Castle had had a will though he was probably not more than forty-five or forty-six. For a moment that struck Anna as a little suspicious; then she remembered what he did for a living. He would've seen many of his friends die at an early age.

She took another pull on her beer. The Bradshaws both seemed to hold Jo in contempt. Was it because she would, as Hawk had put it, weasel Denny out of diving, out of the Musketeers? And, in the process, weasel the *3rd Sister* out from under the Bradshaws? They'd known if Denny died the *3rd Sister* was theirs. Was that reason enough to kill him quick, before the weaseling process began?

They loved Denny. They would have been more likely to kill Jo. Unless there had been a betrayal. To betray one Bradshaw was to betray them both. "Denny's marriage took me by surprise," Anna said carefully. "I'd always just assumed he and Holly had a thing going."

Hawk snorted. "Holly and Denny? No way." He laughed. "No way."

It didn't seem so impossible to Anna. It seemed probable: a shared love of diving, a shared living space, a shared business, shared danger, a boy, a girl. More than probable, it seemed mandatory. Hawk's reaction piqued her curiosity. He'd been amused at the idea. Maybe Holly was gay. Anna made a mental note to ask Christina. The lesbian community in the Upper Peninsula was small, endangered, and therefore close-knit. Christina would have heard.

"The only person I know of that Denny gave more than a wink and a nod was Donna—Scotty's wife," Hawk went on. "I never could see it. Holly thinks she was just old-fashioned enough to catch Denny's imagination. In some ways he'd been born in the wrong century.

"That whole scene was strange. Donna was the first time I think Denny had ever fallen in love. He was crazy, like a kid, like a Romeo and Juliet, *West Side Story*. That crazy obsessive stuff that makes for good fiction but's pretty hard to maintain in real life."

"Especially when Juliet is married," Anna observed dryly.

"Yeah. There was that." Hawk grinned, exposing white teeth, small and strong. Smooth, Anna imagined, under the tip of one's tongue. She hid her smile with the mouth of the beer bottle.

"Denny didn't give old Scotty a thought," Hawk went on. "Not seriously. It was as if he was an inconvenience, not a husband."

"No wonder Scotty hated him. Did Donna feel that way?"

"I don't know. That was the one way Denny's romance differed from kid stuff. It wasn't something he would talk about. At least not with us."

"Us" always meant Hawk and Holly. Anna had been acquainted with them long enough to know that. She wondered if Denny had kept quiet to protect Donna's reputation or because he knew they wouldn't approve. They'd clearly not approved of Jo and she was unencumbered by any "inconveniences." Or, despite Hawk's protests to the contrary, had he not spoken of it because Holly was in love with him, or even his lover? Anna reminded herself again to ask Christina what she knew about Holly's sexual preference.

"Did Denny give Donna a ride to the mainland in the last two weeks?" Anna asked.

"Not on the *Third Sister.* Holly and I have had the boat. Denny was pretty tied up with the wedding. Why? Has Donna gone missing?"

The question was meant as a joke but when Anna made no reply, Hawk asked it again.

"I don't know," she answered truthfully.

The subject had reached a dead end. For a while they sat in silence.

"Pilcher'll go down and Vega—how about you?" Hawk returned to the subject of the body recovery.

"I'll dive. So will Jim Tattinger."

"Tattinger's a squirrel."

A squirrel was a neophyte diver. It was a grave insult. Anna guessed Hawk and Holly were going to carry on the tradition of animosity between the *3rd Sister* and the park's Submerged Cultural Resources Specialist.

"I take it you don't care much for Jim?" Anna invited gossip, hoping for some useful bit of information.

"If he did his job, I could overlook his naturally repugnant self. He's a number cruncher, a bean counter. He couldn't care less about preserving the wrecks."

"He used to work in the Virgin Islands." Anna threw another line in the waters she was fishing.

"I know." Hawk opened a beer and took a drink. He looked over the bottle at Anna. His eyes were a clear hazel. He smiled. "Let's not talk about Jim. It's worse than taking saltpeter." In the slanting light his skin was almost a true bronze and his dark hair showed black. Anna was aware of the warmth from his thigh through the worn denim of her trousers. She remembered she was, after all, off duty and she remembered that there were other things to do with bronzed young men than interrogate them.

"What do you do to relax, Anna?"

She smiled at the answers that rattled through her mind and he smiled back. "Music," she said finally. This evening it was not her first choice but it was the most socially acceptable.

"Put something on the tape deck for me. Anything but a sea chantey."

Anna stood up and held out her hand. Hawk took it and she pulled him to his feet.

A distant growl in the channel penetrated the warm haze of hops and lust. Her first impulse was to hold tight to Hawk's hand and run for the relative privacy of her quarters, to bolt the door and draw the curtains; lose herself for an hour or two in the music of West Texas and, if she was reading the signals correctly, the music of the spheres.

But she waited, her eyes on the channel. Before she could dismiss this boat from her mind, she must run through her litany: Was anybody hurt, sick, or lost? Was anybody on board likely to get that way in the near future?

"They'll have to camp at Belle Isle," Anna said, naming the little island her boat had been called for. "There's no room at the inn." She had dropped Hawk's hand. It would not do to be seen. There was no comfortable mix of business and pleasure for a woman in her profession. Because of the isolation, the predominance of men in middle and higher management, the usual dangers of gossip and backbiting were multiplied a dozenfold for a woman ranger.

The boat came into view: a natty green runabout trailing a frothy wake. "Looks like Patience Bittner's boat," Hawk said.

Anna hadn't known Patience owned a boat. "Do you know her?"

"Know the boat. We've seen it over here three or four times when we've been out with clients. She's always alone, never stops to say hello. Denny thought she was up to something, but Holly and I just figured she was a loner."

"Denny was a little judgmental, it seems," Anna said cautiously.

Hawk laughed. "One of Denny's favorite sayings was: 'It's hard to work well in a group when you're omnipotent.' Denny was always right. He really was. He never cared about himself. Only the lake. It gave him an almost superhuman vision. He saw other people's twists and bends as clearly as if they'd been laid out on graph paper."

"That kind of vision won't get you elected Most Popular Senior Boy," Anna said.

"Denny didn't need to be popular. He didn't need anything but the lake and a jug of air."

Anna sensed that Hawk needed more than that, and that he perceived it as a weakness, a flaw in his character.

There was no place left on the dock and the runabout pulled alongside the *3rd Sister* and rafted off. Patience, her pale hair dyed red by the sinking sun, crossed the deck and stepped onto the dock.

"Amygdaloid gets any more popular and we'll have a floating city to rival Hong Kong's," Anna said. It was too much to hope, she knew, that Patience had just stopped by to use the pit toilet. Her fear was confirmed: The woman walked straight down the dock and turned up the hill toward the ranger station.

"Looks like I've got company," Anna said ruefully.

"I'd better check on Holly. Those three clotheshorses think she's part of their adventure." Briefly, Hawk touched Anna's arm. "Rain check?"

"Sure." I'll pray for foul weather, Anna thought as she watched him walk down the trail. She found herself thinking Hawk Bradshaw would be perfect: he was only in town once or twice a week and would vanish like the honeysuckle when the first snows fell.

Suddenly Anna shuddered. She wasn't sure she cared for the woman who had come to use people in such a calculating way.

CHAPTER 11

Patience stopped at the foot of the steps and looked back over her shoulder at Hawk's retreating form. "Am I interrupting anything?"

"Not a thing."

"Too bad," she said, and they both enjoyed the view a second longer.

Anna sat down again and waited for Patience to tell her what had brought her to the north shore after eight P.M. Patience sat beside her. The light-colored hair was tied back into a ponytail and bound with a cabbage rose ribbon that matched, exactly, her peach shorts and jersey. Her deck shoes were white, even to the leather laces.

When she returned to Houghton in the fall, Anna promised herself, she would go clothes shopping. Levi's and sweatshirts were losing their appeal.

"I'm out on a domestic mission tonight," Patience said. "Carrie's disappeared."

Anna hoped it was not along with another case of pickle relish. "A moderately alarming disappearance or a call-out-the-Coast-Guard disappearance?"

"Moderately alarming. Carrie's started acting out this summer. In ten years some therapist will discover it's my fault. In the meantime I'm blaming her. We are not having fun. She's been coming home at two and three in the morning with that damp, rumpled look. I can't get a word out of her. She's turned from a nice little girl into a sullen tramp. God!" Patience rested her head in one hand. "Sorry. I don't mean that. I'm alternately pissed off and worried sick. It's very tiring."

"Do you think she's out with her boyfriend tonight?"

"I'd bet on it. She was supposed to be home by five-thirty. She knew I had a date. She just doesn't give a damn about anybody but herself. Oh! I sound like a selfish shrew, don't I? Vaguely, I seem to remember promising myself I wouldn't say things like that if I ever became a mom. I just don't want her getting into trouble. I got married too young. I was seventeen. What a fool! She's thirteen and only just barely. All she'll get out of it now is AIDS."

Anna had forgotten about AIDS. Teenage troubles had taken a dire turn since she'd fumbled in the back seat of Steve Duran's parents' Chrysler. "What makes you think she's on the north shore? I'd think she and the boy would just wander around Rock. There's plenty of trails."

"You'd think so, wouldn't you? If she's got to be such a little slut—" Anna winced. "Sorry, sorry, sorry. I was once a little slut myself. I am just so angry," Patience apologized. "I just wish she'd stay on land—then my mad wouldn't be undermined by my worry that some young idiot's got her killed in one of those aluminum death traps we rent out at thirty dollars a day. I'm rambling. I think she's on the north shore because two of the kids who work at the lodge said they saw her on Belle Isle. They didn't put in and she didn't return their wave, so they could be mistaken but it's all I've got to go on at the moment."

"You checked Belle?"

"On the way here. And Merrit Lane, Duncan Bay, and Lane Cove," Patience listed the campgrounds between Rock Harbor and Amygdaloid accessible by water.

"Do you have a marine radio?" Anna asked.

"Yes."

"What do I call you?"

"The *Venture*."

"Why don't you head back around Blake's. Watch the coast, check the camps again. The water's been pretty flat today, even around the point, so I doubt she's come to any harm. I'll head down toward McCargo and see what I can find. She may already be home. Radio if you find anything, or if you don't. We'll look until it's dark. If she's not home by midnight, I'll call Lucas and Ralph. They'll stage a search for tomorrow. I doubt it'll come to that—I need the overtime too badly."

Patience laughed. "You're a comfort, Anna."

"Your tax dollars at work."

"I'll tell Lucas," Patience volunteered.

The dinner date had been with Lucas Vega, Anna realized, and didn't wonder that Patience was so angry with her daughter.

The glow ignited by Hawk and two beers was gone. All that remained was a mild alcohol-induced lethargy. Anna sluiced as much of it away as she could with cold water, pulled on a Levi jacket, and again climbed aboard the *Belle Isle*.

The dock, though still populated, was quiet: people talking softly, listening to the loons calling down the night. The *3rd Sister* was gone. In the distance was the dull thunder of their air compressor filling tanks. Denny had been sensitive about the racket and anchored out when recharging air cylinders. Jamming jugs, he called it. Anna avoided the slang. Where she'd grown up "jugs" did not refer to scuba tanks.

The gold had drained from the water, leaving silver and peach petals of evening on the smooth channel. It was Anna's favorite time of day. Stillness settled over the islands, the winds died, animals came to drink or play.

A great blue heron, the color of the sky, stood on a stone several feet from shore. Two female mergansers sharing a brood of eighteen or twenty ducklings paddled in the shallows. Once Anna had seen two moose swimming the channel, only their magnificent heads above the water. According to the naturalists, the moose population—or the seeds of it—had swum the eighteen miles from the mainland to Isle Royale. It seemed incredible, but fishermen had reported seeing the beasts as much as twenty miles out in the lake.

Puttering down the silent channel, Anna realized she was enjoying herself. It was a pleasure to be looking for someone who wasn't being devoured by a cannibalistic husband, wasn't floating with old corpses, someone who, at worst, was probably having illicit sex with the busboy.

Darkness gathered. Near Kamloops Island, Anna switched on her running lights. Carrie would not be found tonight unless she chose to be. It was time to head for home.

The last fragile light of day glowed in the western sky. Overhead the stars were coming into their own. Anna shut down her engines and went out on deck to enjoy the coming dark. On summer nights in Texas, in Mexico, now here, she promised herself that one day she would learn the constellations. Could she love them better for knowing their human names?

A faint offshore breeze brought her the sweet complex smell of land, and she thought how heady that perfume must have been to sailors months at sea. The smells of the desert had come one at a time: a clear stream of sage on a dry wind, a gust of rain-damp earth on the last hurrah of a sudden thunderstorm. In the vegetation-rich north country Anna could seldom separate out the myriad scents. Layers of wealth and promise, secrets deep under the moss.

The breeze freshened and carried a new fragment of news: the grumbling of a vessel. By the low-pitched sound and the high rev of the engine, Anna guessed it was a small outboard, a hundred to a hundred and seventy-five horsepower. She scanned the water between her and the shoreline. But for an occasional flash of a wave catching the improbable light of the stars, the darkness was unbroken. The growl of the unseen boat continued, a steady hum, growing louder. The boat was coming closer and still Anna saw no running lights.

Traveling after sundown without running lights was dangerous, illegal, and stupid. It was the last of these considerations as much as the first two that decided Anna to give up her meditations.

Having fetched her field glasses from the cabin, she stood in the stern, her eyes trying to follow the cues her ears were receiving. Finally she spotted the perpetrator: a light-colored cabin cruiser just barely big enough to go by that grand title. The boat was powering slowly along just out from the cliffs between Twelve O'Clock Point and Hawk Island. As she watched, it made an apparently senseless dogleg out from the shore, then, squaring the corner, in again.

Whoever the pilot was, he knew there were three barely submerged boulders on that section of shore. No one that well versed in underwater topography would be foolish enough to run without lights. Unless they were up to something—or their electrical system was on the fritz, Anna thought more prosaically.

Though ISRO seldom got involved in the Drug Enforcement Agency's business, this close to the Canadian border, drug running was a reality of life.

Anna took the time to radio in her location and her intended visitor contact before she took her side arm from its briefcase in the bow and laid it next to the radar screen.

The roar of the *Belle*'s inboards swallowed all other sounds. Deafened by her technology, Anna kept the unlit vessel in visual contact.

She switched on the *Belle*'s searchlight and spotlit the cruiser, picking the fiberglass hull out in a circle like the star of a stage show. The vessel speeded up as if the pilot had decided to make a run for it. Anna felt a clutch of fear or excitement tighten her stomach. Then it slowed again to its labored pace. The clutch in her middle did not loosen its grip. In every law enforcement class she'd taken, in every refresher course, instructors in bulletproof vests had exhorted students never to lose the edge fear gave when approaching an unknown. Any officer making a routine traffic stop could be pulling over an armed and wanted felon. One who knows if a radio call is made, he'll be sent back to the penitentiary.

Anna rocked gently on the balls of her feet, her eyes compassing the cruiser in search of anything that was not as it should be. If she saw a crate of Uzis or baggies bursting with white powder, she'd stay back and call for help. There were, she thought with a smile, people for that.

The *Belle Isle* had eaten up the distance. Anna pulled behind and to the starboard of the smaller vessel. Her spotlight picked out the name on the stern: The *Gone Fishin'*. For a minute or two she trailed the boat. The running lights flicked on: sudden red and green eyes to be seen by.

Since the initial impulse to run, it was the first sign that the pilot knew she was there. Anna wondered if he thought this tardy compliance would appease her and she would just go away. Picking up her radio mike, she tuned it to the hailing frequency. "*Gone Fishin', Gone Fishin',* this is the *Belle Isle.*" Three times she called and three times got no response.

Anna turned on the boat's public address system. "*Gone Fishin',* this is the National Park Service patrol boat the *Belle Isle.* Please cut your engine. I'm coming alongside." Ten seconds passed, fifteen. Anna refocused her light on the cabin. Two shadows glared back in the light, reflecting off the boat's windscreen. Then one fell away, dropped like the falling of a veil, and there was only one.

It could have been a trick of the light, or it could have been someone ducking down, hiding. Anna picked up the pistol and stuck it into the waistband of her Levi's. Again she took up the P.A. mike. Before she could repeat her command the *Gone Fishin'* slowed. Anna reduced power, pulled to the starboard side, and cut both throttles.

A fender plopped out of the cabin cruiser's side window, reminding Anna to deploy hers. The boats drifted gently forward eight or ten inches apart. Anna waited half a minute. The pilot did not show himself. "Captain of the *Gone Fishin'* and any others aboard, please come out on deck," Anna said into the mike. She kept the spotlight trained on the cabin, trying to see past the black ovals of Plexiglas in the rear windows.

The cabin door opened a crack, then closed, then opened again just wide enough to let a pale, slender man creep through. He held both hands over his eyes trying to block the glare of the searchlight.

Anna was aware of thin white arms, a stick of neck, too long and too white, long thin fingers crosshatched over a white face. She had that unpleasant sensation one gets when one turns over the wrong rock.

"What the hell is going on?" the nocturnal creature shouted. "Is that you, Anna?"

The white lattice of fingers dropped and Anna recognized Jim Tattinger. She left her .357 on the seat and walked back to the rear deck.

Jim had grabbed a gunwale and was holding the boats together. "What the hell do you think you're doing?" He was angry and letting it show, letting it sharpen on the edge of his voice.

The best defense is a good offense, Anna thought. What could Tattinger be defending?

"Hi, Jim. Your running lights were out." Anna walked over to the port gunwale and leaned close to him. She could smell no alcohol, none of the sweet cloying scent of marijuana. "I pegged you for a desperado on a midnight drug run." She smiled into his eyes. They weren't dilated or pinpointed—no narcotics or amphetamines. They were a little bloodshot but Tattinger's eyes were usually red, as if in sympathy with his red-tipped ears and carroty hair.

"Whose boat?"

"I borrowed it," Jim snapped. "Who authorized you to patrol out of uniform? I bet Lucas didn't."

Anna ignored that. "What brings you to this neck of the woods in the dead of night without running lights?" she asked conversationally.

"I don't see that's any business of yours."

"What's that?" She jerked her chin toward the cabin where four scuba tanks and a pair of fins were piled in an untidy heap. Jim twitched like a puppet on too tight a string. His eyes widened as if he—or more likely Anna—had just seen a ghost.

"Doing a little night diving?"

"Oh. The tanks. No," he retorted and his irritability sounded mixed with relief. Anna wondered how she had let him off the hook—what the hook was. "What are you doing out here?" he demanded. "You can't use NPS boats for personal stuff, you know."

"We've had a report of a missing child. I was checking the usual spots on the north shore."

"Oh gosh!" Tattinger puffed. He seemed genuinely concerned. It caught Anna off guard. "What happened?"

"Carrie Bittner didn't make it home for supper. Patience is worried."

"Oh, for Christ's sake!" Jim's anger was back, though Anna couldn't see why.

"Patience is rechecking all the sites on the way back to Rock," Anna told him. "If Carrie doesn't turn up pretty quick, I'll call in Lucas and get a search under way as soon as it's light."

"For Chr—" Tattinger began his refrain again, then stopped suddenly. "Wait. Bittner? That kid with the brown hair, always hanging around the lodge?"

Anna nodded.

Jim seemed relieved. "I saw her in Lane Cove when I was headed over here. There wasn't any boat so she must've been going back overland on the trail."

"When was that?"

"I don't know—not too long ago."

"Was she alone?"

"Jesus! I got better things to do than look after some snot-nosed kid. You're not Dick Tracy, Anna." Jim curled his lip till the ruffle of pink showed garish in the searchlight. "Nobody authorized you to interfere with my work."

The federal government had authorized Anna to interfere where probable cause could be proved, but she let it pass. "I'll radio Patience," she said, and: "Leave a running light on for me."

Running lights on, the *Gone Fishin'* powered away at high speed.

It was after midnight when Anna got the radio message that Carrie had finally wandered home. Later that same day, Anna knew, she must dive the *Kamloops*. Finally she managed sleep but it was troubled with dreams: Denny holding her fast two hundred feet beneath the lake while air trickled from her tanks like the last stars from the night sky.

CHAPTER 12

"Never to see the sun again," Anna grumbled. Standing in sweats and mismatched wool socks, she drank her morning coffee, staring out the window above her kitchen sink. The day presented a bleak and dismal aspect. An overcast sky pressed down to the top of the cliff that backed Amygdaloid Ranger Station. Oily-looking raindrops crawled down the glass.

"Come on down," Anna hollered. If the cloud settled into fog, obscured the lake, the *Kamloops* dive would be postponed. As it was, the day managed to be completely without sympathy: cold and damp and dark with perfectly adequate visibility.

Anna crossed to the yellow enameled bureau with its chipped edges and olive-green knobs. Amid the clutter of hairpins and badges was an oval box, the lid carved with monkeys frolicking in a jungle of leaves. The handles formed the graceful upward wings the Balinese put on their temples. Anna lifted off the lid. Inside was a handkerchief edged with lace. The creases were yellowed from being so long folded. In the middle of it was the dull gold of a wedding band.

After Zachary died Anna had taken it off and folded it in the "something old" her mother-in-law had given her. Her hand looked ugly without it, she'd never stopped believing that, but in the first years she'd been unable to answer the questions generated by a ring. "What does your husband do? I see you're married—is your husband with you?"

At Molly's suggestion she had taken it off. "It's nobody's damn business," her sister had said.

"People will think I've stopped loving him," Anna worried.

"Fuck 'em," had been the psychiatrist's advice.

Anna thought about putting it back on; a comfort, a talisman for the dive. A thousand times over the years she'd thought of putting it back on. As always, she returned it to its linen nest. She still wasn't ready to answer those questions.

"Three-oh-two, one-two-one." Her radio cracked the solitude and Anna shot it a baleful look. "Three-oh-two, one-two-one."

"Keep your pants on, Lucas." She crossed through the open door into the ranger station and hit the mike button of the base radio. "Three-oh-two," she responded.

"What kind of deck you got over there?"

It crossed Anna's mind to say it was socked in, but she crushed the lie as unworthy—and too easy to detect. "I can see three or four hundred yards. The storm isn't sitting on the water. Some rain. No wind."

"The MAFOR promised more of the same. Waves one to two meters." The MAFOR was shorthand for the marine forecast. All the ranger stations posted the day's MAFOR before they opened shop in the mornings. On busy days there'd be a line three or four boaters deep waiting to read it before the thumbtacks had even cooled.

"Officer Stanton, Ralph, Jim, Scotty, Jo, and I are about to head out." Vega's voice rattled the speaker. "We'll be to Amygdaloid in thirty minutes or so."

"I'll be waiting with bells on," Anna said.

"One-two-one clear."

For whom the bell tolls, Anna thought. It tolls for thee. She laughed aloud, relieved by her sheer morbidity. "I'm wasted in the Park Service," she addressed the mute radio. "Melodrama was my true calling."

Half an hour later, when the *Lorelei* pulled up to the dock, Anna was waiting, surrounded by gear. Only one of the boats that had given the place such a festive air the night before still remained. Rain, slow and cold and with apparently no intention of stopping in the foreseeable future, had driven the fisherpeople back to the more protected amusements on the mainland.

The *3rd Sister* would still be around somewhere. Hawk and Holly were indifferent to comfort. Only a clear and present danger kept them out of the water. When clients paid the *3rd Sister* for an adventure it was not unlike making a contract with the devil. There was almost no way out.

The *Lorelei* glided up parallel with the dock, and Ralph, green from head to foot in foul-weather gear, came out on deck. Lucas didn't shut down the engines.

"How time flies when you'd rather be in bed," Anna said as she handed her air tanks over the gunwale.

Ralph gave her a life vest and she fumbled at the side lacings. ISRO had purchased all Large and Extra Large in the expectation of a future filled with nothing but brawny, strapping rangers. Even having cinched it as tightly as it would go, Anna knew it would probably pop off if she were ever thrown unconscious into the lake.

Lucas motored slowly away from the dock, scrupulous as ever not to create a wake where it could damage another vessel. A crew cut and long brown hair were about all Anna could see of Frederick the Fed and Jo. Scotty and Jim hovered behind the two benches. Ralph stayed out in the rain with Anna. Lightly, he touched her elbow. "How are you doing?"

His kindness irritated because it reminded her of her fear. "Never better," she retorted.

Ralph laughed. "Anna Pigeon: heart of gold, body of iron, nerves of steel."

"Oh pshaw!" Anna pronounced all the letters: "puhshaw." Next to "damn" it was her sister Molly's favorite word. It took the place of "expletive deleted."

Ralph just laughed.

Anna pulled the drawstrings of her Gore-Tex hood close around her face and backed up against the cabin out of the wind. She could put off meeting Officer Stanton a few minutes longer and she preferred the fresh air to the self-inflating chatter Scotty would suffocate the cabin with, given such a prestigious audience.

Besides, she hoped the cold would drive Ralph inside. The last thing she wanted was someone to call her bluff. Two terrors battled for dominance in Anna's belly: that she would dive and that she wouldn't. The latter was worse. She was afraid Pilcher would offer her a way out and she would take it.

He leaned against the cabin next to her, the bulk of his body cutting the wind that curled around the side. Boyish brown curls escaped his hood, contrasting oddly with the broken nose and unsettlingly old eyes. Ralph Pilcher wasn't a handsome man, but Anna guessed it had never stood in his way and she felt a sudden stab of pity for his wife. In sympathy with the unknown woman, she moved a couple inches away from his sheltering warmth.

"A few things," Ralph said as the *Lorelei* motored out of Amygdaloid Channel onto the vast gray bosom of Lake Superior. "The superwoman act works well for you, Anna. Good cover. But you don't need it on a dive. It'll kill you on a dive. This is a team sport. I'll be looking after you. Lucas will watch me. We'll all keep an eye on Jim."

Anna laughed. She was feeling better. She took back her two inches. The hell with Mrs. Pilcher.

Ralph relaxed back against the cabin wall and for a moment they stood in companionable silence watching the wake fold in on itself and disappear.

"Ever do a body recovery?" Ralph asked after a while.

"A few. Always on dry ground."

"In Superior they're not too bad. No smell. Usually we'd take the mask off. If they were diving—breathing compressed air—the change in pressure makes fluids froth out the nose and mouth. The family doesn't need to see that."

Denny's face would be clean when Jo saw him again. No mask. No tanks. No suit. Did Jo know that? Would she be surprised? Could she feign surprise if she was not? Jo had tremendous strength for so small a woman. Years of tramping through forests and swamps with her laboratory on her back had seen to that. She was—or had been—a diver, Anna thought, remembering the distinctive scars on her arms. And she was a determined woman. She had determined to marry Denny Castle and against all odds had finally succeeded. Was removing Donna Butkus a prerequisite for success? Murdering Denny the price of a long madness? Or killing them both revenge for a life squandered on an unrequited love?

The tenor of the engines changed as Lucas throttled down. They were nearing the *Kamloops'* marker buoy. Anna shook her head to clear it of the fog of unanswered questions. First she would dive, just dive.

The *Lorelei* glided gently up to the buoy and stopped. Anna took an instant away from fretting and dedicated it to admiration only slightly sullied by envy: Lucas Vega could sure drive a boat.

The first man out of the cabin was Frederick Stanton. The crew cut had been an optical illusion. His hair was cut close only in the back and over the ears. He wore the top long. When Anna was in seventh grade that configuration had indicated a fresh—and cheap—haircut. On Stanton it smacked of a mild punk rebellion in white socks and hard leather shoes.

Warmed by the possibility that she'd been wrong, that Frederick the Fed might have some redeeming social attributes after all, Anna started to smile.

"Fred Stanton." Scotty, only his head poking out of the cabin, introduced the man from behind. Stanton shook, a sudden convulsion of the shoulders as if freeing himself from any proprietary claims Butkus was trying to stake.

"Frederick," he said clearly and pulled off his glove to shake hands.

"This is Anna Pigeon," Ralph said as she tried to balance her grip between insipid and faux machismo. "She'll be on the wet end of the body recovery."

"Better you than me," Stanton said. His voice was light and gentle for a man. Pleasant and probably misleading, Anna thought. The FBI was a big stick and Stanton may have learned the value of walking softly.

"Excuse me." Lucas was making his way past Scotty, who still hung in the narrow doorway. Butkus, muttering cowboy apologies, clomped to the stern. Vega's eye followed his steps with a sour look, watching for black heel marks on the white deck.

Jim bumped out from the cabin and the Chief Ranger's attention snapped back to the dive. "Ralph?" Raising a dark wing-shaped eyebrow, he officially turned the dive over to the District Ranger.

Quietly, efficiently, Ralph began directing traffic on the crowded deck, lending a hand where buckles needed buckling, rubber hoods straightening. He managed to suit up himself, keep Scotty's great booted feet off the damageable goods, and exchange a few sentences with Jo.

With fingers that tingled, Anna pulled on the bulky suit with boots and hood. The anxiety that was robbing her fingers of feeling filled her throat with a bitter taste. The more she swallowed, the more nauseated she became. Her mind raced with cowardly alternatives: if she dropped a tank and broke her foot, she'd not have to dive; if she stumbled over a fin and rapped her head on the gunwale, she'd be excused with honor intact.

Still, she pulled and jerked and buckled and finally, without mishap, she was encased in gear. Hump-backed, orange-skinned, blue-flippered, they all looked like creatures from an unlikely lagoon.

"Okay," Pilcher said. "Tasmanian cluster fuck." From the corner of her eye, Anna saw a jolt of what could've been alarm or amusement electrify the FBI man's dark eyes. Of the seven people on board, he alone had never before experienced Pilcher's predive ritual. At another time, in another place, Lucas would have said a quiet word against the obscenity. But Pilcher was a first-rate dive leader. Vega was a manager first and a gentleman second: his District Ranger was free to establish trust and camaraderie any way that worked.

Anna, Ralph, Jim, Lucas, even Scotty and Jo closed ranks, forming a tight circle like a football huddle. Through the insulating layers, Anna could feel the bones of Jo Castle's shoulder against hers. A fine mist beaded in her long straight hair, cloaking her in shifting silver. When Anna took her hand it felt clammy. Though it was probably due to the weather, Anna hoped Scotty would have enough sense to monitor Jo for shock.

Ralph's hand closed over Anna's, warm and dry. "Denny's in the engine room," he said, his voice somehow different without in any way being artificial. The pitch was slightly lower, the pace a little slower. Anna could almost feel everyone's heartbeats slowing, respirations evening out.

Everyone except Jim Tattinger. His pale eyes, watery in their pink rims, wandered restlessly. Anna could see his limp fingers refusing to meet the pressure of Lucas's hand on one side and Jo's on the other. If Frederick Stanton was the noticing kind, being unaware this behavior pattern was Jim's usual, he might find the actions suspicious.

Ralph was speaking. "We'll go down pretty quick. I'll lead, Anna will follow me, Jim follows Anna. Lucas, you bring up the rear. We keep each other in sight. Keep me in sight. I get lonely down there. We've plenty of time. We'll be down an hour and twenty-nine minutes. Twenty-two minutes on the bottom's all we got. And we all come up together. Lucas and I will go inside, photograph as best we can, look around a little, and bring Denny out. Jim, you and Anna will check the outside. Go no deeper than the engine room. Take pictures. Look. Stay together. Watch the time. We meet at the line twenty-two minutes exactly after we leave it. Dangers: You two"—he looked at Anna and Jim—"never deviate from the plan. Never lose sight of each other or the time.

"Us two: silt out. Lucas and I'll watch our big feet so we don't get lost in a mud storm inside the wreck."

All this was repetition. Ralph had sought each of them out in the days since the body had been discovered and discussed what they were to do. In true governmental fashion, the plan had been typed up, approved, signed off, and copies given to everyone who needed to know and half a dozen people who didn't. Yet hearing it again in this reassuring voice was visibly knitting the four divers and two tenders into a unit, a team with a single purpose, a single plan.

"Pay attention. Breathe." He laughed. He was alive, excited. "Hey, we're gonna cheat Death," he finished with a dare that was only partly a joke. Anna breathed. Knots of fear in her belly began to loosen.

Once again Ralph checked the gear. They were diving with air. Some divers used roll-your-own heliox on *Kamloops* dives. Mixing gases was fundamentally risky business and the National Park Service stayed with air. The mixture of helium and oxygen eliminated the effects of nitrogen narcosis but compounded the effects of hypothermia.

Ralph gave the go-ahead. One by one they rolled off the port gunwale. For a moment the four of them bobbed in the pockmarked water, the only spots of color in a world gone gray. The lake wasn't just cold but frigging, goddam cold, Anna thought as the frigid water struck her face like the slamming of a two-by-four and her sinuses began to ache. Beneath the layers of suiting she could feel her breasts tighten and shrivel.

With an effort she looked past the pain and concentrated on keeping her mind clear of the flotsam of thoughts washed loose by her intercranial storms.

Tattinger floated into view. With the regulator stretching his rubbery lips and the mask maximizing his watery eyes, he put Anna in mind of Gollum, the pale underearth creature that gave Bilbo Baggins the willies.

Pilcher made eye contact with each of his team, raising his hand in the "okay" signal. In Superior's frigid water there was no chitchat. It hurt to take the regulator out; the cold drilled into teeth, could form ice in the mouthpiece. Each diver returned Pilcher's "okay" and he turned his thumb down.

Time to dive.

Anna was unpleasantly aware that in ancient Rome a thumbs-down was a death sentence.

Pilcher turned bottom up. His iridescent blue flippers breached, a sudden flame suddenly quenched. He was gone.

Anna followed.

Without the sun, the lake was not light even near the surface. Below was complete darkness. It was as if she swam through the twilight toward a night in which there were no stars, no moon, no planets. From behind her, the light Lucas carried poked a beam through the water. Sometimes it caught the yellow line Scotty had dropped. As they descended Anna noted the flash of the marker tape every ten feet. Several yards ahead, she could see the flap of blue that marked Ralph's progress.

Had she been diving alone—or with a less trusted leader—Anna's eyes would have been darting from marker to watch the depth gauge, timing her descent. She'd timed Ralph on their first dives. Easy dives: eighty feet down on the *America*, forty to retrieve buoys tethered below ice level, seventy collecting photos. Ralph swam at a steady sixty-nine feet per minute and never glanced at his watch.

A minute passed: seven marks on the line. The uniform darkness of the lake bottom was changing. A pale form was beginning to take shape, a lighter smudge in the murky depths.

The *Kamloops*.

It was so easy: the swim, finding the wreck, everything. Anna felt quite gay. All the elaborate preparations had been absurd. The dive was a breeze, a piece of cake, a milk run, a pushover. She laughed and air bubbled out, making a chuckling noise near her ears.

Anna was high. Every fifty feet down was like one martini. They were two, maybe three martinis under. She couldn't remember. She had forgotten to watch the time, count the marks. Two? Or three? How many to put a small woman under the table? Six feet under. The moment of hilarity hardened into rising panic.

Ralph was by the line, standing on the lake floor, looking at his watch like a man waiting for a bus. Anna swam down, stood beside him. He touched her shoulders, looked into her eyes, breathed exaggeratedly. Anna mirrored his breath. He raised a circled thumb and forefinger. She'd be okay. In, out: she breathed again.

Jim arrived, then the poking finger of light with Lucas attached. Pilcher checked them as he had Anna. It was subtle, quick. Anna only noticed because she had needed it.

The *Kamloops* rested on her port side, her stern on the top of a slope, her bow one hundred and ninety feet away at the bottom—two hundred and sixty feet below the lake's surface. Very few divers ventured there. Most of the information the NPS had on that end of the wreck—and it wasn't much—they'd gleaned via a remote-control robot camera.

The increasing depth and darkness swallowing the bow gave the wreck the illusion of incredible length. One of the *Kamloops*' twin smokestacks lay across midships. Lines tangled amid hundreds of feet of metal pipe that had spilled when the ship went down. Portholes and doors gaped black. Broken metal showed like bones. The *Kamloops* was a scabby old ghost, one whose soul seemed not to rest. Anna wasn't disappointed that she and Jim would not be prying too deeply into her secrets, would not be the ones to snatch her most recently acquired corpse.

Ralph tapped his watch and flashed twenty-two: open hands twice, then two fingers. They would meet back at the line in twenty-two minutes. Anna flicked on her light. Jim would handle the underwater camera. Without looking at her, he swam off. She followed.

The ship was tipped to the north, the exposed keel line sloping west and sharply downhill. The lake bottom rolled away in every direction. The effect was dizzying. Tattinger moved quickly. He kicked up past the tilted propeller and swam along the hull. The flattened keel of the freighter dropped away into the darkness.

In such a shadowed world, there was little Anna could see at the pace Jim set. As she carried the light, he would be seeing even less. Evidently, his idea of an investigation was limited to feeding data into a computer.

Deliberately, she slowed, moved her beam from his trajectory and played it along the side of the ship, then down to the barren lake floor. No plants, no fishes, even very few stones. The sand lay smooth and untracked like the desert after a windstorm. A red and blue Pepsi-Cola can winked a vivid eye when the light struck it. Anna made no move to swim the fifteen yards to retrieve the litter. "No deviations," Ralph had warned. "That's when accidents happen." Anna believed him and fear made her utterly obedient. Her light picked out a single shoe, colorless but in apparently good condition. It was an old-fashioned work boot, one that had fallen or been carried from the shipment on board. A coffee mug lay half buried in the sand. Bits of metal that had once served some purpose were strewn about. There was more pipe and a wooden crate broken in half with a bright paper sticker still intact.

A jarring clang brought her head up. Tattinger had rapped on the *Kamloops*' hull with the butt of a diving knife. He was hovering near a porthole crooking an admonitory finger. Though she couldn't see his face behind the rubber and plastic, she imagined his scowl.

Once again, she trained the light in his path and he swam on. The beam raked along the hull just ahead of him, across the portholes: blind eyes weeping rust. Between them, near where Tattinger had rapped the hull, something gleamed. Anna kicked once, floated nearer the hull. The rust around one of the portholes had been scraped away. Bright silver scratches as if someone had been hacking at the port with a sharp object. She felt around the edges of the porthole cover. There was just enough purchase to work a fingertip under it.

Jim, losing the light, had returned and hung at her elbow. Pushing Anna's hands aside, he opened the blade of the red-handled knife he still held, and levered it under the metal. The porthole swung in easily. Whoever had pried it open before had broken the latch.

Monstrous and fish-eyed behind their masks, Jim and Anna exchanged a look. The hole was little more than eighteen or twenty inches in diameter. Too small for anybody in tanks to get through. Anna peered inside: the captain's quarters. An out-of-reach heaven for thieves and vandals, but someone had made the effort.

Jim tapped his watch. Seven minutes. Anna tapped his camera, then the porthole. He hesitated, hating to use the film, she knew. Jim was as miserly with government property as he was with his own. He stockpiled everything from toilet paper to engine oil, kept lists of how many of each. Numbers with which to feed his insatiable database programs.

Anna tapped the porthole again and he handed her his diving knife. She held it and the light while he clicked two careful shots.

Four minutes. With efficient haste, they started to swim back. At depth, exertion was a thing to be avoided lest one treble the effects of nitrogen narcosis.

The stern, with its tangle of pipe, rolled by beneath. Anna swept the light in an arc through the water. The snaking yellow of the line did not reflect back and panic pricked again at the back of her throat. Then, at the far right, she saw the faint yellow gleam. Jim saw it in the same instant and they swam.

One minute. Now that the time to ascend was near, Anna felt a crushing impatience. The knowledge that another sixty-four minutes must be spent incarcerated in gear, enveloped in the cold embrace of the lake, seemed almost insupportable. The U.S. Navy Standards would have insisted only on fifty minutes' ascent time but Ralph had chosen to play it safe.

Anxious thoughts began circling in Anna's mind like vultures smelling a corpse. If Ralph and Lucas had kicked up a silt storm and gotten lost, she doubted she would have the courage to go and look for them. Cold ached in the bones of her head.

As she counted her curses she became aware of a non-stop trickle of air through her regulator. It had frozen open. It had happened once before early in the season when she and Ralph dove the docks clearing out rubbish. Once open, it wouldn't take long before the escaping air would fill her mouth with icy slush, numbing her lips with cold until she could no longer feel them to keep them on the mouthpiece.

"Come on, goddammit!" she demanded of Lucas.

Poking her light through the viscous twilight, she strained her eyes in the direction of the engine room. Twenty seconds bottom time left. The darker block that marked the doorway wavered, changed shape, then broke into two separate shadows. Ralph and Lucas swam toward the line. With them was Denny Castle. Eight days dead, he looked the most natural of the three. Jaunty in the uniform, relaxed, he drifted through the water between them, his eyes open and unblinking. The cap was still on his head, the shine still on the black leather boots.

Lucas took Denny. With watch and depth gauge, Ralph swam slowly to thirty feet below the surface. He stopped there, hung in the water. Ten fingers flashed. They waited.

The currents caused by their flippers made Denny's dead hands move as if he, too, grew restless with the waiting. Anna couldn't take her eyes off him. A childish fear that if she looked away he would reach out and touch her kept scuttling through her mind, trailing a nightmare quality.

Martini's Law must have been coined before the advent of Timothy Leary, she thought. For her the experience was proving reminiscent of an acid trip threatening to go sour rather than a good honest drunk.

She glanced at her watch. Another thirty seconds to wait. She looked back at Castle's body.

The dead eyes had not changed expression but the jaw

was dropping. Denny was opening his mouth as if to speak. A froth of reddish-colored bubbles spewed forth and rose toward the lake's surface.

Anna's mind spun. She reached out instinctively for the person next to her as she'd done in countless dark movie theaters when blobs, mummies, and killer lepuses made their moves. Then she remembered: Ralph had warned her. In deep-water body recoveries they removed the mask before the corpse reached the surface to let the water wash away fluids brought forth by the changing pressure.

The phenomenon lasted only a few seconds. Ralph kicked once and floated up the line. Glad to be moving, Anna followed, leaving Jim, Lucas, and the mute but expressive Denny Castle to follow as they might.

Twenty minutes at twenty feet. As the silver of the promised sky grew closer so did Anna's impatience to see it, to breathe deep of air filled with rain, gusts, and eddies, boat exhaust. To breathe again of the varying moods of life that cannot be canned.

The last wait, thirty-four minutes only ten feet below the surface, was provoking enough to amuse and Anna forgot the cold pooling inside her suit, stabbing at the fillings in her teeth, the vacant stare of Denny's corpse.

Finally they reached the surface. Even Scotty's cowboy countenance was a welcome sight. Jo Castle, wan and frightened, reaffirmed if only by way of pain that life went on. Thirty fathoms down, it had seemed a distant and fragile concept.

Jim Tattinger flippered over to the *Lorelei*'s water-level deck and was hauled over the stern like a landed fish by Jo and Officer Stanton. Anna was next, lifted clear of the water's grasp. Ralph pulled himself up as far as the low deck and planted his butt on the two-by-four slats. Gently he took Denny's body from Lucas and held it cradled in his arms while the Chief Ranger floundered on board.

Anna, sitting on deck, a flippered foot held clumsily between two gloved hands, was watching Jo as her wiry brown arms gathered her husband into a one-way embrace. The expression on Jo Castle's face was familiar. Once

Anna had seen it on Christina. She was watching her daughter sleep when Ally had been racked by a fever. A look that was equal parts tenderness and grief.

Either Jo was a complete psychotic, or she had not killed Denny. Remembering the strength in Jo's arms as she had pulled her from the lake, Anna fervently hoped it was the latter.

Awkwardly, Jo bent and kissed her husband. Faint bruises ringed Denny's mouth in blue. The captain's cap, absurd now in the drizzling light of day, fell from his hair. Brass buttons winked as the collar of the uniform fell open. There was no shirt beneath the double-breasted jacket and the flesh of Denny's shoulder was exposed. A livid bruise cut down between neck and shoulder. The discolored flesh was jarring on skin so white, and Anna turned away as if she would protect Denny's modesty.

CHAPTER 13

Anna was thinking about the bruise on Denny's shoulder. Usually on her lieu days she liked to loose her mind from the often paranoia-inducing mental fetters of rangering. Not rangering, she reminded herself: law enforcement. It saddened her that the line between the two grew thinner every year. But recent events were too intrusive to allow her peace of mind.

Postmortem lividity left bruiselike marks on corpses. Blood, no longer circulating, pooled at the lowest point on the body. In Denny, supported by water, pressurized on all sides, lividity might possibly have shown faintly in the lowest extremities but not in hash marks across his chest. The autopsy would tell how much force had been used, if the bruise had been caused by a blow, and if the instrument of trauma had been edged. But it probably wouldn't be able to tell what that instrument had been: baseball bat, crowbar, or just walking into a door.

What was troubling Anna was that the bruise configuration seemed unfamiliar. So, motoring across sparkling blue waters on her day off, she busied her mind flipping back through the endless slides of corpses paraded before her in law enforcement classes. Coroners, policemen, arson investigators, body recovery experts, all with color pictures, each picture telling a story of violent death. Anna dredged up the images, hoping to decode the story Denny's corpse was trying to tell.

At the northern end of Five Finger Bay, the sheer beauty of the day drove the blood and gore from her thoughts. The shores were snowy with thimbleberry blossoms, a lacy skirting between the blue of the water and the green of the trees. The sky had cried itself out the night before and smiled down clear and warm. Anna pushed the *Belle Isle*'s throttles wide and enjoyed the sense of speed.

And of being on the lake's surface, not its floor.

Rock Harbor was bustling. Compared to the great ports of the world, it was a mere hole in the island, but after a week on the north shore it felt like New York Harbor on the Fourth of July.

Heading for the slips reserved for NPS vessels on Mott, Anna maneuvered the *Belle Isle* down the narrow channel between a yacht and the wake of an impertinent eighteen-foot runabout. Only one slip was empty. Effectively preventing her from docking there was a tourist. He was sitting on the quay, white legs dangling over the side. "A tourist's tourist," Anna muttered, noting the soft fishing hat, madras shirt, Bermudas, white socks, and black leather shoes.

It was Frederick the Fed.

Government-issue punk; his superiors must be eternally off balance, unsure whether Stanton merely had bad taste or really was poking fun at them.

"Officer Stanton," she called out the open window. He scrambled ungracefully to his feet and proceeded to louse up her docking efforts with his good intentions. She barely managed to shove her fenders out before he dragged the Bertram into the pilings.

"Yo, Anna," he said as she stepped onto the dock. Anna

had never heard anyone actually use "yo" except in jest. Maybe she still hadn't. Stanton's face was deadpan.

"Morning," she replied neutrally as she tied off to a cleat.

The clatter of leather soles brought him up next to her. His features were overly large but finely shaped, giving him the appearance of a badly carved heroic figure. The goofy hat, the fifties shirt, the hard shoes—everything about him was a study in incongruity. It struck Anna that it might be intentional; it's hard to know a man who defies patterns.

"I've been hoping to get a word with you," he said.

"It's my day off."

"Good. Mine too. We'll have oodles of time."

Yo. Oodles. Anna smiled. "You answer mine, I'll answer yours," she said.

Frederick started to fold himself down again onto the dock but Anna shook her head. She'd had enough of water for a while. This weekend she planned to stay on terra firma.

Together they walked inland, following a well-trodden path lined with bluebead lilies and red eastern columbine. Above them, trees whispered across a narrow ribbon of sky.

Under a white pine, on ground kept bare by fallen needles, Anna sat down.

"Are there snakes?" Frederick asked suspiciously.

"Yup."

"Ish." He curled his muscular legs up close, knees under his chin as he squatted beside her. His slightly bumbling fastidious act put Anna in mind of the disarming foolishness of Lord Peter Wimsey.

"Do you read Dorothy L. Sayers?" she asked abruptly.

"Never heard of her." There might or might not have been a gleam in his eye. "That was your question," he said. "Now mine. Say somebody is trafficking in drugs between Canada and the U.S. Buying it here, selling it there. Your customs checks here are only a formality. Say maybe Isle Royale is the exchange place."

Anna waited. "What's the question?" she asked finally.

Stanton looked surprised, as if it had been obvious. "Who would it be?" he demanded.

Anna laughed. "You tell me."

"Say somebody with a boat. Say somebody who's here regularly. Somebody who's got a reason for repeated trips. Maybe a commercial fishing guide boat, a sightseeing concession, a dive concession." He opened his eyes wide and treated Anna to a friendly, guileless stare.

She looked away, let her gaze rest on the perfect mosaic of leaves and bark beyond the rusty circle of needles. Sun dappled through the foliage, catching and reflecting the living green. Even on dry land on Isle Royale there was a sense of being in a watery world.

"Why do you think it's drug-related? Why a concession boat? Have you corroborating reports?"

"That's three questions, Anna, and no answers. You're running up your tab."

Anna said nothing and after a moment he decided to tell her. "No evidence, just statistics. A border area, not heavily patrolled, an island full of coves, regular international boat traffic, a bizarre murder. I'm working profiles here. This is the profile of a drug-related murder."

All law enforcement people worked with profiles whether they consciously chose to or not—like gamblers working the odds. So did businessmen and shopkeepers and receptionists and streetwalkers. A poorly dressed man, eyes watering, nose running, standing alone in a darkened doorway clutching a heavy object in his pocket, might be a lost country parson with hay fever grasping his Bible for comfort. Profiles said he was not. Given his profile, the police in some places would have probable cause to pull him in for questioning.

Anna rose and dusted off her rump. "I'll let you know if I think of anybody who fits," she said.

Free of Stanton, she found she didn't know what to do with herself. The *Kamloops* dive was behind her.

Denny's body was in the *Ranger III*'s frozen foods locker plowing its way toward Houghton and an autopsy. Under the stress of the dive and the oppression of the weather, Anna had longed for her lieu days. Now that they'd arrived, with the implied time of rest and relaxation, she found her mind still rattling on in its workaday rut. With perfect hindsight she knew she should have stayed on the north shore, hidden out in a quiet cove, watched for wolves, and gathered pretty stones along the water's edge. Those were the things that would have put her right with the world. The bustling atmosphere of Rock bored and stimulated at the same time. Not rest but restlessness was to be the keynote of her weekend.

Anna glanced at her watch. Hours and hours till she could call her sister. At least an hour till the mail would be sorted. Aggravated by the need to be doing something, she sought out Sandra Fox in the dispatcher's office. Delphi looked up from her place beneath the computer printers and dusted a welcome on the linoleum with her gold tail feathers. Anna flopped down beside the dog and fondled the soft ears.

"Can't get enough of the Park Service, huh?" Sandra said, her fingernails clicking against the plastic keyboard. "Got to come in on your days off now for a little bureaucratic fix."

"Quick," Anna said. "Give me something to fill out in triplicate."

Sandra finished typing, the printer blatted out a line of braille, and the dispatcher ran a well-manicured fingertip over it. Into the radio mike she read the line of numbers. "One, forty-two, sixty-four . . ." Fire weather. Anna blew gently on the top of Delphi's head and was chastised with a reproachful stare.

The list complete, Sandra turned with a satisfied sigh and interlocked her fingers over her middle. The signal that chat could commence. "Tinker and Damien were asking after you," she said. "For some reason they thought I might know where you'd be this weekend." She chuckled comfortably.

All plans on ISRO made by phone or radio had a way of finding Sandra's ear. She never broke these unintentionally shared confidences but, like Sherlock Holmes, she took pleasure in amazing people with her arcane knowledge of their lives.

"Ah," Anna said. "And where am I this weekend? More to the point, where should I be?"

"Grumpy, are we?"

"I guess."

"Body recovery got you thinking mortal thoughts?"

"It's got me thinking, at any rate." Anna was nagged by the floating vision of false life the currents had lent the corpse, of the livid bruise. Until the investigation was complete, however, these were not things that could be discussed.

"I take it you don't buy the drug-death scenario Officer Frederick Stanton is so fond of," Sandra remarked.

Anna started and Sandra smiled a Sherlockian smile.

"Do you?" Anna asked.

"Nope. Why come to a national park crawling with rangers and red-necked fisherfolk when there's a million secluded bays and a zillion acres of unpatrolled lake waters to rendezvous in?"

"Stanton seems competent enough," Anna said.

"Stanton's a city boy," Sandra returned. The implication was clear: His mind would make urban profiles of an Isle Royale death. The parks were places apart. Islands of hope, fragments of wilderness in an increasingly developed world, scraps of land trying to be all things to all people: museums, adventures, solitude, recreation, vacation, research, preservation. Different rules, different lusts, different pressures prevailed. People died for different reasons.

"Are you going to see Tinker and Damien?"

Anna had already forgotten about them. She glanced at her pocket watch. Another half hour till the mail. She craved some contact with Chris or Molly, conversation on a meaningful level. Conversation in which she didn't have to protect herself or take care of anyone else. She flashed briefly on Ralph Pilcher's words: "The superwoman act works well for you." It wasn't an act, it was armor. Like all good armor, it was heavy to carry.

"Tinker and Damien. . . . Did it seem urgent?"

Sandra laughed. "With those two it's hard to tell. A few days back they were hiking in Moskey Basin. They radioed in a collision with serious injuries. Scotty rushed a couple of the emergency medical technicians out there. Everybody getting overtime. Everybody rushing around with their hair in a knot having a high old time. They get out to find, in a freak accident, a boater had rammed the dock there at the south end. He wasn't hurt but he'd dislodged a beam under the water level and trapped a young lake otter. Tinker and Damien caught hell but the little otter's going to remember them fondly."

Anna smiled. She was remembering that she liked the Coggins-Clarkes.

D amien was on the paved trail between the lodge and the Visitors' Center at Rock Harbor. Hands folded behind his back, eyes on the ground, he was pacing. Soundlessly, his lips formed words. Clad in the khaki Student Conservation Association's shirt and green uniform trousers, he looked uncharacteristically benign. And young. In Anna's soured mood, he looked about ten years old.

"Damien!" A look of what could have been alarm flitted across his face. His answering wave, a short flick of wrist and fingers, was anything but welcoming.

She walked up to a nearby bench. He continued to pace. She leaned on the back and waited for his next pass. "I've got a nature walk," Damien said ungraciously as he checked his watch. "In seven minutes."

This brusque, nervous fellow was so unlike the cloaked and candlelit boy that Anna was taken aback. It reminded her that she really knew very little about the Coggins-Clarkes.

"Sandra said you wanted to see me," she said easily.

"This is a bad time. I'll catch Tinker." She began moving away.

"Don't bother," he said sharply.

Anna turned, raised an eyebrow.

Under her gaze, the rudeness vanished. "I'm sorry," he said with his old boyish grace. "I got up on the wrong side of the universe this morning. We just wanted to tell you we've stopped with the Donna Butkus thing."

"Ah." Ten minutes before, had she been asked, Anna would have said nothing could have pleased her more. Tinker and Damien's collecting pickle relish jars and general cloak and daggering struck her as just the brand of nonsense that would get them in hot water. Now that they had stopped, she found it more alarming than reassuring. "Why?"

Damien looked past her. A small group was straggling up the pavement. "People for my tour," he said. As he walked away, his tourists all in a row behind like ducklings, Anna wondered why he'd dodged the question, why he didn't just tell a convenient lie. If it had been banal enough, she probably would have believed it and that would have been the end. Evasion was to a law enforcement ranger what undeclared funds were to the IRS.

On some level had he wanted to set her mental alarms off? One of those unspoken cries for help her sister Molly was paid a hundred and fifty dollars an hour to listen for? Or was Damien incapable by choice or disposition of telling a lie?

"Dream on," Anna said aloud. In forty years, she had never met a man, woman, or child who was incapable of lying.

Whether his wish she not speak with Tinker was honest or not, it was in vain. He'd piqued her interest—and on a day when she'd been wanting a little piquing. With renewed energy, she walked down the paved trail and onto the wooded path that led to the seasonals' quarters.

Tinker was sitting on the porch steps of the weathered old house that served as a dormitory. With her head bent over a book she held across her knees, her face was lost in a cloud of blond permed frizz. Hidden somewhere in the draping curtains of fir that glamorized the dilapidated building, a squirrel chattered a warning at Anna's approach and Tinker looked up.

"Sandra said you wanted to see me," Anna said.

"Yes. I wanted to ask if you'd seen peregrines nesting in McCargo."

Isle Royale was one of the many places peregrine falcons were being reintroduced. Resource Management had had some success on the southwest end of the island but the north shore had proved inhospitable. Anna shook her head.

"We've had a sighting."

Anna sat down on the bottom step. A great green caterpillar with electric-blue markings hunched along in the roots of the ferns. Damien said they'd wanted to see her about stopping the Butkus investigation. Tinker said peregrines. Had Anna been inclined to believe either, she would've chosen the falcons. Murder would take a back seat with any serious birder when word came of a rare sighting.

"I haven't seen any peregrines in McCargo," Anna replied. "But I haven't been there all that often in the last couple of weeks."

"Mmmm." Tinker seemed to be considering Anna's viability as a witness. Anna's suspicion that she'd failed to pass muster was confirmed when Tinker said: "Damien and I will go." She closed the heavy book—*Bent's Life Histories of North American Birds,* Volume 10: Birds of Prey, Part 1—and smiled benignly at the woods.

Anna teased the giant caterpillar, trying to make it climb up onto a twig. Several minutes passed. She tossed her caterpillar stick into the hedge of browsed firs. "Damien says you've given up detective work," she said.

Tinker looked pained. In a Garbo-esque gesture, she pushed the fine ruined hair back from her face with both hands.

A scuffle and a grunt from inside the house took Anna's attention. "Pizza Dave," Tinker said, her hands still buried in her hair. "The toilet's stopped up again." As if on cue, heroic slurps of a plunger being plied emanated from the shadowy interior.

Anna turned back to Tinker. "Are you okay?" she asked, more sharply than she had intended.

"I'm fine," Tinker replied and, to Anna's surprise, she began to cry, hugging her knees, her girlish breasts pushed up against the uncompromising corners of her bird book.

Great gulping sobs made a bellows of the thin back. Images of Heinz pickle relish jars jammed with fingers, ears, and eyeballs flashed through Anna's mind. "What is it? What?" she demanded.

"Just leave me alone!" Tinker cried out. Springing to her feet, sending *Bent*'s sprawling onto the moss, she rushed inside the house.

Anna debated the wisdom of following. For whatever reason, for the moment at least, her presence was more alarming than comforting. She restored the book to the porch where the damp wouldn't ruin it and retreated down the path the way she had come.

Halfway back to the harbor she was overtaken by the roar of machinery. Tractors used by Maintenance were the only land vehicles allowed on the island and even they were banned from Amygdaloid.

The driver was Pizza Dave, returning from his plumbing job. He was the fattest man Anna had ever seen. The tractor seat was lost beneath his vast rump, and the machine, a small four-cylinder John Deere, looked no bigger than a lawn mower. R&R, the company that made all the National Park Service uniforms, didn't come close to carrying his size. Consequently, on duty and off, he lived in bright slogan-sporting tee-shirts, denim trousers, and black high-topped sneakers.

As he drew level with Anna, he engulfed the gearshirt knob in a palm the size of a Frisbee and brought the tractor to a halt. "Afternoon," he called over the roar of the engine.

"Afternoon," Anna agreed, wishing he'd shut the tractor off. Wishing, not hoping: Dave loved the noise. He was part machine. He never walked. He bragged that there wasn't anything he couldn't do given the right equipment.

He was saying something.

Anna shouted: "What?" and he shouted back: ". . . in the head." She looked blank, shrugged. "The head, the john, the terlit, the loo," he shouted. "I couldn't help hearing. Here. Found this." He dug something out of his hip pocket and held it out in a closed fist. Both her hands were about the size of one of his. Anna cupped her hands, not daring to think what gem he'd found in the "terlit" that was about to be dropped into her grasp.

Dave's fingers uncurled and several crumpled slips of paper fluttered out. "Found it tore up," he hollered over his engine.

"What is it?"

"Can't hear you. Found it," he called. Anna suspected he was using the engine's noise to drown out all the questions he didn't want to answer. "Donna Butkus is okay," he said suddenly.

"How do you know?" Anna yelled.

"Gut feeling." He laughed, passed his hand over an immense expanse of red double-knit. "Can't ignore a gut this big." He pushed the gear lever forward and roared on down the trail before Anna had time to respond.

She waited till the aggravation of sound had passed completely away, then crouched down on the trail and pieced together the bits of paper. It was a dot matrix printout. Any computer could have been used. In an odd mixture of metaphors it said: "Before you go looking for skeletons under other people's rocks don't forget your own dirty laundry can be dragged out of the closet." Then the word "Hopkins" and the numbers "1978."

"Jesus H. Christ," Anna muttered. "Nobody writes notes this mysterious." Then she laughed, thinking of the messages Christina left stuck to the refrigerator with duck-shaped magnets: "Ally tippy-toe. Me in the salt mines. Save yourself." Meaning: Alison was at ballet class and Chris was working late. Literal translation: Don't wait dinner. Everything was mysterious when it was unexplained.

Doubly so if a corpse or two was factored in.

Anna read the note again. A threat—you expose mine, I'll expose yours. Hopkins—the name of a person or a town; 1978. At a guess, Tinker or Damien had done something to a person or in a place called Hopkins in 1978 they were ashamed enough of or scared enough about that they would drop their investigation into Donna Butkus's disappearance to keep it from coming to light. That was thirteen years back. In 1978 Damien would have been eleven or twelve, Tinker maybe twenty. Tinker, then, was probably the threatened party. It would fit with both Damien's reaction and her own.

Anna folded the bits of paper carefully and buttoned them in her shirt pocket. Who would threaten Tinker? Scotty was the obvious choice. But not the only one. If Donna's disappearance and Denny's death were connected—and Scotty didn't do it—whoever did was definitely in the running.

CHAPTER 14

The rest of the afternoon Anna spent taking her medicine. Abandoning the populous marina, she strapped a water bottle to her belt and hiked the trails to Ojibway Tower, six and a half miles from Rock Harbor. Several times her path crossed that of backpackers but she spoke to no one. She was out of uniform, off duty with no obligation to be helpful or even polite. When she heard voices ahead of her on the trail she stepped softly into the trees and, wreathed in silence, watched unseen until they had passed.

On a stony ridge, rising above the green canopy of summer leaves, Anna climbed the old fire tower and stretched her legs in the sun. From Ojibway she could see white sails out on Superior, watch the flashing backs of birds cutting through the air. The sun-baked perfume from the pines. She breathed it in like a narcotic and felt her brain losing its ferret ways, ceasing to chase around inside her skull. A breeze, cool, separate from the ambient air, soothed the aches left by invisible burdens.

Near six o'clock, refreshed, her mind clear, she started back.

She was third in line to use the phone at Rock. Sitting on the bench with a redheaded girl of twenty or so and a wide-shouldered natural blonde with jaw-length hair, Anna stared at the occupied phone booth and listened to the desultory conversation of the other women. Most of it centered on the doings of T.O.A.D.s—tourists on a detour—the interpretive rangers' usually affectionate term for island visitors. One had taken his fiancée down the Minong Trail. They ran out of water, her feet were covered with blisters, her left eye was swollen shut from blackfly bites, the wedding was off. Two boys had wrecked a concession rental on Blake's Point. The boat looked like a crumpled ball of aluminum foil but, miraculously, the boys were unhurt. There'd been complaints that the *Spirogyra*, the party boat out of Two Harbors, had people dancing naked on the flying bridge.

The phone booth door opened. "All yours," came a voice.

"You want to go next, Trixy?" the red-haired girl asked.

"You go ahead," replied the blonde.

Trixy, the interpreter, Donna Butkus's friend: Had Anna been a terrier, her ears would have pricked up. She waited till the redhead was dialing. "Trixy, isn't it? I'm Anna Pigeon." They shook hands in a manly fashion, Anna, as always, feeling slightly ridiculous.

"You're the North Shore Ranger," Trixy identified her. She had a slightly fruity voice that could easily slip into a singsong pattern.

Anna admitted that she was and cast about for a comfortable way to bring the subject around to Donna Butkus's disappearance. "I'm Scotty's counterpart on the north shore," she said finally. "You must know Scotty. This is your fifth season at Rock, isn't it?"

"Sixth," Trixy said, then added grimly: "I know Scotty."

Anna took the grimness as a good sign. It invited Pandora to open the gossip box. "You sound a little sour on the subject of Mr. Butkus." Anna turned the key and the box popped open.

"Scotty Butkus is an asshole," Trixy said. "I hope he's not a friend of yours. . . ."

Anna laughed. "I give him a pretty wide berth. Good old boys make me nervous. I've met his wife a couple of times though. She seemed pretty straightforward. Haven't seen her around for a while."

"Her sister Roberta hurt her back. Donna had to go look after her," Trixy volunteered.

"Scotty tell you that?" Anna kept her voice neutral but still Trixy reacted with some alarm.

"Yes. He did. Said Donna had to leave in a rush. Why? Have you heard something to the contrary?"

"There's nothing wrong with Roberta's back," Anna said carefully. "She's a good friend of my housemate in Houghton."

"What an asshole!" Trixy snapped.

"I assume you mean Scotty. What did he do—besides lie to you?"

"Oh, he and Donna had a big fight. He knocked her around some. Not that that was all that unusual. But Donna came over crying. She had a big shiner and a split lip. That was unusual. Usually he'd hit her where she'd be embarrassed to show anybody the bruises. Scotty was drunk. Mega-asshole."

"Did she say she was going anywhere?"

"No. She was going back to Scotty. She can put up with a lot. I don't know whether that's a compliment or not. Scotty is killing her. He does that pedestal thing: In public he brags about her in front of her like she's this thing he won. Then when they're alone he picks and undercuts till she doesn't know if she's a princess or a prick-tease. I guess he didn't start smacking her till fairly recently. A couple months. Donna covers for him. She's everything a good South Texas wife is supposed to be: supportive, warm, covers up his flaws, takes his abuse, and still looks pretty."

"Like a handwoven Navajo rug," Anna said.

"You got it."

The phone booth door opened. The redhead stepped out. As Trixy rose to make her call, Anna asked one last question. "Did you see Donna after that night? The night they had the fight?"

"Nope. I had to go do an evening program. She was pretty upset. I gave her some ice for her eye. Dave said he'd walk her home. That was it."

Trixy's call was short. The redhead waited with Anna on the bench; then the two interpreters left together. Anna shut herself up in the booth and dialed New York. After innumerable clicks and whirs—the sound of her paycheck going down the drain—a machine answered. "Nobody's here. Leave a message," was the command. Anna waited for the beep.

"It's me," she said. "Are you lying doggo?"

A click and a fumble. " 'Lying doggo'?" Molly said. "Is that a law enforcement term: 'The perpetrators were found in Macy's lingerie department *lying doggo'*?"

"I'm backsliding. They don't have a support group in Houghton for women suffering from colloquialisms." The familiar hush, the sigh of air. Anna hated it. "Can't you talk on the phone without a cigarette?"

"Can't. Hipbone connected to the thighbone—it's like that with cigarettes and phones. Oral fixation, premature potty training, early childhood trauma, can't help myself. How did the corpse dive go?"

Anna told her, glad to be able to drag out all her fears and panics, expose them to Molly's harsh, reasoning mind. She told her sister of the corpse's half life, the bubbles and the floating hands, the porthole vandalism, about Donna, about Scotty.

"What an asshole!" was Dr. Pigeon's concurring diagnosis.

"Do you think he could've killed her?" Anna asked.

"Sure. Emergency rooms are full of battered wives.

Some die. I see the rich ones who live. They come to me to find out what's wrong with them, why they keep making a good man act so bad. That's not saying this Butkus individual did kill his wife. He may just be a batterer and an asshole."

"Donna's not the type to press charges and there's no law against assholery," Anna said.

"If it weren't so profitable for psychiatrists, I'd lobby for one."

"How about eating the body?" Anna asked.

"The old Hannibal Lecter thing? Cannibalism? Pretty unlikely. It's a very rare form of psychosis. Very rare. And even the loonies don't eat the bones and hair and eyeballs and fingernails. They have their favorite cuts. Usually something visceral—heart, liver. Like Dracula's Renfield, they're often trying in some way to gather life or power from the victim and into themselves."

"What if he wasn't psychotic? What if he just ate her to dispose of the corpse?"

"Anna, you've been out in the woods too long. If he ate her, for whatever reason, doesn't that seem a teensy-weensy bit psycho to you?"

"I guess," Anna conceded.

"I guess," Molly confirmed.

Anna listened to a second cigarette being lit. Molly was going to die first, leave Anna to flounder through life without a guide. Half a dozen cancer-related remarks danced on the tip of her tongue but she didn't give them voice. It would only elicit remarks in kind about cirrhosis of the liver. Who was going to die first was an old argument, one neither of them wanted to win.

"I don't suppose you'd come visit me?" Anna asked. "I'd get you a room with an ashtray and a flush toilet."

"From the sound of things, I could hang out my shingle there and do a pretty good business."

"Not at a hundred and fifty dollars an hour. You make more between coffee breaks than the average ranger takes home in a week."

"Jesus! No wonder you eat your spouses. Not psychosis: lunch. With just enough salary left over to buy a decent table wine. Speaking of which, remember my ten o'clock? The gourmet with vintage envy?"

"I remember."

"He's taken a turn for the worse," Molly laughed. "Another reason I can't come to Wherever right now. He's developed a fashion disorder. He's taken to wearing canary-yellow suspenders with his Armani suits. Buttons them right over a belt of some no doubt endangered reptile."

"Here in Wherever we'd call him careful, not crazy."

"You're forgetting motive, Anna. You of all people. He's smug about it. He's doing it in the belief it will infuriate his rival. He's so pleased with this deviltry he won't tell me how this particular brand of revenge is supposed to wreak its havoc. Maybe he'll start a new trend."

Anna laughed. "Remind me to tell you about Frederick Stanton, next time," she said, thinking of his Joe-Friday-goes-Hawaiian outfit. "I gotta go. The line is forming to the left." Two shadows had come to darken the waiting bench outside the phone booth.

"Ciao," Molly said. "Or is it 'Happy trails'?" Stay off the menu."

Before the line wend dead, Anna just had time to squeeze in, "Okay, bye."

L est her sister should precede her through the pearly gates by too great a margin, Anna decided to work on her cirrhosis. Instead of a glass, she bought a bottle. Ordinarily Patience sold only house wine and only by the glass. For Anna she'd found a bottle of Graves Villages, 1984. At eighteen dollars Anna guessed she was getting it at cost.

The sharp flinty taste was a perfect accompaniment to the night. Out on the patio behind the lodge, the air was full of moisture and lay on her skin like damp velvet.

She relaxed into the Adirondack-style lounge chair, enjoying the gentle bite of the wooden slats across her back and thighs. Taking a sip of the Graves, she held it in her

mouth, letting her tongue savor the taste, her body antici-
pate the alcohol. Onto the mysteries of the night, Anna pro-
jected the petty mysteries of the days, listing them for
herself in no particular order.

Number one: Denny Castle, dead, one hundred and
ninety-five feet below the lake's surface, dressed in a costume that was supposed to be in a trunk in his mother's
attic.

Frederick Stanton believed the death was drug-related.
Profiles indicated traffic between the U.S. and Canada.
Profiles indicated the *3rd Sister* as a red-hot possibility.
And she was the only concession working the island that
week with known dive capabilities. If Stanton could get a
case up, the *3rd Sister* would be impounded. The Bradshaws would be out of a living and, more to the point, out
of a life. Diving was all they had, all they cared about.

Number two: Mrs. Scotty Butkus had vanished, beaten
certainly, and, if Tinker and Damien were right, consumed
as if by a Windigo, the cannibalistic demon said to haunt
the north woods.

Number three: Tinker and Damien now had a mystery
all their own. Who was threatening them? What happened
in 1978 to, in, or because of "Hopkins"?

Four: Why had Jim Tattinger been running without
lights near the *Kamloops* wreck forty-eight hours before
the body was scheduled to be brought up?

And five—or was she already to six? What was Denny
to Holly, and why was it so laughable to Hawk that there
could be a romance there?

Why was Molly's client wearing suspenders and a belt?
More to the point, how was Hawk Bradshaw in bed?

Anna laughed. The wine was kicking in. In the close
darkness, she smiled over her list. Some of the mysteries
were going to be a whole lot more fun to solve than others.

A clatter of footsteps broke into her thoughts. Invisible
in the shadowless dark, she lay still. The clatter ended in a
flop. A pale shape dumped itself on the wooden step a couple of yards from Anna. The shape was fidgety. Anna could
hear the scuffling, plucking sounds as of restless fingers

and feet fiddling about. The breathing was slightly adenoidal.

"Evening, Carrie Ann." There was a satisfying squawk
from the girl. "Sorry if I startled you," Anna lied mildly.
"Out to enjoy the evening?"

"Not hardly." Carrie, at thirteen, had already mastered
the art of adolescent sullenness. Two words, and the night,
the stars, the glittering lake, were dismissed as entertain-
ments for the aged.

"Ah." Anna wished the child would sulk and flop back
to where she'd come from.

Carrie squirmed a shush of denimed buttocks over the
wood. "Mom send you out here to keep an eye on me?"

"I was here first," Anna replied, repressing the urge to
add: "You silly little shit."

Mystery number seven—or was it eight? Who was Carrie Ann's boyfriend, and, outside a small circle of friends,
who the fuck cared? The wine was very much in control.
Anna noticed her vocabulary deteriorating. Till she'd
moved in with Christina, she'd never given it a thought except at her mother-in-law's dinner table. Christina'd never
said anything, but the first time Alison had announced that
Jimmy Fulton was a fuckhead, one perfectly shaped brown
eyebrow had been raised in Anna's direction. Since then
she had weeded the four-letter words from her conversations.

Anna knocked back the last swallow of the Graves as if
it were a shot of vodka and refilled her glass. "Why would
Patience want me to keep an eye on you? Are you harass-
ing the wildlife, camping out of bounds, running a white
slave trade, what?"

"Nothing," Carrie grumbled. "Mom thinks I'm a baby."

Anna forbore comment.

With the teenager's paranoid ear, Carrie heard the implied agreement. "I'm not. I'm thirteen. Juliet Whatser-
name was married when she was thirteen."

"And dead at thirteen and a half. Careful of your allu-
sions."

"Mom grew up in the sixties. She probably slept with

every guy in Santa Cruz. Now it's like sex has been recalled or something. Like a Pinto. Rear-ended once and it
blows up."

Anna laughed. Carrie didn't join her. The sentence
hadn't been meant as a joke. "There's AIDS," Anna offered.

"Oh. Yeah. Like everybody's got AIDS," Carrie sneered.
"Can I have some of that wine?"

"Nope."

"You drink too much."

Anna was glad she had never had children.

Carrie began scooting over to where Anna sat. Anna
hoped she would get splinters in her butt, but the gods
were not with her and Carrie arrived unharmed. She
snatched up the Graves from where Anna had it sitting on
the deck and held it close to her face. "Graves. Mom's giving you the good stuff," she said.

Anna guessed she'd already picked up more about
wines than most adults would ever know. "I'm impressed,"
she admitted.

"Mom likes to pretend she's cosmopolitan." Carrie
shrugged off the compliment she'd worked so hard for.
"I've been drinking wine since I was five."

"Watered?" Anna needled.

"I guess," Carrie replied indifferently. "You ought to
ask her for some of her secret stash. But you can't guzzle
it."

Anna was growing tired of the company. Not wanting
to relinquish her corner of the night, she chose silence hoping Carrie would grow bored and go away.

"Carrie!" came a call.

"Oh God," the girl moaned. "Mom." She lumbered off.
Whether to or from the voice, Anna didn't care. Just as
long as it was away from her.

"Carrie!"

Evidently Carrie Ann had run from, not to. Short stac-
cato steps announced the arrival of high-heeled pumps on
the wooden deck. A faint scent of perfume invaded the
clean night air as Patience came round the bulge of thim-

bleberry branches. A flashlight raked across Anna's face and she winced.

"Sorry," Patience said curtly. "Have you seen Carrie? I'm going to strangle her."

"In that case, yes I have. She went thataway." Anna waved into the darkness back the way Patience had come.

"She must've slipped off the edge of the deck and run around through the bushes. Little beast." Patience sighed, clicked off the flashlight, and sat down on the step. "I'm damned if I'm going to go running after her. She'll come home eventually."

"You can strangle her then," Anna suggested.

"Don't think I won't."

"I encourage it," Anna said, inadvertently awakening the protective maternal instincts.

"Carrie Ann is not like she is," Patience defended her offspring. "She was always a biddable child. Who thought she'd go through the terrible twos eleven years later than most children? It's this damn boyfriend. If I knew who he was I'd have him off this island in a second. I don't know why Carrie is being such a little ass about it. Why she doesn't just let me meet the boy. I'm such a monster? She's old enough to have a date. It's this sneaking that's got me so crazy. What's the big deal about this boy? We haven't any coloreds working up here this summer."

"Coloreds." Anna hadn't heard that term in a long time. If Patience wanted to nurture a cosmopolitan image she would have to update her bigotries.

"What else could generate all this creeping around and lying?" Patience asked.

Anna could think of a dozen answers. Not feeling particularly soothing at the moment, she began to list them: "Married men, convicted felon, illegal alien, older man, older woman, drug dealer, alcoholic—"

"Enough!" Patience cried. "I feel better already just talking with you." She laughed. "Any Graves left?"

"A glass or two." Anna handed the bottle to Patience.

"I never do this." A white flutter blurred the darkness.

She took a swig from the bottle, then neatly wiped the mouth clean with her hankie.

"Keep it," Anna offered. "I owe you a drink for procuring good wines. A touch of class. Helps maintain our civilized veneer in the wilderness."

"Damn Carrie," Patience returned to her former theme. "You'd think she'd . . ." She seemed to be mentally listing things any sensible person would do under like circumstances and rejecting the possibility that her daughter would do likewise. "Damn, damn, damn, double damn, hell!" she fumed, and Anna laughed.

"Why don't we go look for her?" Anna suggested. "We won't find her unless she wants to be found, but it'll give you something to do. Nothing personal, but you're not your usual scintillating self."

"I suppose you're right." Again Patience sighed. She pushed herself to her feet and flicked on the flashlight. The beam caught the swirl of her skirt. Flame-orange silk; it moved like a vapor in the still air. Dainty flame-colored suede shoes burned against the dark wood of the deck.

"Half of the fun of coming to Rock is seeing what you're wearing," Anna said as she levered herself unsteadily out of the lounge chair. "I have a feeling by the end of the season I'm going to be heartily sick of Patagonia and L. L. Bean; of anything functional, durable, or fuzzy."

"No more feety pajamas?"

"Never give up your feety pajamas," Anna said. Upright, she realized she was slightly inebriated. Maybe even more than slightly. The feeling was of lightheaded well-being. And on a good vintage there wasn't even the shadow of an impending hangover to sully it.

Below the lodge, along the bay, two harsh intruder lights threw their glare out onto the water. Quays poked concrete fingers into the mooring area. Boats, many still showing lights, lined them bow to stern. The effect was of magic lanterns, or, Anna thought, luminarias on the snow.

She turned and walked out on the second of the piers.

"Where are you going?" Patience sounded alarmed.

"Thought we'd check your boat. See if Carrie is holed up there. Or took it. You never know."

"No, that's not it."

"Does Carrie only like boats with cute boys on them? I can sympathize with that." Anna arrived at the *Venture*. The green striping showed black under the lamps. No light inside, no sign of life. If Carrie and the unauthorized beau were in the cabin, they were lying low.

Or dead. Anna shuddered at the unwelcome thought. Off duty she allowed herself the luxury of cowardice. "You want to look?" she asked Patience, who was still hanging back as if checking her boat was ridiculous.

"I guess if anybody has to play Miss Coitus Interruptus it may as well be the outraged mom." Patience sounded too sour to permit Anna to laugh.

Patience rapped out a sharp shave-and-a-haircut on the fiberglass. No reply. She stepped off the dock into the boat. Anna followed. Both cupped their hands around their eyes and peered in the small windows. What little space there was inside was filled with gear: tanks, a dry suit, flippers. No naked little girls, no half-clad sheepish boys.

"Told you," Patience said.

Anna said nothing. Patience had ceased being any fun. The warm glow of the expensive wine was being wasted. "I didn't know you were a diver," Anna said in hopes of turning the conversation into more pleasant byways.

"I'm not."

Anna retreated into silence. As it soaked in around them, Patience seemed to put together Anna's remark with the cabin full of gear. "Not like you, I mean. Not really. I'm a dilettante at diving as at life. Just playing at it." Her humor was back, the bantering tone, the sharp commentary, but Anna was no longer in the mood for it. It fell on her ears like lines from a play.

"Think I'll turn in," she told Patience. "Suddenly the bottom fell out. The week is catching up to me, I guess."

"Are you in the *Belle Isle*?"

Anna nodded.

"You're welcome to our couch."

Anna declined. This night, a little damp seemed a small price to pay for quiet.

The *Belle* was moored beyond the harbor lights in a horseshoe of concrete. Anna sat down on a wooden bench on the quay to enjoy a silence made deeper by the mousy squeaks of boats rubbing against their fenders.

"Anna."

Her name was called so softly she could believe it had been whispered by the lake. Little hairs on her neck began to prickle.

"Anna."

She hadn't imagined it. A shadow coalesced in the back of the *Belle Isle* and sprang noiselessly onto the concrete.

"It's me, Hawk," the incubus said before Anna had recovered enough breath to shout. "I guess there's no way to spring yourself on somebody at midnight without scaring them half to death. Sorry."

He sat beside her on the bench, very near. The warm glow began to creep back.

"I couldn't sleep," he said. "Too many squirrels on the boat."

"I couldn't sleep either," Anna said, knowing it was true, though she'd not yet attempted it.

"Shall we try it together?"

"Strength in numbers?"

"Comrades in arms," Hawk said.

CHAPTER 15

Hawk and Anna sat a while longer on the bench enjoying the warmth where their bodies touched. Anna counted back on mental fingers. Many months and sixteen hundred miles had gone by since she'd last lain with a man. Remembering put the heat of the Mexican desert and a lover's touch into her bones.

Hawk put his arm around her shoulders. His touch was light but firm. Anna relaxed against him, enjoying simple contact. At forty was there such a thing as casual sex? Somehow, she doubted it; too many memories.

An absurd desire to say the words "I love you" came over her. Not because she meant them, merely because she remembered how good it had felt when she had.

Suddenly she was sorry she'd imbibed so heavily. Her mind was wandering from lust. Anna schooled it. The body had its own life. Hungers of the spirit could be dealt with in the morning.

"I'm sleeping on the *Belle* tonight," she said. "Can I offer you a nightcap?"

"Only if the night comes with it."

"It does."

They walked together, not touching, to the boat. Anna latched the cabin door behind them. Beyond the pilot's area and down a step, a small door led into the bow. Anna secured it open with a metal hook made for the purpose, then lit two candles. The *Belle Isle*'s cabin lights would run off battery power but this was not an occasion for stark electric reality.

Hawk sat on the blue-vinyl-covered bench and watched without speaking as Anna cranked open the hatch, letting in the soft night air, the light of the stars. He watched while she put two cassettes in her well-used player and punched play on one side and pause/play on the other. As Cher's voice sang, "It's in his kiss," he smiled.

"Be gentle with me," he said and Anna laughed.

"Your first time?"

"Might as well be."

"Orphans in the storm." She sat beside him and he took her face in his hands, smoothed her hair back with callused fingers.

If anything was new to Anna it was the sadness. As they made love, sweetly, gently, she felt Hawk's tears falling on her neck and breast. She found herself crying too, without knowing why. In sympathy, she realized, but whether for Hawk or herself she couldn't tell.

The "Mermaids" tape ended. "Wolf Eyes" filled the *Belle* with music of the north. Anna felt herself drifting to sleep until a thought jarred her. "Damn," she whispered.

"Vasectomy," Hawk said as if he'd read her mind. He pulled her closer, kissed her hair. "Sleep, Anna."

She slept without dreaming till sometime after moonrise. The silvery beam, powerful as a spotlight at the forty-eighth parallel, pouring down through the hatch woke her. Finally the harbor was utterly still. Hawk had rolled away from her on the triangular-shaped sleeping platform and lay curled up as neat and independent as a cat. Anna slipped from under the sleeping bag that covered them both.

She needed to escape the narrow confines of the hull, to get out where she could breathe. I have grown addicted to solitude, she thought as she dragged on Levi's and a sweat-shirt, too many nights alone. Something fell from the pouch pocket of the shirt and rattled to the floor. She scooped it up along with her socks. Not looking at Hawk lest the pressure of her gaze awaken him, she crept to the stern.

The scrubbed deck caught the moonlight, held it like milk in a glass. Anna's shadow was black, its edges clearly delineated. She looked across the water to the piers lined with fishing boats. Every crack in the concrete was ink-black, every bolt visible. The boats, though colorless, kept no secrets from the night. The moon picked out their names: *Marie III, Gladdest Night, Fisherman's Home, I.O.U., The Office.* The only one with lights still burning was the *Spirogyra.*

Anna sat down on the engine cover to pull on her socks. What had fallen from her pocket was still balled inside them. It was Tattinger's diving knife, the one he'd handed her when he'd taken the photographs of the porthole in the *Kamloops'* captain's cabin. Anna had brought it to Rock to return it.

As she turned it over she felt letters scratched into the plastic handle. Dive knives were all pretty similar. It wasn't unusual for divers to mark their equipment. Anna ran her thumb over the initials. The letters were not J.T., not R.M. for Resource Management. Not S.C.R. for Sub-merged Cultural Resources. Tilting the knife in the moon-light, she read the marking: "d'A." Some computer code, she thought, and, Tattinger is such a dink.

She didn't realize she'd whispered the last half of the thought until Hawk said: "Casting spells by the light of the moon?"

He stood in the doorway, his dark hair falling over his forehead. The silvery light blessed him as the setting sun had done on Amygdaloid. Instead of bronze, his body shone like living granite.

"You're a beautiful man," Anna said.

He looked shy. "What've you got there?"

"Nothing. Jim's dive knife. He gave it to me on the *Kamloops* dive and I forgot to give it back." Because she could think of nothing else to do, she handed the clasp knife to Hawk.

He turned it in his well-made hands. "It's a dive knife all right." He sat down beside her, nude, perfect. "Would you take it wrong if I didn't spend the night?"

"No," Anna said and meant it. "We don't know each other that well."

He sat a moment longer. Finally he said: "You're wearing my pants."

Clad only in a long sweatshirt, Anna stayed on deck while he dressed, then watched him as he walked down the dock, leaving as he had come: noiselessly, privately, in the wee hours like a young girl's fantasy. There would be no morning stares, no sly remarks, no gossip. He was a good man. Watching him go, Anna wished he were someone she loved.

Waking alone, the sensible light of day a square of gold overhead, Anna took a moment to decide whether Hawk Bradshaw's night visit had really occurred. When she decided it had, she was unsure how she felt about it. She chose not to worry. She'd ask Christina how she should feel, and if that failed, she'd bring out the big guns: She'd ask Molly.

Physically she felt terrific; relaxed and energized. She pulled on trousers—her own this time—and a red tee-shirt with "Frijole Fire" silkscreened across the front and a line drawing of El Capitan in West Texas. Her hair, incarcerated in two braids, reminiscent of a hundred drawings of Minnehaha, was in need of a shampoo. Anna fired up the *Belle*'s twin engines and motored slowly over to Mott.

Docking, she saw the *Loon*, the boat Jim Tattinger used,

and was reminded of her last Rock Harbor chore: returning his knife.

Having secured the Bertram, she climbed back aboard. The knife was gone. In the finite space of cabin and bow, she knew she was not mistaken. The knife was gone. Hawk had taken it.

Anna sat down on the bench in the bow and stared at the small space of linoleum between her feet, the place where the knife had fallen from her pocket the night before. The last she'd seen it, Hawk had it in his hand.

Had he pocketed it by accident? Force of habit? Doubtful, Anna thought. By the time she'd divested herself of his Levi's and he'd put them on, he would have had to put the knife down somewhere. His taking it had been deliberate. Was his leaving so abruptly merely a way to steal an eleven- or twelve-dollar knife, a knife no different from half a dozen or so he and Holly must own between them? A kleptomaniac? Unlikely—a rash of petty thefts in such a closed society wouldn't go unnoticed and anything noticed would never go unremarked upon. Hawk disliked Jim. Could the theft have been spite?

"No!" Anna stood abruptly, knocking her head on the low ceiling. All the disparate facts had tumbled into line with this sudden thought: It wasn't Jim's knife.

Time had come for a trip to the mainland. Talk with Christina and the lesbian community in Houghton. Pay a visit to Mother Castle in Duluth.

CHAPTER 16

"The 'd.A': d'Artagnan."

"Dartanyon?" Christina shook her head.

"The Three Musketeers," Anna explained. "Porthos, whoever, and d'Artagnan."

"Yes!" Christina remembered. "Okay. D'Artagnan . . . ?"

"Hawk, Holly, and Denny. One night, just before he got married, Holly called Denny 'd'Artagnan.' "

"So, d'A—the knife was Denny Castle's?"

"Yes," Anna said, excited. "Jim found it down there, found it under the porthole. I just thought it was his."

Christina looked at Anna expectantly. "And?"

"There was a straplike bruise on Denny's body. A mark left, I'm willing to bet, by his diving harness. It was in the right place. When I first dove, I got panicky and buckled my stuff on way too tight. After an hour or so I had red marks like that on my shoulders."

"Like girdle marks."

"Exactly."

"Denny dove a lot. Wouldn't he know how to adjust his harness thing?"

"Maybe the tanks or the hoses were pulled around, dragged off him."

"Then he was killed on the *Kamloops*? Down under all that water?"

"I think so. I think he was in full dive gear. I think he fought, somehow his tanks were jerked or something, and he dropped his knife. I think he was killed down there."

"You said he wasn't wearing dive gear," Christina said, confused.

"No. When we found him, he wasn't. He was dressed in this ship captain's clothes, but when we were ascending bloody bubbles frothed out of his mouth from his lungs. That only happens if the body recovered was breathing compressed air. And I saw his diving gear—tank, fins, the whole nine yards—on the deck of the *Third Sister*."

"Goodness," Chris expelled a long breath. "Oh my goodness. This calls for serious sugar."

As the two women picked at a shared slice of the cheesecake Christina kept in the freezer for such emergencies, Chris told her news. "Holly Bradshaw is not gay," she said. "But whatever else Holly may be—Democrat, Sierra Club member, murderess—I can't say. Maybe you'd better ask Hawk what was so funny about the idea of her and Denny—maybe Denny was gay. Maybe they were triplets separated at birth. But she's not a lesbian. We'd know."

Anna nodded. They would know. Chris would know.

"She could be asexual," Chris suggested hopefully.

Anna shook her head. "There's vibes, signals, pheromones. If not homo, then hetero, but definitely sexual. It is a motive—the only good one I've come up with. The 'hell hath no fury' stuff comes up true every now and then."

"Mmm." Christina scraped the last of the cheesecake up with the side of her fork and smeared it sensuously on her tongue. "So. She and Denny. Then Denny and Jo. Then Denny and the Lady of the Lake?"

"Maybe," Anna agreed. "Maybe."

• • •

Anna enjoyed the long drive to Duluth. After two months without so much as seeing an automobile, it was a novelty. She fiddled with the tape deck, sang to herself, and reveled in the true and glorious privacy that could only be had when one was free of tourists and two-way radios. She couldn't imagine putting a telephone in her car. Or in her bathroom. Some places must remain sacrosanct.

Superior, Duluth's sister city, located to the east just over the canal, dampened Anna's spirits somewhat. When the life had gone out of northwest Minnesota's iron country, the blood of commerce had ceased to flow through this industrial shipping town. Row houses, poor imitations of eastern brownstones, crumbled along streets in need of repair. Men of working age loitered in groups around the entrances to mini-marts. Rusting skeletons whose forms suggested the lifting and moving of great loads scratched the skyline.

Anna fished a scrap of paper out of her pocket. Drawn in Jo's precise scientific hand were directions to Denny Castle's childhood home. Mrs. Castle lived on the Duluth side of the canal but just barely. According to Jo's sketch the house backed up on a waterway. Anna had assumed Mrs. Castle had money. Houses on waterways usually meant prime real estate. But this canal was dying. A thin brackish stream trickled down a muddy causeway pocked with tin cans, used tires and burned-out car bodies.

At 103rd Street Anna turned her old Rambler to the right. Shortly after the intersection the asphalt ended. Small clapboard homes, once identical but diversified over the years by individual abuses, littered one side of the road. On the other, old foundations and lilac bushes framing vanished porches indicated that a like row had once faced them before fire or an aborted land development plan had razed it.

Number 1047 had nothing to recommend it but Jo's assertion that Denny's mother lived there. Anna pulled up in front of the house and switched off the ignition. For a moment she sat looking at the dead lawn and faltering front porch. The poverty and neglect embarrassed her, as if she'd stumbled across a dirty secret. Denny had evidently taken greater care of things past than things present. Or things wet than things dry.

Lest her sitting there alarm the occupant—the neighborhood was seedy and Anna's Rambler far from reassuring—she climbed out and let herself in through the garden gate.

Half a minute after her third knock, as she was about to give the house up as empty, she heard the whisper of slippered feet on the inside hall floor. The door opened wide. Behind the torn screen a tiny woman blinked from under thick glasses with dark plastic frames; the kind Medicaid provides for the poor. She was older than Anna would have guessed, maybe in her late eighties or even early nineties. As if in defiance, she wore carmine lipstick, expertly applied, and pink powdered rouge. Bobbed chin-length white hair was held out of her eyes with a child's barrette: two bears on a pink plastic log.

"Mrs. Castle?" Anna asked. "Denny Castle's mom?"

"Oh, yes," the old woman replied, and her smile showed a line of large regular teeth that clicked when she talked. "Denny's my boy. Do you want to see him?"

Anna wasn't sure how to respond to that.

"He's at school," Mrs. Castle said. "But he should be home around three o'clock." Her face firmed up and she suddenly looked terribly sad. "Oh dear. Denny's not at school. Were you a friend of my son's?"

She asked the question with such sympathy Anna knew she had remembered Denny was dead. "Yes. I worked with him on Isle Royale."

"Won't you come in?" Mrs. Castle invited graciously. "Denny will be home from school—oh dear. Come in. Come in. I don't think I have any Pepsi-Colas. That's what young people drink now, isn't it? Pepsi-Cola? tea? No . . . tea's for us oldsters. . . ." Mrs. Castle stopped between the living room and the kitchen, unsure of beverage protocol.

"I don't need anything," Anna said gently. "I just came—" She had started to say "to ask you some questions," but the phrase seemed too abrupt for such a fragile old person. "To visit," Anna amended.

"Tea . . ." Mrs. Castle began again on the beverage question.

"That would be fine. Tea would be nice. I like tea."

"That's settled then." Mrs. Castle sighed with relief, showed Anna into the living room, then disappeared in the direction of the kitchen.

Anna began to revise her opinion of Denny-as-son. The inside of the house was neat and well appointed. The sparkling window glass and lack of cobwebs in high places suggested a spryer cleaning lady than Mrs. Castle. The room had been papered in recent years and the furniture, though worn, was of good quality and kept in good repair.

In such a neighborhood the dilapidated exterior could very well have been left as protective coloration to keep the old woman from being the envy—and therefore the target—of her neighbors.

An old-fashioned upright piano took up all of one wall of the living room. The top was covered with framed photographs. Anna studied them. An extended family was represented: lots of group shots with the very old holding the very young on their laps. A young Denny was in many, cutting watermelons, showing off a skateboard, always grinning. Then he disappeared. Photo to photo Anna watched Mrs. Castle growing old without her son. Then he was back; in his thirties now, the grin gone. This was the Denny Anna had known, the one who carried the world on his shoulders, who could not fit watermelons or skateboards into his work schedule.

A few snapshots tucked into the frames of more formal pictures showed Hawk and Holly. There was only one of Jo. She wore an Empire-waisted pink brocade prom dress, her hair, as always, parted in the center and stick-straight. A boy whom Anna didn't know stood beside her, proud in a rented tux.

Jo was an enigma, Anna thought, seldom remembered but never gone.

Shuffling, slow, careful, Mrs. Castle came in with the

tea things. Anna hurried to take the heavy tray. A short struggle ensued. Anna won and set the tea service down on a low coffee table. After the tea had been poured and the packaged cookies discussed, Mrs. Castle said matter-of-factly: "You want to talk about Denny. He's dead, you know."

"I know," Anna replied, glad Mrs. Castle was lucid for the moment. "It's his death I want to talk about. We're trying to find out all we can about it."

"So it won't happen again?"

"Something like that."

Mrs. Castle nodded approvingly. Anna sipped her tea and turned over in her mind ways to approach her question. "I was looking at your picture collection while you made tea," she said. "I hope you don't mind."

"Oh, no." Mrs. Castle got up and carried her tea over to the piano. She was so small she had to look up to see the photographs. "I'm very proud of them. They are my family now."

The way she said it made Anna wonder how many of them were dead. "I was looking at Jo's pictures the other day," Anna began.

"Oh, yes," Mrs. Castle interrupted. She set down cup and saucer and stood on tiptoe to retrieve the picture of the girl in the prom dress. "This is it. It's the only one left. I used to have more, but Denny got in one of his moods and took them all down one Sunday after church. He never gave them back. Jo sent me this one."

Mrs. Castle brought it over to the sofa and held it out for Anna to look at but not to touch. "Who's the boy?" Anna asked to be polite.

"I don't know his name. He's the boy who took Jo to the winter formal the year Denny wouldn't. He could be a stinker sometimes. I think maybe Jo sent me this hoping Denny would see it and get jealous. That's why I kept it out. I don't think Denny ever did notice it, but I got kind of attached to it. Jo's got a pretty dress on, don't you think?"

Anna admired the dress. "I recognized Hawk and Holly Bradshaw in some of the snaps," she said.

"They're good kids. Wild though," Mrs. Castle said sadly. "They came to visit me a while back."

"When?" Anna realized she'd spoken too abruptly. Mrs. Castle looked startled, as if her thoughts had fled.

"I don't know really. . . ."

Anna worried she had frightened the old lady back out of a reality in which she'd not been too firmly rooted in the first place. She changed the subject, trying her original tack a second time. "Jo was showing me some pictures she had of Denny. One was particularly nice. It was Denny in a ship captain's uniform."

"That was my brother's," Mrs. Castle said, pleased either with the memory or with her ability to recall it.

"Do you still have it? The uniform?"

"Why yes! Yes, I do. Those kids wanted to play with it. It's with Denny's old things in the upstairs bedroom. Do you want to see it?"

That was exactly what Anna wanted. She was grateful her prying seemed to give the woman some pleasure.

Denny's upstairs bedroom had long been out of use for anything but storage and had taken on the dust-and-dead-flies smell of an attic. Old clothes hung on racks. Tattered books and ruined long-playing records were stacked along the walls. There were boxes of shoes and belts and a shelf of dusty vases. Mrs. Castle wended her way through these relics to a blue plastic and aluminum trunk—a cheap recreation of an old steamer trunk.

"Denny's. He wanted to be a seafaring man since he was a little boy," she said as she opened the trunk. "Oh dear."

Anna came to look over her shoulder. The trunk was very nearly empty. Only a half-dozen books and a child's cowboy hat remained. It reeked of mothballs.

"I was sure it was in this trunk." Mrs. Castle's hands began to flutter, her eyes to wander over the clutter.

"Was it here when you showed it to the kids—to Hawk and Holly?" Anna asked gently. "When they came to visit you."

"Why yes! Yes, it was."

"Maybe they borrowed it," Anna suggested.

"No," Mrs. Castle said firmly. "I would have remembered. They stole it. They're wild, those two. They're horrid bad children. They were playing up here and they took it. They'll not play with any of Denny's toys again until they apologize."

Denny was once again alive in his mother's mind. Anna was glad to leave it that way.

On the drive back the facts lined themselves up oppressively in Anna's mind. Holly was not gay and could have been Denny's lover. The bruise indicated that Denny had been wearing his diving gear; the bloody froth, that he had been breathing compressed air; and the knife, that he had dived the *Kamloops*. It was logical to assume he had been killed there. That meant he had been killed by another diver, an experienced one. He had been found in a costume Hawk and Holly had stolen. Anna had seen his gear back aboard the *3rd Sister.*

She remembered the night aboard the *Belle Isle*, remembered Hawk's tears on her throat, and wondered if he cried for his sins.

CHAPTER 17

Christina found Anna sitting in the glider under the white lilac bush in the backyard. A low fog had rolled in off the lake and, though it was July, the night was cold. Anna had draped one of Ally's dinosaur-covered beach towels around her shoulders to ward off the chill. Hugging herself in an old Levi's jacket, Christina sat down next to her and began rocking.

A popping noise came, as of distant gunfire. In the fog the sound was directionless.

"Somebody is getting off to an early start," Anna remarked.

"Mmm." They rocked in silence. The lilacs were long since blown. Glossy leaves shone black all around and overhead. Light glowed from the back porch, illuminating without penetrating the mist. "Ally's preschool is having a Fourth of July picnic tomorrow down on the lake."

"Can't go," Anna said. "I'm going back to the island. If it's clear enough, I'll fly. Otherwise I'll take the *Ranger Three*."

"Are you missing Zach?" Chris asked gently.

"Today's his birthday."

"I know."

Anna looked at her friend. The smooth oval of her face was ageless in the diffused light: idealized. She looked like a woman from another time, a time before aerobics and Nautilus machines, when women were rounder and, of necessity, kinder. "I don't make a big commemorative occasion out of it," Anna said, irritated at being so transparent. "I just think of things."

"Why don't you call your sister?"

As Chris said it, Anna realized how much she wanted to talk with Molly. Childishly, she sat a bit longer lest Christina know how surely she had hit the proverbial nail's head. "Do you see much of Roberta these days?" she asked.

"Mmmhmm." Chris had a self-satisfied smile that made Anna nervous. It was selfish to hope Christina would never marry, never set up housekeeping with a lover, but that was what Anna wished.

"I don't desert my friends because I find a lover," Christina said quietly.

Anna stood abruptly. The glider clanked in protest. "I'm going to call my sister. I can hide more from a psychiatrist than a psychic," she grumbled as she plowed through the fog toward the porch light.

Molly picked up on the second ring.

"Can you listen without a cigarette?" Anna demanded peevishly, not bothering to say hello.

"Nope." A shush, a scratch, a sigh followed, proving that more than one of Mrs. Pigeon's daughters could be stubborn.

"You're on hold," Anna said. "I'm getting a drink." When she got back to the phone she could hear Molly's laughter even before she put the receiver to her ear. It was a distinctive cackle, a "heh, heh, heh" usually associated with caricatures of dirty old men.

"Well," Molly said as Anna's presence crackled down the wires. "Now that we've both got one foot in the grave and one on a banana peel, what's up?"

"There's this guy—" Anna began.

"So far so good. Sex, adventure, romance. I like this story."

"He's seven or eight years younger than I am—" Anna pushed on.

"Better and better. Endurance, virility, flexibility, longevity. Does he have a baby brother?"

"I spent the night with Hawk last week."

"'Hawk'? Lordy, Lordy, to be just forty," Molly cackled.

"Dammit, will you shut up and listen?"

"Sorry," Molly said, suddenly businesslike. "What do you feel about all this?"

"Goddammit," Anna exploded. "Nothing. Let me finish. Then I'll feel something, okay?"

"Mmmm"—a yes murmured with tobacco smoke.

Anna counted to ten in her head, took a deep breath. "Erase, erase," she said, their childhood code for a clear slate, a new start.

"Erase, erase," Molly agreed. "So, you slept with a guy named Hawk."

"Yes. It was okay. Kind of strange but okay. I could like him."

"Like? Don't go hog-wild, Anna. You don't want to put yourself out on an emotional limb here. 'Like' could lead to 'like pretty much,' and that's just two jumps from 'real fond.' You don't want to rush into anything."

"Do people really pay you a hundred and fifty dollars an hour for this?" Anna asked sourly, but she was smiling and let it show in her voice.

"Why? Do you think I'm selling myself too cheap? I'm thinking of starting an Inner Child Baby-sitting Service to bring in a little pin money."

Anna laughed. "Okay. Back to me. Here's the rub: It's looking a whole lot like Hawk and probably his sister, Holly, committed the Denny Castle murder. Maybe a love triangle thing. Maybe to get a boat worth a quarter of a million. Maybe drugs."

There followed a moment of stunned silence which Anna thoroughly enjoyed.

"Jesus," Molly said finally. "No wonder you never watch the soaps. They pale by comparison."

"Thank you," Anna said with dignity. "Now, may I get to the confusing part?"

"Lord! Yes, by all means. Please do."

"Given the givens—"

"Sex, drugs, and murder."

"Given the givens," Anna repeated firmly, "I want to talk with Hawk before I go to the FBI and feed him and his sister—and their only means of livelihood, their boat—into the bureaucratic meat grinder. Give him a chance."

"Let me get this straight. You have fallen in 'like' with a sinister stranger you believe killed a man. Now you want to confront him face-to-face with his murderous deed. Have you picked out a windblown cliff or an isolated tower to go to all alone and unprotected in the dead of a dark and stormy night?"

"I get the point," Anna said. She changed the subject: "Tell me about gourmet suspenders."

"Another mysterious bottle retailing for ten grand, another tasting, three more sessions on the couch. Anna, are you going to do this thing?"

"I don't know," Anna admitted wearily.

"If you do it, promise me it'll be in a crowded cafeteria at noon," Molly insisted. "No drama, no glamour. Egg salad sandwiches and bad coffee. Oops. Gotta go. David Letterman's on."

The click and the "goodbye" were almost simultaneous.

Anna put down the receiver and promised herself a trip to New York. She'd go for Christmas. Angels in Rockefeller Center, holiday scenes in the windows on Fifth Avenue, elves in Macy's, New Yorkers moderately cheerful. The city was at its best at Christmas.

"Are you done on the phone?" Christina poked her head in the door to Anna's room. "Ally wants you to kiss her goodnight."

"I can do that," Anna said.

Alison Walters went to bed each night with more animals than the keeper at the San Diego Zoo. Three of them were alive. Two sleek black cats curled up like bowling balls near the foot of the bed and Piedmont, Anna's yellow tiger cat, stretched almost the full length of the child, his white belly turned up to be petted. A low rattling purr emanated from somewhere.

Anna kissed Ally's cheek and Piedmont's belly. Christina turned out the light and pulled the door closed but for a catsized gap for nocturnal comings and goings.

By habit more than design the two women went into the kitchen. Anna sat down at the small round table where they took most of their meals. Christina rummaged through the refrigerator for an appropriate evening snack.

"Ally and I won't ever leave you, you know," she said without turning to look at her housemate.

Anna started to lay her head down on the table, started to cry, but since she didn't know why she was doing it, she stopped herself. Later, alone in her room, she could cry. Then there would be no burden of sympathy or understanding.

Approached by air, the island took on the jewel-like quality of the islands of the South Seas: an emerald set in sapphire. When Anna flew in from Houghton the effect was heightened by veils of retreating fog that wreathed the island like tissue paper in a fancy gift box.

The seaplane landed in Tobin Harbor and Anna walked over the narrow peninsula to Rock just as people were disembarking from the *Queen*. She picked up the *Belle Isle* and motored down toward Mott. The narrow ribbon of water was crowded with Fourth of July revelers. A red speedboat towed a water skier bent on an illegal death. Anna saw the *Cisco* pull out. Scotty in hot pursuit.

She turned in at Mott Harbor, secured the boat, and walked the short gravel road to Ralph Pilcher's quarters. It was one of Ralph's lieu days but Anna knew he would want a report.

The permanent employees lived in apartments arranged in rows like the rooms of a cheap motel. In front of each was a small weedy patch that passed for a lawn.

Hawk Bradshaw sat cross-legged on Pilcher's plot tossing a baby into the air and making those crooning noises understood by infants the world over.

Anna would have turned and run, ducked for cover behind one of the old white pines that lined the road, but she knew it was only a fraction of a second before Hawk would see her. Not even time enough to compose her features. It occurred to her that perhaps she was glad not to be gay after all. A woman lover could too easily read one's thoughts. The lack of understanding between the sexes provided each species with at least a modicum of privacy.

Hawk caught the baby. Against its delicate skin, his hands looked to be made of mahogany. Laughingly he nuzzled the child's cheek. Still Anna remained rooted to the gravel drive. Something in the charming scene struck her as odd. Hawk and the infant, so comfortable at play. She combed through her tangled thoughts to find the snarl.

Vasectomy: Hawk, thirty-two, had a vasectomy. Why would a young man who so clearly loved babies have ensured that he would never father one?

"Anna!" Hawk had seen her. He cuddled the baby to his shoulder like someone who knows how, and rose smoothly to his feet.

"Morning, Hawk. Ralph around?" she asked casually.

Hawk looked hurt, then annoyed. "Was the other night nothing?" he asked quietly.

"The other night was the other night," Anna said with a shrug. She wanted to smile, touch his arm, say something more, but there was no graceful way out of the situation.

"I'm sorry, Anna." He sounded like a man accepting his own failure. That didn't seem in keeping with what had transpired between them, but since she would probably have to arrest him in the immediate future, Anna didn't think this was the time to pursue the details of their aborted romance.

"Me too," she said. "Is Ralph around?"

"He got called to Houghton, he and Lucas, I guess. It's a shame. Mrs. Pilcher and Max"—he wiggled the baby between his hands like a bit of Play-Doh—"just got here yesterday. Max's mom is over at Rock, visiting. I asked if I could baby-sit."

Ralph and Lucas were off the island. They'd be gone at least a day and a night and part of the following day. Anna considered going to Frederick Stanton with her burden of proof. But if he clung to the drug-death theory, the *3rd Sister* would be impounded as evidence immediately, long before Hawk and Holly were proven guilty. With the ensuing investigation and governmental red tape, there was no telling when she'd be released. Clients would be canceled. Goodwill in a small industry lost. Insurance payments, dock fees, gear maintenance cost, would go unpaid. It wouldn't take much to break the back of *3rd Sister* Dive Adventures, Inc. If, by some chance, Hawk and his sister were innocent, they would have paid a stiff price for her suspicions.

Hawk kissed the baby's ear.

"Are you free for lunch?" Anna asked.

"Are you cooking?"

"Better. A crowded cafeteria at noon, egg salad, bad coffee."

"Are you buying?"

"Dutch treat."

Hawk laughed. "Never go into sales, Anna. How about twelve-thirty? Max's mom won't be back till noon."

"Twelve-thirty."

At central dispatch Anna left a message for Stanton: "URGENT. MEET ME AT ROCK HARBOR LODGE LUNCHROOM AT 1:30." Sandra said she'd give it to the Fed if she saw him, but Anna knew behind the joke was the promise to track him down at all cost.

Ninety minutes to kill. Since she was out of uniform, Anna decided to play tourist. She motored back to Rock, took her place on the bench above the harbor, and waited

for the eleven o'clock nature walk to begin. Visitors trickled up. Soon the bench was full, and half a dozen people
milled around on the asphalt path. Anna didn't talk much.
It was restful to be incognito, not to have to feign interest
in anybody's little adventures.

At five of eleven the group perked and stirred meaning-
fully. The ranger was coming. It was Tinker. She looked
markedly older than when Anna had seen her several days
before. Her face was thinner and drawn, as if she'd not
been eating or sleeping well. Her hair needed shampooing
and her uniform shirt, usually worn like a flag of honor,
was crumpled. Tinker noted Anna in the group with a dis-
interest that smacked of lethargy.

The nature walk seemed to pick up her spirits to some
degree. Teaching distracted her perhaps from her private
terrors. But Tinker's usual joy, her religious reverence for
the natural world, seemed blighted. Something was eating
away at her.

After the walk, Anna returned to the *Belle Isle* and put
on her uniform. Body armor came in all sizes and colors.
The LAPD had bulletproof vests, Molly had Anne Klein
suits, Anna had the green and gray.

At the lodge, she picked a table near a window. Sunlight
flooded across the white cloth, splashed into the empty
chair. Anna left that seat for Hawk: her back to the wall,
the light in his eyes. Clichéd TV choices, Anna thought
with a smile, but making them gave her something to do.
Stress management, Molly would call it. Dicking around,
Anna said to herself.

Hawk was late. Anna flicked all the real and imaginary
crumbs from the cloth, checked and rechecked her watch,
went through the reasons Hawk might have chosen to
stand her up. None of them were reassuring.

At ten of one the *Loon,* piloted by Tattinger, motored up
to the near dock. Through the window, she saw Hawk
jump off the boat, wave a thanks, and sprint up the quay.
The sun caught his curls where the breeze ruffled them.
Cold-blooded killer or not, Anna thought, he was lovely.

She did not like to think of the man he would be after a few years in the federal penitentiary.

"Sorry I'm late. Couldn't cadge a lift," he said, smiling, folding himself into the chair opposite, whisking up the paper napkin and cracking it open as if it were made of linen. "Will you order for both of us?" Hawk was grinning wickedly. The waitress was standing at their table, pen poised, an interested expression pasted politely on her face.

"Two egg salads, two coffees. No dessert." Handcuffs were dessert, Anna thought acidly.

"To what do I owe this honor? Is it to be: 'About last night . . . I think the world of you but . . .'? No? Let me guess. You're married."

"Sort of," Anna said. The conversation, planned and rehearsed so carefully in her head, had gotten away from her and was running amok.

"Ohmygod!" One word gusted out on a laugh. "Sort of? Sort of?"

"I'm married. He's dead. Till death do us part," Anna explained awkwardly.

"Only sometimes it doesn't. Dead men are tricky. Memories are tough to beat. They only improve with age."

"Dead people," Anna echoed. "Let's talk about Denny." So much for smooth segues.

Hawk sobered. Like a light going out, the hazel eyes dimmed, the full lips stilled and thinned. "Okay," he said evenly. "Denny."

The waitress came then with two egg salads on white bread, bread-and-butter pickles on the side. Neither was tempted. Coffee came and got a slightly better reception. Hawk sipped. Anna pretended to.

"I went to see Denny's mother," she said. "She showed me the trunk in the spare bedroom. There'd been a suit of clothes there—a sea captain's uniform. It was gone. Mrs. Castle said you and Holly had stolen it. 'Wild children,' she called you. Did you take it?"

Hawk thought over his reply. Took a drink of the coffee. "Denny thought a lot of that uniform. He said if he believed in previous lives—which he didn't—he'd've believed he'd once dressed that way. That's how he saw himself."

Not a yes, not a no. Like a character in a Greek tragedy, Anna pushed on with an unpleasant sense of the inevitable. "Denny's corpse was found dressed in that uniform. No dry suit, no tanks, no mask, just that old sea costume. Mrs. Castle said she showed it to you and Holly around the time Denny died."

"When did he die?" Hawk asked abruptly. "Exactly?"

"The autopsy will tell us—today, maybe tomorrow. Why?"

Hawk didn't answer. It was as if he hadn't heard. He pushed a bit of egg salad around his plate with the edge of a chip but didn't look as if he was inclined to eat it.

"I saw Denny's tank—the oversized single—on the *Third Sister* when Lucas and I came to tell you of the death. Yours and Holly's were charged but Denny's was down by nearly half. You'd not bothered to top it."

"Why should we? Denny was dead."

"How did you know? At the time you were filling tanks the body had not yet been discovered. And there was a bruise on the body. A mark like one that would be left by a dive harness. My guess is Denny was wearing the tank when he died, or just before."

"Ah. Gotcha! That it?"

Anna waited, watched his face. Emotions flickered and flooded over the smooth brown skin but she couldn't separate any one out as stronger than the rest. Unless, perhaps, it was sorrow.

"It's crossed my mind," she said, "that Denny was killed by two divers, divers who dressed him in that costume, who retrieved his gear, who stood to inherit his boat and his business."

Hawk looked up from his plate. His eyes were hard. "The *Third Sister* has got a load of debt that should sink her. Collateral so we could buy gear for the squirrels. Do you think I'd kill Denny for a boat even if it were free and clear? I can build a damn boat." The voice was so cold, had

Anna not seen him speak she would not have recognized it as his.

"Maybe not for the *Third Sister,* but for your sister? For Holly."

Hawk looked blank. "Holly loved Denny," he said.

"And then there was Jo?"

"No. Nothing like that. Holly couldn't love Denny like that. Never."

"I find that hard to believe," Anna said. A shadow fell across the table, drawing their eyes to the window. It belonged to Frederick the Fed, clad in a suit and tie reminiscent of a Mormon missionary witnessing door to door. He was heading for the lodge.

Instantly Hawk understood what the apparently coincidental arrival of the Bureau man meant.

"No," he said hurriedly. "No."

"Holly's not gay," Anna said. "I checked."

"Gay!" Hawk laughed. "No." The restaurant door opened. Anna could see Frederick looking around him in that vague half-blind way people seek a familiar face in a crowd. She started to raise her hand to signal him. Hawk caught it and held it. He leaned across the table, his face close to hers.

"There's never been any man for Holly but me. Never any woman in my world but Holly."

The truth jarred more deeply than Anna would have admitted, more deeply than if the man she'd slept with had been a murderer. "The vasectomy!"

"No half-wit children," Hawk said bitterly.

"Why did you go to bed with me?"

"You for me; the three clotheshorse clients for Holly. Denny was our savior, our cover; after he died we tried to go straight. You were my best bet. But it was too lonely. Holly's my other self. If, after I die, I burn in hell for it, I burn in hell. I won't live in hell now."

"Denny?"

"We found him," Hawk said. "Two days before you did. Floating near the ship. His gear was on him, there was air in his tank. Maybe ecstasy of the deep. Stupidity. Accident.

It doesn't matter—not even if it was murder. We gave him the burial he wanted in the grave he would have chosen. We owed him at least that."

"Howdy, howdy, howdy." Frederick Stanton had arrived at their table. Somewhere along the way he had picked up a coffeepot, and proceeded to refill their cups. "Nothing for me, thanks," he said when an irritated waitress steamed over to retrieve her pot.

Anna was too stunned to speak. Stanton flopped down in the chair beside Hawk and leaned back. His carefully blank eyes moved between the two of them. Anna doubted he missed a thing. Hawk began wolfing down his sandwich, his face burning red under the tan. Anna had lost what little appetite she had. The sight of egg salad nauseated her. So did the sight of Hawk.

Watching the boats come and go in the harbor, she stared out of the window. Nothing broke the silence but Hawk's muffled chewing. Stanton had grown so good at waiting Anna scarcely even felt him there.

Twins and lovers. Denny knew. Denny was their employer, protector. Denny understood. They had risked imprisonment to give him the burial he had wanted.

Stanton caught her eye. She smiled. "Sorry to drag you all the way down here. I just wondered if the autopsy report had come back."

The FBI man's look of expectancy evaporated. "Ah. Well. Meet me in Ralph's office." Looking crestfallen, a disappointed child, he rose from the table.

Anna felt a stab of guilt. "There are some things I'd like to talk over with you." He brightened. Anna wondered what technique he used on other people. Whatever worked, probably. "An hour okay?" She looked at her watch. "Around two-thirty?"

"Two-thirty it is." For a moment he hovered near the table. "You going to eat that sandwich?" he said finally.

"It's all yours." Anna pushed the plate toward him, and he shoveled the entire sandwich onto one flat palm and wandered out, eating as he walked.

Hawk stopped chewing as abruptly as he had begun but

remained staring down at his plate. "I'm sorry, Anna. We were so young. We never knew better. Then we knew better and we tried to quit. Holly broke hearts. I made a lot of women hate me. Holly and I cried and fought. I drank. Holly did coke. We'd sit across the room from each other at parties, some pretty boy panting over her, some bimbo hanging on me. It was sick, Anna, sicker a hundred times more than anything we could ever do together. Denny hired us. Out on the lake days at a time, the world kind of fades. Old rules seem like nonsense. We made new rules. Our parents are dead. We'll never have kids. New rules for a new world. Who were we hurting?"

"Denny knew?"

"Denny was our friend."

"Jo?"

"Nobody. Just Denny."

"Now me." A number of stock phrases marched across the tip of Anna's tongue: How could you? You lied to me. You used me. But he hadn't lied and she had used him. And to the same ends: to forget, for a moment, a love that had come to hurt more than it healed. "It's okay," she said.

"Is it really?" Hawk sounded as if her answer genuinely mattered to him.

" 'Okay' is relative, I guess," Anna said. "But yeah."

CHAPTER 18

Frederick was in Ralph's chair, tilted back, his ankles crossed atop the clutter on the desk. In the cheap suit he presented a perfect parody of the 1930 shamus. Anna couldn't tell if it was intentional or not.

She finished her story: "So they dressed Denny in his favorite clothes, stuck him in the engine room, and left him to his eternal rest."

"That was two days before those divers—Whosis and Bozo—discovered the body."

"Two days."

Stanton picked up a blue For Your Eyes Only envelope and tapped it without showing the contents to Anna. "The autopsy says Denny died the day before that."

"Four? Four days before the Canadians found him?"

"Yup. Nobody reported him missing? Nobody wondered where he was?"

"He was on his honeymoon," Anna replied a little defensively. "You expect people to disappear on their honeymoon."

"Three days."

"He died on his wedding night!" Anna realized aloud.

"You'd think the bride would have noticed," Stanton said.

J o was camped up on Lake Richie just southwest of Moskey Basin, working on her freshwater quality study. When Denny died, the NPS had offered her any length of leave she required to settle personal business. Jo had taken just enough time to finalize the plans for planting Denny's body deep in Michigan's soil where, as Holly put it one bitter evening, he could never drift away from her.

Within a couple of days Jo had been back on Isle Royale working. Anna understood. It was what she would have done. Had done, once she'd sobered up.

Jo's camp was a two-mile hike in. The trail was muddy. Blackflies, tiny airborne carnivores called "all-jaws" by the local Michigan children, bit without warning. Mosquitoes and Frederick Stanton whined.

"Tell me about the autopsy report," Anna said, hoping to distract him. Or hoping the bugs would've distracted him enough he'd accidentally tell her something worth knowing.

"Good of you to come along, Anna. Oh, ish!"

Anna looked back. Stanton was staring ruefully at one black leather shoe, brown now with mud. She laughed. "If you're for real, you're scary."

He looked the offended innocent.

"The autopsy . . ." she led in.

"Dead since the seventeenth of June, four days before the Canadians discovered the body. Cause of death: drowning."

"Drowning? With his tank nearly full?"

Stanton chuckled. "The corpse wasn't wearing a tank."

Anna made no comment. She walked on, listening for the rest of the report. "What about the bruises?" she asked when nothing more was forthcoming.

"You knew about that, too? Jeez, Anna. Why ask? You tell me."

"There was a bruise across his shoulder where his harness would've been. He was in dive gear when he died. That's my guess anyway."

"Wow." Stanton sounded genuinely impressed. "Gee, you think?"

"Occasionally." Anna was losing patience.

"Remind me not to deal drugs in your park."

"You don't buy that anymore."

Stanton neither agreed nor disagreed.

Anna stopped, turned. "Do you want to work together, or do you want to keep dicking around?"

Stanton looked at his shoes, at the canopy of aspen closing overhead. He grinned, he shrugged, he shuffled.

Anna was unimpressed. "You never bought it, did you? You just hoped by threatening to impound the *Third Sister,* you'd get somebody setting out to clear the Bradshaws. Or convict them."

"I swear by local talent," he said at last. "They know where the bodies are buried, who's sleeping with whom."

"Help me then."

Stanton seemed to weigh the efficacy of interagency co-operation. "Okay," he said after a moment. "Castle drowned. Water was in his lungs. If you're right about the bruise being caused by his harness, he drowned with plenty of breathing air on him. Too weird for me."

Anna told him about the knife. If there'd been any kind of struggle at that depth, Denny could have blacked out. His assailant could have pulled off his mouthpiece.

"Left him to wake up dead?"

"That's what crossed my mind," Anna said.

"Why?"

"Beats me." She turned and began walking again, the moisture-laden thimbleberry branches slapping dark patterns on her trousers.

"Drugs," Stanton said. "When you've ruled out the impossible, whatever's left, however improbable, is drugs."

"One-size-fits-all motive?"

"It's perfect," Stanton said, and: "Damn!" The sound of slapping, a mosquito or blackfly departing the quick and joining the dead. "I'm all for drugs," he babbled on. "Takes the guesswork out of law enforcement."

They found Jo's camp on a rocky bluff overlooking Lake Richie. Set like an orange Easter egg amid the froth of wild sarsaparilla, her tent was pitched on the hardened site.

Frederick crawled halfway inside. "Not searching," he called out. "Can't search without a warrant. Checking for guns and bombs. Officer safety."

Anna sat down on a rock screened by Juneberry bushes where she could see the trail that wound up from the lake. Search finished, Stanton came and curled his long body neatly down beside her, hugging his bony knees to his chest. Despite his grumbling the hike hadn't even winded him.

"Do you think Jo killed Denny?" Anna asked impulsively.

"The spouse is always a prime suspect."

"Better than drugs?"

"Nothing's better than drugs."

"No more profiles. Do you, personally, think Jo did it?"

"I don't think," Stanton replied solemnly. "I'm a government employee."

Anna gave up. His reticence had ceased to amuse or challenge. It merely irritated.

Out in the lake, silver rings were beginning to appear on the blue, fish rising to eat their suppers. Soon Jo Castle would be returning. Anna ran scenes in her head: Jo, jealous, following or luring Denny down on the *Kamloops* for a midnight dive on the night of their wedding; a struggle, a death. Maybe Jo had found, despite the marriage, Denny still pursued Donna. Maybe she had killed them both.

The story didn't feel right. The knife: Anna couldn't picture Denny defending himself from his wife with a knife. The location: too difficult to execute a planned murder, and without words, what could ignite that kind of passion under two hundred feet of water?

Still, in Anna's mind, the greatest argument against Jo-as-killer had nothing to do with clues or evidence. Jo Castle lacked passion. She was a trudger. If Denny was unfaithful, Jo was more the type to outlive the mistress than kill the mister. It was why she had finally won Denny, and why it had taken her twenty years to do it.

A figure, humpbacked like a forest gnome, appeared on the trail at the far end of the lake. "That'll be Jo," Anna said. "I recognize the pack."

"Shh," Stanton returned. "Sound carries across water."

His oversized face was hard with concentration. The angles of his usually gawky body were knifelike.

The distant figure disappeared into the trees. Frederick and Anna waited. She felt as if she were sitting by a crouching lion. She had an irrational urge to holler and warn Jo away.

Twenty minutes passed. The lake was absolutely still, a perfect mirror. Across the water, two backpackers had dumped their gear against a tree and were wading in the shallows. Muted, indecipherable, their conversation floated up to the bluff. A crunching from the trail: footsteps. With no more warning than that, Jo Castle walked into the clearing.

"Hi." She seemed unsurprised and disinterested, as if most evenings law enforcement agents were waiting in camp for her.

Anna remembered that apathy. The dullness that followed had, in some ways, been harder to bear than the pain. It came when one accepted the death as fact: immutable, forever. Then, for a while, the world no longer held any wonder. Anna wanted to tell Jo if she lived through this, life would get better. But it was not a good time.

Jo dropped the pack with a thud. It weighed close to a hundred pounds.

"I'm Frederick Stanton," the FBI man said. He moved easily between Jo and the pack. Officer safety. "We talked a week or so ago."

"I remember." Jo looked around as if for a place to sit,

didn't see one and lost interest. "Do you guys want coffee or something?"

"Nothing," Stanton said as she moved toward the tent. "We came to talk with you about the death of your husband."

"Yes."

"Why don't you sit down, Jo? Sit here by me." Anna patted the rock. Obediently, Jo came over. Stanton shot Anna a look of professional annoyance and Anna guessed he meant to keep Jo standing, literally and figuratively, alone and unsupported. Anna didn't care. "You were saying, Frederick?" she said helpfully.

Stanton waited, letting the sarcasm clear from the air. "When did your husband die, Mrs. Castle?" It was not so much a question as a demand for information. Irritation nibbled at Anna's self-control. Officer Stanton was seldom what he seemed. He preferred circuitous routes, but he usually got where he was going.

"When?" he repeated.

"Anna and Lucas told me Denny . . . Denny's body . . . had been found on the twenty-second of June. I'm pretty sure it was the twenty-second. I was . . . What was I doing, Anna?"

"Not when did you hear, Mrs. Castle," Stanton pressed. "When did he die?"

Jo turned to Anna as if for help. Anna looked sympathetic but still said nothing. Jo turned back to Stanton. "I don't know," she said distinctly.

"He died on June seventeenth. Four days before the body was found. Five days before you were notified."

Jo raised her chin slightly, her face set and stubborn.

"You must have known your husband was missing. You were just married, on your honeymoon, your husband disappeared and you didn't report it. I mean to find out why." Stanton waited perhaps ten seconds after the end of the speech, then pointed a long finger at Jo. "Break camp. Come in for questioning. Pilcher's office, eight a.m. tomorrow." He dropped his arm, turned, and marched down the trail toward Moskey Basin and the *Belle Isle*.

"What an asshole!" Anna said. "Are you okay, Jo?"

Jo rose to her feet. The defiance had gone with Stanton's departure. She looked tired to the point of exhaustion. "I can't break camp now," she said wearily. "I'm in the middle of things. It'll shoot weeks of work. God!" She crumpled down, legs crossed tailor-fashion, and hid her face in her hands.

"Why didn't you report Denny missing?" Anna asked gently.

Jo didn't look, didn't take her hands from her eyes. "I thought he was with Donna. If she'd given him the nod, he'd've come running. Even on my fucking wedding night."

Anna sat on the rock, looked over the lake to give Jo a moment's privacy. Denny and Donna: they could have run off together, left brides and husbands; could have turned up in a quickie-divorce court in Reno. But Denny had turned up dead, and Donna had gone missing.

"Don't break camp quite yet," Anna said. "No need to louse up your experiments. I'll square it with Stanton."

"Thanks. Work is what I've got now. It's got to be right."

She left Jo still sitting in the dirt hiding her face from her memories.

Anna almost stumbled over Frederick the Fed. His back against a fallen log, his long legs across the trail, he sat twenty feet or so down from Jo's camp just out of sight behind a dense screen of vegetation.

"Jesus!"

"Interesting," Frederick remarked. He levered himself up. "Sounded pretty convincing to me. What a drag. I knew there was a reason I've never married. I mean other than nobody's ever asked me."

Anna quickly recovered from being startled, but the entire situation had put her in a foul mood. Being used was an unpleasant sensation, one she was growing altogether too familiar with.

She struck off down the trail at a good clip, hoping to walk away from Stanton and his bag of tricks. Muttering and fussing, he bumbled along behind. Several times he turned on his idle chatter, the stuff Anna had come to suppose was designed to disarm the listener. She ignored it.

In less than an hour they reached the shoreline of Moskey. Seven P.M. and the shadows had yet to grow long. The *Belle Isle* sat quietly at the dock. The basin was still. A cold breeze from the lake shivered the grass near the tree line. Covering the finger of land between Moskey and Superior was a curtain of white fog.

A green fiberglass canoe was beached down from the dock, and a thin line of smoke, the color of the mist, curled up from the fire pit in front of the lean-to shelter. It pleased Anna that for once the place hadn't been taken by powerboaters.

The shelter door opened, and a woman in a sweatshirt with a red hood stepped out. Blond hair frizzed, making a halo around her face. "Tinker!" Anna called.

Stanton came up behind her, so close she could feel the heat radiating from his body. The chill of the fog had reached the shore and the sensation would have been pleasant if Anna hadn't considered the source.

"Friends?" Stanton asked, then: "Oh, it's your Cannibal Jamboree folks."

"You wait in the boat," Anna commanded. Looking positively hangdog, Frederick shambled off down the beach toward the *Belle Isle*. Though the shore offered no cover, Anna watched him till he reached the dock. The lean-to backed up against the trees and she had had enough of Stanton's false exits and surprise appearances for one day.

"I thought it must be you when I saw the *Belle*," Tinker said as Anna walked up. "Damien's gathering firewood. Where have you been?"

"Visiting Jo," Anna replied. Uninvited, she sat down on the picnic table, her feet on the wooden bench. Stones were laid out creating a circle divided into three parts. Several small cloth bags, closed with drawstrings like old-time tobacco sacks, were scattered nearby. Anna picked one up and smelled it: a spice tea, orange and clove or cinnamon.

"Ah," Tinker said apropos of nothing, and: "Okay, okay." She went into the shelter. A moment later she reappeared with the stuffed bear in her hands and put him down on the table near Anna. The bear stared at her with interested button eyes.

"Oscar worries," Tinker explained. "You are always putting yourself in places a body could get its fur wet."

"I hope stress isn't causing him to smoke too much," Anna joked.

"It's hard to tell," Tinker replied in all apparent seriousness.

Anna laughed anyway and picked the bear up. She felt comforted. "I read somewhere hugging teddy bears reduces blood pressure and pulse rates."

"It does."

Anna kept Oscar on her lap. In Tinker's world it was not a foolish thing to do, and she did not feel a fool for doing it. She watched as the other woman busied herself about the camp, feeding bits of wood into the fire, arranging metal pots on the grill. Tinker's face was tight, her movements heavy as if she labored under great weariness. Clinical signs of depression: Anna remembered Molly ticking them off with her porcelain fingernails after Zach had died.

"You look like you could do with a little more hugging of bears," Anna remarked. "Could it be you who's keeping Oscar up nights worrying?"

"Oscar's an old fusspot," Tinker said affectionately.

"Who's blackmailing you?" Anna asked abruptly.

Tinker's hands, busy breaking beans into a pot of water, twitched. In a voice almost too low to be heard, Tinker said: "Nobody's blackmailing me."

"I read the cryptic note about Hopkins and dirty laundry," Anna countered.

"I don't know anything about that." Tinker dragged her sleeve across her eyes.

"My mistake," Anna apologized. "Like I said, the note was pretty cryptic." She stayed a bit longer, fondling Oscar's ears. The fog enveloped them. The *Belle Isle* took on a ghostly aspect. The land spit that held Moskey safe from the moods of the lake had vanished.

Finally Anna put the bear down and stood up. "Whatever it is, it can't be that bad," she said.

"Yes it can," Tinker replied shortly.

Anna left her to whatever peace she could salvage for herself among her pots and pans and herbs.

Relying on radar, ragged green lines on a black screen taking the place of shoreline, the *Belle Isle* crept back up Moskey toward Rock. Stanton hummed old Donovan tunes. Anna kept her irritation to a tolerable level by reordering her thoughts. She'd decided she would share none of them with Frederick the Fed until he offered her something substantial in the way of information or insight.

With the Bradshaws and Jo out of the picture—at least in Anna's mind, and she didn't doubt that with the autopsy and time of death, alibis would be found—the investigation was back to square one. Back to the FBI's drug death and Tinker and Damien's Windigo. Denny and Donna; cocaine and cannibalism.

It would have been tragic, but simple, if Hawk and Holly had done it. Motive, means, opportunity: they'd seemed to have it all. The pieces had fit so nicely. But they'd been guilty only of loving Denny more than the law. And of incest.

The remaining possibilities each lacked one of the big three: motive or means or opportunity.

Jim Tattinger had the means: access to boats and dive gear, and he was a certified diver. The opportunity had been there. Jim was on the island that night. Anna had seen him at the reception. On the day before they were scheduled to recover the body, she had caught him running without lights near the dive site in a boat with full gear. He was clearly hoping to avoid detection. He was defensive at being stopped and questioned. Knowing the investigation was to begin in the morning, he could have been diving the *Kamloops* destroying evidence.

Motive was a little weak for Tattinger. Generalized dislike and professional squabbling seemed inadequate cause for such an elaborate and risky murder. Unless it stemmed from a deeper rift between the two men. Jim had left his job on St. John's in the Caribbean under a considerable cloud. St. John's was largely an undersea-oriented park. Had Jim been suspected of pilfering from any sunken archaeological site? Was he doing the same thing at ISRO? Did Denny suspect? Catch him at it? Pilfering what? The dive was so perilous any recovered artifact would have to be of considerable value. The *Kamloops*'s bill of lading showed no treasure. She was a package freighter; she carried pipe and shoes. Not a glamorous lady.

The most damning thing against Tattinger was Tattinger. He was a creep. Anna wanted him to be the guilty party. She smiled remembering a crusty old county sheriff telling her law enforcement class that most people were arrested because they were guilty of P.O.P.: pissing off the police.

"A ruble for your thoughts," Stanton said.

"Not worth even a *glasnost* ruble," Anna replied, glad her thoughts, at least, were not for sale. As children, she and Molly had fantasized endlessly about living in a telepathic world. As an adult the idea gave her chills. There were days, weeks, when the only real privacy to be had was inside one's own skull.

Stanton began whistling "Sunshine, Superman." Anna returned to her musings.

Scotty Butkus had motive: the classic—a cuckolded husband committing a crime of passion. He had opportunity: He was on the island that night. Means was the weak link in this chain. Though he had access to boats and dive gear, he was no diver. His health and, more important, his nerve had failed him. And Anna doubted he had the courage for a midnight dive. She doubted he could stay sober past six P.M. At depth, Dutch courage would kill him.

Casting about for other suspects, she considered Pilcher and Vega—both could do it but had no reason to. Blackmail? There was a blackmailer on the island but he was still in business. And, too, blackmail didn't seem Denny's style.

Patience had means, a boat—Hawk had even mentioned seeing it near the *Kamloops*'s marker buoy a time or two—and she had the gear. Much as she claimed to be a dilettante, Anna assumed that she could use it. She was on the island the night Denny was killed. It was motive that failed with Patience. She had liked and respected Denny. Where was the gain? Not inheritance. Not love.

A shadowy green blot the shape of Rabbit Island materialized on the radar screen. Mott was two islands farther up the channel. "Where can I drop you?" Anna asked.

Stanton was staying on Mott in the V.I.P. quarters. She docked the *Belle*. The FBI man learned quickly: He deployed fenders and secured lines like an old salt.

As she stepped onto the concrete pier, he shook her hand enthusiastically. "You've been a great help. Terrific!"

Anna didn't feel particularly gratified at the commendation. "A flea in a flea circus can be prodded to jump through fiery hoops. It doesn't make it a Flying Wallenda," she said ungraciously.

"Nope, but it sure can make folks scratch." Flapping the autopsy envelope he'd carried from the boat, he said gleefully: "Got a time of death. Now I can check alibis. I like doing alibis. Makes me feel sleuthy."

The fog swallowed up his ambling form and muffled the crunch of his hard-soled shoes on the gravel.

Much of the day's last light had been swallowed as well. Anna was cold and depressed. The *Belle Isle,* rocking gently on the wake of some passing boat, invisible forty yards out, was uninviting: a cluttered, damp, floating office. It was the end of a long hard day and she wanted nothing better than to go home. Wherever that was. Amygdaloid with marine radio, cobwebs, and single bed would have been a relief. Houghton with Chris and Ally and the cats, a pleasure. A double bed with Zachary, heaven.

"Cut that shit out," Anna said aloud. In the fog, her voice sounded strange.

Laughter percolated incongruously through the cold mist. Trail crew. Or the maintenance men. Both had bunkhouses on Mott. Both drank enough vodka to qualify for detox on either coast. On the Upper Peninsula of Michigan, where most of them hailed from, it was just a way to unwind, let off a little steam.

Scotty would be there no doubt, telling lies and opening beer bottles with his teeth to impress the new recruits. Dave would be eating the pepperoni pizzas he seemed to procure from nowhere. The TV would be blaring. Talk would be of outboard motors, dead fish, or female body parts. Still, needing heat and light, Anna gravitated toward the noise.

Pizza Dave was always good for a beer. If the sauna wasn't booked she could retreat there with a couple of Leinenkugels, strip down, smell the sweet scent of cedar and feel the dry heat of the desert.

CHAPTER 19

After two Leinenkugels had been poured in and sweated out, and Anna had showered and washed her hair, she felt life was once again worth living.

The fog had not lifted. If anything it lay more heavily over the island than before. Steam boiled off her overheated flesh and Anna felt herself a creature of the mist, no longer oppressed by it but at one with it. Fairy tales of a cloak of invisibility returned to memory and she drifted silently down the wooden steps of the sauna.

Trees, robbed of color by the fog, appeared as black smoke around the NPS housing area. Wooden barracks, built in the thirties by the CCC boys and held together over the years with mouse nests and multitudinous coats of paint, gave the housing the aspect of a ghost town.

A clamor of cowboy laughter added to the sense of a place out of time. There was the ring of booted feet on a wooden floor: Scotty. Wrapped in fog, Anna walked soundlessly toward the source of the racket—trail crew's bunkhouse.

Perhaps *in vino* there wasn't always *veritas,* but one

could usually count on a lack of discretion. With luck, she might learn something.

Blobs of muted color swam through the mist. Trail crew was cooking out. A barrel cut in half, metal fenceposts welded on for legs, served as their kitchen even when they were not on the trail. The smell of grilled meat warmed the damp. Once it had smelled good to Anna, like food. After years without it, it smelled only like death.

A grating sound, a pop, ragged cheering: another beer bottle opened with Scotty's teeth. "Now you're a bachelor again, you going to go with us over to Thunder Bay?" A coarse voice cut through the fog, making Anna wince as if she'd been suddenly exposed. Thunder Bay had one of the best-known houses of ill repute on the lake. From what Anna picked up, it sounded drunken, loud, and cheap. A surefire appeal.

"Naw," Scotty drawled. "Donna ever found out, she'd skin me alive. She keeps a pretty tight rein on this old stallion."

A growing nausea began creeping through Anna's wraithlike detachment.

"Not what I heard . . ." Anna recognized the dissenting voice. An enormous field of purple moved along the darker wall of the barracks. It could only be Pizza Dave. Or Moby Grape. Anna stifled a giggle. Two beers in a sauna had the kick of four anywhere else.

"Now what son of a bitch told you that?" Scotty growled.

"Told me what?" Dave asked innocently.

Scotty wasn't to be drawn or trapped. "Goddamn little intwerps," he muttered. Anna could barely make out the words but she knew her cloak of invisibility wouldn't hold up under closer scrutiny, so she stayed where she was. "Some little hippy-dippy seasonals were trying to drive a wedge between me and my wife," Scotty explained belligerently. Then he looked sly, an old cow-dog narrowing of the eyes and curling of the lip. "I made 'em an offer they couldn't refuse," he said, quoting a movie older than at least two of the boys on the crew. "Tonight I got a reminder for 'em in case they've forgotten you don't fuck with the old stallion."

There was a satisfied grumble, then laughter. These men were as old as the world, Anna thought. These were the men who'd gone to bear baitings, dogfights, beatings, hangings, witch burnings. Their heyday was over. Now they contented themselves with football and hunting— sports where they could either watch the pain from a safe distance or inflict it on creatures with only teeth and claws with which to defend themselves.

The talk settled on baseball. Fingers of mist moved in from the trees, curled around the hot metal of the grill. When the fingers felt their way back into the surrounding woods, Anna went with them.

Shivering, she let herself into the ranger station and clicked on the electric space heater Sandra Fox kept in the dispatch room. The heat smelled faintly of Delphi's fur. Anna sat in the dispatcher's chair, lost in thought. Fog pressed close, blinding the window Sandra would never see out of.

Anna had guessed Scotty was the author of the cryptic Hopkins note; now she was sure. There were several reasons he might have stooped to blackmail. Tinker and Damien could have rubbed him the wrong way once too often. The attention they were focusing on his marital problems could have been too great an embarrassment. But the most compelling reason was that the Coggins-Clarkes were getting too close to a truth Scotty didn't want brought to light; namely, where his wife had disappeared to.

Despite the capes and incense and Windigo stories, there was nothing fundamentally wrong with Tinker's or Damien's mind. If they put their heads together they would unravel most knotty mysteries. Scotty might have sensed that.

On impulse, Anna went into Ralph Pilcher's office. His desk, as always, looked like a sorting bin for recycled paper. Five minutes' shuffling turned up the key to his filing cabinet. It had been five minutes wasted: Pilcher had forgotten to lock it. She flipped quickly to the seasonal personnel file and pulled the Coggins-Clarkes' folders. Crossing her ankles on Pilcher's desk, she settled in for a good read.

A lot of it she already knew. Tinker, thirty-three, and Damien, twenty-four, had been married three years. Both had mentioned on the "previous employment" section that they had been married on the south rim of the Grand Canyon while working at that park. Skills and schools were listed, evaluations from other jobs. "Flaky but fine" seemed to be the consensus, though the District Ranger from Voyageurs had described Tinker as "sensitive, moody," the implication of instability being unmistakable.

On the final page—the one that invariably threw Anna into a frustrated rage, the page where the government asked for a list of the addresses of all residences used in the previous ten years—was the information she had been looking for.

From 1974 to 1980 Tinker had lived in Hopkins, Minnesota.

Anna dialed central dispatch at the police department in Houghton, trusting Pilcher would back her when the phone bill came. A woman answered. Anna identified herself and asked if she could run two 10-29s. The answer was yes. Anna read off first Tinker's, then Damien's driver's license numbers and their dates of birth, then waited through several minutes of computer clickings.

"No wants or warrants out on either Theresa Lynn Coggins nor Daryl Thomas Clarke."

"Thanks." Anna hung up. She could see why the two of them had changed their names. Theresa and Daryl: under those monikers no cape would swirl, no ritual candle flicker. Coggins and Clarke, no hyphen—the computer had yet to receive input of their marriage, or, more likely, the ceremony hadn't been formalized through legal channels.

Name changes and a nontraditional marriage but no warrants out for their arrest, not so much as an unpaid speeding ticket.

Whatever Scotty was threatening them with either wasn't illegal or was, as yet, unknown to the law. "Dirty laundry," he had called it. Tinker had said, if not in so many words, that the crime was a bad one. Pilfering? Vandalism? Grand theft auto? Child molestation? Ritual killings? The sheer variety of evils human beings thought up to perpetrate upon their fellows was enough to hint at the existence of a Satan or cast doubt upon the existence of a God.

Anna switched off the desk light and opened the window a few inches. Somewhere above the fog the light of a northern moon burned. Nature, in all her stunning beauty, was cruel, Anna knew, cruel but never vindictive. It was a wolf-eat-moose world out there. The storms that ravaged the lake, claimed lives, and the snows that drove men to madness, to cannibalism, did so without malice, without love or hatred. "Mother" Nature was a misnomer. It implied love and nurturing. The freedom Anna felt in the deserts and, now, in the woods of Isle Royale, was freedom from ties that bind, from envy, anger, friendship.

No wonder man was always out to conquer Nature, Anna thought. He can't bear it that she doesn't love him, or even hate him. She simply doesn't give a damn.

Scuffling sounds came in with the fog, then laughter, then laughter receding. Trail crew were settling into their second phase. The light drunks had dined and were wending their still somewhat steady way homeward. The hard core were settling in for the evening's sodden festivities.

Anna removed her feet from Pilcher's desk and peered through the mist, which grew more opaque with the coming night, to see who had chosen the better part of valor.

Scotty Butkus passed within a yard or two of the window where Anna sat. His leathery face was twisted in the same sly smile he'd worn when he'd mentioned his intention to deliver a reminder to the "intwerps."

Tinker and Damien were camped in Moskey. In July, the height of the season, even if they had told anyone of their destination, it would have been impossible to foretell precisely which camp they would find empty when they arrived. Knowing they were well hidden, Anna wasn't so much afraid for them as curious.

Without taking the time to replace the files or lock the cabinet, she slid the window up the rest of the way and stepped out onto the gravel. Keeping in step with Scotty's boot-shod stride, she used his noise to cover hers.

Once past the dock he veered left, following a dirt road into the heavily forested center of Mott. On the windblown duff, he made less of a racket and Anna found herself having to fall further behind to remain undetected.

Trees pressed like shadows onto the road. Without them it would have been possible to lose one's way even on a track rutted by two-wheeled carts. Fog robbed Anna of any sense of direction. She concentrated on the ever fainter sound of Scotty's footfalls.

The road forked. The left fork led up to the water tank that served the island. The right fork led to the permanent employees' apartments. It seemed years since she had walked that road, found Hawk in the District Ranger's yard playing with a baby, but it had been less than twelve hours.

Scotty passed Pilcher's door, passed the Chief of Interpretation's apartment. He was going home. To drink himself to sleep, probably, Anna thought as he went inside.

The hunt was finished. She turned to retrace her steps but a sense that the evening's activities were not over stopped her. The gift of the cloak of invisibility had been bestowed for a reason, and that reason had yet to manifest itself. "You're getting as bad as Tinker," Anna grumbled, but she stepped off the road, leaned against a tree, and slid down to wait in the cold.

Mudroom, hall, living room: a trail of light preceded Scotty through the apartment. Though Anna'd never been inside the Butkus residence, she could picture it in her mind: ruffled throws, pictures hung, artsy-craftsy attempts to soften the edges of government architecture. These feminine touches would be made pathetic now by a litter of beer cans, cigarette butts, and dirty underwear.

The overhead in the bedroom came on, and the parade

of lights was at an end. Anna's butt was growing damp from the loam, and the bark was beginning to bite through her shirt.

Scotty might have passed out, she reasoned, though he'd not seemed nearly that drunk. More likely he'd wandered back into the living room and was settled comfortably in front of the television while she refrigerated her posterior out in the dark.

With a sigh, she pulled herself to her feet. It was time to go home, and the *Belle Isle,* however unappealing, was home.

Twenty yards up the trail, she heard a door slam. Once again the fog became her friend. She stepped off the path into the shrouded darkness. Footsteps, sounding stealthy only because she waited in stealth, came up from the dwellings. Booted feet: Scotty Butkus passed her. He'd changed into dark clothing and carried a bundle a little larger than a human head under his left arm.

Windigo stories flooded Anna's mind and her flesh began to creep. Things that seemed laughable by the light of day took on a more forbidding aspect on a foggy night. She fell into step twenty or thirty paces behind him.

He stopped. Anna stopped. She almost believed she could feel him listening, feel him groping around in the fog with his mind. Feet planted in crushed gravel, she didn't dare move. Her breath rasped at the silence like a crosscut saw. Logically, she knew Scotty was at least eight or ten yards ahead of her, knew he couldn't move without noise any more than she could. Yet in the thick darkness she waited for the sudden hand clutching at her throat.

Scotty began to move away from her. Whatever had been the cause of his halt, the result must've been reassuring. He went on with a confident step. Anna went with him.

The fog moved in sinuous waves, some so dense she could see scarcely two yards, some thinning till she could see him in the glare of the few intruder lights scattered along the path.

Scotty kept on till he reached the docking area in front

of the Administration Building. Showing more sneakiness than he had to date, he studied the dock, peered at the office, then, satisfied he was alone, boarded the *Lorelei*.

Anna understood the sudden increase in caution. Blackmail was one thing, but using a government vehicle for personal reasons was serious business. Leeway was given to the North and South Shore Rangers due to the isolated nature of their duty stations, but in Rock Harbor Lucas held a hard line. It was a firing offense.

The *Lorelei*'s running lights flicked on, then the engines. Anna knew she'd never be able to follow in the *Belle Isle* without being detected. Even in the fog Scotty would recognize the familiar growl of the Bertram's engines.

She ran lightly across the quay, her rubber-soled shoes making no sound on the concrete. Just as the *Lorelei* eased away from the dock Anna sprang aboard. Two of the cabin windows faced the stern; between them was the door. Quick as a cat, she stepped to the door and put her back against it. In the cabin's blind spot she would be safe.

Faint green light glowed from the windows. Radar was on. The *Lorelei* crept out of the little harbor. In the middle of the channel, shores invisible in the fog, Scotty pulled back the throttles to an idle. A click: The cabin window slid open. Soft bumping—the rubber fenders. Scotty had forgotten them. Now he was pulling them in. In less than a minute he would come out on deck to pull up the stern fender.

For an irrational moment, Anna thought to do it for him.

The bow fender thumped in place. Boots clumped. Anna ducked down under the window and moved to the port side. As the cabin door swung open she got both feet on the narrow gunwale. Using the chrome rail that ran around the cabin roof, she clung to the side of the boat like a barnacle. Scotty hauled the starboard fender dripping onto the deck. He was so close she could smell his heavy cologne.

Anna became acutely aware of the vulnerability of her situation. He had but to pick up a boat hook and shove her

into the lake. In the frigid water, she would never make it
to shore. He was so close it seemed he must sense her,
smell her.

The much touted sixth sense in humans being more ev-
ident in the relating of incidents after the fact than the ex-
periencing of them, he didn't feel her. He secured the
fender and, with the tunnel vision common to people who
believe themselves alone, returned to the cabin.

Anna pulled herself up onto the roof, out of sight of the
windows. She felt the boat turning right. The wake curved
away to her left, corroborating the sensation. Dead reck-
oning said they would reach the mouth of the Rock Harbor
marina in a few minutes. Her guess was right—that was
where Scotty was headed. The *Lorelei* swung to the starboard, her wake forming a vanishing hook to port. Scotty
cut power. Anna lay still, straining her eyes for the first
glimpse of the dock.

The *Lorelei* coasted almost to a stop. Then, to the port
side, the concrete slab hove into view. Scotty had mis-
judged, and Anna spent a miserable minute exposed on the
cabin roof while he clawed at the shore with a boat hook,
his back to her. Using his scrabbling with the metal hook
to cover the sound of her own slitherings, she slid back off
the roof and perched again on the seaward gunwale. When
Scotty turned to go back into the cabin, though he passed
within four feet of her, she was no longer in sight.

Within seconds he reappeared, the bundle under his
arm, and stepped onto the quay. Anna waited till she heard
him step off the concrete and onto the wood-chip path that
led up from the water before she swung onto the deck.

In the *Lorelei*'s bow, in a compartment under the bench,
she found the District Ranger's briefcase. Inside, amid
brochures and charts, was a loaded .357, handcuffs, and a
canister of Mace. Despite the sinister cast of the night, the
.357 seemed too melodramatic. As nearly as she could tell,
Scotty wasn't armed. Anna slipped the Mace and cuffs in
her hip pockets.

Overhead, silver flickered by in scraps and fragments
where the moon poured through the overcast. Anna

watched till Scotty reached the tree line, then followed at a trot.

Once they were in the trees, the darkness was absolute. Hand extended like a Hollywood rendition of the blind, Anna inched forward, cringing at the thought that she was walking into Scotty's waiting hands.

The glare of an intruder light ignited the fog, and she moved more confidently toward it. All residence areas were kept safe from the magic of the night by the intrusive glare of blue floodlights. This one marked the enclave of the seasonals.

From the porch of the house where Tinker and Damien roomed, a yellow light softened the heartless glow. Anna stood still, trying to pierce the fog with eyes and ears. Just when she was beginning to think Scotty had been bound for a different destination, one she had not even guessed at, she heard the complaining screech of a window screen being pried from its seating.

She forgot the cold, her fear. Careful of the placement of each foot, but moving quickly for all of that, she crept to the corner of the house. A scraping sound followed by a thump announced the screen had been jerked clear of the frame and dropped to the ground. For several seconds, Anna stayed where she was, back pressed to the wall. When she looked around the corner, Scotty's boots were disappearing over the sill into Tinker and Damien's room.

Anna retreated to the front steps. No lights shone inside. Tinker and Damien's housemates either were out or had already gone to bed. She tried the door. It was unlocked, as she had expected it to be. Old boards, complaining of abuse, creaked as she crossed the living room. Trailing her fingers lightly along the walls, she moved down the dark hallway. At the second door on her right, she stopped and pressed an ear against the paneling. Furtive scuffling sounds came from within.

Silently, she turned the knob. When she was sure the latch was clear, she opened the door and stepped inside. The light switch was to her left. With the palm of her hand she shoved it on.

Scotty was crouched beside the bunk beds. In front of him on the floor was the package. Anna had come upon him in the act of unwrapping it.

"Howdy, Scotty, what's happening?"

Anna had expected surprise; she had counted on it. What she'd not bargained for was panic. From his crouched position, Scotty lunged. His considerable weight struck her in the thighs and slammed her against the door so hard her thoughts scattered.

An instant later her mind refocused and she took in the situation as a camera would take a still shot. Near her waist, Butkus's dark hair beaded with condensation from the fog; one booted foot trailed, the other, coiled beneath him, was lost from sight. His arm was locked behind her back, his shoulder wedged under her rib cage.

When the trailing foot recoiled, Scotty would lunge again, cracking her ribs and maybe her spine against the door.

Anna grabbed a handful of hair and, holding his head fast, gouged her right thumb up under his left ear where the angle of his jaw met his skull. The pressure on her rib cage increased. She dug the thumb deeper.

A little pain goes a long way. Even through his alcoholic haze, he had to be feeling the bite of the compliance hold. "Let go. Let go," she repeated clearly and she pushed harder. She could feel him becoming paralyzed. "Do as I say. Do it. Let go."

His arms dropped. He tried to say something. It could have been the word "Okay."

Still holding his head between her fist and the gouging thumb, Anna eased herself from the door. He fell onto both knees. His hands came up to pry her thumb away, but she screwed her knuckle into the nerve. "Hands down. On the floor. All the way. Do it. Do it."

Scotty did it. She followed, pressing till he was face-down on the worn linoleum. "Hands on the small of your back. Cross your wrists. Hands back."

Anna put one knee on his neck and one on his butt, then fished Pilcher's handcuffs from her pocket. Scotty twitched when he heard the familiar ratcheting noise, but it was too late. She rapped them on his wristbones and quickly made them fast.

Less than a minute had elapsed since she had entered the room. Her heart was pounding and her vision growing fuzzy. Anna sat down on the edge of the bunk. Scotty lay at her feet. One of her peers, a fellow ranger, a commissioned federal law enforcement officer, was bound like a piglet. Anna didn't know what to do with him. Odds were good she was nearly as surprised at the turn of events as he was. And probably in more trouble.

The National Park Service would not be anxious to believe breaking and entering to further an employee's blackmailing another employee to keep her from exposing God knew what. If Scotty pieced together a good story—a practical joke, climbed in the wrong window—Anna would end up at best with egg on her face, at worst on charges for assaulting an officer. She fervently hoped either Butkus wasn't thinking that clearly, or the package contained a severed human head or at least a kilo of something incriminating.

"Jesus, Scotty, what the hell is going on?" she asked peevishly.

"None of your goddamn business," he said from the floor.

Anna thought about that one. "It is," she decided. "You're blackmailing a friend of mine. What're you holding over Tinker?"

"You can't prove I know a goddamn thing about those two."

"Then tell me what you know about the late Denny Castle. Like what made him 'late'?"

No answer.

"Where's Donna?" Anna tried. Scotty said something that could've been "Goddam intwerps." Anna was tired. And she was tired of Scotty Butkus. "Leave Tinker alone," she said. "Stop the blackmail. It's killing her."

"The hell I will." He began to struggle, trying to sit up. Anna pushed him down with her foot. He banged against the board-and-brick bookcase the Coggins-Clarkes had assembled beneath the room's one window. Candles rocked precariously. A cheap Instamatic flash camera teetered near the edge.

Anna picked it up. Click! Flash! "Gotcha!" she said. Scotty actually screamed as if the light had burned him. "The 'old stallion' knocked down and trussed up like a steer by a rangerette," Anna said. Click. Flash. Scotty scraped his face away, turning it against the floor. "Too late. Got a good one," she told him.

"This camera is Tinker's. So is the film. I'll see that she gets it. If you bother her, if whatever her big secret is leaks out in any way, I'll encourage her to have the negatives blown up poster-size and put on trail crew's bunkhouse door."

For a moment Scotty neither spoke nor moved, and Anna began to be afraid the shock had been too much and he'd died of a massive coronary.

"You'll pay for this," he growled finally. Despite the threat, she was relieved to hear him speak. "I got friends in damn near every park in this country. Every one of 'em's getting a call from me. I'll by God smear your name from Acadia to Joshua Tree. You want a career in the Park Service? After this little stunt, you haven't got a snowball's chance in hell. Not a hope."

"These people known you long?" Anna asked.

"Damn right they have."

"Then I can always hope they'll consider the source."

Scotty struggled to his knees. Anna let him. "Unlock these goddamn cuffs," he demanded.

Anna just looked at him, not rising from the bed where she sat. "Ralph keeps the key in his briefcase on the *Lorelei*. I didn't bring it." She got up then, held open the bedroom door. Scotty crawled through and she watched as he worked his way to his feet using the walls of the narrow hallway.

She closed and locked the door. Scotty would get the cuffs off, but it would take him a while. It would keep him away from her.

Suddenly too tired to stand, she sat back down on the bottom bunk. At her feet was the plastic-wrapped bundle Scotty had come across land and water to leave in Tinker's way.

A growing dread would not allow her to open it slowly, scientifically. Grabbing two corners, Anna yanked the bag and shook it. The body of a baby tumbled out, and she screamed.

But it wasn't a baby. It was a plastic baby doll and it had been painted blue from head to foot.

CHAPTER 20

Anna clicked through the rest of the pictures in Tinker's Instamatic. She took two of the doll and two of the torn screen. When the film was used up, she rewound it and dropped the roll into her pocket. Tinker could not be trusted to be sufficiently hard-hearted. Anna could.

She wrapped the blue baby in its plastic shroud, then glanced at the clock: a rhinestone Sylvester, tail and eyes twitching off the seconds. After ten P.M. and she was marooned in Rock Harbor with no food, no wine, no dry clothes, no change of underwear, and no place to sleep.

Patience would just be closing the restaurant at the lodge. All Anna needed to do was look moderately pitiful and she would provide everything but the underwear. Anna bundled herself and the baby out the window, replaced the screen, and set off through the fog at a trot.

The lights of the lodge glowed a warm welcome. Coming out of the darkness of the trees, Anna felt as if she'd been lost in the wilderness for a month. "I once was lost, but now am found." Whistling the old hymn, she felt her spirits rise.

Two parties, one of six and one of eight, still lingered in the dining room. Though they were subject to the glares of a waitress and two busboys, Anna was grateful to them. They had forced the kitchen to stay open. And the bar. She ordered pasta Alfredo and a glass of Chianti. The pasta was gooey and the bread reheated but, glad to be in a warm well-lit place where nice people brought food, she was not inclined to be picky.

Patience, looking tired but well groomed, had drifted over to Anna's table and been wheedled out of an invitation to sleep on her sofa. By the time a pretty young waiter, angling for a tip, brought over a second glass of Chianti, Anna had begun to feel downright expansive. Even the snufflings of Carrie Ann, trying to chip the crockery at the sideboard, seemed more homey than sullen.

Near eleven the larger party called for their check, and Patience felt she could go home. Carrie Ann in tow, she came by Anna's table. Scarcely into her teens, Carrie was already taller and bigger than her mother.

"We are practicing togetherness." Patience explained Carrie's late hours as Anna pushed up out of her chair, then finished the last swallow of Chianti. "Surveillance in the guise of Motherly Love has taken the place of trust and 'do your own thing.' Certain persons of the childish persuasion seemed to think three A.M. was a good hour to retire."

Anna found herself wishing Patience would address her insults/parables/whatevers to her daughter instead of banking them like an expert billiard player off Anna. No such thing as a free lunch, she reminded herself. She was to be had for a meal and a bed.

"More star-crossed disappearances?" Anna said to say something.

"In spades," Patience replied.

"Oh God!" Carrie Ann rolled her oversized brown eyes. "What speech now? AIDS or 'when I was your age'?"

"Shut up!" her mother snapped. To Anna she said: "Get your tubes tied."

Anna began to wonder if partaking in this dispute was going to be too much to pay for a dry bed.

Shortly after they reached the Bittners' apartment, Carrie disappeared into her room.

"Gad!" Patience threw herself onto the vinyl of an institutional rendition of an overstuffed chair. "I need a drink. Need, not want: the point when connoisseur becomes addict. Can I pour you something?"

"Whatever," Anna replied. She wanted the hot shower, the flannel gown, the sofa Patience had lent her in the past, but, ever mindful of her beggar-not-chooser status, she schooled herself to listen to anything from confession to kvetching.

"Wine! Lord, what would we do without it?" Patience asked rhetorically. "Wine is about the only thing you can count on. Too bad you can't choose vintage children. Can't say, 'Ah, yes, '78, that was an excellent year for children. Sweet, a little precocious, but not impertinent.' Do you remember Prohibition?"

"Not firsthand," Anna replied. "I've seen the movies. Loved Sean Connery in *The Untouchables*."

"It almost killed the California wine industry. A crippling blow." Patience brought two glasses of red wine over to the couch where Anna huddled dreaming of dry flannel gowns. "Some kept going in secret—like the Catholics in Communist Russia or the secular artists during the Inquisition—artists smuggling their art out of a repressive country."

"Mmm." Anna drank of the red. It slid down rich, uncompromising. "California?" she guessed.

"No!" Patience laughed. "Hungarian. Who cares?" she said with a sudden change of attitude. "Wine's wine. It'll get you there."

" 'There's' not where it used to be," Anna said wearily and, with the words, realized she'd probably consumed enough alcohol for one night.

"You sound like a woman who's had a long day," Patience observed.

"Long day," Anna agreed. She found she didn't want to talk about it, about Jo, Stanton and his pointed questions, about Scotty or blackmail or blue plastic baby dolls. What she wanted, she realized, was to watch TV. Preferably something familiar, something without too much violence.

"Isn't *Murder, She Wrote* on tonight?" she asked. "I haven't looked at television for a while."

CHAPTER 21

A good night's sleep had cleared Anna's head. Sitting on Patience's couch, warm in a tangle of bedclothes, she turned the doll between her hands. It was fairly realistic: The legs bowed, the arms were pudgy, the glassy blue eyes closed when the little body was placed on the horizontal. There were no marks of violence, no tiny broken legs, no doll-sized knife in its back. Nothing that Anna could see to indicate a threat. The blue was the only abnormality.

Blue to indicate death by suffocation or drowning, immersion in the icy waters of Superior; a death, or a burial like Denny Castle's? Then why the "Hopkins" in the blackmail note?

Anna put the toy back in its garbage bag. "Patience, can I use your phone?" she hollered. From behind the bathroom door came a muffled affirmative.

A private phone: Anna felt the luxury of it as she lifted the receiver. Dutifully she recited her credit card number to a user-friendly AT&T operator and was channeled through long-distance information to the Hopkins Public Library. An efficient-sounding woman answered on the first ring.

Anna introduced herself. "I'm doing a background check on a Theresa Coggins," she told the librarian. "She lived in Hopkins from 1974 to 1980. Is there any way you could check the local paper for any reference to her during those years?"

Normally, no, but it wasn't a busy morning and the librarian had always wanted to be a park ranger, so yes, this once. She would call back.

Patience emerged from the bath in a cloud of commercial scent. Her slender frame was draped with tasteful elegance in dove-gray linen with shoes to match. "How do you do it?" Anna asked.

"Perhaps I didn't marry well," Patience said with a wink, "but I divorced brilliantly. Carrie Ann!"

Looking dull as an ox beside her mother, Carrie trudged up the hall and was taken off to the lodge in maternal custody.

Anna showered with the bathroom door open so she could hear the phone. As she was toweling dry, it rang. Mindful of her guest manners, she answered, "Bittner residence, Anna Pigeon speaking."

It was the librarian from Hopkins. Yes, there had been a number of articles on Theresa Coggins published in the newspaper between 1978 and 1980. Ms. Coggins and her husband, David Coggins, had been on trial for manslaughter. They had been accused of the wrongful death of their daughter, Constantina, aged ten months, twelve days.

"Whoa!" Anna breathed.

"What?"

"Nothing. Go on."

"They were finally acquitted," the librarian said, sounding mildly disappointed. "That's everything, except a wedding announcement two years later: David Coggins marrying a woman named Agnes Larson. Nothing else on Theresa Coggins. She may have left town or changed her name."

"Do you have a fax machine?" Anna asked abruptly.

"There's one at the post office."

Anna gave the librarian the park's fax number and her own profuse thanks.

The newspaper articles beat her to the ranger station on Mott. Seventeen articles in all, covering the death of the child, the trial, the public outcry, the acquittal.

The first paragraph of the first article told the story. "During last Sunday's cold snap, when temperatures were hovering at thirteen below with a windchill factor in the minus forties, David and Theresa Coggins went cross-country skiing on Winetka Lake near their home in south Hopkins. They took their ten-month-old daughter, Constantina, along in a backpack worn by Mrs. Coggins. Exertion kept David and Theresa from feeling the cold, but the baby, confined to the backpack froze to death.

" 'I thought she was sleeping,' said the nineteen-year-old mother. 'Then she just wouldn't wake up.' "

Anna leaned back and rested her head against the wall in the dispatch room. A blue baby doll: "Scotty should have his heart cut out with a dull Boy Scout knife."

"Put me on your list of volunteers," Sandra Fox said, never taking her fingers from the printout she was reading. "What is it?"

"Nothing."

"You're a shit, you know that, Anna Pigeon?"

"I'm just postponing the inevitable. You always find out everything eventually. Think of it as a challenge."

"I hate that damn fax machine," Sandra said without rancor. "Messages blatting in and out of my dispatch and I can't read them."

Anna chuckled aloud to let Sandra know she knew it was a joke. Sandra went on with her reading, fingers keeping her place when she was interrupted by the phone or the radio. Anna slipped off her shoe and buried her toes in Delphi's warm fur. The dog thumped the floor with her tail.

Scotty was blackmailing Tinker to stop her and her husband from investigating the disappearance of his wife, the alleged lover of the dead man.

Damning as it was, Anna was not convinced Scotty had killed Denny. She could see Scotty, in a drunken rage, accidentally killing his wife. But the Castle murder appeared calculating, dangerous, clever.

"Scotty hasn't got the balls," she muttered.

"Beginning, middle, and end," Sandra said, "or I don't want to hear any of the story."

Anna relapsed into thought. If not Scotty, who? Jim Tattinger, because he was a creep? Because Castle was a threat to him professionally? Tattinger had left the Virgin Islands under a pall. Had Denny known why? Had Tattinger been suspected of plundering the shipwrecks? Suspected but not proven guilty, so the accusation was never made public? Or, more likely, to avoid bad press had the NPS decided to "handle it from within"?

Was Tattinger continuing those activities at ISRO?

"Sandra, do me a favor?"

"No. No way. Not possible. Tit for tat. Eye for an eye. You scratch my back, et cetera."

"Find out why Jim Tattinger left the Virgin Islands."

"Is Jim being investigated in the Castle thing?"

"No," Anna admitted. "There's not a scrap of evidence against him. That's why I need you to find out for me. Personnel, the District Ranger—the official channels will be closed."

"Island dispatcher to island dispatcher?" Sandra said with a smile. "The centers through which all information flows? You want me to abuse my position of trust to wheedle gossip from an unsuspecting peer?"

"That's it in a nutshell."

"Tit for tat," Sandra replied.

Anna told her what she could of the circumstantial evidence built up around Tattinger, of finding him sneaking around near where the *Kamloops* went down after the murder but before the body recovery. She wanted to hint at Jo's and the Bradshaws' innocence, but until they were officially cleared by the FBI, she didn't dare. It wasn't much, but Sandra took it as a sign of good faith.

"I'll see what I can do," she promised.

Anna thanked her and left for the sunshine on the dock. The fog had burned away and the day promised to reach close to seventy degrees. She was anxious to get back to the north shore, resume her routine duties.

The *Belle Isle* needed refueling, and Anna's supply of candy bars was perilously low, so she made a stop at Rock. Pacing in front of the bench above the harbor was Damien Coggins-Clarke, preparing for his nature walk. Anna jogged up the path in his direction. Once again she was given a less than enthusiastic greeting.

"It's okay," Anna said gently. "There'll be no more threats. The past won't be dragged out. It's been taken care of."

Damien stopped pacing and looked at her squarely for the first time. "The Windigo is so powerful. People eaten up with fear. They must devour others but they'll never be sealed. I thought I could take care of her," he added simply. "But all I could do was love her."

"In the end that will be all she'll remember ever needing," Anna said.

Damien paced the length of the bench again, his eyes on something farther away than the mountains. "Is it over?" he asked when he'd returned to where Anna was standing.

"The blackmail is over," Anna replied. For a mother the death of a child would never be over.

Two beats of silence passed in which Damien's face slowly lit up from within. "I want to give you something."

Inwardly, Anna began to squirm. Gifts made her uncomfortable. Before she could voice her concern and wriggle away, Damien had fished something out of his trouser pocket. "Here. It's a greenstone. We found it out from shore," he assured Anna. Collecting greenstones on the island was illegal but off shore the practice was allowed. "It's the nicest one I've ever found." He pushed it into her hands.

Anna looked at the glossy jade-colored rock fitting as neatly as a robin's egg in her palm. It was a beautiful specimen, rounded from years of wave action, deep clear green with veins of a lighter color running through it in an un-characteristic pattern.

"You were always supposed to have it," Damien said earnestly, as if afraid she was going to give it back. "I just didn't know till today. When I brought it up, Tinker said, 'Look how the gray zigzags, like the gray through Anna's braids.' See? It's always been yours."

"Thank you," Anna said, and closed her fingers around the stone.

Damien looked pleased. Behind him a noisy group of mostly teenage girls was coming up from the lodge. "Looks like your audience is arriving," Anna said.

"I want to run and tell Tinker the good news—will you take my nature walk, Anna?"

He enjoyed the look of stark terror on her face for a moment before he said: "Just kidding."

As Anna made her escape she heard Damien's girlish voice calling "Thanks!" after her and: "Oscar says you are one stout fella."

Oscar, it seemed, could communicate telepathically over fairly good distances. The whimsy pleased Anna.

CHAPTER 22

The week passed peacefully, and for that Anna was grateful. The most traumatic incident on the north shore was cutting a fishhook out of the thigh of an urbanite up from the Twin Cities on his first fishing trip. He got no sympathy from his companions, all seasoned lake fishermen, who felt he should dig it out himself.

Lucas Vega came by Amygdaloid on his way up from Windigo on one of his periodic tours of the island. He had a cup of coffee with Anna and told her the results of the autopsy and Stanton's alibi sleuthing.

With the time of death established, Stanton had been able to check alibis. Hawk and Holly had been cleared of committing the murder. On the night Denny had been killed they were in Grand Marais. The *3rd Sister* was in the Voyageur Marine undergoing minor repairs. Hawk and Holly had closed the bar at the hotel toasting Denny's nuptials. At three o'clock in the morning the bartender had taken them back to his place and stored them in his guest room. Brother and sister were too drunk to drive.

Unwilling to abandon his drug theory completely, Stanton still considered them possible accomplices. If Denny had been killed by drug dealers, the Bradshaws might have been involved in his alleged drug-running business.

Jo Castle had been completely cleared of suspicion. She had been alone on her wedding night but had been so distraught by what she believed to be the groom's defection to another woman's bed that she had spent the night on the phone to her mother. Jo's mom corroborated the story, as did AT&T. The call had started near midnight and gone till nearly dawn. Denny'd been seen alive around ten-thirty P.M. when he and Scotty had had their little scuffle. The ninety minutes Jo was unaccounted for wasn't time enough to commit a murder on the other side of the island at the bottom of the lake.

Anna was unsurprised at the news. In her mind they'd all three ceased to be suspects. She was sorry Hawk and Holly had not been freed from the entangling web that was being spun around the crime. The *3rd Sister* was still not safe from impoundment.

The Chief Ranger went on to tell Anna that the autopsy and the ensuing investigation noted that the dive knife Jim found had been open and the blade chipped from recent use, and the corpse had lacerations on the fingers, as did the diving suit's gloves. Particles of paint were found on the gloves. Findings indicated something more than a death by natural causes. The investigation was far from closed.

Vega commended Anna on her unraveling of the Bradshaws' part in the mystery and suggested she take a couple of days off from patrol and clean the ranger station at Amygdaloid. He was not amused by her assertion that the rat droppings and spiderwebs were historical artifacts and necessary to maintain the building's rustic allure.

With a charming shyness, he declined a second cup of coffee. He had a dinner date, he said, with Patience Bittner.

For all the gentility of delivery, a Chief Ranger's suggestions were orders. The last two days of Anna's work week were spent elbow-deep in soapy water swamping out the office and putting up with the good-humored ribbing of the fishermen about finding her true calling.

On Monday evening, the day before her two lieu days, the *3rd Sister* docked at Amygdaloid. Anna was rehanging the door on the pit toilet, moving the hinges slightly to give the screws a better bite into the weathered wood.

She'd seen neither Hawk nor Holly since Hawk's confession over egg salad. Feeling cowardly, she pretended not to see him walking up from the dock.

"The glamour never stops, huh?"

Mustering a smile, she turned. He stood a few yards away, out of the pit toilet's olfactory range. "Never does," Anna said. She reapplied herself to her screwdriver, keeping eyes and hands busy. "I hear you and Holly have lost the distinction of being prime suspects."

"Mostly thanks to you."

"I heard it was thanks to public drunkenness in Grand Marais."

Hawk laughed obligingly. Anna began to feel a little more at ease. Still, fearing silence, she asked: "Any squirrels this trip?"

"No squirrels. Next week. A couple out of Florida. He knows all there is to know about diving. Told Holly so on the phone. But a client's a client. We've got to make hay—or payments—while the sun shines."

Anna finished the top hinge, tested the door, and then, for the first time, really looked at Hawk. He appeared tired and worn. "Are you worried about losing the *Third Sister*?" she asked.

"Stanton's still nosing around. There are enough rumors floating on this lake to keep him interested a long while."

"What rumors?" Anna asked.

"The usual. That there's drug traffic. Secondhand stories of wild parties out on the lake."

"Anything to the rumors?" she asked.

"Probably. But Holly and I don't mix enough to know where the stories point. At the moment, I think if I did I'd run and tattle to Stanton. Everybody's got their price. Mine's that boat."

"And Holly."

He looked pained, and Anna was sorry she'd needled him. She turned back to the pit toilet and began gathering her tools. "Lucas put a moratorium on staff diving the *Kamloops.* Too dangerous, he said. He's right. None of us but Ralph dive enough to be really good at it. But something was going on down there. Something to do with the porthole where Denny's knife was found," Anna said. "Another look at the site couldn't hurt."

She could see the suggestion filtering into Hawk's mind. He and Holly were professional divers, the best, and they had a vested interest in the outcome of the investigation. "You're a jewel," Hawk said suddenly and kissed her lightly on the cheek. "If nothing else, it'll keep us from feeling so helpless."

"Take pictures," Anna called after him as he ran back toward the dock.

Tuesday morning, the first day of Anna's weekend, she motored over to Lane Cove, then walked overland the five miles to Rock Harbor. Mid-July, and the island had settled into the heart of a summer so lush her desert-born-and-bred mind could scarcely conceive of the largess. In clearings between stands of pine and aspen were meadows waist-deep in wildflowers. Red wood lilies, fire-colored jewelweed, the delicate blue flags of the wild iris, joe-pye weed; and everywhere the brilliant yellows of the Canada hawkweed.

In Texas each fragile blossom had been cause for celebration. Many times Anna had left Gideon to munch the dry grasses while she crawled among the rocks for a better view of a solitary claret cup. Isle Royale had such wild abundance she found herself taking it for granted, walking blind through a shimmering patchwork of living color while her mind toiled away on some tedious detail of human interaction.

The bustle of Rock Harbor came almost as a relief. She was freed from the responsibility of appreciating a beauty so complex it was nearly a burden. "Let's get small," Anna said, and loosed her mind to its petty pursuits.

Jim Tattinger gave her a lift to Mott Island in the *Loon,* Resource Management's runabout. He was full of the autopsy and the alibis. It was his contention that the Bradshaws had been let off too lightly. "I thought that Holly might be okay, but Denny'd gotten to her. She had that hard edge women get when they're older. She'd do anything, I bet. There's that twin thing," he insisted. "Like in the movies. One's in the bar while the other one kills somebody and everybody thinks it's the same person."

How the one in the bar could toast himself all night in front of dozens of witnesses, Jim didn't say.

Though she often found herself hoping he was the culprit, in her heart of hearts Anna suspected Jim Tattinger was too little to have murdered Denny Castle. Not just physically spare but psychologically shriveled. Kicking dogs or pulling the wings off flies seemed more his style. Anna knew he would feel no guilt. His self-justifications were rock-solid from years of exercise. Had Jim committed a murder, he would never give himself away from remorse, and would feel only anger and resentment if his crime was brought to light.

Were he stealing artifacts, destroying their historical significance, and robbing the public trust, Anna could easily imagine him on the stand, his Adam's apple bobbing in his skinny neck, nasal voice whining: "It was just a bunch of old junk hardly anybody got to see anyway. At least now it's where people can look at it. . . ."

Anna let him rattle on. Tattinger had become what Christina always referred to as "a bit of a pill." There was no arguing with him because there was no substance to his complaints. Just sourness born of disappointment.

Even in this generous and understanding mood, Anna was glad to escape his company when the *Loon* docked at Mott.

Sandra Fox was in the dispatch office. For once both

radio and phone were silent. She sat with her feet up on the printer table reading *Peyton Place.*

"Reviewing the classics, I see." Anna flopped down in the visitor chair and winked at Delphi.

"I only read the underlined parts." Sandra set the book aside. "It's sociological research. I'm gathering tons of insight into the Park Service in general and Isle Royale in particular."

"It's beginning to feel a little like that, isn't it?"

"You make it sound like a bad thing," the dispatcher said with a comfortable chuckle. "All part of the grand comedy, Anna. A veritable combination pizza of life laid out on our dinner plate."

Anna laughed. She'd been taking things too seriously. Monomania did that. And she was not yet cured. "Find anything out about Jim's quitting the Virgin Island job?"

"Oh, Anna, you user you! No flowers, no candy, you never call me the next day." Sandra chortled and Anna squirmed. "As a matter of fact, I did garner the odd tidbit. Alicia Folk is the dispatcher down there. Good talker. Nice gal. After a few preliminaries, I got the goods. It seems our Jimmy boy was having a torrid affair with the District Ranger's daughter. The DR raised a modest stink, and Jimmy left for a healthier climate. Who would've thunk it? Still waters and all that . . ."

Anna shook her head. "That can't be it. Affairs in the Park Service are so common as to be de rigueur. I'm surprised first wives haven't been declared a threatened and endangered species. An affair with a woman—even the boss's daughter—"

Sandra interrupted with a clucking of her tongue. "You are jumping to conclusions, Anna. Making assumptions. Did I say the affair was with a woman?"

Anna waited with a blank mind and a blank look on her face.

"The District Ranger's daughter was twelve years old."

Anna had a sour taste in her mouth. She needed to talk with Patience.

Sandra looked fire from blind eyes. "Kinda makes you proud to be human, don't it?"

"What happened to the little girl?" Anna asked.

"Who knows? Little girls are always spirited away in cases like this. What could happen? Hopefully she wasn't pregnant. Hopefully she wasn't punished. Who knows?"

"Why didn't Jim get canned? Seems there were grounds enough."

"You know the gub'mint. It's harder to fire somebody than it is to get a tax bill passed in an election year. He was counseled. Had to serve a little time on the couch. That stuff seldom seems to take."

Anna made a mental note to ask Molly why. And if anybody ever got their money back. She stood, stretched. The joints in her ankles cracked, and Delphi cocked a concerned eyebrow. Sandra picked up *Peyton Place* and settled it against her thighs.

"Let me know when you're finished with that," Anna said. "I think it should be required reading for all law enforcement personnel."

"You dig, you get dirt," Sandra replied philosophically.

Lunchtime had come and gone. Anna was beginning to feel light-headed. Back out in the sunshine, she found a warm, windless place on the dock and dug her sandwich and water bottle out of her daypack.

Twenty yards away Scotty Butkus and Jim Tattinger stood together near the fire-weather box in front of the ranger station. There was just enough of a breeze to move the line on the flagpole, and the low grumble of their words was punctuated by ringing as the metal fasteners hit against the pole.

Anna could tell by the looks they shot her way that they were not only talking about her but wanted her to know it. She'd not made a friend of either. For all her bravado, she knew Scotty could and would make trouble for her. Even if it was only the burr-under-the-saddle variety, it would be tiring to deal with. It was already tiring. She chose to ignore them.

Ducklings—black ducks—feathered now but still in the

impossibly cute stage, rocked around the stern of the *Loon*. As if on cue, they'd all flip bottoms up and for several seconds Anna could see nothing but orange feet and brown feathery rumps. The mother paddled nearby, a running commentary of instructional quacks percolating from her bill.

Anna chewed her cheese sandwich and resisted the urge to throw so much as an illegal crumb to the baby ducks.

The ducklings put her in mind of Donna Butkus, who fed the birds every morning on a secluded stretch of shore; Tinker and Damien standing by, opportunistic birders who'd never dream of feeding the wildlife—or missing a chance to view it if someone else did.

She pictured Donna from the descriptions she'd been given since the woman was first reported missing: an old-fashioned pretty, gentle, southern dumpling, the perfect Texas wife. Married young and—one presumed from the rest of the package—innocent, to a man more than twice her age, then swept away from family and sunshine and home to a snowed-in Houghton winter.

Anna imagined her loneliness before her sister, Roberta, had come, her disorientation. Scotty would react the only way he knew how: with anger and alcohol. Denny, with his gentleman's ways and fanatic's intensity, had stepped into the breach. Donna's confusion must have deepened into pain, all her training, socialization, upbringing cleaving her to a husband whom she may not ever have really loved. A husband who beat her. Scotty's jealousy would grow. There would be drunken scenes, tears, more violence.

Then what? Anna asked as the ducklings followed their mom out of sight around the port side of the *Loon*. One day Donna disappears and Scotty lies about it. Even her sister doesn't know where she's gone. Scotty orders a case of pickle relish. Damien swears Scotty is the human personification of the Windigo. Donna's best friend reports Scotty was ". . . killing Donna . . . eating her alive . . ."

Woman's intuition or just an unfortunate choice of words?

Scotty and Jim finished their tête-à-tête. Butkus disappeared into the Administration Building. Jim crossed the concrete to where the *Loon* was moored. Both pointedly refused to acknowledge Anna. She had to holler Jim's name twice before he responded, and then she thought he was going to refuse her a ride to Rock. Good sense, if not manners, prevailed, and he acquiesced.

On the short trip Anna had trouble not staring at him. She'd never seen a pedophile before. In every seminar she'd ever attended on sexual deviants, the instructors had stressed what normal, guy-next-door types they often were, attractive men with good personalities, with wives and children. Jim Tattinger broke with tradition. He looked like a child molester right out of Central Casting's Obvious Perverts book.

For half the trip she debated the wisdom of letting him know she was aware of his propensity; debated whether it would scare him into walking the straight and narrow, or push him into taking a risk that might be damaging to his latest inamorata.

She chose silence. She would talk with Patience, then the Chief Ranger. After all, that's what he was paid the big bucks for.

At the lodge, Anna was told Patience and her daughter had gone to the mainland for a few days to get Carrie's braces tightened. She was glad of the reprieve. This was one hornet's nest she did not look forward to stirring up.

CHAPTER 23

Anna stayed around Rock Harbor just long enough to collect her mail from the *Ranger III.* As always, there was a letter from Chris to be treasured away for later. As she headed overland toward Lane Cove and her duty station, an unexpected bit of good news came her way.

Damien ran after her. Boyish again, joyous, he loped along the asphalt path as graceful as a greyhound. "She's birding again!" he told Anna of his wife. Anna gathered that to bird was to live and was glad that Tinker's burden had been one that she could ease, if only a little. "We're spending our weekends at McCargo Cove. If there's a nesting peregrine, she'll see it. She sees *everything.*"

The stress he gave the word seemed to indicate that Tinker saw both the visible and the invisible, the corporeal and the existential. Anna did not disagree.

On the walk over Greenstone Ridge Anna dawdled along, enjoying the sense of time and immortality the long summer days engendered. In several places where the island's backbone had been rubbed free of its fur of trees and shrubs, the trail cut across solid stone, the way picked out only by rock cairns.

On one such expanse of bare ridge, Anna went off the trail till she was out of sight, divested herself of her pack, and lay down. The gray rock soaked up and savored the weak rays of Michigan's sun, the heat soothing her back and shoulders.

Her mind wandered back to New York City, the apartment in Hell's Kitchen, Zachary waiting on tables at a little Mexican restaurant on Ninth Avenue, waiting for his big break. There was no money. Cockroaches scuttled like evil spirits every time a light was switched on. The kids in apartment 1C spray-painted obscenities on the walls of the foyer and smashed the mailboxes. The lady across the air shaft slept all day and screamed at her husband all night. And that was the summer the city was infested with rats. The *Post* was running headlines on it. Zach reported seeing a rat so big coming down the tracks into the Forty-second Street subway station that nine tourists tried to board, thinking it was the number 7 train.

Yet Anna had been happy then. There was Zachary and there was hope. It doesn't take much, she thought. You'd think it would be easier to hang on to.

She stared up at the sky, felt the stone warm beneath her spine. Playing in her mind, she began replacing her body, molecule by molecule, with bits of the earth.

There would be peace in shedding one's humanity, rest in moving to the slower geological rhythms, charm in feeling the skittering of animal feet over one's chest, the brush of autumn leaves settling in the wrinkles of one's skin, blankets of snow cooling the body into a long sleep.

Mosquitoes woke Anna. It was dusk and she was laid out like a smorgasbord. She awakened from her dream of the earth thinking: You can't get blood from a stone.

But if any mosquitoes could, it would be the mosquitoes of Isle Royale. Pursued by bloodsucking demons, she ran the last mile through the gathering darkness and escaped out onto the water in the *Belle Isle*.

• • •

Two days later as she grumbled around Amygdaloid dock with buckets, sluicing off the fish guts some slob fisherman had deposited in her absence, the *3rd Sister* motored up the channel and glided effortlessly to her mooring. Without looking, Anna knew that Holly was the pilot.

She waded through the herring gulls her impromptu bouillabaisse had collected, and helped Hawk tether the lines to the cleats.

Holly sprang from the deck with a grace born of strength. Both she and her brother looked better than they had since Denny had been killed. Some of the arrogance that was an integral part of their charm was beginning to creep back into their bearing.

By now Hawk must have told his sister that Anna knew of the incest. Anna suspected that Hawk seldom had a thought he did not share with her; that things did not exist for him until they existed for Holly as well.

Either Holly didn't mind, or she was hiding it well. She greeted Anna with the same short, sharp smile she always had. "We've got the pictures," she said. "Picked them up in Grand Marais this morning."

For a moment Anna was at a loss. Then she remembered they were going to do a bounce dive on the *Kamloops* to see what they could find.

Like most underwater photos, those Holly had taken seemed slightly out of focus. Time had been severely limited. She and Hawk had confined themselves to the area along the hull where they had found Denny's corpse floating. Three of the shots were of the porthole where Jim and Anna had noticed the scratches. The remaining seven were of the surrounding area.

Since the body recovery dive, Anna had collected the stats on the *Kamloops,* garnered not only from the original builder's specifications but from the findings of the Submerged Cultural Resources Unit out of Santa Fe. Information on the ship was not hard to come by. Like all ISRO's wrecks, it was quite celebrated.

Having perfunctorily cleared her desk in the ranger station, Anna spread out a diagram of the ship and the ten photographs the Bradshaws provided. Brother and sister hovered interestedly while she gathered her thoughts.

As she had guessed, the scratched porthole led into the captain's quarters. According to the builder's specs and corroborated by Anna's memory, the diameter of the opening was just over a foot and a half, 19.6 inches to be exact.

Anna picked up the photos of the porthole and examined them carefully. Then she took an envelope from her desk, removed two pictures from it, and compared them with the Bradshaws' photos.

"Jim took these the day we recovered Denny's body. Look." Anna laid both sets of pictures back on the desk. "There's more scratches. Somebody's been down there since the murder messing around at that porthole. The latch was broken when Jim and I were down there. There were these scratches. They're dulled a little in your pictures. Here they're not so deep. These old ones look like they were made with something sharp. These are new, more like scrapes, as if someone were repeatedly vandalizing this one porthole. Dragging something through."

For several moments they all three stared at the photographs. "You couldn't get through that porthole in tanks," Anna observed.

Hawk held the close-up of the scratches so the sunlight illuminated it clearly. "Maybe the marks could have been made with a chain or a wire. Somebody fishing through the hole, fishing something out of the cabin."

"What could they be after in the captain's quarters?" Holly asked. "I mean, there's the usual trinkets, but nobody dives the *Kamloops* for trinkets. Too dangerous. All I saw anywhere near the porthole were some busted-up wooden crates and pieces of broken crockery."

Anna sorted through the folder of papers she'd collected on the *Kamloops* and pulled out a Xerox copy of the bill of lading. "Fence wire, machinery from England, pipe, shoes, steel cable," she began aloud. She ran through the list of goods. The *Kamloops* was a package freighter; she carried everyday fare. Time and circumstances might have made some of them worth more than they had been originally, but nothing that would be worth repeatedly risking one's life for, or committing murder for.

"You're barking up the wrong list," Holly said. "If whoever's stealing artifacts is fiddling around the captain's cabin, my guess is they're looking for personal effects."

"Gold doubloons," Hawk said with an exaggerated air of mystery.

"Wrong century," Holly retorted.

"Wrong sea," Anna said.

"Right touch of glamour," he offered.

"Captains of freighters weren't rich," Anna thought aloud. "Contraband?"

"Maybe," Holly agreed. "What was contraband in 1927?"

"We are close enough to Chicago. There was that whole gangster thing. Maybe dirty money, drugs—" Anna began.

"Guys in cement overcoats," Hawk interjected.

The women ignored him.

"Stocks, bonds, stolen goods: jewelry, gold, silver—"

"Hooch," Hawk added unhelpfully.

"Do you want to go out and play?" Holly asked. Despite her preoccupation, Anna was glad to see Hawk smile.

"I'll be good," he promised.

"Whatever it is, it had to be small enough to get through a porthole, close enough to the porthole it could be fished out, and worth a lot to somebody," Anna went on.

"You forgot easy," Hawk said, finally serious. "There's no time down there. It's too cold for much in the way of decompression stops. A bounce dive is about it. Maybe twenty minutes max if you know what you're doing. You'd have to grab the thing and get back to the surface in a short space of time."

"Or things," Anna corrected and pointed to the scratches that indicated more than one attempt at entry. Rubbing her eyes, she leaned back in her chair. Idly, she moved the photos around as if they were pieces in a jigsaw puzzle she was putting together. "I wish this made more sense."

"Me too," Holly said. "Stanton's been asking questions

on the mainland—both at the Voyageur Marina and in Grand Marais. The locals are beginning to look at us funny. It doesn't take much to lose your reputation in this business."

"Better than losing your boat," Anna said.

"Without it we won't need the boat."

Anna picked up the remaining seven pictures and fanned them out like a poker hand: the hull vanishing into the somber depths, a shot of the hull in the other direction with the vague light of the surface beckoning, mud hills rolling away, the Pepsi can she remembered from her dive, a shot of Hawk by the porthole, and a coffee mug half buried in the lake bottom.

"I wish I hadn't been so scared when I went down," Anna said. "It's hard to remember what, exactly, was there."

"That's true of almost everybody on a deep dive," Holly reassured her.

"Particularly squirrels," Hawk added.

"I think I liked you better depressed," Anna countered. "Why don't you guys go back to work or whatever it is you do?" She rose from her chair and gathered the papers and pictures together to replace them in the manila folder. "I've got things to do."

"Like gather nuts for the winter?" Hawk asked.

Anna laughed. "A lot like that."

That evening, as most evenings when the tourist trade had died down and the dock had grown quiet, Anna poured herself a glass of wine and carried it out onto the steps of the ranger station to sit and sip and watch the day turn to silver.

Christina's letter, still unread, was folded in her pocket. Anna took it out along with the packet of underwater photos she'd been meaning to study, and ran a finger under the flap in pleasant anticipation of a touch of home. This note was short and businesslike, scribbled on the back of an old memo. Chris had written it over her lunch break. It started with an apology for the orange thumbprint in the corner. An arrow pointed to the smudge. On the arrow's tail was written, "Oops. Doritos." Anna read the rest of the letter, written in Christina's graceful looping hand. Bertie had finally grown alarmed. Repeated efforts to get information out of Scotty had resulted in conflicting stories and outright lies. Bertie had alerted the Houghton police to her sister's disappearance. As the waiting period on missing persons was long since past, the investigation had begun. Ally was studying dinosaurs in preschool. Chris was thinking of taking a cooking class on Tuesday evenings. Piedmont was said to be missing Anna.

Piedmont. Anna folded the letter and wished she could have a cat on her lap, an orange tail to pull. As if granting her wish, a flash of reddish fur illuminated the dark green of the thimbleberry not four yards from where she sat.

Knucklehead's kits were old enough to leave the den. Several times Anna had seen them poking shy black faces out of the bushes. Often at night she heard their sharp cries and muffled tumblings in the thick underbrush. Tonight they had grown quite bold and pounced and tumbled, playing like kittens while their mother watched with her chin on her paws. Knucklehead, however tame, never took her eyes from Anna or any other human being now that her kits had outgrown the safety of the den.

Beside Anna, on the step, were the underwater photographs of the *Kamloops*. A breeze stirred them, and she tucked them under her thigh lest they blow into the dirt. "Maybe I'll learn something by osmosis," she said to Knucklehead.

There was so much information, and no one piece of it seemed to connect up with any other. A murder committed in an impossible place, for improbable reasons, by an unidentified person. Maybe Stanton was right, maybe it was drugs: buying or selling or taking.

"Not bloody likely," Anna said to the fox. She began forcing mismatched facts together, snapping one to the next like pop beads on a child's necklace. Someone wanted something they knew or believed to be in the captain's cabin. The broken latch and the scratches attested to the fact that they had attempted or succeeded in dragging that something out through the porthole.

Denny had been found dead by that porthole. Anna married the two bits of information: Therefore Denny had seen whoever doing whatever, and so they had killed him.

The careful, professional Denny had done a solo midnight bounce dive on an extremely dangerous wreck. Denny hadn't told anyone he was going to dive. Anna hammered the disparate facts into a third: Therefore Denny hadn't known beforehand that he was going to make the dive, and as there was no radio in the *Blackduck*, he couldn't broadcast it after he decided to do it.

Denny, then, had followed someone, someone he suspected. After the reception he had followed them in the *Blackduck*. They had dived, he had dived.

Denny Castle was a superb diver. Denny Castle had been killed. Therefore either the murderer was a better diver, was someone Denny was not afraid of, or had caught Denny off guard.

The sound of a scuffle interrupted Anna's thoughts. The kits were growling, lowering their noses to their paws, their hind ends high in the air in a three-way standoff. The tableau erupted into a spout of fur and Anna laughed. It was hard to remember they were wild things. The desire to pet them, name them, feed them was almost irresistible.

The roar of a motorboat broke up the fray. Flashes of red enlivened the bushes as they all disappeared, running as if they'd not been born and raised with the sound of boat engines.

Anna stood to see who was causing the ruckus. A green and white cabin cruiser was shearing the silver fabric of the channel: Patience Bittner's boat, the *Venture*. She pulled up at a speed that waked the boats at their moorings and set the fishermen to squawking.

Anna began to run toward the quay.

Patience didn't disembark. She stood on the deck holding the *Venture* to the dock with her hands. Her usually well-coiffed hair had come loose and hung in strands accentuating the deep lines etched in her face. One of Carrie's old sweat-shirts rendered her for the first time in Anna's recollection shapeless and unstylish.

Tourists, hunched over bourbons and beers, pricked their ears for any sound of adventure. Anna crouched on the pier, eye-level with Patience standing in the boat. "What is it? Carrie?" As she asked and was answered with a grim nod, Anna suffered a stab of guilt. Denny Castle's murder, Donna's disappearance—both damage already done—had absorbed her attention so completely she had forgotten her primary duty: to protect and preserve. She had forgotten Jim Tattinger and his proven penchant for little girls, forgotten Carrie Bittner and her sullen and secretive affair with the mysterious beau.

"She's run off," Patience said. "She was supposed to be busing in the dining room. I was busy with the inventory brought on the *Ranger Three* and was at the dock. My night manager said Carrie left for supper and never came back. I've looked everywhere I can think of. I came to the north shore because that's where she ran to the last time— Lane Cove, remember? She left this at the apartment. It must've been about an hour before I got home."

Anna took the paper Patience pulled from the pocket of her trousers. On a piece of stationery with little faceless girls in oversized bonnets brightening one corner, written with pencil so dull that at first Anna thought it was crayon, were the words: "Living with you is like being in jail. You think you're the only person that deserves a life. Not everybody thinks I'm a little kid anymore. Like you made my childhood so great! I'm going to end it and you can pretend to all your friends that it's a big deal."

"I wasn't paying attention," Patience said, and water started in eyes already reddened. "I've had so much on my mind this summer. Carrie's boy troubles were a complication I didn't have time for. She was sulky but I didn't think she was depressed. I know she won't kill herself—she's too big a baby—but even to leave a note . . ." Patience's throat closed with tears and she stopped talking rather than break down.

"What day is it?" Anna demanded.

The unexpected nature of the question startled Patience momentarily from her fears. "Friday." She waited for an explanation.

"Tattinger's lieu day," Anna said. "My guess is when Carrie said she was going to 'end it' she meant her childhood, not her life." Anna dropped into the *Venture* and dragged a life vest out from under the seat. As she buckled it on she told Patience what she had learned of Tattinger.

"The first time she ran off it was Jim who told me where she was," Anna said. "He was acting fishy, but I wrote it off to general assholery, and after Denny was found, I figured his running without lights and creeping around had something to do with that. Carrie was with him, I'm willing to bet. That's what he was hiding. She was the second shadow I thought I saw in the cabin."

"What kind of boy could be so unacceptable?" Patience repeated her question of several weeks before. "A boy pushing forty. I'll kill her."

Had she been a mother, Anna thought, her first impulse would have been to kill Jim Tattinger. Tattinger couldn't charm, dominate, or compete with women, so he'd turned his sexual attention to girls so young he could still wow them with his wisdom and maturity. Carrie Ann, awkward, plain, wanting to grow up sooner than her mother thought fit, would be the perfect choice.

Anna said: "Unless you saw a light-colored cabin cruiser called the *Gone Fishin'* on your way here, head south. That's where I found him that first time. I expect he's scouted out some little cove." Patience turned south down Amygdaloid Channel. "I wouldn't blame Carrie," Anna said.

"I'm going to kill her for lying and for scaring her mother half to death," Patience explained. "I'm going to kill Jim Tattinger for the good of the human race." She shoved the throttle to full and the *Venture* leapt forward with a speed that took Anna by surprise. Clearly the engine had been overhauled, souped up. It was more powerful by far than the engine in a standard Chris-Craft cabin cruiser.

The roar ripped the stillness of the evening as the keel ripped the stillness of the water. Habitually watchful for snags and other water hazards, Anna kept her eyes on the channel. Her mind rattled on the Fate Worse Than Death they raced to stop, or interrupt. End her childhood: "Do you think Carrie was a virgin?" Anna asked.

"Yes. I'm pretty sure of it. She's not boy-crazy at all. And it's not like the seventh-grade boys were lining up to walk her home. Eighth grade was scaring her. They start having dances, dates, all that. God!" Patience exploded. "Barely thirteen. Eight weeks ago she was twelve. I will rip Tattinger in two. It's not like she's a Lolita. She's just a goofy-looking little girl."

Anna didn't doubt that that attitude had done half of Tattinger's work for him, but she didn't say anything.

Finding Carrie and Jim together, the ensuing scene— certainly if the scandal was made public—the fuss and notoriety, might do Carrie more harm than simply waiting for her to return and dealing with it quietly in the morning. Unless Jim was exerting undue pressure, unless she'd been resisting because she'd not felt ready to commit her body to anyone, unless she was planning on "ending it" tonight not because she wished to enter into a sexual relationship at thirteen but to spite her mother. And at thirteen, does one know the difference?

"Do you think Carrie Ann has had sex with Jim yet? Has she seemed different, said anything?" Anna asked.

"How would I know? I'm only her mother," Patience snapped. The anger momentarily vented, she gave the question due thought. "Carrie seems dull but she's not stupid and she feels things. She's never been any good at hiding things either. If she'd been sexually active I think she'd either have gone religious and remorseful or smug and insufferable—depending on how it went. Mostly she's just been sulky. My guess is no, she's too scared, too confused. Damn him! She hasn't even had her first period."

No fear of pregnancy, Anna thought. Somehow it made things worse, not better. It made Carrie such a child.

Silence was drummed deep by the throb of the engine.

The *Venture* carried her cargo of anger and worry forward, the peace of the summer night descending in her wake.

"I know it seems like I stopped caring," Patience said without looking at Anna. "But I didn't. I just got tired. Single parenting: the formula for guilt. I got tired of feeling guilty because I wasn't Supermom. I took the last year off, I guess. Kind of a sabbatical from motherhood. Bad timing, but I just ran out of gas."

There was nothing Anna could say. Merely looking at Carrie Ann shuffling sullen-faced through puberty had made Anna tired. Still, she pitied the girl. Nobody chooses to be from a broken home. Maybe Carrie Ann just needed a dad, and Tattinger had chosen to exact a price for playing the part.

"Little girls should never have to pay for love," Anna said, but she'd spoken only to herself and Patience didn't hear over the noise of the engine.

They found the *Gone Fishin'* anchored in Little Todd Harbor. A white light bobbed dutifully at the stern. Tattinger was taking no chances on this rendezvous getting interrupted for a petty maritime misdemeanor.

No one was on deck but there was a faint glow from the cabin. Anna wasn't surprised. Tattinger harbored no affection for nature. He would choose the civilized discomfort of a cramped but man-made cabin to the glories of a summer night.

Patience headed the *Venture* straight for the side of the anchored vessel and didn't cut power. For a sickening moment, Anna thought she meant to ram the other boat.

With an accuracy that would have done Holly Bradshaw credit, Patience pulled up short, came alongside, and caught the *Gone Fishin'* with her stern line before the wake could wash it out of reach.

"Let me handle this," she said as Anna belatedly deployed the fenders.

Anna was more than happy to let her do the honors. She put herself in the stern of the *Venture* where she had a clear view, and settled in to watch the fireworks.

Patience stopped at the cabin door and drew her five

feet two inches up to what appeared a quite formidable height. Anna was glad it was not she who was about to be discovered in flagrante delicato.

Patience knocked, opened the door a crack, and softly called: "Carrie, honey, it's Mom." Then she waited a few moments as if to give her daughter time to drag on enough clothes to cover the worst of her embarrassment.

From within the cabin came a frantic scuffling that, despite the situation, made Anna smile. One of her least favorite aspects of being a park ranger was coitus interruptus. She'd inadvertently waded into more than one wilderness frolic.

The cabin light flicked out. Patience pushed open the door and stepped inside. "It's me, baby. You're not in any trouble," Anna heard her say. Seconds later a huddled form was pushed gently out. Patience followed. She tried to put her arms around her daughter, but the girl shrugged them violently off.

At some point in the two hours it had taken to locate Carrie, she had lost her blouse. She crossed her arms protectively over her flat chest. She'd retained black denim trousers, and her high-topped sneakers were on and still laced. They'd arrived in time to save her, if not from sex, Anna thought uncharitably, then from the memory of having had it with Jim Tattinger.

Carrie was crying like a baby, great whooping sobs and hiccups. Whether from humiliation or fear or just plain anger at being caught, Anna couldn't tell.

Patience pulled off the sweatshirt she was wearing and Carrie struggled into it awkwardly, twitching away from her mother's helping hands.

"Get on the *Venture*," Patience ordered, maternal softness turned back to asperity by rejection. She caught up something from the floor just inside the cabin door. "You forgot this," she added acidly, dangling a white bit of cloth from her fingers. It was a training bra. In the light from the stern, Anna could see the little spandex cups and the thick sensible straps.

With a shriek Carrie grabbed it and, gulping air and

sobs, clambered over the gunwale into her mother's boat and disappeared into the cabin, slamming the door behind her. From the muffled sounds that followed, Anna guessed she had thrown herself down on the seat and cried into folded arms.

During all this Jim Tattinger had not appeared. The light in the cabin on the *Gone Fishin'* had stayed resolutely out, and there hadn't been a single sound from within.

Patience pushed the cabin door wide. An unseen hand pushed it shut again. With a force that made Anna flinch, Patience kicked the thin wood. The veneer cracked and the door banged inward. There was a sharp scream of hinges or of pain. Anna hoped it was the latter. Patience stood to one side of the black opening. "Come out or I will burn your fucking boat to the waterline," she said quietly. "I swear to God I will."

A rustling followed, then a pale shape began to insinuate itself into the darkness of the doorway.

"All the way out," Patience said coldly. "I've never seen a child molester up close."

Tattinger came out into the unflattering white light. He'd either retained or dragged on his T-shirt and underpants. They were white Fruit of the Looms, baggy like ill-fitting diapers. The undershirt was tucked into the panties. He had blue socks on his feet and his carroty hair was standing on end.

From the shadows of the *Venture,* Anna braced herself for the familiar whine, the stream of self-justification that was bound to follow. Just as she began to think that for once he had the good taste to be ashamed of himself, he began to speak.

"Look here, Mrs. Bittner," he said as if Patience, instead of being his peer, were decades older than he. "It's not what you think."

One graceful hand shot out, plucked the blue and white band of his underpants away from his bony frame and let it snap back. Tattinger turned pigeon-toed and grabbed his crotch in a parody of masculine modesty.

"It's what I think," Patience said. "Just shriveled and

uglier." Tattinger opened his mouth to speak, but she forestalled him. "You will not talk to me," she commanded. "You will not talk to nor come near Carrie. If you do I will kill you. Really. If you stay away, I will content myself with telling Lucas, getting you fired, getting you sent to jail. There you will be the little girl the ugly men want and I shall rejoice in every day you spend facedown bent over some bench with your trousers down around your ankles."

Finished, Patience stepped away from him, took a solid stance, doubled one fist inside the other, and, straight-armed, swung a roundhouse. Her knuckles collided with Jim's jaw just below his left ear and he went down.

As the *Venture* motored away, Anna could hear him screaming, "That's assault! That's assault! I'll press charges!"

"He will, you know," she said. "He's that slimy."

"So will I," Patience returned. "And mine will stick."

Carrie Ann began to howl.

CHAPTER 24

"**C**ounseled!" Patience fumed, spitting out the word.

At Patience's request Anna had followed her and her daughter back to Rock Harbor in the *Belle Isle,* then accompanied them to the Chief Ranger's house on Mott Island. After talking with Lucas Vega, the two women and the eternally weeping thirteen-year-old returned to Patience's apartment behind the lodge. Carrie had stumbled off to bed to cry into her stuffed animals. Anna sat on the couch watching Patience stomp around the tiny kitchen.

"Counseled *again,*" Anna said unhelpfully. She wasn't feeling much like defending the Park Service. Though Lucas had been as shocked as they, if the flashing of his usually somber dark eyes was to be believed, all he could promise was that Jim Tattinger would be forced to undergo psychological counseling. For reasons Anna could understand, Patience didn't want to drag her daughter—or herself—through the courts trying to prove attempted statutory rape or child molestation. Lucas would lodge a complaint, but without Patience pressing charges, he didn't have the power to fire or even suspend Tattinger without pay. Chances were good the higher-ups wouldn't want to be tainted by the tawdry goings-on below. As in any bureaucracy, the best way up in the Park Service was to produce a smokescreen of paperwork, an avalanche of plans and studies and proposals, but to be very careful to never actually *do* anything.

"I'm getting cynical in my old age," Anna said to break her train of thought.

"Cynicism is the fool's synonym for realism," Patience snarled. Anna laughed. At first the other woman looked angry; then her face cracked and she laughed. "Pretty bad, aren't I? This has been one of those life's-a-bitch-and-then-you-die days. The worst of it is, I remember being happy. I remember when I was a nice woman: cheerful, optimistic, fun. I remember, but just barely. The good old days are getting older by the minute." There was a satisfying pop as she eased a cork from a bottle and the familiar, comforting glugging noise as the wine was decanted.

Patience brought the glasses over to the couch and handed Anna one. "To counseling," she said and raised the glass.

"To old friends and better days," Anna said.

Patience would drink to that. Tonight, Anna suspected, Patience would drink to anything. "Too much light," the woman said. She turned off the lamps at the ends of the sofa and opened the drapes that had obscured the black square of night beyond the picture window.

With the lights out, the window ceased to show a blind eye, but looked out across the sparkling waters of Rock Harbor. Raspberry Island was a ragged silhouette against a pearl-gray curtain of fog that hung further out on the lake.

"It doesn't take much here," Patience said as she curled her little body up in an armchair. "Even a halfmoon throws enough light. I do this all the time. Not all the time," she amended. "When I can browbeat little Miss Video into turning off the television. You never had kids?"

Anna thought she sounded a bit wistful. "Never did." She drank her wine.

"Never wanted them?"

"Never wanted them."

"You were married, though," Patience said. "I got that from Sandra. Widowed, she said, not divorced. Supposedly that's easier to take. Probably depends. I would like to have been widowed, like to have widowed myself with my bare hands a time or two—" Patience stopped abruptly and fifteen seconds ticked by audibly on a clock Anna couldn't place. "If I'd had more than a couple of tablespoons of wine I'd blame it on the drink. As it is, I shall have to accept the fact that I am an insensitive clod. Nerves—will you buy that? My mouth is just running away with me. I hope I haven't been riding roughshod over any old wounds."

"Talk doesn't open them," Anna answered truthfully.

"What does?"

"Forgetting. Thinking you're healed, you're as strong as you used to be, that you can leap those old buildings at a single bound. Then the wounds open and you fall and you wonder if you'll ever be the woman you were."

They sipped in silence, watching a late-arriving sailboat, sails furled, motoring up the channel.

"Divorce isn't like that," Patience said. "The wounds maybe aren't as deep—certainly aren't as deep—but everybody, everything rubs salt in them. Other women that look like the Other Woman, his friends, your friends, things he kept, things he didn't get, kids that want to call Daddy every time you yell at them and come to Mommy anytime they want money. Money. God yes, money! Suddenly at thirty-five you're shopping for clothes at Wal-Mart and dusting off your library card because you can't afford even a paperback. At least with death you can look tragically beautiful in something black and silk you bought with the insurance money."

Anna laughed. "Patience, you would sell orphaned virgins into white slavery before you would wear anything from Wal-Mart."

"I would," Patience admitted.

"Zachary wasn't insured." Anna wasn't sure why she told that to Patience, it just seemed natural. "He's been dead seven years."

"What happened?"

"Hit by a cab crossing Ninth Avenue in New York City." Both women laughed.

"Sorry," Patience said.

"It's okay. It strikes everybody funny. Me too. Comedy of the absurd, I guess. Divorce: is that when you went to work in the winery? After the divorce?" Anna moved the subject back to Patience.

"It seemed genteel somehow," Patience said. "Paid genteel too: eleven sixty-five an hour. How anyone is expected to live on that is a mystery to me."

Since joining the Park Service, Anna had never made anywhere near $11.65 an hour but she didn't say so.

Patience poured the last of the wine into their glasses. Alcohol was beginning to warm Anna's muscles, relax her brain. "Did you grow up rich?" she asked rudely.

Patience didn't seem to mind the question. "We had 'plenty,' as Mother endlessly reminds me, but not rich, no. My parents own a pig farm in Elkhart, Iowa." She said it in the tone of a nineteenth-century gentlewoman admitting to a fallen sister or an idiot child.

"Good honest work," Anna remarked mildly.

"The place smelled of pigs. All my clothes, my hair, the boys I dated, the food I ate, smelled of pigs. I can't remember not wanting something better. Even when I was tiny, I had this little kid's vision of heaven. You know those ornate white iron lawn chairs—the ones that look as if they're welded from fat vines?"

Anna nodded.

"Somehow that was the height of class in my little pea brain. I'd fantasize for hours about sitting in a lawn chair like that, wearing something chiffon, and snubbing boys that had manure on their boots." She laughed. "Silly. But the dreams got me out of there. That's what I needed them for."

"What do you dream of now?" Anna asked.

"Bigger lawn chairs, finer chiffon, and tycoons to snub." Patience unfolded herself from the armchair. "Dead soldier," she announced and carried away the empty bottle. Anna stayed where she was, enjoying the moonlight on the

fog, enjoying the buzz of the wine. Another pop, more gur-
gling: Patience was opening a second bottle.

"I'm working in the morning," Anna protested.

"Not to worry." Patience brought the wine and two
fresh glasses. "This is the good stuff. Too good for me, I
kept telling myself, but this talk of pigs has driven me to
open it. Once in this life I will have the best. You lucked
into it by sheer accident. Here."

Anna sipped. It was the best; the best she had ever had.
A red wine, though it showed black with only the moon for
light, rich and so warm Anna finally understood all the ef-
fete talk of sunshine and hillsides and aging in wood.

They drank without talking. The wine was the event. In
silence they finished the bottle. Patience said good-night by
a simple touch on Anna's arm. Anna lay in the moonlight a
while longer enjoying the solitude. She picked up the wine
bottle and turned it in her hand. The stuff was excellent. On
an NPS salary Anna doubted she'd ever have the money to
buy a vintage that fine. The bottle looked the worse for
wear, the label wrinkled and faded. Something was vaguely
familiar about it. Anna thought of turning on the lamp, but
moonlight and alcohol won out over curiosity.

Tonight, it was enough that it had gotten her high.

Regardless of the quality of the wine, Anna had had too
much. Near two in the morning she awoke with the jit-
ters. The bit of moon had continued on its wanderings and
the channel was now in shadow. The island was so still she
could hear the faint creaks as the apartment building talked
to itself.

Alcohol poisoning and the cold hour of the night
crowded in. The world seemed a sordid place; people a
cancer that was spreading, killing the earth, killing one another.

Wishing she were a cat or a shadow or at least sober,
Anna lay on the sofa and stared into the dark until uncon-
sciousness finally took pity on her and returned.

When she awoke again it was light but fog hid any trace

of the coming sunrise. She looked at her watch: 5:40 A.M. A dull ache at the base of her skull and a parched feeling told her she would be getting no more rest for a while. Giving in to her hard-earned hangover, she got up and stumbled into the kitchen for a glass of water.

The wine bottles were gone and the glasses set tidily on the counter near the sink. Patience must have had as bad a time as she, Anna thought, creeping about her apartment in the dead of night doing domestic chores. Anna drank off half a glass of water standing at the sink, then refilled the glass. Theoretically, rehydration helped a hangover. Theoretically a lot of things helped a hangover. In reality only the passage of time worked out the poisons. Anna looked at her watch again: 5:42. It was going to be a long day.

Molly would be up at six. She always was. A woman of strong habits, Anna's sister rose with coffee and a cigarette to watch the six o'clock news and went to bed with Scotch and a cigarette and *The Tonight Show*'s opening monologue.

Anna killed twenty minutes standing under a hot shower. At 6:05, wishing she had coffee but lacking the courage to rummage through Patience's kitchen, she dialed her sister's number in New York. Molly picked up on the first ring. "Dr. Pigeon," she said curtly. The formality threw Anna for a moment.

"It's me, Anna," she said. "You sound further up than five minutes. Are you okay?"

"Had a rough night." The sounds of crockery and metal rattled behind Molly's words.

"Making coffee?" Anna asked enviously.

"Second pot." There was a clicking on the line. "Hold," Molly said. "I'm expecting another call." She was back within seconds. "False alarm. Nobody there. Phone must be acting up."

"Migraine?" Anna asked. Her sister had suffered migraines since her twenties but she'd not had one in a while.

"No. That's for later if this clenched feeling behind my eyes means anything. I lost a patient last night. I thought you might be the police. Lots of questions. I've got answers that satisfy them. None that satisfy me."

"Suicide?" Anna asked. Molly had only had two in twenty years of practice. She'd taken both of them hard for a psychiatrist. Anna loved her the better for it.

"Not exactly. At least I doubt that was the primary motivation. Remember my crazy connoisseur?"

"The disgruntled food writer?"

"Him. He climbed the outside of a three-story building in Brooklyn Heights last night. The man is—was—in his late fifties with the figure of a confirmed food worshiper. He hadn't climbed more than stairs in the past ten years and never those if there was an elevator nearby."

"Jumped?"

"The police thought jumped at first, but he fell. All the windows were locked on the inside. He had to have climbed up."

"Do you know why? I mean, did he live there or something?"

"No. He was trying to get to the food lab and kitchens of his rival. I think he figured if he could get in, he could find something to prove the Great Discovery was a hoax."

"Jesus," Anna breathed. "You'd think anybody who can afford you would hire someone to do their stunt work."

"Not this man. I should have seen it coming. The obsessions amused me, Anna. Amused me. I thought it was funny. I just didn't see it as something that could drive anybody to do something that desperate. The last couple of sessions he talked of revenge, said the yellow braces weren't enough. He talked of plans to mock, to expose, even to kill his rival. The plans were all overblown—comic book stuff. You know: plastic explosives on the violent end and intricate Rube Goldberg devices to deliver a public pie in the face on the silly end. Boyish. I wasn't paying attention. I've got that article coming out in *Psychology Today* and that conference I'm chairing at Princeton in August. Like some damned TV star, I sat there primping while this poor man cried out. The system failed him. I failed him. Dr. Quick Fix. I fell in love with my own glib theories. And Gustav Claben died."

"I'm sorry," was all Anna could say. Molly was never to

be comforted when she believed she had failed. People found it hard to love a woman to whom they could give nothing. The pain would pass and Molly would never let it happen again, at least not in the same way.

Again there was a clicking on the line. This time it was another call: the hospital where Molly's client had been taken. Molly rang off abruptly, leaving Anna with the depressing feeling that she should have done something more, said something wiser. Just once she wished Molly would need something that she was equipped to deliver.

Like what? Anna mocked herself. Need someone arrested for camping out of bounds in Central Park? A horse shod or a boat engine tuned for her Park View practice?

Anna promised herself she would call again soon and make a point to listen more than talk. She had to satisfy herself with that.

When she looked up from the phone, Patience was standing in the hall between the living room and the bath. Her face was twisted, as though she couldn't decide whether to come ahead into the front room or retreat back to the bedroom.

"It's all right," Anna said. "I'm off the phone."

Patience gave her a hard look, angry—or so it seemed through the medium of a hangover.

"I used my credit card," Anna said, feeling childish.

The look faded and was replaced by Patience's usual dry smile. "I'm not worried," she said lightly. "I know where you live. Carrie!" she called back down the hall.

Carrie Ann plodded slowly out. Her usual sullenness had hardened into a look very near hatred. On so young a person, it was unsettling.

As Patience herded her daughter into a morning blanked with fog, Anna rubbed her face and groaned. Apparently it was destined to be another life's-a-bitch-and-then-you-die kind of day.

CHAPTER 25

Fog seemed to penetrate everything, obscure everything. Motoring slowly down the channel toward Mott, her eyes on the radar screen, Anna felt it penetrated her very skull, obscured her thoughts. It was hard to tell where the hangover ended and the fog began. She ached for the clarity of the high desert, strong clean sunshine not filtered through atmospheres of water, air so transparent mountains a hundred miles distant looked as if they were but a day's walk away.

Another boat loomed suddenly out of the fog behind and just barely to the port of the *Belle Isle*. Anna shoved her throttles forward to avoid a collision. The leap was unnecessary as it turned out but it had been a close call and she swore under her breath. Slowing, she watched, deciding whether or not to call the other pilot onto the carpet.

The other vessel pulled alongside and Anna reached for the public-address-system mike, but it was the *Lorelei*, Scotty Butkus piloting.

He cut power, clearly wanting a word. Anna followed suit and walked back to the stern. The water was absolutely flat. Fog hung in close curtains, absorbing all sound, all color. The boats could have been meeting in a vacuum, a windowless white room.

"Hey, Scotty, what's up?" Anna opened the conversation as he clomped out of the *Lorelei*'s cabin.

"Just routine. Bound to be some fender benders in this stuff. I'll be sticking pretty close to Rock today."

Anna suspected it was less out of concern for the health and welfare of the tourists than because Scotty'd never gotten the hang of Loran, and wasn't too comfortable running on radar. "It's soupy all right," Anna concurred. "I'll need a red and white cane to find my way back to the north shore."

Something was different about Scotty. As usual, his shirt was crisply pressed and his boots shiny. It was the set of his shoulders, the cock of his head that was different, Anna decided. He was smug, puffed up. She waited to hear why. He didn't keep her on tenterhooks.

"Yup." Scotty narrowed his eyes against a nonexistent sun and stared into a nonexistent distance. "It's one hell of a day to be left with half a damn island to look after." Putting a booted foot on the gunwale, he leaned his elbow on his knee. He would have looked right at home in Texas. Anna wished he were there.

Butkus was waiting for her to ask him why he was in charge of half the island but she wasn't going to do it. He cracked before she did. "I don't mind being Acting District Ranger," he continued. "Hell, I'm used to that. But they don't pay me enough to be Acting Chief Ranger."

So that was it. Scotty was in pig heaven: both Ralph and Lucas were off duty. "Where is everybody?"

"Right. I forget. Hidden away over there on Amygdaloid, you miss out. Backcountry Management Group meeting. Be out till tomorrow."

Several times a season Lucas, Ralph, Marilyn—the Chief Naturalist—and Lyle, the head of Roads and Trails, spent three days in the backcountry camping and hashing out wilderness-management issues.

"Ah. Well, I'd better get on with it before we get run down out here," Anna said.

"Whatever your business is here, finish it up pronto," Scotty said, enjoying himself. "I need you on the north shore on a day like today."

"Will do."

Inside and out of Anna's head, the fog grew denser. Scotty and the *Lorelei* faded like specters come sunup. The *Belle Isle* fired up at a touch and Anna cracked the throttles. In the thick mist there was no sensation of movement. Following the jagged green map on her radar screen, she felt her way into the little harbor at Mott Island and inched up to the dock. The *Loon,* the *Blackduck,* and Pizza Dave's little aluminum runabout were all snugged up to the concrete. No one who didn't have to would be out on the water today.

Anna tied off her lines and followed the gravel path to the Administration Building, invisible thirty yards away.

"Coffee . . ." she croaked at the door of the dispatch room and Sandra returned a throaty chuckle.

"Fresh pot," she said without turning from her keyboard.

"When you die you shall be canonized," Anna promised. Secure in the knowledge the Chief Ranger was deep in the woods, she took Lucas's personal coffee cup, a white mug with "Smokey the Bear's a Communist" emblazoned on it in red. Fresh coffee in a real cup; the day was beginning to look less bleak.

"Not your cup," Sandra admonished as Anna poured, and she realized she'd given herself away by the tiny clicking sound the neck of the pot made when it touched the rim of the cup.

"I'm using Lucas's," she confessed.

"That's tantamount to sitting in the emperor's chair," Sandra warned. She'd finished whatever she'd been working on and turned to face Anna.

"I'll polish my prints off when I'm finished." Anna took a drink and sighed with satisfaction.

"Are you working over here today so Scotty won't be

all by his lonesome? Terrible to be all dressed up and nobody to boss."

"Nope. Already got my marching orders from the Acting Chief: back to Amygdaloid ASAP. Suits me fine. I just came by to dish the dirt."

By way of repayment for the information Sandra had provided, Anna told her of the Jim and Carrie affair and that it had been stopped. The dispatcher echoed Patience's reaction with a shocked "Counseled!" But being less cynical than either Carrie's mother or Anna, Sandra put her faith in Lucas Vega.

"He'll come up with something," she said confidently. "His mother owns half of San Diego County. There's bound to be a few pocket senators or congressmen he can lean on to lean on somebody."

Over a second cup of coffee Anna asked after Jo. Sandra had seen her several times, had her over to dinner once. "She's working hard," the dispatcher said. "Talks about PCBs and fish and slime and percentages of whatever in the whatever. She's nailed down every minute of every day."

"Whatever works," Anna said, but she wondered how Jo fared during the endless minutes of her nights.

Tinker and Damien provided the only good news. Evidently Scotty had ceased his blackmail and they were of good cheer. Sandra said they were haunting McCargo Cove every spare minute in search of the mythical peregrine.

"They won't find it today," Anna said.

"Rumor has it it's foggy."

Anna drained her coffee cup. "Come on, Delphi," she said. "Lead me back to Amygdaloid."

Coming around Blake's Point, eyes glued to the Loran, Anna was half sorry the water was so flat. Even the slamming of the hull against hard water would have been preferable to the absolute nothing she felt.

Between Blake's Point and Steamboat Island, Anna executed a turn to the 248-degree heading dictated by experience and charting. Amygdaloid Channel, usually a narrow comforting waterway, took on a different aspect when neither shore was visible. She threaded her way carefully down the center.

The dock at the ranger station was deserted. Having eased the *Belle Isle* into her space, Anna disembarked.

Indoors, with four cluttered walls and a fire roaring in the woodstove, the fog seemed less malevolent. Anna took a couple of Advil for her head, made a pot of strong tea, and sat down at her desk to catch up on the month's paperwork. How many diving permits issued, how many fishing licenses sold, how much in revenues to be sent to the Michigan Fish and Game. She wrote up a 10-343 Case Incident Report on two fire rings she'd destroyed and rehabilitated on Green Island and a half-page on the removal of the fishhook from the Minneapolis man's thigh. There was a short form to be completed on two visitor complaints that the party boat, the *Spirogyra*, had been making undue noise after quiet hour. For Ralph's amusement, Anna included one visitor's statement that the denizens of the *Spirogyra* were calling down aliens from outer space. She deliberated on whether or not to write up a 10-343 Case Incident Report on the Jim Tattinger situation or a 10-344 Criminal Incident Record. Knowing Lucas would wish to decide along with Patience and the Superintendent whether or not to treat the incident as a criminal act, she contented herself with writing a summary narrative that could be typed on either form later on.

Over a tuna fish sandwich and soggy potato chips, Anna opened the packet of interoffice mail she'd brought back from Mott. There was a memo regarding the Backcountry Management Group meeting dated four days earlier, and an announcement for the coming Chrismoose festivities held on the island every twenty-fifth of July. One memorandum piqued her interest for a moment. Lucas had written up a report on the FBI's investigation of the Castle murder. No new information, it said, and ended with the vague threat: "Frederick Stanton will continue to head the ongoing investigation."

Tea, food, and routine paperwork had a normalizing effect. Anna's brain no longer felt so fog-choked. Relief at this modest clarity was soon paid for with the nagging sense of something forgotten. Pushing away the papers that cluttered her desktop, she put her feet up and teetered back in her chair, her fingers intertwined and cradling her head. It had always been her private contention that this was the pose Rodin should have chosen for *The Thinker*.

Staring into the blankness beyond the window, Anna let her mind wander back over the day. The sense of uneasiness stemmed from her early-morning conversation with her sister.

Molly was her arbiter of sanity, her rock, anchor, and reality check. Without a doubt, Anna knew she owed Molly her life. There were days after Zachary had died when only the knowledge that her death would make her sister angry beyond recovery had kept Anna from taking her wine-wrung grief out on the Henry Hudson Parkway at eighty miles an hour.

Molly didn't hold with suicide. "You've got to stay in the game. Your luck's bound to change. Be a shame to miss it," she liked to say.

And this morning, when her sister was in trouble, all Anna had found to say was: "Gee, gosh, I'm really sorry. . . ."

Somewhere in the conversation there must have been a word or a phrase that should have meant more to Anna than it did. Molly based her practice on the belief that if you listened hard enough and long enough even the most troubled person could tell you how to help them.

The sense of something missed might have been the squandered chance to repay even a fraction of the debt she owed her sister. Anna rocked her chair down. Next time she would listen harder, longer.

Beyond the window dusk was robbing the world of light. Two of Knucklehead's kits had come to play near the clearing. Their red-orange fur provided the only color on the scene. The smaller of the two stood up on his hind legs and danced, trying to reach a fat bunch of thimbleberries. The pose was so like that of the fox trying for the "sour" grapes in *Aesop's Fables* that Anna laughed.

Her laughter came to an abrupt stop. Grapes. All at once she knew what it was that she'd missed in Molly's conversation, what had plagued her all afternoon. It had nothing to do with her sister's peace of mind. It was the dead gourmet's braces, his yellow suspenders worn to mock his rival. Canary-yellow suspenders tying up a bunch of purple-black grapes. That was what had seemed so familiar about the wine label she'd seen in Patience's apartment. Anna recalled the bottle. Moonlight shining through the window; an outline of black grapes, lines, robbed of color, traced over it, ending in the familiar Y of old-fashioned men's suspenders.

Pacing the cluttered office, Anna pushed her mind back to the story Molly had told her of the winetasting in Westchester, of the rivalry between the two connoisseurs. A rare California wine had been spirited out of the Napa Valley during Prohibition, a shipment that had vanished on its way out of the country. A wine so rare it had become almost mythical. So rare it retailed for thousands of dollars a bottle. So rare Molly's client had been willing to risk—and lose—his life rather than admit a rival had actually found the lost shipment.

But the shipment must have been found, tracked down by a woman who worked in a California winery, who lived and breathed wine, who wanted money more than just about anything. Patience had tracked the missing vintage to the *Kamloops*. It wasn't on the bill of lading because it was contraband being smuggled into Canada among the personal effects of the captain.

Denny had suspected some depredation. Had followed. Arrogance would have robbed him of the good sense to be frightened of one small woman immersed in his world. So Patience had killed him somehow—drowned him.

One hip on her desk, Anna lost herself in thoughts of the cynical blond woman she was becoming friends with. The courage, the brains, the daring—all the things that made Patience a fascinating companion—must have served her well in her criminal activities. Even a brilliant divorce wouldn't keep her in silk dresses indefinitely, and Patience was a greedy woman. Greed had usurped the higher emotions. Greed had become the driving force. Greed had made theft easy and murder possible.

"One-two-one, three-oh-two," Anna snapped into her base radio. Three times brought no response. The glacier-broken interior of the island was riddled with places where radios couldn't reach in or out. Evidently Ralph and Lucas had pitched camp in one of them.

"Damn," Anna whispered. Mike in hand, she debated the wisdom of broaching the subject over the airwaves with Scotty. Patience was clever, quick. If Scotty botched it, fog or no, she would be gone before anyone had a chance to stop her. And Scotty would botch it. Anna had seen the label, she had heard the story, but as yet there was no real evidence. Scotty wouldn't have the forbearance to wait and watch without hinting or pseudo heroics. By the time Lucas and Ralph were out of the backcountry, Patience would be long gone.

The situation would keep better without interference, Anna decided. Tomorrow she would go to Rock Harbor. Lucas would be back. They would talk.

She put down the mike, stared out into the fog. The kits were gone.

"How the hell did she get into the captain's cabin to bring the stuff up?" she demanded of the world at large.

CHAPTER 26

Before the coming night robbed the fog of the last light, Anna had to make her evening patrol. A moment passed in evil thoughts: a glass of red wine by the stove instead of a blind boat tour, who would know? Tonight, there would be little in the way of visitor contact.

But anyone out could be in trouble if they didn't know the waters. Anna sighed and shrugged into her Gore-Tex.

The channel was empty. Two boats were snugged in Herring Bay near Belle Isle, a dozen more anchored in the secure waters of McCargo Cove. Anna turned a blinded windscreen back toward home and crept through a mist turning from white to gray with the setting of the sun. As she reached Twelve O'Clock Point, seven miles from Amygdaloid Island, she began to debate whether to pour her wine or divest herself of her uniform first upon reaching home.

These heavy deliberations were interrupted by the sudden coming to life of the *Belle Isle*'s marine radio.

Three or four cracking pops warned that someone was

fiddling with their mike button, then a hesitant, childish voice. "Hello? Hello? SOS. Please. SOS."

Anna snatched up the mike and waited for the caller to stop keying her radio. Finally the click came. She forced down her transmitter button. "I hear you," she said clearly. "My name's Anna. When I stop talking you push down the button on the microphone again, tell me where you are, then let the button up, okay? I'm stopping talking now."

There was a silence that seemed long because Anna held her breath but it was no more than fifteen or twenty seconds. A few fumbling clicks, then the child's voice again. "I'm out by the *Kamloops*," she said. "My mom's in trouble. I think she's dead. Please come."

"Carrie Ann? Is that you?" Anna demanded.

There was a confusion of clicks as the girl tried to talk at the same time Anna was transmitting. "Carrie Ann?" Anna tried again. This time she got through.

"Yeah?"

"Are you at the *Kamloops*'s dive buoy or Kamloops Island?"

"The buoy."

"And your mom's in trouble. What kind of trouble?" As she talked Anna changed course. She was less than two minutes from the wreck site. Carrie didn't respond. Anna tried again but the girl held her silence.

"Two-oh-two, three-oh-two, did you copy that?" Anna put in a radio call to Rock Harbor. Scotty was her only option for backup. Even if she could raise them on her radio, Ralph and Lucas were too deep in the woods to be of any help.

"Ah . . . negative."

Anna repeated the gist of the conversation with Carrie. "I'm headed over to the *Kamloops* now. I'll keep you posted." Again Anna tried Ralph Pilcher. There was no response. Scotty was monitoring. He promised to try Ralph from the east side.

Four hours into the wilderness and dark coming on, there was little Ralph or Lucas could do, but it was policy to keep them informed. And, Anna admitted to herself, a comfort to be in radio contact with them when there was an emergency.

This situation was double-edged: Patience might genuinely be in trouble, or she might be setting a trap.

Innocent until proven guilty, Anna reminded herself. She didn't dare ignore a distress call, the lake was too dangerous a place. And she could think of no reason Patience should risk a confrontation; no reason she would think Anna had figured out the deadly business she had undertaken. Anna picked up her radio mike again and called Rock Harbor. "Scotty, there may be more to this. I've stumbled across some complications," she said, being purposely vague since there was no way to keep the conversation private on the airwaves. "If you could start around, I may need the backup."

There was a silence, then two clicks as if he was fingering his mike uncertainly. "ASAP," he said after a moment. "Having some engine trouble on the *Lorelei*."

"Fuck you," Anna hissed but not into the mike. Scotty was lying. He couldn't navigate in the fog and he was trying to cover himself. "Did you get ahold of Ralph or Lucas?"

"Negative."

Loran took Anna to the buoy. Radar kept her from ramming the *Venture*. None of the Chris-Craft's lights were on and she was all but invisible in the fog. Anna rafted the *Belle Isle* off her starboard side. Taking the precaution of removing her Smith and Wesson from the briefcase and putting it in her raincoat pocket, Anna climbed over the gunwale. "Carrie! Carrie Ann!"

The cabin door opened slowly. A kid's sleeping bag wrapped around her against the chill, Carrie Ann Bittner shuffled out.

"What's happened?" Anna asked. "Where's your mother?"

"She went diving." Carrie replied in the sulky tone Anna was accustomed to. "She dived down a while ago. She must be hurt or caught on something."

Anna couldn't see the child's face clearly and could

read nothing from her voice. Without explaining why, she moved past her and checked the cabin. It was empty.

Why would Patience come out in the fog, dragging her daughter with her? The question jogged Anna's memory and she remembered the click on the line when she was on the phone with Molly—the click Molly had thought was another call but had turned out not to be. Patience could have picked up the phone in Carrie's room, heard of the death of the gourmet clad in yellow suspenders, and known Anna would put it all together sooner or later.

If Patience did know, it made sense she would rush the last dive, try and get the remainder of the wine out before she was stopped. Carrie must have been brought along in the capacity of prisoner. Left alone, she would undoubtedly have found her way to Mr. Tattinger's for solace.

"How long has your mom been down?" Anna asked.

"I said," Carrie grumbled, "awhile. Maybe half an hour."

At first Anna thought Carrie was unaware that half an hour at depth could be her mother's death warrant but the girl had said on the radio, "I think she's dead."

"Why is she diving here?" Anna asked.

Carrie shrugged. "How would I know?" She sounded more aggrieved than concerned. "Anyway, she's down there."

Anna radioed Scotty of her intentions. "I'm going to do a bounce dive," she said and thanked the gods that her voice did not betray the fear that was spreading through her veins like poison.

"Ten-four," Scotty replied. "I'll stay on this damn engine. Hell of a time to have your horse go lame."

Anna repeated her earlier obscenities. Focusing on anger to keep the terror at bay, she struggled into dry suit, fins, weights, and tanks. "Turn on every light on the *Venture*," she ordered Carrie, who'd stood bundled and silent watching the process.

Before she entered the lake, Anna raked the surface carefully with her handheld lamp looking for bubbles, disturbance, anything that smacked of ambush and watery graves. Fog impeded her investigation.

Finally, there was nothing left but to dive. The water was black and looked for all the world like death. Concentrating only on breathing, she clutched her light and rolled backward off the *Belle Isle*'s stern.

Cold cracked in her sinuses with such force it felt as if her eyes were being gouged out from inside her skull. For several seconds pain left her breathless and disoriented. The universe shrank to the single paralyzing sensation of utter, damning cold.

Forcing her ribs to expand, accepting the icy stabs and letting them pass through her, she righted herself and located the line Patience had dropped. With "follow the yellow brick road" singing irritatingly through her mind, Anna pursued the lemon-colored line down into increasing darkness. Ten seconds, fifteen, two white depth markers flashed by on the line. Anna kept her eyes on her watch and counted. The bright line weaving gently in the probe of light, black pressing close, the world was no bigger than her gauges.

Atmospheres crushed in and terrifying giddiness tried to spin her mind away from counting. An ache started at the base of her skull. Stringing her thoughts together cohesively became increasingly difficult. Fear that had been murmuring at her aboard the *Belle Isle* shrieked through all the organs of her body. Sixty-three seconds had elapsed since she had left the lake's surface.

The snaking of the line through liquid space began having a hypnotic effect and Anna found herself forgetting the dangers not only of the icy depths but of the woman she swam to save. Somehow, she must fix her mind on Patience as an enemy, a killer of persons. Denny had not, and Denny's mind worked better at six atmospheres than hers ever would.

Two minutes, fifty-six seconds: the bottom blocked the beam of her light. She stopped, stood with one hand on the yellow line for security, and switched off her lamp. In her years with the Park Service, she'd worked on a dozen or more searches and rescues. Habit demanded she blow a whistle, shout a name. All she had in the malevolent shadow world was light or lack of it. Cloaked in darkness, Anna searched the lake bottom.

A flash, another, then burning steady: Patience was on the south side of the wreck. Without relighting her own lamp Anna swam toward the light.

As she closed the distance down the side of the ship, she could see that Patience's lamp had been set on the hull. In the wedge-shaped beam it threw, Patience—or at least a heavily suited person she assumed was Patience Bittner— was kneeling, slipping efficiently into dive tanks. The tanks were unlike any Anna had ever used. They fit singly, one to each side of the dive harness. Beside Patience was a net bag filled with dark objects.

For a moment Anna's nitrogen-befuddled brain refused to grasp the situation. Then, with a suddenness that made her feel a fool, it fell into place. The porthole into the captain's cabin was too small to get through in tanks. Patience, hardly bigger than a child even in the bulky dry suit, used side-mounted tanks, each with its own regulator, and clipped on for easy removal. They were the kind worn by cave divers who needed to squeeze through small spaces. She could take them off, feed them through one at a time, then follow them.

Anna's flippered foot trailed against the hull, making a faint metallic sound as the buckle scraped the ship's skin. Patience's head jerked and Anna stopped her glide, waited, realized she had stopped breathing, began again.

Bittner's flicker of interest was only momentary. With the mask and the darkness it was impossible to tell, but Anna didn't think Patience realized she was no longer alone.

Dive tanks in place, Patience grasped the neck of the sack and began swimming up the hull. Her light was trained toward the tilting deck. She was obviously in no need of rescue, nor did she look as if she was expecting company. Clearly she had not been down half an hour. Like Anna, she would have chosen bounce dives. Dangerous but doable for the kind of money she would get for the wine in the net bag. Bottom time would have dictated more than one dive; one load at a time. Carrie had never been worried for her mother; she had informed on her, getting revenge for the loss of her first lover.

Sharper than a serpent's tooth, Anna thought.

With time so short, Anna assumed Patience would head immediately back to the surface with her prize, but she swam for the deck.

Safe in her shroud of darkness, Anna followed, grateful for once for the depths. Stalking in absolute silence was not difficult.

Without pausing even an instant at the lightless portal, Patience swam into the engine room.

Anna glided up to the right of the door, shielded from view from within, and waited. One minute passed, then two. From far back in the tangle of equipment and narrow passages, she could see a flicker of light on the bulkhead.

There could be little of value in the engine room, nothing worth the precious time Patience was spending. Anna wondered what she needed to do with a hundred thousand dollars' worth of wine and five sixty-four-year-old corpses. She looked at her watch: in minutes her bottom line time would be used up. Any longer and she would be into twenty to forty minutes' decompression time.

Switching on her light, she followed Patience into the interior of the *Kamloops*.

Claustrophobia met her just inside the portal. The engine room was low-ceilinged and the passages were narrow. Bulkheads showed gray in the beam of her light. To the right the passage opened into a space filled with machinery separated by walkways just wide enough to accommodate a man. Ahead, the corridor branched into several narrower passages fanning out amid the once working organs of the dead ship.

In the clear, still waters at one hundred and ninety-five feet, the wrecks were amazingly clean, as if they'd settled just weeks before. Still, over everything was a softening shroud of silt so fine it scarcely dulled the outlines of the machinery. Each flick of her feet stirred up eddies in the fine-grained mud, and Anna swam with great delicacy.

Keeping her light trained on the floor so it wouldn't alert Patience to her presence, Anna trailed down the passage. Knowing somewhere five corpses kept vigil, she had a sense of being watched, a prickling feeling down her back that at any second a half-fleshed hand would clutch at her.

The circle of light that Patience's lamp produced continued to flicker on the bulkhead at the end of the passage. Tricky, unnatural, the light flitted here and there, always on bulkhead or machinery, always in sight, as if Patience shined it constantly behind her looking for pursuers. Like a will-o'-the-wisp, it vanished as Anna reached the corner. Like a will-o'-the-wisp it led her down another, smaller walkway.

Like a will-o'-the-wisp, Anna thought and suddenly knew, like other unwary travelers, she was intentionally being led astray. Patience must have seen her light as she descended from the *Belle Isle,* and had lured her into the ship.

Anna stopped. The feeling of clutching hands grew till she could feel her heart pounding in her ears and wondered if the sound carried through water. Slowly, warily, keeping an eye on the light beckoning her still deeper into the wreck, she swam back the way she had come. Corpses no longer seemed of any consequence. Compared to the living, they were benevolent.

Something was wrong with Patience's lamp.

The light, once a clear stabbing white, began to fade, then diffuse in a strange fog. Silt. Patience was silting out the engine room. An impenetrable fog was boiling down the corridor. Panic rising, Anna fled.

Patience had circled round, found her way through the twisting passageways until she was between Anna and the door. The brownish-gray wall swept down, blotting out everything. In seconds, Anna's light was rendered useless. The water was thick with silt. Bulkhead, deck, engine parts half a foot away, were hidden behind liquid mud.

The world dwindled, closed in. Lake and ship and now the very space she moved through crushed down. There was no way out, no choices left to make. A scream built in Anna's chest, pressing hard against her sternum until the pain brought tears to her eyes. Fear flushed through her bowels and she was weak with it. Air gulped through her mouthpiece burned her throat with icy slush and her head spun. The need to run like a wild thing blindsided her and Anna kicked hard, swam madly through the opaque waters.

A racking pain took her in the left shoulder. Kicking free, she hit her knees on an unyielding surface. Wildly, she scrabbled her hands over it. The deck. She had swum hard into the floor of the passage. Equilibrium was gone, sight was gone, hearing, everything. Nothing was left to tell her if she swam deeper into the ship, up toward the ceiling, or sideways into the maze of machine parts that cut the engine room into winding passages. With blunt, gloved fingers, Anna clawed at the metal of the decking, or was it the bulkhead? The ceiling?

The insanity of the act caught her mind, held it still long enough so she could think. Forcing herself to stillness, she retreated back to basics, to Ralph's remembered instructions: Breathe. Concentrating on the mechanics of her diaphragm drawing down, her rib cage lifting and expanding, air pulling through the rubber hose filling the vacuum, Anna breathed in, breathed out. Her lips had lost feeling, her mouth felt like a snow cone. In. Out. Rational thought, not opposable thumbs, is what makes us more dangerous than the apes, she thought.

Rational thought. First she must discover, microscopically, where she was in the ship. She stopped even the gentle movement of her flippered feet and waited, feeling time, the essence she had less of than air, slipping away. Slowly, in her stillness, the weight she wore to counteract her buoyancy sought its natural state and she began to settle. Her knees, then her hands struck the deck.

You're no longer lost, she told herself, mostly because she needed the reassurance of banal conversation. You are on the deck of the *Kamloops*'s engine room. Not the ceiling. Not the bulkhead. Good.

Closing her eyes to shut away the brown haze that seemed the physical manifestation of pure confusion, Anna mentally retraced the path she had taken following Patience. Into the ship, then down a corridor walled on the left, open on the right where machinery was housed, past one doorway on the left, then a left turn, another passage, narrower, left again at an open door.

Careful not to lose contact with the deck, she spread-eagled herself. Her left hand hit the bulkhead, her right, nothing. Changing the light over to her right hand and keeping her belly pressed to the deck, she pushed her left hand into the angle where bulkhead met deck, and began to work her way back down the short hallway. At least she hoped she headed back and had not turned herself around in her frenzy and was now swimming deeper into the ship. Her hand lost contact and she felt a spark of hope. It would be the right place for the door she had seen as she turned up the last passage in pursuit of Patience. Inching to the right, she felt along the deck till her lamp collided with the bulkhead on that side. Again she switched the useless light to her free hand. Fingers trailing, she made the first turn, then a second.

If her mind map was accurate she would come to another doorway. A break in the wall: She began to believe she might escape and swam on with more confidence. Another twenty-five feet or so and she should swim free into the lake.

Keeping her hand firmly in the angle of the bulkhead and deck, she swam. No change in the silt miasma heralded open water. No slightly lighter square in the hopeless darkness relieved her eyes.

The bulkhead ended in another. No open door, no freedom, another wall made a ninety-degree angle to the left.

Panic, held at bay by hope and action, flooded back. Anna couldn't breathe. The mechanism of her tanks had malfunctioned. Air wasn't coming through the mouthpiece. She fought down the urge to rip her mask off, to get some space around her.

"Breathe," Ralph said clearly.

Her mouth was completely numb with cold inside and out. She grabbed her lips with gloved fingers and pressed them down, molding them around a regulator she could no longer feel. Sitting with her back to the wall, Anna breathed. There was air. She took it in; let it go. I will die calmly, she thought. And preferably not today.

The map she'd drawn in her head was shattered. Exploring the unexpected bulkhead with her hands, she felt for something that would jog her memory, give her a place to begin drawing a new map. One that would take her out of this hell and back to the world of the living.

A seam ran up vertically eight inches out from the corner. Anna pursued it with fingers grown clumsy with cold and fear. The seam made a right angle, then another. A door: her mental map had not failed her. Patience had closed the door to the engine room. A lever, slanting down at a forty-five-degree angle, was located to the left and center. Anna's hand closed on the metal. For a second or two she hesitated. If the door didn't open, she would die.

With a control that both surprised and reassured her, Anna pressed down. The lever didn't move. Control slipping, she jerked the metal handle upward. It was ungiving, jammed in place. A desperate moment passed as she struggled with iron forged to withstand storms a thousand times greater than any human arms could foment.

Exertion at depth began to take its toll. The darkness without was becoming a darkness within. Anna felt her hands drifting from the lever, her mind receding as a light would vanish in the night. She was falling back, her flippered feet losing touch with the reality of the decking. Strength born of desperation closed her fingers and she clung to the metal lever. Still she drifted, still she fell away into mud-blanketed darkness, the lamp at her feet kicked aside by a trailing flipper.

As from a great distance, Anna found herself staring at the tumbling light. The beam was losing the gray-brown dullness of the silt fog, gaining clarity, sharpness. She blinked, breathed, fought to stay awake and so alive. Her back bumped gently against something and her fall was stopped. Against all logic, she was still clinging to the door handle.

As the mud fog cleared, so did Anna's brain. The lever had been welded in the open position by more than half a century of immersion in Superior's waters. Patience had closed the door but been unable to lock it. Had Anna died, her corpse would have been found floating against an unlocked door, forever mysterious: the woman who had chosen death behind an open portal.

A kick brought Anna back to the relative freedom of the lake bottom. What fragile light there had been in Michigan's fog-ridden skies was gone. The surface of the lake no longer showed lighter. But for the lamp she'd retrieved, there was a total absence of light. It was as if she swam in India ink.

Anna looked at the time. Six minutes had elapsed since she had entered the *Kamloops'* engine room; fifteen since she had toppled out of her patrol boat. Ten was the maximum bottom time for a bounce dive, for surfacing with minimal decompression stops.

Vague and fumbling in mind and body, Anna looked for the lifeline, the line that would lead her back up, time her stops. It had been withdrawn: Patience banking on the fact there would be no one left alive needing a road home. Without light from the surface, the water was as directionless as deep space. To swim could be death if one was swimming in the wrong direction.

Anna pushed a button on her low-pressure inflator hose. Slowly she began to ascend. Like Winnie-the-Pooh with his balloon, she thought with the closest approximation to optimism she had felt since tumbling off the *Belle Isle*'s stern.

The small circle of light her lamp cast on the *Kamloops*'s deck dwindled. Finally it no longer touched the dead ship. Anna lost all sense of movement. Try as she might, the effort of watching both timepiece and depth gauge proved too much. She lost count, forgot her numbers. All concept of how fast she was ascending, how long she'd been down, was lost.

From below, where her finger of light poked into the blackness came a white amorphous shape. Anna tried to train the light on it but it moved in and out of the beam as if it chose to be seen only for a second, then to hide in the black recesses. Fear of the known evil of bends or an embolism with blood frothing from her lungs kept Anna from kicking into sudden flight. Then it was upon her; a corpse from the *Kamloops*. Pale. Dead.

Not dead: hands trailing ribbons of saponified flesh reached for her. Before the fingers could close, the body drifted away into the dark. Denny Castle replaced it. He floated near her; not a corpse but alive and clad only in the captain's uniform.

In and out of dreams, Anna was carried upward. Ralph swam by, looking at her and tapping on the face of a watch she couldn't read. Formal, a maître d' in gossamer silks that shimmered around her, Patience offered wine for Anna's approval. Molly was there but Anna was unsurprised. Always, when she was in trouble, Molly had been there.

Then Anna dreamed fishes were flapping wet tails in her face. Whether she opened her eyes or regained consciousness she was unsure, but the darkness was no longer absolute. The fish tails were waves. She had reached the surface and she was alive. Fog still clamped down on the lake. She began to swim but faltered, not knowing if she swam to or away from the safety of land. And the cold had worked its way through the layers of her dry suit, sapping the vitality from her muscles, wrapping deadening fingers around her already slow-moving thoughts.

To lie back, to sleep, to stop struggling, would be heaven but Molly was nagging at her, something about staying in the game. After she had rested, Anna thought, she would figure out what her sister was babbling about. The fishes flapped their tails and cigar smoke wafted across the water.

Cigar smoke and fishes: the note was jarring. Anna forced herself awake. Fish tails turned back into waves. Cigar smoke remained cigar smoke; sweet and fruity. To shake the hallucination, Anna forced her arms to stroke, her legs to kick. The lake felt as if it had turned to concrete and was setting, heavy and rock-hard around her limbs.

The strange smoke, clear as a beacon, stayed in the air. Blind and deaf and aching in every joint, she floundered on, kicking away the cold, kicking away death for one more minute.

Her mind narrowed to the odor of exotic tobacco and the need to keep moving.

Stay in the game.

Finally death, tired of waiting for life's leftovers, overtook her. Her leaden arms were pinioned, dragged forward. "No!" she screamed around the mouthpiece that choked her.

Voices were burbling in her ears again. "We've got you. Don't fight. We've got you," they were saying. The voices of the dead in the engine room. Anna fought to come out of the dreams.

Her regulator, the breath of life, was pulled from her numbed lips. She stopped breathing to cheat death another few seconds. Her face mask was ripped away.

"Anna!" came a surprised cry. The sound of her own name startled the hard-won breath from her lungs. She gulped cold living air. "Anna, it's us."

Fight faded. Anna's mind opened. Without her mask, she could see. Tinker Coggins-Clarke was bending over her. She held fast to one arm. Damien clasped the other.

"Don't flop," Tinker said gently. "You'll overturn us. Come into the boat. Death can't follow you into the boat."

Anna willed the wood that was her legs to some semblance of action and Damien and Tinker dragged her over the gunwale of the aluminum runabout.

"What're you doing out in the fog?" Anna demanded faintly, a half-formed idea of citing them for running without lights dissolving unspoken into weary laughter.

"An experiment in sensory deprivation," Damien told her seriously.

"And Oscar was stinking up the tent," Tinker added. "I told him if he had to smoke his smelly old cigars, he could brave the elements."

Anna looked to the bow. Wearing a tiny yellow slicker and lashed to the bow with what looked like a hair ribbon was the brown-eyed teddy bear.

"I'm buying you a case of Havanas," Anna promised. "And a red sports car."

CHAPTER 27

The Coggins-Clarkes had been floating in darkness and silence—feeling the lake breathe, they said—several miles off Kamloops Point. Near as Anna could figure, she had swum just over a mile.

Free of tanks, mask, and flippers, but still swaddled in the dry suit, she lay like a landed fish amidships of the little runabout. At his own request—transmitted via Tinker—Oscar had been zipped inside her suit. Not without great risk of wetting his fur, as the little bear had pointed out.

After the surreal quality of the dive, Tinker and Damien arguing good-naturedly with a stuffed bear in a rain jacket didn't strike Anna as even moderately peculiar. Given the choice between a bat-blind airless dimension nearly two hundred feet below and this gentle insanity, she gave the latter more credence.

Half sitting, she leaned against Tinker's knees. She could feel the other woman's long slender fingers resting along the side of her head. To keep it from rolling off, Anna thought foolishly and was comforted. Tinker's other hand was at the tiller of the seventy-five-horsepower out-board motor.

Anna's arms and legs felt heavy as stone. She could scarcely move them, yet, without her volition, they twitched occasionally, knocking with loud violence against the side of the aluminum boat. When Anna talked her voice sounded far away and the tale she was telling of Patience and the wine and the *Kamloops*, absurd.

Damien, head bent over a compass strung around his neck on a cord, was navigating the little craft through the black and drifting waterscape. A flashlight duct-taped to the bow provided all they had of running lights.

"Watch it!" Anna barked suddenly. She'd sensed as much as seen a shape in the fog beyond Damien. Immediately Tinker cut what little power the engine produced and helped Anna as she struggled to sit upright.

"Oops!" Damien said cheerfully as the nose of the run-about bumped into the floating obstacle. "A boat," he announced.

"Of course a boat," Anna growled peevishly as she tried to get her useless legs folded underneath her.

Tinker noted the cranky tone: "You're feeling better," she approved.

Anna laughed and was alarmed at the sharp pain it caused in her left lung, near her heart. "Yes," she said, her breath coming in a gasp. "Unh!" The grunt was to alleviate the pain in her right knee as she pulled herself up holding on to the gunwale of the vessel they'd run against.

Standing half erect, she could see over the gunwale onto the stern deck. "It's the *Belle Isle*. She must have been cut loose. Give me a boost."

Damien wedged a shoulder awkwardly under her rump and managed to spill her over into the Bertram without overturning his own boat. Tinker and he scrambled aboard with more agility and tied the aluminum runabout to the stern cleat.

On unsteady legs, Anna staggered to the helm. Restored to life, the surface, and her patrol boat, her vision had tunneled: She would find Patience Bittner.

Tinker and Damien settled quietly on the bench across from the pilot's and, hands intertwined, watched the drama unfold with great interest but no apparent surprise or concern. Soon Anna forgot they were there.

Her mind, usually a fairly tractable organ, was hardly clearer on the surface than it had been under the confusing effects of Martini's Law at thirty-two fathoms. Waves of dizziness shook her and it seemed as though her eyesight was blurred at the edges, though it was difficult to tell with the sinuous fog moving through her running lights. She didn't care to hazard a guess which problems were internal and which external. Definitely internal was the intense, sharp aching in her knee and left shoulder. The bends: Anna had been down too long, gotten too cold, ascended too fast.

Trusting the radar to keep her from ramming any night-crawling fools, she nudged the throttles further open. Never had time been so much of the essence as it had been this day. Ascent time, bottom time, decompression time, time immersed in frigid water, now—if she'd been down much too long, or come up much too fast—time till she could reach a recompression facility. For deep-water divers, *tempus* not only *fugit*ed but killed.

"I'll leave you in Rock." Anna remembered her passengers as she rounded Blake's Point and started down the protected channel between Edwards Island and Isle Royale.

"We'll stay till you've got somebody else," Tinker said.

"You'll get out at Rock," Anna reiterated.

"No."

Anna didn't pursue it. She'd seen women like Tinker, fragile, gossamer creatures, chain themselves to trees, lie down in front of bulldozers, tangle themselves in the nets of tuna boats till it took half a dozen burly policemen to dislodge them.

"Two-oh-two." Anna tried to raise Scotty on the radio. He didn't respond and she glanced at her pocket watch tethered to the depth finder where she'd left it for safekeeping when she'd donned her diving gear. "Past cocktail hour," she observed sourly. "He's turned his radio off."

"Somebody else, then," Tinker suggested.

Refocusing on her radar screen, Anna forbore comment. The fog in her peripheral vision was definitely internal and she was unable to blink or wish it away.

Rock Harbor was as quiet as she had seen it since early in the season. Half a dozen boats, as still in the flat water as if they were set in concrete, lined the dock. The only one showing any sign of life was the *Spirogyra*. Her rear deck was strung with paper lanterns that made diffused spots of pink and yellow and green in the fog. Disembodied laughter floated from her direction.

The low growl of an engine starting up intruded. The sound was clean and high-pitched: a motor that had been souped up. "The *Venture*," Anna guessed aloud. "She decided not to hang around until the body turned up." She glanced sharply at Tinker and Damien on the bench still handfast like teenagers on a date.

"No," Tinker said firmly.

"Damn," Anna breathed. Undoubtedly Patience would be headed for Canada with a good chunk of cash and all the evidence in an improbable—and, without the wine, possibly unprovable—theft of historical artifacts. Even with the evidence, Denny's death would be tough to pin on Bittner beyond a reasonable doubt. A good defense attorney could easily make the attempt on Anna's life sound like an accident.

"Damn," Anna said again.

"Go," Damien urged. "The Windigo has found modern form: greed. It feeds on the human spirit." His eyes were sparking, more boy than magician at the thought of this adventure.

"Cut that damn sea anchor loose," Anna ordered and he ran to loosen the runabout.

Shifting one engine to reverse, the other forward, Anna turned the *Belle Isle* in a tight, hard circle and was rewarded by yelps of protest emanating from the heavily waked and fog-bound *Spirogyra*.

There was just the one moving blip on the radar screen. She followed. Either Patience had holed up in the few seconds it had taken to turn the *Belle Isle* and been replaced by another vessel, or the lime-green blot moving south down Rock Harbor was the *Venture.* As Anna pushed the throttle forward, she sent up a prayer to a god so vague it and hope had come to mean the same thing, that the waterway harbored no half-submerged snags.

Catching Patience in the channel was her only chance. Once the *Venture* hit open water she would be lost. The Bertram was a powerful, well-built boat but she wasn't particularly fast, not when compared to the reworked engine replacing the standard-issue on Bittner's Chris-Craft.

If Patience realized she was being pursued, even in the close quarters of the channel she could make a successful run for it.

"There are a few advantages to being dead," Anna mused. "It's a good cover."

"Yes," Tinker agreed and Anna wondered what it would take to surprise the Coggins-Clarkes.

"Tinker, my three fifty-seven is just inside the door to the bow on the bench to the left under my trousers. Get it."

Without a word, Tinker hopped down from the bench and opened the small door. Seconds later she reappeared holding the revolver on both palms like a sacred offering. "This will be a complication," she said as Anna set the revolver on the dash between the depth finder and the radar screen. Tinker spoke with such assurance Anna wondered if she could see, along with things corporeal and existential, the immediate future.

The green mark on the radar grew larger. Reaching across Damien and his wife, curled together again like sweethearts, Anna banged open the side window. Cold air burst in and with it came a sound that was not made by the Bertram's powerful engines.

"Can either of you drive a boat?" Anna demanded. She thought of the aluminum runabout and amended her question: "A real boat?"

"Damien can," Tinker replied. At another time Anna

might have found the pride in her voice touching. As it was, it only served to deepen her natural skepticism.

"Mmm," she returned noncommittally, but she had no choices. "When I tell you, take the helm—the wheel," she told Damien, who had crowded out past Tinker to stand near the pilot's bench. "Do nothing till I'm clear of the deck. Then pull these back. Both of them. At the same time. All the way." Anna laid her hands on the twin throttles. "Shove these two levers down halfway. That's neutral." Anna put her left hand on the gear levers. "Then just wait. Don't drive anywhere. If you don't hear from me in twenty minutes or so, start calling for help on the radio. Eventually, somebody'll come get you. Got it?"

"Got it," Damien replied, with such boyish earnestness that Anna's misgivings increased substantially.

On some level she knew she should let Patience escape, knew she worked without backup, endangered Tinker and Damien, knew, at best, she was courting a tort claim against the National Park Service by enlisting the aid of noncommissioned employees, SCAs—scarcely more professional by legal standards than tourists. But Anna's joints were aching as if they'd been bent backward to just short of snapping and her vision had narrowed till, unless she concentrated, it was as if she viewed the world through the wrong end of a pair of binoculars. The bends. The truly bent could sometimes never get straight.

And Patience Bittner was not going to get away with it.

The green blip lost focus. Half a dozen yards ahead the *Belle Isle*'s spotlight illuminated the ghostly outlines of a boat's stern. In the soft green tones of folding money, the name *Venture* was blazoned across it.

Anna held the *Belle Isle* back a little longer. The instant Patience recognized it she would run. The *Belle* couldn't outrun her and Anna hadn't the firepower to stop her. Wouldn't use it if she had. Carrie would be with her mother. Risking a child's life—however unpleasant the child—didn't fall under the direction to Protect and Preserve.

"Here." Anna traded places with Damien but kept her

hands on the wheel and throttles as she would have with a
student driver in a hazardous situation. "I'll pull alongside.
You hold it there till I've cleared the *Belle Isle* and am
aboard the *Venture*. Then what?"

"Pull back the throttles, put her in neutral, and wait,"
Damien repeated dutifully.

"Hand," Anna demanded. He raised his right hand. She
moved hers from the throttle and he laid palm and fingers
over the handles as if he'd been doing it all his life. A
flicker of hope, not bright enough to be called optimism
but welcome anyway, sparked in Anna's breast.

She placed her hand over his and opened the throttle all
the way. The *Belle Isle* surged ahead, came alongside the
Chris-Craft, her port gunwale less than a yard from the
smaller boat's starboard side.

Trading action for thought, Anna snatched up her .357
and ran from the cabin back to the *Belle Isle*'s deck. The
ribbon of water between the two moving boats boiled
black, reminding her of the cold and lightless death she
had cheated and was, perhaps, still waiting for her. "Because I could not stop for Death," she whispered, "he
kindly . . ."

Using the seven feet of deck to get a running start, she
threw herself across the widening gap between the boats.
Through fog, all visible surfaces moving at differing
speeds, through dark and fleeting arms of white light, she
had an uncanny sense of flying as one flies in a dream.

The dream came to an abrupt end when the toe of one
foot caught the *Belle*'s gunwale. The rushing black water
came up. Throwing her arms forward, Anna grasped the
Venture's gunwale but her lower body was sucked down
into the lake. The dry suit kept the cold from her.

The ache in her shoulder pried between the bones, letting what strength had returned after the exhaustion of the
swim leak away. The lake was reclaiming her. The drag of
the water, the pull of the *Venture* cutting through it, was
ripping Anna in two, pulling her arms from their sockets.

Slowly, she loosed her grip, let the water and momen-
tum pull her back along the gunwale toward the boat's

stern. The jets of water where the wake turned under made a last try for her, but Anna had one foot up on the waterline diving deck. A foot, a knee, another knee, and the lake had to relinquish its claim. Anna tumbled over the stern rail onto the deck.

She landed on Patience's cast-off dive suit and fins. Damage and noise were somewhat alleviated. But the revolver was gone, dropped in the channel.

"Shit," Anna muttered.

For a moment she stayed where she'd fallen, watching the twin Plexiglas windows in the rear of the cabin. No alarmed face appeared, no concerned head peeked out of the cabin door. Either the noise of her arrival had been masked by the roaring of the engines, or Patience had assumed the thump was due to the flapping of unstowed fenders or a sideswipe by the *Belle Isle*.

Anna pushed herself up far enough to look back. The *Venture*'s wake curled in two tight lines of pale water on the black lake. The sudden appearance of another boat had put Patience into high gear. The *Belle Isle*, engines silent, was already losing herself in the fog. Only the red and green glow on her bow gave away her whereabouts. Damien had done his part admirably.

Now Anna must do hers.

No gun, no way off the boat: it was not a good corner to have painted oneself into. Surprise was on Anna's side, height, weight, and training. Maybe training, she amended as she eased herself noiselessly to her feet. Patience could drive a boat, could dive like a pro, and could choose the right wine to go with the fish. If there'd been aikido or tae kwan do mixed in with the ballet and cooking classes, Anna might be in for a more entertaining evening than she'd bargained for.

And the thought of facing even a tiny murderer without a revolver was nearly as daunting as the thought of all the government forms she would have to fill out explaining how she lost it.

Perhaps Patience would give up without a struggle, bend to the will of the law as personified by Ranger Pigeon. It could happen. "Yeah," Anna said and looked around the crowded deck for something she could use as a weapon.

In addition to Patience's dive gear, the pockets along the gunwales just above deck level had the usual maritime paraphernalia. There were several hundred yards of line, scrub brushes, a fish gaff on a long wooden handle, and cleaning supplies: detergent and something blue in a plastic bottle with a metal spray-pump top.

Anna lowered herself gingerly onto her aching knee and unscrewed the top from the spray bottle. Closed in her fist, it might pass muster if she maximized her shock value—people never saw much when they were frightened.

It crossed Anna's mind to kick down the door like John Wayne in *McQ*, uttering only a terse dry "Knock, knock" as the wood splintered. But doors, even cabin doors on boats, were a good deal tougher than one might think. There was the possibility she'd only break a few bones in her foot and alert Patience to her presence.

The engine slowed. The *Venture* was nearing the end of the channel and would head out into open water at the marker buoys in Middle Islands Passage. The upcoming interview was not one Anna cared to conduct any farther from land than she had to.

The customized Evinrude engine that propelled the small boat was housed in an engine box to the rear of the stern deck. Anna turned the butterfly nuts and lifted back the cover. Though it was of higher caliber and horsepower, the engine was much the same as the twin engines on the Bertram. Black spark plug wires popped up to meet her grasp. With a jerk, she pulled them loose, and dropped them overboard.

The engine coughed once and died. In the ensuing silence Anna felt naked, exposed. At any moment Patience would come out on deck to see why the engine had failed.

Bent double to avoid the windows, Anna stepped across the narrow deck. Bracing one shoulder against the cabin wall on the port side where the opening door would help shield her, she waited with the aluminum spray nozzle held in what she sincerely hoped was a sufficiently fierce and businesslike grip to discourage close inspection.

Surrounded by an insulating blanket of fog, the sounds from the cabin were at the same time very clear and quite unreal, as if they were happening inside Anna's skull. Muffled clicks: Patience trying the key. Muttered words as there was no answering surge from the engine. Dull thumps: Patience closing the choke, shutting down the throttle, turning off the ignition in preparation for coming to check the engine. More murmurings: probably instructions to Carrie Ann.

Anna tensed, then forced herself to relax, to clear her mind. A shadow across the window, then the cabin door opened with a bang. Looking neither right nor left, Patience made a beeline for the engine.

Anna reached out, caught the door, and quietly closed it. Moving her body to block it, she wedged one rubber heel against the wood.

"Stop where you are," she said softly.

Throwing up her hands and collapsing to her knees like an old-time rivalist, Patience screamed: "My Lord!" She pressed her hands theatrically over her heart, but such was the shock registered on her face, Anna guessed the gesture was unplanned.

"Stay on your knees and turn around," Anna said evenly. "Face the stern." She held the spray nozzle in two hands, her arms extended from her body, elbows locked. "Do it."

Patience turned all but her head. Chin on shoulder, she continued to stare back at Anna. The initial shock was wearing off. Anna could see thought and sense rushing back behind her eyes, unlocking the stony set of her facial muscles. "Face away," Anna commanded. "Eyes on the engine box. Do it."

Patience faced away.

"Lie down slowly on your stomach," Anna ordered.

"Mom!"

The door hit Anna's back and she wedged her heel more firmly against it to keep it closed.

"Mom!"

The distraction was giving Patience courage. Anna could see it in the restless twitch of her arms and legs. "Don't even think about it, Patience. What with one thing and another, my nerves have been pretty much shot to hell today. Killing you is a real possibility.

"Carrie Ann," Anna called without taking her eyes off where Patience Bittner sprawled. "Carrie Ann, this is Anna Pigeon. Stay away from the door. Stay quiet."

"Mom!" Carrie hollered again and rattled the door.

"Sit down and shut up!" Anna barked. Silence from within except for a snuffling sound that could have been either shuffling feet or adenoidal aggrievement.

"Face down," Anna reminded Patience.

There was nothing with which to secure her prisoner but the dive line stowed near Patience's right hand. In close quarters Anna didn't care to wade into the midst of the other woman to retrieve it.

"Reach out with your right hand, Patience. Do it slowly. Good. Take hold of the dive line and pull it slowly into the middle of your back."

With a short growl that telegraphed her intentions, Patience's fist closed round the coiled line. Twisting like a stepped-on snake, she rolled and flung the line at Anna's face.

Instinct and training held Anna steady. Her finger squeezed the trigger. A trickle of foam dripped from the nozzle. Her own playacting had caught her up. The instant was enough. Patience pulled the fish gaff free of its clamps and sprang to her feet.

"Jump, Anna," she said. "Jump. Maybe you'll make it. I hope you'll make it. Jump." Slashing at Anna with a power born of desperation and adrenaline, she lunged.

There was nowhere to go but back into the black water, and Anna held her ground. The gaff was sharp. Anna felt it cutting through the dive suit, catching the flesh of her breasts, ripping. She saw it come free on the other side.

There was no time to wonder if she'd been badly hurt. Her hand shot after the shaft before Patience could make another swing. Fingers closing around the wood, Anna jerked hard, but Patience kept her footing, kept her hold on the gaff. Blond hair fell wild around her face and her jaw was set like a bulldog's.

"Mexican standoff," Anna said reasonably, holding tight to her end of the long staff. "Eight or ten hours and it will be light. Somebody will come along. The ranger always gets to win. Why don't we stop now? Save ourselves a miserable night?"

Patience was not lulled, convinced, or amused. "You won't last till daylight, Anna. I will. You're hurt. I hurt you. You're sick. The bends. Maybe an embolism. I can see it in your face. Your lungs are filling up with blood. Blood is pouring from where the boat hook got you. You'll be dead long before the sun comes up and I'll still be here."

"Okay," Anna agreed. "Then I haven't got all night." Hand over hand she began working her way down the wooden handle. "How about this then: I'm taller, stronger, outweigh you by ten pounds and am really pissed off?"

Anna's hand reached Patience's. The other woman gripped the haft of the fish gaff more tightly but the battle for that was over. Laying one hand across Patience's wrist, Anna began to peel her thumb off the wood in what must have seemed a childish gesture until the pain set in. By the time Patience realized what was happening agony had become paralysis. Pain has a way of taking the place of thought. Finally, like the animals humans pretend to be above, people will do anything to get away from it.

"Down," Anna suggested, pushing Patience's thumb back toward her wrist. "Lie down."

Patience complied.

"Stay still. Soon it will be over. Stay still." Anna looped the dive line around Patience's slender wrists and pulled the plastic rope tight. The rope would bite deep, perhaps cut off the blood to her prisoner's hands. To cripple the graceful little woman would be a shame.

"Not a crying shame," Anna said aloud. The meaningless words scared her. Her mind was not in top working order, her vision was fogged. Knowing her condition was worsening, she tied Patience's slim ankles together and anchored the woman to both the stern and midship cleats so she couldn't wriggle around the deck.

"Carrie Ann!" Patience yelled. "Come out, honey."

"Stay put," Anna ordered.

No sound came from within the cabin.

"Smash the radio," Patience screamed.

"Jesus!" Anna jerked at the door.

"I'll get you your own phone," Patience cried. Immediately there followed the sound of electronic equipment being pulverized. Patience laughed. "It's an unnatural mother who does not know her own offspring."

Dizziness took Anna then. She put her back against the cabin door and allowed herself to slide down till her butt met the deck. For an instant she thought her clarity of vision was returning but realized it was the fog, the real fog, the fog outside her brain. It was lifting.

"You're dying," Patience said. "Drowning in your own blood. You're dizzy, aren't you? Eyes playing tricks?"

Anna shook her head but the motion made the deck spin and she stopped.

"Your joints hurt, don't they? This is only the beginning."

"Quiet," Anna said wearily and let her head rest against the cabin door. Overhead, through moving tendrils of fog, she thought she saw a star, but as she watched, it vanished.

"Bleeding inside and out," Patience continued. "Lungs and chest. The gaff got you. Soon you will faint. Carrie will come out then. Trust me. A mother's plea and all that. I'll throw you to the fishes, Anna. Untie me now and I'll put you ashore somewhere close, where they can find you and get you to treatment. I can do it. You're too far gone to be any danger to me. Untie me, Anna. I don't want you to die."

Another star. Then it, too, was gone. "Did you want Denny to die?" Anna asked in an effort to keep her mind from wandering, consciousness from dripping away.

"God!" Patience exploded. Thrashing sounds forced

Anna to turn her head. Bittner was fighting but the rope held secure.

"Did you?" Anna pressed.

"Denny was a fool."

"He grabbed an oversized single with a Y valve out of the *Third Sister* and followed you in the *Blackduck*," Anna prompted.

"Denny was a diver. He'd dived all over the world. Australia. Mexico. He'd dived caves. He knew how I'd gotten into the captain's cabin. He took off his tank, fed it through the porthole."

Two stars now. Anna could feel herself losing touch and she tried to focus her eyes on the distant points of light. "While you were inside the cabin?" she pursued.

"I was inside. What did he think I'd do? He'd jerk his thumb and I'd follow him docilely up to prison? A fool. I grabbed the tank, pulled it through, yanked the regulator out of his mouth and slammed the port. Two seconds, three at most."

In her mind's eyes, Anna saw Denny scrabbling at the porthole with his dive knife. The movements growing jerky as his lungs began to burst. The gush of bubbles, the frantic breath that filled him with water. Drowning. Dead.

"I'd've bolted for the surface," Anna said. "So would Denny. So would anybody."

"Denny got the porthole open."

Anna forced her eyes open. Patience was looking at her, one cheek pressed against the deck, hair falling in strands across her eyes. She looked like a caged animal. "I grabbed his arm when he reached in, cranked it up against the bulkhead, and braced my feet on either side till he stopped struggling." Patience spoke with deliberation. The threat in her words was unmistakable.

Fear stirred Anna's torpor. Patience was telling her of Denny's death. She tried to pull herself up straighter, look alive, formidable. "Then you put the tanks back on his body, surfaced, and cut the *Blackduck* adrift." Anna tried to take back control of the conversation.

"Rest," Patience said. "Lie back, Anna. Let yourself

sleep for just a second. Nothing bad can happen in a second."

"Fuck you," Anna whispered. Taking a fold of flesh from the inside of her cheek, Anna bit down till she tasted salt, hoping this new pain would focus her mind, but it was lost in myriad others.

White light came, surrounded her, surrounded the *Venture*. Tendrils of fog glowed like fingers lifting her to the stars.

"Anna. Anna." A sweet and gentle voice filled the illumined air; a voice bigger than anything human, a voice booming from all directions at once. A voice so kind Anna knew now, finally, she could let go of this world and glide into the next.

"Damn," she said. "I'm in for it now."

CHAPTER 28

"Cut nearly in half. Look: it's blood, blood in the sawdust."

"Immortality is in your hands . . ."

"A needle and thread is all."

"And a Dustbuster."

"Put her down there, Dave."

"Carrie . . ."

Anna's mind tuned in and out of the world around her.
Twice she'd asked: "Whose blood?"

Tinker was there somehow. She'd answered, "Yours.
Mixed with his."

"Sawdust," Damien had corrected his wife and Anna
had lost the thread. She'd felt herself lifted easily, as easily as if she were a kitten, and knew it was not by Damien.
Once she'd forced open her eyes and thought she'd seen
Pizza Dave's face, big as a harvest moon, floating above
her.

"That can't be right," she'd said and heard vaguely
someone saying, "Hush. Rest now."

Somewhere in the distance she thought she heard Patience's low voice pitched in persuasive tones as if selling something. "Don't buy it," she had mumbled, wishing she could speak more clearly.

Then there was Ralph's voice and engines roaring. Anna came fully awake in a small compartment made up of equal parts of noise and darkness. She stared up through a window. The sky was glittering with stars and a half-moon. Her feet were raised and stretched toward a panel lit by subdued, green, circular lights. She lay on her left side, her head lower than her feet.

Every part of her hurt. Her chest burned and sharp points of pain pierced her shoulder and knees. Tentatively, she wriggled her toes. They worked just fine. Over the years she had taken a few tumbles; bones had broken, muscles torn. The terror was always for the spine—paralysis. Again she'd gotten off lightly.

Then she remembered she'd not fallen off a Texas mountain, not been tossed from a horse. The lake had crushed her in its dark embrace. The damage would be internal, as dangerous and inexorable as the deep. "Oh dear . . ." she whispered.

"'Bout time," came a friendly voice.

Carefully, so as not to dislodge it from her shoulders, Anna turned her head to see who had spoken. "Ralph." The District Ranger sat in the seat next to the board she was lashed to. She was glad to see him and felt bad that her voice sounded so dull. To let him know how welcome a sight he was, she tried to pat his knee, but her arm was tied down. "Ralph." She repeated his name. It was all she could manage.

"It's okay, Anna. You're okay. We're in the seaplane. Sid is flying low as he can so your decompression sickness won't be made any worse. We're almost to Duluth. There's a medevac helicopter waiting there. They've got everything—even hot and cold running paramedics. They'll be taking you to the hyperbaric chamber in Minneapolis. You're going to be okay."

"Backcountry . . ."

Ralph put a warm hand on her forehead to quiet her.

"Lucas and I heard your little radio drama," he said. "We just couldn't call out. I was for going to bed and letting you fight off the forces of evil alone, but you know Lucas, he's a belt-and-suspenders kind of guy. Made us do a forced march out in the dark. We got there just as the kids were dragging the bodies back into Rock. Lucas got the perpetrator to take care of. I got you."

For a second time Anna tried to touch him, to let him know she'd heard, understood, appreciated. "My arm," she complained, encountering the bandages.

"Routine packaging," Ralph reassured her. "There's nothing wrong with your arm. I just bandaged it to keep you from moving it and opening the cut on your chest. Nothing too serious," he went on. "You'll still look terrific in a bathing suit. Just a scratch half an inch deep or so and about ten inches long. Looks worse than it is and it bled a lot. You were quite a mess of blood and sawdust when Lucas and I saw you."

"Sawdust?" Anna remembered hearing the word before. It had made as little sense to her then as it did now.

"Yeah. What were you doing with a teddy bear stuffed down the front of your dry suit anyway? Patience cut it in half. The suit was full of stuffing. Worked, though. She would have done a lot more damage with that fish gaff, maybe killed you. The bear took the blow, then the sawdust stopped your bleeding. Tomorrow I'll put in a wire to the LAPD. Body armor is out. Toy bears are in for officer safety."

"Oscar." Anna turned her head away, felt the tears stinging her eyes, rolling down into her hair.

The paramedics on the medevac helicopter were efficient and kind. Anna was unsurprised. In her brief stay in the northern Midwest, she had found most Minnesotans to be efficient and kind. The helicopter—an Augusta, she was proudly informed—hovered the distance between Duluth and Minneapolis in just over an hour.

Ralph stayed beside her. Demoted from primary caregiver to companion, he was strapped into a seat at the foot of her stretcher. "I feel like the mother of the bride," he joked.

Anna's mind could not make sense of the remark. "Why?" she demanded.

"Just something to say," Ralph soothed her. "Seeing you all in white and fussed over, nobody knowing where to put me. Take it easy, Anna. I won't try to be funny anymore."

"Good." As she drifted off, she heard him laughing.

When she reasserted herself in the conscious world, the helicopter was setting down.

"We're there," said one of the paramedics, a strong, handsome woman with big teeth and hair badly in need of reperming. "Ninth floor, Hennepin Medical Center. We'll have you in Jo's submarine shortly."

"Lost my sense of humor," Anna apologized wearily, guessing the paramedic, like Ralph, had made a joke. The woman just smiled and squeezed Anna's shoulder gently.

"Don't you worry about a thing," she said.

"Submarine" was an apt description of the hyperbaric chamber. An oxygen mask on her face, Anna managed to sleep out most of her seven-hour stint as the pressure was dropped and slowly brought back up. The last thing she remembered clearly was a friendly smile and the woman behind it saying, "Relax. We work well under pressure."

Hospital rooms always put Anna in a foul mood. Even more so when she was the inmate. Disconsolately, she stared out over the roofscape. Black asphalt sent up shimmering curtains of heat. Turkish-domed ventilators and galvanized aluminum excrescences completed the monotony. Minneapolis's ultra-urban skyline blotted out most of the blue. A thin line of green trees advertised Marquette Avenue but so feeble an outpouring of life in the concrete only depressed Anna further.

To cheer herself, she contemplated a shopping spree when the doctors turned her loose. Cities were for Things. Anna began to list all the things she would buy. On a GS-

7's twenty-two thousand a year, the list was necessarily short and only kept her amused for a couple of minutes. Channels 4, 5, 9, and 11 didn't hold her attention that long.

Boredom had set in so solidly that when a nurse poked her head in the door Anna was actually glad to see her. Even a shot or a pill would be a diversion. The news was better yet: "You've got visitors," the woman announced and was replaced by Christina Walters.

"Thank God!" Anna said. "A person, a real, live human being who doesn't smell like antiseptic. Come here and let me smell you."

Christina laughed and crossed the room to kiss Anna's cheek.

"Ahhh." Anna collapsed back against her pillows. "'White Shoulders.' So much more pleasing on females than benzene."

Ally bounded up on the opposite side of the bed. "Smell me, Aunt Anna."

Anna grabbed the little girl by the ears and sniffed deeply on the top of her head. "Hmmm . . . What is that divine scent you're wearing?" She sniffed again. "Rotting squirrel guts? No . . ." Ally squirmed and giggled. "'Eau de Road-kill'? No . . . I've got it! 'Essence of Dog Vomit'!" Ally squealed with delight.

"For heaven's sake," Christina sighed. "Ally will be completely beyond redemption by the time she's old enough to drive."

"You must be ladylike or the boys won't like you," Anna intoned ominously. "No more bat-dung hair mousse."

"Boys. Ish." Ally tossed her head with such disdain that Anna and her mother laughed.

"Ally, settle down," Christina said comfortably. "Get your Aunt Anna her present and then we'll see what can be done with her. If anything."

Alison thumped off the bed and ran to dig through the oversized shoulder bag her mother had dropped just inside the doorway. She returned with a paper sack and climbed back up onto the bed.

"Don't bounce Aunt Anna," Christina cautioned her. "She's been saving the free world. It's not as easy on her as it used to be."

Anna sniffed.

"It's in the bag," Alison said. "We didn't wrap it because it's not your birthday or anything."

Anna reached into the proffered sack and pulled out a plastic-wrapped package.

"Pajamas," Ally announced.

Anna ripped them free of the cellophane. "They've got little Garfields on them," she complained ungraciously.

Christina arched a perfect eyebrow. "Ally picked them out," she reproved. "She thought the orange cat motif would keep you from missing Piedmont."

"Nobody wants to be sick without a cat," Ally added.

"I love them," Anna said. "Almost as much as I love you." She captured the child and covered her head with loud smoochy kisses.

"Stop!" Ally cried, but she was holding tightly to Anna's neck. "Put 'em on," she demanded when the attack was subsiding.

Dutifully Anna took off her hospital gown. The ten-inch slash was exposed. The bandages had been removed to let the air get to it. Encrusted black with blood, the edges pale, the laceration ran from her left shoulder almost to her right nipple.

"Oh, honey . . ." Christina ran out of words. Even Ally was quiet.

Sympathy unmanned Anna. So far, sheer cantankerousness had kept her from feeling sorry for herself. Ralph had been wrong. She wouldn't be admired in a bathing suit. Not unless her date was Freddy Krueger.

"Boy, Aunt Anna," Alison breathed. "Like Zorro. Will it make a scar?" she asked hopefully.

"Alison!" her mother exclaimed. "Whose little girl are you?"

"We can keep our fingers crossed," Anna laughed, feeling suddenly better.

"I have news, but it can wait." Christina took charge of

the situation. "The nurse here may be efficient, but they have no sense of aesthetics. You look like last season's prom dress. Get me my bag, honey." Somewhat subdued after her mild reprimand, Alison fetched the shoulder bag without comment. Chris took out what she deemed life's necessities: a natural-bristle brush, a lipstick, cream rouge.

"Last time I landed in the hospital you played the role of administering angel. Doesn't it get a bit old?" Anna asked.

"Very old," Christina retorted crisply. "Take better care of yourself in the future."

In a high, piping voice, Ally began to sing: "Button up your overcoat . . ."

Anna relaxed. Christina knew the best medicine. Healed in body by antibiotics and the hyperbaric chamber, healed in soul by well-dressed hair and a little cheek color. Healed in soul, Anna admitted as the other woman deftly brushed and French-braided her hair, by knowing someone was genuinely glad you had lived.

"What's your news?" Anna asked when Christina, satisfied with her efforts, was stowing away the hairbrush and makeup in her capacious bag.

"The Houghton police found Donna Butkus's body," she replied without preamble.

"Jesus!" Anna sat up straight and felt the sudden pull of the torn flesh of her chest.

"He didn't eat her up after all," Alison said disappointedly.

"Where?" Anna demanded.

"In the police station of all places." Chris sat down in the vinyl armchair beside the bed.

"Nitrogen narcosis." Anna rubbed her eyes. "Does this make sense to you?" she appealed to the five-year-old Alison who, ensconced at the foot of the bed, was folding the pajama wrapping into a transparent fan.

"Yup. She wasn't eaten at all. She wasn't even dead. She was only hiding."

"Once Roberta made a formal missing persons report to the police, they started looking. Donna got nervous and came back to Houghton to get Bertie to hush things up. Scotty was—" Christina shot a look at her daughter. Ally seemed absorbed. "Beating Donna."

"I guessed that."

"Oh. Anyway, Donna told Bertie it was only when he drank and it wasn't too bad—"

Anna snorted her disgust.

Chris touched her arm. "We don't all have the courage of a lion or a big gun to back it up with."

"I know," Anna apologized. "Go on."

"Then he started having—" Again the look at her daughter. Ally showed no sign of interest. Chris continued in a lowered voice: "Impotency problems. The beatings got bad then. Denny's wedding really set him off. I guess he thought Donna was pining or something. He beat her bad. She ran off. Pizza Dave found her and took her to Thunder Bay in his boat."

"In the taxpayers' boat," Anna corrected. "Dave doesn't own a boat. It's a firing offense. That must have been why he didn't tell me what had happened to Donna." Then she remembered the short exchange over the racket of Dave's tractor. He had tried to tell her Donna was all right.

"Donna asked him not to tell anyone," Christina said. "She was afraid Scotty would find her."

"And Scotty told lies because he was afraid we'd all find out his pretty young wife had run out on him."

"Donna's staying with her sister," Chris finished. "Bertie was going to help her with the divorce papers and everything."

"The old stallion is destined for the glue factory," Anna said unsympathetically.

Around four o'clock Christina and Ally deserted to go shopping. They placated Anna with the promise of another visit the following day before they started the long drive back up to Houghton.

Anna was left with her new pajamas, two glossy fashion magazines, a bundle of mail Chris had brought down from the park headquarters office in Houghton and, because Chris truly loved her, a Leinenkugel smuggled in past what Christina had been sure were vice cops in the uniforms of hospital orderlies.

Camouflaging the beer in a moderately clean sock, Anna began to sort through her interoffice mail. Lucas had put out another FYI memo regarding the status of the Denny Castle murder. The case had been officially closed with the arrest of Patience Eva Bittner on suspicion of murder, attempted murder, assault on a federal officer, theft of federally protected historical artifacts, vandalism, and diving without a permit. At the bottom of the memorandum, written in the Chief Ranger's hasty scrawl was a note: "Carrie Ann's been shipped off to her dad in redwood, CA. J. T. offered to look after her till plane time—" Anna smiled. She'd read enough of Lucas Vega's memos to recognize the dash. He used it as a literary version of putting his tongue in his cheek.

Anna shuffled through the tedious bits: a flier announcing the July 25 Chrismoose festivities, a copy of the Superintendent's schedule, minutes from the last safety meeting. Government offices always seemed anxious to put in writing and circulate all information of no interest or value. The important things had to be discovered through the grapevine.

A plain white envelope with "PIGEON" printed on it in block letters looked promising. Anna ripped the end off and tipped the contents out into her lap. There was a clipping from the Duluth paper with a yellow Post-it note stuck to it. "WHATEVER WE CAN THINK UP, SOMEBODY IS OUT THERE DOING IT. F. S."

Anna removed the note and read the clipping. Federal Agent Frederick Stanton had made his drug bust. He'd nailed the captain of the *Spirogyra* on two felony counts. The man had been purchasing peyote for resale as part of the entertainment experience on *Spirogyra* party excursions, and, as a sideline, transporting cocaine across international boundaries.

"Go Frederick," Anna said. She had nothing against the

Spirogyra, but the excitement generated by the bust would knock the *3rd Sister* out of the local gossip ring. Hawk and Holly deserved a break.

The following morning Anna was told by her doctor that she'd be incarcerated in Hennepin County Medical Center for another day and a half. On hearing the news, it was her intention to give way utterly to sullen peevish depression. The ninth-floor nurses were spared this event by the arrival of Christina and Ally. They brought in apple turnovers and fresh-ground deli coffee just as Anna was preparing to complain about her breakfast.

When they left, she was in such a good mood it lasted till her next visitors arrived in midafternoon.

As Student Conservation Associates, Tinker and Damien had only a six weeks' long season. They'd come to Minneapolis to catch a plane to Damien's mother's place on Nantucket Island.

"Nantucket," Anna remarked. "So you did know how to drive a boat."

"Yes. When we didn't hear from you, we fetched Pizza Dave," Damien told her.

"He was the largest person we could think of," Tinker explained.

"Large," Anna agreed.

For a time they sat in silence, Tinker in the chair, Damien perched on the arm, Anna, resplendent in her Garfield pajamas, propped up on pillows.

In an urban setting, without their uniforms, the two interpreters looked ordinary: like elves in a shopping mall or water sprites in a horse trough. The island itself was the magic; Tinker and Damien just the dwellers therein. Anna was aware of a feeling of disappointment.

"We've got winter jobs in Everglades National Park," Tinker said. "There's magic there."

Anna smiled. "If that fails, you can always get on with a traveling show, reading people's thoughts."

After due consideration, Damien declared: "Too dull."

Another long but in no way awkward silence passed. "I'm sorry about Oscar," Anna said finally.

"Yes," Tinker returned. "He was the purest of bears."

Another silence began. Anna didn't know quite where to look. Funerals, memorial services—dead people—were hard enough to deal with. Dead teddy bears presented a whole new realm of social obstacles.

"He was pure," Damien mused. "But there are compensations. Now that he's part human he's thinking of taking up whiskey to keep his more esoteric vices company."

"Human?" Anna repeated stupidly.

"We got most of his sawdust back," Tinker explained patiently. "Your dive suit caught almost all of it, but it was pretty well soaked with blood."

"We dried it out in our fruit dehydrator." Damien picked up the thread of the story. "Stuffed it back in and sewed him up. He's got a scar on his chest, but Tinker tried to keep the stitches small."

"Oscar's a bit vain," Tinker confided.

Anna fingered the wound on her own chest. "During bathing suit season, he and I'll stick together," she said. "Is he . . . here?" She felt absurd at the hope she heard in her voice.

"He sends his regards," Tinker apologized. "He wanted to stay at the hotel."

"Nothing personal," Damien put in quickly. "He thinks the world of you. It's just that our room has a color TV."

"Ah." Reality was becoming less and less important to the conversation. Anna changed the subject. Brightly, she said: "So, tell me what's happened on the island. Did they find somebody to run the lodge? Has Carrie left for her father's? Did Scotty ever get the fog-sensitive engine on the *Lorelei* running again?"

"Didn't you hear the big news?" Tinker asked cautiously.

Anna thought *she* was the big news.

"Scotty was drinking like he does and started opening beer bottles with his teeth."

"What a jerk. Were trail crew properly impressed?"

"No. Wait." Tinker looked pained. She had no reason to be a friend to Scotty Butkus. Anna wondered at it and waited.

"He choked to death on a bottle cap," Tinker said slowly. "No kidding," she added as Anna began to laugh. "Nobody knew the Heimlich maneuver—or they thought he was just horsing around. By the time they figured it out, he was dead."

Banal, embarrassing, meaningless: an accidental death. After all the mysteries on the island, Anna had forgotten there was such a thing. "Bummer," she said.

"Sometimes the wrong people die," Tinker said philosophically. "But sometimes they don't."

"Time," Damien broke in.

"Meeting of the Survivors of the Harmonic Convergence?" Anna teased.

Tinker shook her head. "Lyle Lovett's playing at the Guthrie."

Another perfectly good pigeonhole evaded by the Coggins-Clarkes, Anna thought as they gathered their things and headed for the door.

"Oh, you've a message from Ralph," Tinker remembered. "He said to tell you to get well soon. Now that Scotty is gone, you are to be stuck with organizing the Chrismoose picnic. Scotty ordered the paper plates and all the condiments, but nothing else has been done."

Anna groaned.

Tinker waved goodbye as Damien swirled her away in the crook of his arm.

"Condiments!" Anna exclaimed, sitting up abruptly. "That's why Scotty ordered the case of pickle relish!" she hollered after them. But the Coggins-Clarkes were on to other things.